A PART...

DI ALEC MCKAY #BOOK 6

ALEX WALTERS

www.bloodhoundbooks.com

Print ISBN 978-1-5040-7639-5

ALSO BY ALEX WALTERS
BOOKS PUBLISHED BY BLOODHOUND BOOKS

THE DI ALEC MCKAY SERIES

Candles and Roses (Book 1)

Death Parts Us (Book 2)

Their Final Act (Book 3)

Expiry Date (Book 4)

For Their Sins (Book 5)

Winterman

CHAPTER ONE

Murray Johnson turned off the main road, shifted down a gear for the steep hill, and made his way up the winding track towards the chalet park. He was always cautious coming up here. Visibility was limited by the hedgerows, and guests occasionally came racing down at speeds far in excess of the specified 10mph.

There wasn't much more he could do to prevent it. There were large warning signs at the top and bottom of the track, and similar exhortations in the information pack provided in each of the chalets. He'd considered adding speed bumps, but he knew that would just provoke complaints. Fortunately, they'd so far avoided any serious collisions, though they'd had the odd near miss.

Today, he reached the top of the track without incident. It wasn't yet 8am, but it was changeover day at the end of August. Some of the guests would be setting off early to get a head start on the crowds heading back before the start of the English school year.

Sure enough, as he passed through the gates into the site, he saw there were cars being loaded outside a couple of the chalets, parents and children coming and going with suitcases and bags, all trying to pack too many items into too small a space. Murray waved as he passed, and continued along the track towards his destination, one of the chalets at the rear of the park.

It was Murray's favourite time of the day at one of his favourite times of the year. The sun was well up, sparkling on the blue waters of Rosemarkie Bay but the first taste of autumn was in the air. They were reaching the end of the main season with plenty of bookings continuing into October and beyond. This was typically a more relaxed period, the guests less demanding and less inclined to inflict excessive wear and tear to the chalets.

He parked at the rear of the park and climbed out into the chilly morning air. From here, a twisting path led down through the woodland to the beach below. Murray took the opportunity to stand for a few moments to enjoy the panorama. He'd lived in the area all his life but had never tired of the place. The view changed from hour to hour, day to day, month to month across the seasons.

'Looks like another fine day,' a voice said from behind him.

'Aye, it does that.' Murray turned. 'Morning, Fergus. How's the world treating you?'

'Not so bad, considering.' Fergus Campbell never specified what it might be he was considering, but he wasn't a man to express unalloyed enthusiasm. He was a short, slightly squat individual, seemingly wider than he was tall, although most of what was under his thick sweater was muscle rather than fat. His skin was dark from outdoor working and he looked twenty years younger than his sixty-odd years.

Murray gestured towards the chalet behind them. 'How's it going? All ready in time?' Fergus, a qualified electrician who could turn his hand to most trades when needed, was Murray's assistant at the farm, and doubled as the site's handyman. The chalet behind them had needed some internal redecoration following a water overflow a few weeks earlier. At the time, Fergus had carried out the repair and some cosmetic work on the decor, with the intention of completing the job at the end of the season. In the event, the most recent guests had departed a couple of days early because of some family crisis, giving Fergus time to finish the redecoration before the next group arrived.

'All done,' Fergus said. 'Just been checking it's drying okay. It'll be ready by the time they arrive. Looks good, though I say so myself.'

'I'd expect nothing less. Well done, Fergus. One less job at the end of the season.'

'Aye. Unless some other daft bugger leaves a tap running.'

That was always the problem in the height of the season. All the units were booked back to back, and there was never time to do anything other than running repairs between each set of guests arriving and the next turning up. You just had to hope no major problems occurred. But Fergus, as the man himself knew very well, was worth his weight in almost any material you chose to name. He just had a knack for making things work, and he understood the constraints they had to work under. Between here and the farm, he'd saved Murray a fortune over the years.

'All full for next week, I'm assuming?' Fergus asked.

'What do you think? And we're still getting calls enquiring if we've got vacancies, would you believe? Having to tell people we've had no vacancies since this time last year.'

'It's been bloody manic, this year. Same everywhere.' Fergus shook his head as if baffled by the madness of holiday crowds. 'Thought we might struggle without the Americans but every bugger in Britain's come here instead.'

It wasn't too much of an exaggeration. With foreign travel still uncertain as a result of the previous year's pandemic lockdowns, large numbers had opted to book holidays in the UK instead. From Murray's perspective, it had been an even more challenging season than usual. Generally, he knew and was fond of the people who came to stay here. They were people who loved the Highlands, often people who came up here year after year. Some were Scots who'd moved away, some were Americans with roots here, some were English or Europeans who loved the wilderness and the landscapes. They knew what to expect, and most expected nothing more than tranquillity, some half-decent food with the odd dram, and this glorious backdrop.

This year's visitors had been harder work. Most of them had been likeable enough, but some had clearly had a desire for entertainment or experiences unlikely to be available in the Highlands. They'd complained about the weather, the lack of amenities, or – most commonly – simply the cost of holiday accommodation in the UK. There hadn't been much that Murray could do about any of that, other than smile politely and direct them towards the many pleasures the area actually did have to offer.

'Aye, well,' he said to Fergus now, 'it keeps us in business. We needed it after last year.'

He left Fergus to finish clearing up his equipment in the chalet, ready for the cleaners who'd be arriving at ten. Murray didn't usually bother coming up here for changeover day, trusting the two cleaners to make sure everything went smoothly. They'd worked for him for years now, knew the place better than he did and were generally more than capable of handling any issues that might arise. Not that many did. Occasionally, a family overslept, accidentally or otherwise, and weren't ready by the designated checkout, but they could work around that. Sometimes there was some last-minute complaint or damage to be dealt with, but Murray was available at the end of a phone if needed.

This year, though, given the different profile of the clientele, his presence might be useful. If there were problems, he'd prefer to deal with them straightaway rather than waiting till the guest filed a snotty review on some online site weeks later. He strolled slowly down through the site, enjoying the green patchwork of the trees, the patterns of sun and shadow on the undergrowth.

'Morning,' a voice called from the side of the chalet he was passing. Murray turned to see a man loading luggage into the boot of a sizeable Volvo estate. 'Lovely day,' the man said. 'Pity we're heading back now.'

Murray braced himself for a complaint about the previous week's weather which had been, even by the most generous interpretation, mixed. But the man seemed content enough. 'Pity we didn't get this earlier in the week,' he continued. 'But you don't come up here for the weather, do you?'

'Not unless you're terminally optimistic,' Murray agreed. 'Been hit and miss this year. Decent at the start of the summer but not so good since. I'm crossing my fingers for a better autumn.' He gestured vaguely towards the car. 'Heading far today?'

'Manchester,' the man said. 'Bit of a drive but not excessive. As long as we stop a couple of times to keep the kids from killing each other.'

'Hope the traffic's not too bad,' Murray said. 'You all had a good time?'

'Great, thanks. I've been wanting to do this for years, but not been able to wean the wife away from the Greek islands. We ought to spend more time exploring our own country.'

As if she'd been summoned by his mention of her, a woman stepped through the front door of the chalet. She was carrying a couple of bulging supermarket carrier bags. 'I heard that. I hadn't realised I'd been singlehandedly responsible for dragging us to Santorini.' She nodded to Murray. 'Morning, Mr Johnson.'

He'd always made a point of greeting new guests on their arrival, introducing himself, showing them round the chalets and giving them a few pointers about the local area. He recalled meeting these two when they'd first arrived, but he couldn't remember their names.

'You're very lucky to own a place like this, Mr Johnson,' the woman said.

'I'm lucky even to live here,' Murray said. 'It's a glorious spot.'

'It certainly is.' The woman turned to her husband. 'Did you tell Mr Johnson about it?'

Here it comes, Murray thought. The last-minute whinge about something in the chalet. When they left it this late to complain, that usually meant they were either angling for a refund or they were launching a pre-emptive strike because they'd left some damage themselves.

The man straightened up from the car he'd been loading while they talked. 'It's none of our business, Cath. I'm sure it's nothing.'

'Some problem?' If they were going to raise some dissatisfaction, he might as well get it out of the way.

The man gestured towards another chalet in the woods along from where they were standing. 'The people in there. Dawson, I think the name is.'

Murray suppressed a groan. A complaint about another set of guests, then. As if there was anything he could do about that. If they'd raised the issue earlier in their stay, he might have been able to take some action. As if was, he was damned if he was going to agree to a refund just because the neighbours had been noisy or disruptive or whatever the problem was. 'What about them?'

The man exchanged a glance with his wife. 'Well, like I say, none of our business, really...'

'It was last night,' the woman said. 'A hell of a lot of shouting and screaming.'

Murray looked over at the chalet in question. It looked to be in darkness, though there was still a car – an imposing Audi saloon – sitting beside it. Most likely, the buggers had got themselves pissed on their last night and were still sleeping it off. He glanced at his watch. Not yet nine, so they had over an hour to get themselves together. 'I'm sorry if they disturbed you. I can have a word, but there's not a lot I can do now, I'm afraid. Have they disturbed you previously?'

The man shook his head. 'No, that's the point. It seemed out of character. They'd seemed a nice enough couple, and their kids have been playing with ours. We were just a bit surprised.'

Murray frowned. 'You said screaming?'

Again, the man looked over at his wife, as if hoping she'd take over the conversation. 'Something like that. What did you think, Cath?'

'I don't know, really,' she said. 'They must have had the patio doors open at the back.' Each chalet had rear patio doors which opened on to a decking area where guests could eat al fresco or enjoy barbecues. 'We could hear some noise earlier. Nothing that was a problem, but it sounded like they might be having an argument.'

'It was odd because it looked like they had visitors,' the man said. 'There was another car parked outside last night.'

'The real noise was later,' the woman said. 'Maybe about ten. We were getting ready to go to bed because we knew we'd have to be up fairly early this morning. I came out for a last breath of air when I heard it.'

'Cath called me out because she was a bit worried,' the man said. 'There was a lot of noise from over there. Shouting, at first. I just thought, well, it's not our place to interrupt, but it seemed to go on and on.' He laughed awkwardly. 'Even Cath and I don't make that much noise.'

'Then it seemed to get worse,' the woman said. 'I thought it sounded like someone screaming. I was wondering if we ought to do something but I didn't really know what.'

'Then it just stopped,' the man said. 'Just like that. It was weird. One minute there'd been this – I don't know, cacophony's the word, I suppose. Then there was silence. We both just stood there. I heard an owl hooting.' He shrugged at his own anticlimactic conclusion. 'We didn't know what to do.'

'Or if we should do anything. I mean, you can't just go across and ring someone's doorbell and ask if they're all right, can you?'

Although, Murray thought, that was exactly what the couple clearly wanted him to do. He glanced uneasily over at the other chalet. 'What about the car?'

'Car?'

'You said there was another car outside there last night. Was it still there when all this was happening?'

The man frowned. 'I'm not sure. What do you think, Cath? Do you remember seeing it?'

'I think it had gone. I wasn't really focused on that. Does it matter?'

'Probably not,' Murray said. 'I just wondered.'

'I wonder if you should go and check that everything's okay?' the woman prompted.

Murray's first instinct was to tell the woman, just as her husband had done earlier, that this was really none of their business. People had arguments all the time. The last thing they'd want was for some busybody stranger to come poking his nose into their business. He was the owner of a bunch of holiday cottages, not a police officer or a counsellor.

Even so, something about the silence and darkness in the

chalet made him uneasy. He glanced at his watch. Still only 8.40. If they'd done their packing the night before, there was time for them to be up and about before checkout time. He didn't want to appear to be chivvying them unreasonably.

Even so.

'They need to be out by ten,' the woman said, as if Murray might be unaware of his own rules. 'Not much sign of them getting ready.'

'I don't like to hassle people before I need to,' Murray said finally. 'If they're not up and about in a while, I'll see what's going on.' Murray offered the couple a smile. 'I hope you all have a decent trip south. Maybe we'll see you again next year?'

'If Santorini's not calling.'

He left them to their packing and continued on through the site. As he reached the far side of the chalet they'd been discussing, he looked back. His discomfort was increasing, though he couldn't pin down why. There were no lights showing and no sign of any movement. The man and woman were still standing by their car, watching him as if willing him to act. He took a few more steps, then paused and turned back.

At the front door of the chalet he hesitated momentarily, then reached out and raised the knocker. There was no doorbell – he'd reasoned that guests wouldn't normally want or need one – and the knocker was primarily ornamental. Even so, it made a noise that would be difficult to ignore.

He looked along the length of the wood-built buildings. The blinds were still down in the two windows at the front of the house. Those were both bedrooms, with the third, master bedroom at the side, offering a partial view of the firth.

He raised the knocker and gave a second sharp rap on the door. Murray glanced over his shoulder and saw he was still being watched by the couple opposite. Ignoring them, he walked round the side of the chalet. The blinds on the side window – the master bedroom, with its en suite and its views of the sea – were also down, and there was no light showing behind them. Murray looked at his watch. Getting on for nine, now.

He reached the front of the chalet. Here, the partial view of the sea opened up to reveal the full breadth of the Moray Firth, the stone ramparts of Fort George on the far side of the water, Chanonry Point jutting into the sea to the right.

The patio windows were standing wide open.

The windows opened from the large living room, allowing guests to sit inside and enjoy the full view. There were no lights visible either in the living room or in the window of the kitchen beside it.

Murray's discomfort had intensified. He could conceive of reasons why guests might have opened the windows even at this time of day before leaving. Perhaps they'd wanted to make the most of the fine weather and enjoy a last breakfast out on the decking. Perhaps they'd eaten outside to prevent the children making more mess after they'd cleared up. Perhaps they'd just wanted one last taste of the Highland air. But why was the whole bloody place still in darkness?

If they'd had too much to drink the night before, maybe they'd simply forgotten to close the windows. You'd have to be pretty bloody pissed not to notice, though, particularly now the nights were growing colder. If they'd left the doors wide open all night, at least Murray would have reasonable grounds for complaint.

He climbed the steps on to the decking. 'Hello! Anyone around?'

There was no wind and the silence felt intense. From up here, he couldn't even hear the wash of the sea on the beach. Somewhere in the distance he could hear the barking of a dog, but that sounded like it might be coming from another world.

'Hello! It's Murray Johnson. I've just come...' He trailed off, unsure how to finish the sentence. Then, feeling uncomfortably voyeuristic, he peered into the gloom of the living room.

It took him a moment to register what he was seeing, as if his brain were refusing to process it. Then he recoiled to the edge of the decking, bile rising in his throat.

'Oh, my sweet Jesus.'

CHAPTER TWO

This was a first.

A first in more than one way, Alec McKay thought. The first time he could recall seeing Jock Henderson not fully enclosed in his white protective suit. The first time, at least in a very long time, that McKay had been seriously tempted to accept Henderson's semi-ironic offering of a cigarette. Definitely the first time that both he and Henderson had been almost lost for words. They could generally find something to say, even if it was only trading half-hearted insults.

They were sitting on a bench at the top of the cliff, a few hundred metres from the chalet. McKay had been patiently waiting for some feedback from the team of examiners who had been working on the scene all morning, making a series of calls back to the office to get the necessary processes underway. He'd decided the view out over the firth might distract his brain from what had taken place just behind him. So far, that hadn't worked, but he'd been glad of the fresh air.

Eventually Jock Henderson had made his ungainly way along the cliff path to join him. McKay had been expecting Henderson to summon him for a debrief back at the scene, but

Henderson had clearly opted to ditch his protective clothing for the moment to join McKay out here. McKay couldn't say he blamed him. Henderson had taken a seat beside him and then silently waved his cigarette pack in McKay's direction. It was a long-running joke between them, but McKay had found himself hesitating for a moment before shaking his head. Henderson had nodded and lit his own cigarette. McKay had pulled out his familiar pack of gum and, with the air of a chess grandmaster making a counter-move, briefly held it under Henderson's nose. It was as close as they were likely to get to their usual verbal sparring.

Henderson had sat in silence for several minutes, his attention apparently focused on his cigarette. McKay watched the play of the morning sun on the water. Finally, Henderson said, 'The bloody kiddies, though.'

'Aye,' McKay agreed.

'What sort of cold-hearted bastard does something like that?'

McKay stretched out his legs. 'The working assumption is that it's the kind of cold-hearted bastard currently sitting in that living room half-decapitated. Unless you're about to tell me differently, Jock.'

'We've seen nothing so far to contradict that idea.'

McKay thought back to the moment, an hour or so before, when he'd taken a brief look at the crime scene. Henderson had grumbled, in his usual slightly tetchy manner, that McKay shouldn't trouble himself, but McKay was damned if he was going to allow Henderson to tell him what to do. Apart from anything else, if McKay had showed any sign of squeamishness, Henderson would never have allowed him to forget it.

More importantly, though, McKay had wanted a real sense of the crime scene. By the time Henderson and his team had completed their work, the room would have been rendered tidier, more sterile. It would be captured in literally forensic detail, but that would be different from the initial technicolour-reeking reality. McKay felt he needed a sense of that.

McKay had never thought of himself as faint-hearted, and there wasn't much he hadn't witnessed in his police career. But a brief glimpse into that living room, standing at the patio windows, had been more than enough. He'd used the term 'bloodbath' once or twice over the years, but he knew now he'd really never used it appropriately. This was like nothing he'd seen. The blood was everywhere, soaking the carpet, spattering the walls, the heavy stench almost unbearable.

There were five bodies, five sets of human remains, among the endless gore. All dead from multiple stab wounds, the apparent murder weapon still buried in the nearly severed throat of an adult male. The others were an adult female, and three children – two female, one male – of varying ages.

The Dawson family. Paul. Maria. And the three children. Lily. Amelia. Will.

McKay had already extracted what information he could from the site owner, Murray Johnson. The Dawsons had been staying here for two weeks, due to leave today. Johnson had had little contact with them, other than a brief welcome on their arrival.

'Why would someone do something like that, though?' Henderson asked now. 'And to their own bloody family.' It sounded like more than a rhetorical question, as if he was hoping that McKay might genuinely provide an answer. People always wanted to know why, McKay thought, but often there was no answer or at least nothing that came close to an explanation.

Both men lapsed back into silence. Henderson smoked another cigarette and looked at his watch. 'They'll think I've got lost. Better be heading back.'

'Anything else you can tell me, Jock? Anything else I should know?'

He could see the other man bite back his usual sarcastic response. 'Not really. Not at this stage. It seems to be just what it looks like.'

'What it looks like,' McKay said, 'is a glimpse into hell.'

'Aye, you're not wrong about that.' Henderson dropped his cigarette butt into the undergrowth and ground it firmly under his heel. McKay couldn't even be bothered to offer some caustic remark about the risk of wildfires. Henderson stood for another moment staring out to sea then, as he turned to leave, muttered again, 'The bloody kiddies, though.'

CHAPTER THREE

Henderson was a tall skinny man, who moved back along the path with all the grace of a crane with knee problems. He looked as if, at any moment, he might miss a step and topple awkwardly over the cliff edge, but somehow maintained his equilibrium long enough to make it to the rear entrance to the chalet.

McKay closed his eyes for a moment, as if summoning some telepathic power. 'You can come out now.'

DS Ginny Horton stepped out from among the trees. 'How did you know I was there?'

'I'm a bloody detective, Ginny. I have the gift of being able to spot people standing ten feet away. You should have joined me and Jock.'

'You seemed to be having a moment. I didn't like to interrupt.'

McKay gave a snort of disgust. 'Jock was having a moment. I was just listening. Or, rather, not listening.'

'Not like Jock,' Ginny observed. 'He's not one for moments.'

'I never imagined the undead had feelings.'

'If this one doesn't get to you,' Ginny said pointedly, 'I don't know what would.'

'Aye, you're not wrong. One hell of a business. How were our friends over the way?'

Despite his shock at the discovery, Murray Johnson had done a decent job of persuading the guests in the other chalets not to leave until the police arrived. A couple of families had ignored his request to stay put, but the majority had co-operated and were being interviewed by a team of uniformed officers.

Ginny Horton had taken on the task of interviewing Mark and Catherine Fanning, the couple who'd first drawn Murray Johnson's attention to the disturbance the previous night. She sat herself down on the bench beside McKay. 'They're a bit in shock, to be honest. I didn't tell them what had happened, but they'd worked out it was something serious. They'd obviously got to know the Dawsons a bit – kids played together and all that – so it's knocked them back. And of course they're blaming themselves. Wishing they'd done something when they first heard all the noise.'

'Would probably have made bugger all difference. At best, we'd have just been on the scene twelve hours earlier.'

'That might have made a difference.'

'You reckon? Looked to me like they'd all have died pretty instantly. And the perpetrator's not gone anywhere in the meantime, except maybe to the fiery furnaces.'

'We don't know that for sure yet.'

'You have a different view? I mean, I'm keeping an open mind till we've had all the pathology and forensic reports but only because that's what they taught us back in detective school. Doesn't seem to me that this is likely to be anything other than some crazy bastard topping his wife and kids and then plunging the knife into his own throat. The question is why.'

'The Fannings reckoned they'd seen no sign of any

problems. Paul and Maria Dawson seemed a perfect couple and there were no signs of any issues with the children.'

'They're always the ones to watch, though, aren't they? The idyllic families who seem to live the perfect lovey-dovey existence. Who knows what poison is churning below the surface? What else did they tell you?'

'There wasn't a lot to add to what they'd already told Johnson. Last time they spoke to any of the Dawsons was yesterday afternoon, when Catherine Fanning had a brief chat with Maria Dawson. Again, no sign of anything out of the ordinary. Catherine Fanning had suggested they eat dinner together as it was their last night here, but Maria Dawson said her husband was expecting a visitor.'

'She didn't say what kind of visitor?'

'That was all she said. Apparently, there was a car parked outside the Dawsons' place in the earlier part of yesterday evening, but the Fannings didn't see it arrive or leave.'

'I assume they couldn't provide any information on the car?'

Ginny shrugged. 'Something big. Dark coloured – maybe black or dark grey. Maybe a BMW or an Audi, something like that.'

McKay sighed. 'Aye, that and two quid gets me a cup of coffee. We can check whether Johnson's got any CCTV set up here, I suppose. Was this car still there when they heard all the shouting later?'

'Have a guess.'

'They don't know. What do I win?'

'My undying loyalty and admiration, obviously. But, yes, you're right. They weren't sure. Though they thought it probably wasn't.'

'Sometimes I wonder why we even bother. So what was it they heard?'

'Something that started like an argument, but then got

increasingly heated. Screaming, she reckoned, and probably not just one person.'

'The children?'

'Seems likely.'

'So a lot depends on this mysterious car,' McKay said. 'Who was the visitor? Did they somehow contribute to whatever the argument was about? And – above all – what time did they leave? Shall we go to see what else our friend Murray Johnson has to say?' He pushed himself to his feet, his eyes still focused on the sea, as if he were trying to erase the images he'd witnessed earlier.

They walked back through the trees to the central track that led down through the cluster of chalets. The area around the crime scene was still busy with uniformed officers, and the site was cluttered with marked vehicles. 'Not ideal publicity for the place,' Horton commented.

'Not in the short term,' McKay said. 'Next year the place'll be packed with people wanting to see the crime scene.'

'He might have more difficulty letting the scene itself.'

'They'll be flocking to stay in there. There's no shortage of ghouls.'

They found Murray Johnson in a small office and workshop near the entrance to the site. McKay tapped on the window and Johnson waved him to come in. 'I'm afraid there's not much room,' he said, as they crowded into the small space. Another man had been sitting in the corner and now rose to greet the arrivals.

'Fergus Campbell, my deputy,' Johnson explained.

'Deputy and general dogsbody. I'll leave you to it if you need a bit of space.'

'No bother, Mr Campbell. I'm sure we can all squeeze in. Might be useful to talk to you both together.'

'Aye, you'll get twice as much blether.' Campbell lowered himself back down on to a stool in the corner.

The office contained little more than a desk, a handful of stacked chairs and a filing cabinet. The rear of the room led through a small workshop with a workbench and a row of racks containing what McKay assumed were spare parts relating to the chalets. Johnson looked apologetic. 'We don't often use this place. Fergus had the workshop mainly to do running repairs on items from the chalets. I come up occasionally to deal with suppliers, but that's about it. It's not exactly a home from home.'

'I'm sure we'll manage.' McKay slid one of the chairs across to Horton, and then sat down himself, gesturing to Johnson and Campbell to do the same. 'It's not exactly a social call. We'll try not to detain you any longer than we need to. I'm sure you've plenty on your plate.'

'You can say that again. Your people reckoned it was okay for me to continue letting the other chalets? I hope that's true because most of the new guests are already on their way.'

'I don't see why not. As long as we keep the crime scene well protected. We'll need to be in there for a while yet. What about the people who were due to rent that?'

'I've been in touch with them. Told them what had happened – not in any detail, just as you said, but just to say there's been an incident which requires police investigation. Luckily, I've been able to find them a place at another site up the coast. Not quite as convenient, but more luxurious. I've taken the hit on the cost, but they're happy enough.'

'You reckon the other guests will be okay to stay with something like this in their midst?' Horton asked.

Johnson shrugged. 'I've explained it to the ones I could get hold of. They seemed happy enough but it might be different if word gets out on the grapevine about what's really happened.'

'And it will,' McKay growled.

'We'll just have to play it by ear, then.' Johnson shook his head. 'I still can't quite believe it.'

'How long have you been running this place, Mr Johnson?'

'Over ten years now. Attempt to diversify from the farming. I've still got the farm, arable and livestock, but it's a precarious business. This place gives a solid income for a good part of the year.'

'What about the Covid lockdown?' Horton asked. 'That must have been tough for you.'

'Bloody tough. We more or less had to shut down the place. Got some bits and pieces of support from the government, but nothing like we really needed. Just hope all this doesn't finally pull the rug from under the place. Sorry, that probably sounds a bit insensitive.'

'You've a business to run,' McKay said. 'Nice place, too. You must get a lot of repeat visitors?'

'We do. Some people book for next year as soon as they've finished this. This year's been a bit different, though, with the lockdown. People were worried about booking overseas holidays, so they've booked to come here instead. So we've had a lot of first-timers over the summer.'

'Including the Dawsons?'

'They were actually Scottish, unlike most of our guests over the summer, and seemed familiar with the Highlands – more than a lot of this year's crowd, anyway – but they hadn't stayed here before.'

'What can you tell us about them?'

'Not a great deal, I'm afraid. I printed off their booking details in case it's of any use to you. But it doesn't tell you much. Husband, wife, three children. Home address in the Borders. Paid the deposit and balance promptly on credit card. That's about it.'

McKay scanned through the papers. 'What did you make of them?'

'I didn't see a lot of them. I try to make a point of greeting all the new arrivals when they first get here. Just makes the whole thing a bit more personal. Say hello. Give them a quick tour of the chalet. Tell them a bit about the area, places to eat and drink locally, bit of a chat about what sort of things they want to do on the holiday, and give them a few recommendations if they don't know the area. That sort of stuff. But I only met them for a few minutes, really. Seemed pleasant enough. Made all the right polite noises about the location and the chalet itself. Like I say, they seemed to know the area reasonably well. Not the Black Isle in particular, but the Highlands in general. I think the husband had done some work up here.'

'What sort of stuff were they looking to do on their holiday?' Horton asked.

'Mainly just get a bit of rest, from what they said. Husband was in business in some form. He was just looking for a couple of weeks with the family not doing too much. I remember his wife making some mildly caustic remark about there always being a first time.'

McKay raised an eyebrow. 'Some tension between them?'

'Just the usual married couple banter, I thought. But it was just a brief chat. To be honest, I was a bit surprised they'd chosen to come here.'

'Why do you say that?'

'We're proud of the old place, but it's not the most upmarket set-up. I'd have expected someone with their money either to stay in one of the hotels or to have booked one of the posher holiday cottages. And probably on the west coast rather than here, if that's not too disloyal to the Black Isle. The real money tends to head west.'

'Maybe they left it too late?'

'That's what I assumed. We were worried it might be slim pickings this year without the Americans and the Europeans, but everywhere's been booked solid. The Dawsons booked fairly early in the year, but it might still have been too late to get what they really wanted.'

'What about the children?' McKay asked. 'How did they seem?'

Johnson was silent for a second, clearly thinking back to what he had witnessed in the chalet earlier in the morning. 'Just kids. The boy looked only about five or six, the two girls a bit older. They were running around slightly manically, but I imagine that was because they'd been cooped up in the car for hours.' He stopped suddenly and swallowed. 'Sorry. It's just...'

'I know,' McKay said, in a tone that sounded uncharacteristically tender. 'Take your time.'

'It just seems such a bloody shame.' Johnson blinked. 'How the hell could someone do that?'

'That's what we need to find out,' McKay said. 'What motivated this. Why it happened.'

'I'm assuming the father...'

'It's too early to offer a view, Mr Johnson. We've a lot of work to do first.'

'Aye, of course. I didn't mean...'

'We're keeping an open mind at present, at least till we've finished the preliminary investigations. Is there anything else you can tell us about the Dawsons you think might be pertinent to the inquiry?'

'I don't think so. As I say, I only met them for a few minutes.'

'What about you, Mr Campbell?'

'Not much I can add,' Campbell said. 'I spoke to them a couple of times, but that was about it.'

'Do you spend a lot of time up here?' Horton asked.

'Maybe a day a week on average during the season. My main work's down on the farm, but I come up here to keep things ticking over. Bit of grass cutting round the chalets, the odd repair, even stuff like replacing light bulbs if guests ask for it. Whatever needs doing. I've been up a bit more than usual in the last couple of days because we were doing some work in one of the chalets. Happened to be walking through the site when they were on their way in or out the chalet, so said hello and had a brief chat. Just to show willing, really.'

'How did they seem?'

'Like Murray said, pleasant enough. Comfortable in chatting to the hired help, if you get my drift. If I'm honest, I thought the husband had a slightly condescending air. A boss who's used to talking down to the workforce. Not unpleasantly, but as if he saw himself as a cut above.'

McKay nodded. 'What about Maria Dawson?'

'The wife? Not sure. I did notice that he did most of the talking. She just stood there smiling. She looked a bit bored, to be honest.'

'Bored?'

'Not sure how else to describe it. As if she'd seen her husband do his country squire bit before and wasn't keen to sit through it again. Sorry if I'm talking out of turn.'

'Not at all. That's very helpful. Anything else, Mr Campbell?'

'Don't think so. I bumped into them one other time, but they were just getting into the car, so it was nothing more than a nod and a hello.'

'If anything else does occur to you both, please let us know. Anything you think might be relevant, even if it's just something trivial. There's one other question. Do you have CCTV on site?'

'Some,' Johnson said. 'There's a camera at the entrance, and a couple of others around the site. We mainly put them in because we've had the odd bit of vandalism over the winter months.'

'Anything on the chalets themselves?'

'We've talked about it, but I didn't want anything that would feel too intrusive for guests. Some of them don't like it if they think they're being watched, even if it's for their own safety and security.'

'Can you let us have any footage from yesterday?'

'Sure. It's all electronic, but I can give you the data. Do you think it's likely to be useful?'

'We're at the stage where every little helps. Or might do. We'll leave you to it.' McKay paused. 'I ought to warn you that, once word gets out, the media will be all over this. We'll do our best to keep them away from you and your guests, but they're cunning and tenacious buggers, if you get my drift.'

Johnson nodded, wearily. 'What do I say to them?'

'If you want my advice, as little as possible. You may find that you even get financial offers for your "exclusive story". I can't stop you talking to them, but I wouldn't advise it. And don't believe a word the buggers tell you about what they'll pay.'

Johnson gave an involuntary shudder. 'I wouldn't want to profit from – well, from that.'

'No decent person would,' McKay agreed. 'Unfortunately, not all tabloid journalists fit into that category. Let us know if you have any problems.'

'I will.' Johnson still looked mildly stunned, as if his understanding of the world had been shifted irrevocably by what he'd witnessed that morning. *Join the club, pal,* McKay thought. Except that, in McKay's case, this kind of event tended mostly to confirm everything he'd always assumed about his fellow man.

CHAPTER FOUR

DCI Helena Grant slammed down the phone and uttered a mild expletive. Alec McKay would no doubt have come up with a more imaginative profanity, but straightforward invective was good enough for her.

This was not how she wanted to spend Saturday morning. Any Saturday morning, but particularly not this one. She'd had plans for this one. Not major plans. Just the same low-key ritual she enacted every year at this time. It always felt mildly melancholy, and not only for the obvious reasons. It was as if she were marking the end of yet another summer, as well as commemorating a more significant loss.

Another summer. Another year passing. Another year in which nothing much had happened to her.

That wasn't quite true, of course. Plenty had happened in the past twelve months. It was just that none of it was positive. She'd spent the first part of the year recovering from the impact of the last. Literally recovering, in that she'd been encouraged to take medical leave even though her physical injuries had been minor. She supposed the emotional and psychological damage was likely to be deeper and longer lasting, but it hadn't felt that way and, in truth, it still didn't. She just felt numb, bereft of any real feeling or emotion. That probably wasn't a good thing.

Since then she'd thrown herself back into work, knowing it was the only way she could keep going. As matters had turned out, it had proved to be a wise move.

Everything had changed back in April. None of them had realised that at the time, of course. It was just another new appointment, and the first rumblings of rumour drifting up from the south. The appointment had been that of Chief Superintendent Michael Everly, late of police headquarters in Tulliallan, as divisional commander. There was nothing particularly surprising about the appointment itself. The previous incumbent had retired, and the expectation had been that the post would be filled from outside the division. Everly seemed both capable and personable, a combination which – at least in Alec McKay's eyes – was all too rare at senior levels in the force.

But it was clear from the moment of Everly's arrival that something had changed, or was in the process of changing. Since the establishment of the national force, there'd been an increasing drive towards conformity and centralisation. That was fair enough up to a point, Grant thought. The creation of the national force was supposedly to increase consistency of practice, improve communications, deliver economies of scale, all the stuff that they printed in their glossy annual reports. That inevitably involved breaking up some of the fiefdoms that had developed over the preceding decades. That, equally inevitably, resulted in growing resistance from those who, for good reasons or ill, remained wedded to the way they'd always worked.

For these and other reasons, the pace of change had been

slower than many at the top had initially expected and wanted. Some centralisation initiatives had succeeded, but many others had failed. As far as Helena Grant was concerned, this was just organisational life – those with new brooms wanted to use them, the older hands were concerned about what might be swept away in the process. Like most officers at her level, she'd largely just kept her head down.

It had been clear from the start that, pleasant and easy-going as he might seem, Michael Everly was firmly grasping a brand-new broom and had every intention of using it. Within weeks of his arrival, he'd introduced a series of restructurings and changes, most of which had reduced divisional autonomy. An ill-informed observer might have wondered why Everly would want to reduce his own authority, but the obvious answer was that he already had an eye on the next rung on his career ladder.

The changes had worried Alec McKay more than Helena Grant. Her preference was simply to get on with the job, and she didn't much mind whether authority lay here in divisional HQ or somewhere further south. McKay, on the other hand, preferred to operate without what he saw as undue constraints and pointless bureaucracy. When it suited him, he was all too happy to exploit any ambiguity in the major investigation team's chain of command, even if that ambiguity existed mainly in McKay's own head.

Michael Everly, by contrast, was a man with a low tolerance of ambiguity. He wanted matters to be clear-cut and unequivocal, and his preference was for specialist teams to be co-ordinated and managed from the centre. And that, increasingly, was what was happening, with more and more activities – from restructuring projects to criminal investigations – led by officers from the south, while local staff simply provided the supporting resource.

Grant had been sceptical as to how well this would work in

practice. Her experience was that the major investigation team up here was largely left alone simply because ambitious officers couldn't be bothered to drag their backsides up the A9 to deal with what they thought of as 'trouble in sheep-shagger land'. In McKay's acerbic phrase, 'Most of them don't believe in life after Perth.'

So far, her scepticism had been largely vindicated. Even when an officer from outside the division had been placed in notional charge of an inquiry, in practice she'd found herself operating as senior investigating officer, subject to little more than regular debriefs to her supposed boss and the receipt of unwanted and generally unhelpful advice on how to do her job. McKay had had an acerbic phrase for that too, but it was one Grant preferred not to articulate out loud.

'Penny for them.'

Grant looked up in surprise, wondering if her not entirely positive thoughts on Michael Every had somehow managed to summon his presence. However he'd been invoked, he was now leaning on the doorway to her office. 'You'd be getting a bargain.'

'That right? Profound stuff then.'

'Always. What can I do for you, Mike? You do know it's Saturday?'

'No peace for the wicked, especially at my level. Was just wondering what the latest was on this case up on the Black Isle? Sounds a nasty one.'

'Very. I'm just trying to drum up resources for it.'

'Having problems?'

'No more than usual. But it's going to be a big one. Especially over the next few days.'

'I'm assuming it'll be relatively straightforward, though? As an investigation, I mean.'

'In theory. If it's what it appears to be.'

'Family annihilation?'

She raised an eyebrow. It was a piece of jargon she'd come across only relatively recently, and it seemed unnecessarily brutal. 'Something like that. Most likely murder-suicide. And most likely the father as perpetrator. But obviously all that's to be confirmed.'

'Obviously. Media's going to be all over it, though.'

'I'd have thought so. At least for a day or two till they get bored.'

'I've just been talking to comms. They're getting a media statement ready. Do you think we need anything else?'

'My inclination would be to keep it low-key for the moment. We don't want to release names until we've identified and contacted the next of kin. And then we need to be conscious of their sensitivities.'

'Yes, of course.' Everly had remained in the doorway while they'd been talking. Now he entered the office and seated himself in the chair opposite Grant's desk. 'Speaking of sensitivities,' he said, 'I believe Alec McKay's dealing with this?'

She looked up. 'I was expecting to be SIO. But, yes, I was intending Alec to lead the work on the ground. Is that a problem?'

'Not at all. I've heard good things about him. He seems a bit of a character?'

'He'd like you to think so. A lot of it's an act.' Grant wasn't remotely sure this was really true, but she wasn't going to acknowledge anything else to Everly.

'An act?'

'Alec's the best I've got. He's an instinctive investigator who knows what stone to turn over, what hole to start poking his metaphorical stick into. His manner's just one of his techniques. He likes to wrong-foot people sometimes, to stir things up. It works.'

Everly's expression suggested he remained unconvinced. 'But underneath he's got a heart of gold?'

'I wouldn't go that far. But underneath is a real foundation of integrity, let's put it that way. He's not your clichéd maverick cop who doesn't play by the rules. He just likes you to think he is.' She'd resisted crossing her fingers under the desk while saying all this. After all, it was largely true. Largely.

'I know the type. I was just wondering how he'd react if, on this occasion, the SIO was someone from outside the division?'

'How do you mean?'

'I've been talking to major investigations at HQ. They're keen to improve co-ordination across the divisions. Get things more on a consistent footing.'

'Is that right?'

'Don't you think it's a good idea?'

'I can see the logic.'

'They want to encourage more cross-divisional working. We thought this might be a good one to start on.'

Grant noted the *we*. 'Why this one?'

'It's likely to be high profile, but should be relatively straightforward in that we already know who the likely perpetrator is. As far as the Fiscal's concerned, it'll largely be a matter of confirming that and providing some insights into the likely motivation.'

'We don't know for sure who the perpetrator is.'

'You think it's likely to be anyone other than the father?'

'I don't imagine so.'

'There you are then. So what do you think of the idea?' It wasn't clear whether he was seeking her approval or just asking her opinion. The latter, she assumed.

'Who do they have in mind as SIO?'

'Chap called Nightingale. Brian Nightingale.'

'Name sounds familiar. Where's he based?'

'Glasgow.' Everly paused. 'I understand he started out up here.'

'Think I remember him. He was a few years older than me. He moved on just about the time I joined CID, I think, so I never really knew him.' *Except by reputation,* she added to herself. If her recollection was correct, Nightingale had been another one of DCI Jackie Galloway's young acolytes. That didn't necessarily mean much, of course. Both she and Alec McKay had both briefly been part of Galloway's team and hadn't been tainted by Galloway's dubious example. Some of Galloway's coterie had been closer to him than others, and the smarter ones had always maintained a cautious distance from his practices. That might explain why Nightingale had chosen to depart for the south.

Except she had a vague recollection that Nightingale's departure had been clouded by some hint of scandal. Even at the time this hadn't been much more than canteen gossip, with no coherent story emerging. She'd been a trainee at the time so no one had confided in her. All she'd had was the tail-end of others' tittle-tattle.

'Has a decent track record anyway. So if his presence isn't going to put your nose out of joint...'

And what if it did? she thought. It was quite clear the decision had already been taken and nothing that she might say would make any difference. 'Fine by me. It's not as if I'm short of work.'

'Well, that was another consideration. I know how hard pressed you all are.'

Grant couldn't think of an immediate response that wouldn't have sounded sarcastic. Not for the first time in her recent career, she found herself feeling grateful that Alec McKay wasn't in the room. 'So when's he joining us?'

'He's driving up tomorrow to join us first thing Monday

morning. Can I leave you to brief Alec? I'm assuming Brian will still want him on the team.'

That's likely to depend, Grant thought, on whether Nightingale is more interested in a successful outcome or a quiet life. 'I'll let him know.'

'Excellent.' Everly began to rise from his seat then paused, as if struck by a sudden thought. 'There was one other thing while I'm here.'

'Yes?'

'I'm not sure if this is appropriate or if I'm speaking out of turn, but I understand your late husband was Rory Grant?'

The question took her by surprise, especially given the timing. 'You knew him?'

'Way back. We both started in Strathclyde at roughly the same time. He was a good man. And a good cop, too, for what that's worth.'

It had been worth a lot in Rory's eyes, she thought. He'd always said he'd lived for two things – her and the job. Not necessarily in that order, he'd usually added with a laugh. He'd not been one of those who were wedded to the job rather than their spouse, but he'd taken the job very seriously. 'In my eyes, he was both.'

'I'm afraid I'd lost touch with him. It was only when I moved up here and someone mentioned your name that I made the connection. I was sorry to hear the news. It must have been a dreadful shock for you.'

'It was bad at the time. Not least because it was so sudden and unexpected. Time passes, though.'

'Well, I'm very sorry.'

'It's funny you should mention him today.'

'Is it?'

'It would have been his birthday. I used to rib him about it because he was a few years older than I was. If I'd known what was going to happen, I might have put more force into saying "many happy returns".'

'I'm sorry, I didn't realise...'

'Don't worry. It's really a time for positive thoughts.'

'Not an ideal time to be in the office, though?'

'I've been telling myself it's what he would have wanted. Which is probably true. But it doesn't really matter. It's not as if I'd have been having a party at home. But I do like to commemorate it.'

'In what way?'

She looked mildly embarrassed. 'I usually drive over to Rosemarkie to be honest. Over on the Black Isle. I live over there now, but it used to be one of the places we went walking. Just on the beach there. If it's a fine day, I usually follow the track we'd have taken. Come back and have a coffee at the beach café. I just sit and think about it. It doesn't sound much. It's just one of those rituals you get into.'

'I understand. Pity you weren't able to do it today.'

'I'll take a drive over there once I've finished here. Could use it as an excuse to visit the crime scene and break the news to Alec.'

'Ah, yes, of course. That's over that way, isn't it? Sorry, I'm still getting used to the area. Anyway, I just wanted to let you know I'd known Rory. He was a decent man. I'll leave you to it. I'll bring Brian round to introduce him to everyone on Monday. Let me know if there's anything you need in the meantime.'

'I'll get everything ready to hand over to him. Wouldn't want him to think we were unprofessional.'

'Exactly.' Everly stood for a moment, as if wanting to say more, but finally turned to leave. 'Right. See you Monday.'

After he'd disappeared down the corridor, Grant sat staring at the spot where he'd been sitting. What, she wondered, had that been all about? There'd been something mildly awkward about Everly's tone throughout. Partly discomfort at the news he was bringing, no doubt. Partly discomfort at raising the personal topic of her late husband, perhaps. But it had felt a little more than that.

If she hadn't known better, she might have thought he'd been very ineptly trying to chat her up.

CHAPTER FIVE

I sla Bennett turned into the drive and pulled into her usual parking spot in front of the house. Ginny's car was still absent, which meant Ginny was most likely still at work. That wasn't a surprise. From the little Ginny had been able to tell her that morning, it was clear she had another big one on her hands. Those kind of cases didn't come along too often, but when they did they were all-consuming.

Isla didn't really mind too much. She'd known what she was signing up for with Ginny, and it wasn't as if Isla was exactly a home-bird herself. Like Ginny, she worked long hours and often had to shuttle up and down to London. There'd been much less of that during the Covid lockdown, of course, and many of her associates and clients seemed finally to have weaned themselves off face-to-face meetings, accepting that much of their business could be carried out remotely. That had been something of a blessing, but in practice it just meant she spent even more of her time in the office in Inverness.

Even so, today was Saturday, and Isla hadn't really needed to go into the office. Her original intention had been to spend the day at home with Ginny and actually try to relax for a change. But once Ginny had been called in, Isla had thought she might as well use the time to deal with her backlog of paperwork.

She let herself into the house, picking up the mail as she did so. She checked her phone but there was no further message or text from Ginny, so no more indication of when she was likely to be home.

While she waited for the kettle to boil, Isla flicked aimlessly through the small stack of mail. Virtually all of them were junk of one variety or other – leaflets from supermarkets in Inverness, menus from local carry-outs, a 'once in a lifetime' opportunity to own a worthless gold sovereign commemorating some unimportant national event. At the bottom of the small pile there was a white envelope that looked more personalised, her name and address printed on to a label, the envelope carrying stamps rather than a machine franking. She took the envelope, along with her coffee, into the living room.

She turned on the television, flicking till she found one of the news channels. It was nearly five and there'd be a news bulletin on the hour, but for the moment the announcer was running through the day's football results. Isla turned her attention to the envelope, prising it open with her fingernail.

Inside, there was a single sheet, a letter addressed to her. The letter was typed and printed rather than handwritten, but signed with a personal signature, scrawled in blue ink.

Shit.

It took her only a few minutes more to skim through the rest of the content. It was more or less what she expected, given the identity of the sender. She was tempted to toss it straight in the bin, but in the end she refolded it and slipped it back in the envelope. As she did so, her phone buzzed on the table. Ginny.

'Hi, Isla. You back home?'

'Just. How are you doing?'

'Just about finishing up here for the day. Examiners are still doing their stuff, but we've done as much as we can for the moment. Was just going to have a quick debrief over a drink, then I'll head back.'

'That's good. How's it looking?'

'Not great. It's going to be a big one.'

'Won't be seeing much of you for a while then?'

'For a few days at least. It looks fairly straightforward. Not pleasant but straightforward.'

Isla was silent for a second. 'I've had a letter.'

'A letter? What sort of letter?'

'From Tristram.'

'Your brother Tristram?'

'How many Tristrams do you think I know?'

'Isla, you went to boarding school, and you've got degrees from Durham and St Andrew's. You're not going to tell me you only know one Tristram.'

'Fair point. But, no, this is my brother.'

'Christ. How long's it been?'

'Not long enough, as far as I'm concerned. I'd hoped he'd given up on me.'

'Is he still inside?'

'Unfortunately not. At least for the moment.'

'Maybe he's turned over a new leaf.'

'Maybe the Pope's embraced Protestantism, but I'm not putting any money on it.'

'So what does he want?'

'He wants to see me.'

'Do you want to see him?'

'Not in a million years. I mean, I feel bad even saying it.

He's flesh and blood, after all. But it's how I feel. He's nothing but bad news.'

'There's no law that says you have to get on with your relatives. I know that better than anyone.'

'Yeah, I suppose you do.' Isla could tell they were both thinking of the moment, a couple of years earlier, when Ginny's stepfather had turned up unexpectedly on their doorstep. 'I guess it's a similar deal.'

'So why does he want to see you?'

'The usual bollocks. Rebuild bridges. Catch up. Put the past behind us.'

'Maybe he means it.'

'I refer you to my previous comment about the religious preferences of the head of the Catholic church. He doesn't mean a word of it.'

'So what does he really want?'

'Who knows? Money, probably. That's usually what he wants. Preferably for nothing.'

'You don't have to see him if you don't want to.'

'I know. But I don't know how best to handle it. My inclination's to ignore the letter. But he can be a persistent bugger when he wants to be. On the other hand, if I write back, even just to tell him to piss off, it'll probably only encourage him.'

'How'd he get your address anyway? I assume you didn't give it to him.'

'I've not had any contact with him for ten years or more. But that's Tristram for you. He has his methods. If he could ever bring himself to turn his hand to something constructive he could make a fortune.'

'Often the way, isn't it? Look, Alec's making characteristically unsubtle "hurry up" gestures to me. I'd better go. Let's discuss this properly when I get back.'

'That'll be best. I'll get some supper going.'

'I won't be long. See you soon.'

Isla ended the call and sat back on the sofa. After a moment, she picked up the envelope, slid out the letter, and began to read it again.

CHAPTER SIX

'That's not exactly tasteful in the circumstances,' Horton said.

She'd gone out into the car park to make the call, and for the last few seconds Alec McKay had been standing in the pub doorway, making a throat-cutting gesture to tell her to hurry up.

'You think?' he said. 'Hadn't occurred to me.'

She raised an eyebrow as she followed him back into the welcoming gloom of the bar. 'Where's the fire, anyway?'

'Sorry. Didn't want to hassle you. It's just that Hel's got some business after she finishes here, so I didn't want to keep her too long.'

'Business?'

McKay said in an unexpectedly quiet voice, 'Rory's birthday.'

'Oh, God. Is it? I didn't realise.'

'She wants to take a walk along the beach at Rosemarkie. For old times' sake.'

'We'd better not keep her then. She's got some news to break to us, apparently.'

'What sort of news?'

'I don't know, but serious enough to break the news in a pub.'

'That's seriously serious.'

'What I thought. Let's find out.'

They were in the public bar at the Culbokie Inn, the nearest McKay had to a local, not that he was much of a drinker these days. But he enjoyed the odd pint with Chrissie and the place offered decent food and a convivial atmosphere. They were off-duty now and he could walk home from here, so he could afford to treat himself to a pint. Grant was on some alcohol-free beer and Horton on a lime and soda.

'Sorry to keep you,' Horton said as they sat down.

'Just want to get to the beach while the light holds. Don't want to find myself walking in the dark.'

McKay took a swallow of his beer. 'So what's this all about, Hel? Sounds like something serious.'

'It's just an organisational thing.'

'That sounds worse. What kind of organisational thing?'

'I had a visit from Mike Everly today.'

'You must feel honoured. I bet he doesn't deign to visit just anyone. I've never seen him near my desk, for example. What did he want?'

'You know he's keen to promote cross-divisional working.'

'So we can all work in locations that we don't know or understand. Smart thinking.' McKay already had an inkling of where this was heading. For all his casual manner, he had a knack for keeping his ear close to the ground.

'He doesn't want me to be SIO on this one.'

'So which bugger does he have in mind?'

'A guy called Brian Nightingale from Glasgow.'

'Nightingale? Another bad penny.'

'Who's Brian Nightingale?' Horton was accustomed to

playing spectator to these kinds of exchanges between Grant and McKay.

'He's a DCI now,' McKay said. 'Bafflingly. Just shows how much lower standards are down south. He started out up here, a year or two ahead of Helena and myself. One of the late unlamented Jackie Galloway's crew for a while. Then departed for the Elysian Fields of the central belt.'

'Another of Galloway's?' Horton said. 'With the usual characteristics?' Galloway had been a DCI in the force early in Grant and McKay's career, with a well-merited reputation for corruption and questionable practices. His presence still hung over the division like a malign spirit, his unfortunate influence living on in unexpected ways.

'I don't know,' Grant said. 'He always seemed a bit detached from the rest of Galloway's team. I'm not sure he shared their proclivities.'

'From what I've heard,' McKay said, 'he had proclivities of his own.'

'I hope you're not going to gossip unprofessionally, Alec.'

'Trust me, Hel, when I gossip it's always with the utmost professionalism. If Ginny's going to be working with this guy, she deserves to know.'

'Know what?' Horton looked from Grant to McKay.

Grant shrugged. 'Alec's obviously got information that's not reached me yet. All I know is that Nightingale supposedly left the Highlands under something of a cloud.'

'You might say that,' McKay said. 'It was all hushed up at the time. But there were complaints. I heard sexual harassment and some kind of drink problem.'

'And it wasn't dealt with?' Horton said.

Grant swirled the beer in her glass, as if hoping to conjure up some image of justice. 'Even today stuff like that gets swept under the carpet. Jackie Galloway probably pulled a few strings. But it's all just gossip. We need to keep this between ourselves. And give Nightingale a warm welcome.' She looked at her watch. 'I ought to be going. Want me to drop you off on my way past, Alec?'

'No, you get on. I could do with the walk. Give me a bit of time to get over today.'

'Not good, then?' Grant said.

'I'm not sorry I took the opportunity to view the crime scene. It's part of the job, and we can't hide from it. But it's not something I'd rush to see again. Don't ever tell Jock Henderson I said so, but I don't know how he copes. We owe it to the victims to do a proper job here. I hope Nightingale realises that. I don't want him breezing in, doing the minimum to satisfy the Fiscal, then taking the credit and buggering off.'

'I'm sure it won't be like that.'

To McKay's ears, Grant sounded far from confident. He took a final mouthful of his beer. 'How are you feeling today, anyway?'

She hesitated before responding. 'Not so bad, considering. It's become less painful with every year, and it's a long while ago now. It's just that this year, well...'

'Aye,' McKay said. 'I'm sorry.' It was less than a year since Grant had seemed to be heading into another serious relationship, which had been snatched from her in the cruellest possible circumstances. He wondered how she was feeling now about everything that had happened. Maybe she'd tell him in her own time. Or maybe she wouldn't.

'I'll survive,' she said. 'And a brisk walk on the beach is just what I need.'

'Aye. You get on.' He waited till Grant had said her goodbyes and left before turning back to Ginny Horton. 'You reckon she's okay?'

'I was just wondering that myself. It's always hard to tell

with Helena. Do you think she's had her nose put out of joint by the arrival of this Nightingale guy?'

'I didn't get the sense she was really concerned about that. Not in itself. The bigger question is whether this is just a one-off or whether this guy Everly really is looking to make serious changes.'

'How would you feel about that?'

'You know me, Gin. Easy come, easy go. I drift where the winds of change take me.'

'Is that so, Alec?'

'Aye. As long as they're taking me in the direction I want to go.'

CHAPTER SEVEN

'You're earlier than I thought. Weren't you holding the debrief in a pub?'

'Strictly one drink. Non-alcoholic in my case.' Ginny paused in the doorway and smiled at Isla, who was stretched out on the sofa.

Isla gestured towards the television screen. 'This you?' The local news presenter was referring to a report of unexplained deaths in a Highland location north of Inverness. Few other details were provided – no indication, for example, of the number of deaths or the circumstances of the killings. It sounded as if the information had been derived largely from the media release issued by the force. She suspected the low-key reporting wouldn't last.

'There'll be more to come.'

'Bad one?'

'About as bad and tragic as they come. Murder-suicide. Probably not a lot to consider from an investigatory point of view, other than to confirm that it's what it appears to be.' She'd become accustomed to providing these kinds of stripped-back summaries of her work to Isla. Just enough to ensure Isla understood what she was dealing with.

'Family thing?'

'Three kids involved. You don't want to know.'

'I probably don't.'

Ginny took the hint. 'Cooking smells good.'

'Thought I'd roast a chicken for a change. Shouldn't be too long.'

Ginny disappeared into the kitchen and returned a few minutes later bearing two glasses of wine. She sat on the sofa by Isla's feet and gestured to a letter on the coffee table in front of them. 'That the famous missive?'

'Tristram breaks the silence.'

'So tell me about Tristram.' She'd been aware that Isla had a brother, and she'd known he was in some way the black sheep of the family and had spent time in prison. But that was about all she knew.

'Where to start? We were the only two kids, and he was older than me. I always felt that he was the favoured child, if you get my drift, but I'm not sure that's really true. Our parents probably treated us both pretty equally – which is to say with financial generosity but not much in the way of love or affection. But Tristram was skilled at making me think he was getting all the attention. I spent most of my childhood and teenage years resenting what I thought was my parents' favouritism.'

'Not sure how to put this delicately,' Ginny said, 'but you're sure this was his problem rather than yours?'

'It's a fair question, but I think so. At the time, I genuinely felt my parents loved him more. It was only later that I looked back and realised there was no real evidence for that. I could think of times when he seemed to have been treated better than me. But if I'm honest I can think of plenty of times when it was the other way round. As far I can see now, my parents bent over backwards to try to treat us equally. They sent us to similar schools, they spent the same amount of money on us at birthdays and Christmas, they made the same effort with both of us. More than I might have expected, to be honest. They were pretty old-fashioned conservative types. It wouldn't have surprised me if they'd seen him as the favoured son and heir. But they didn't. So I asked myself how I'd formed that impression at the time and I realised that it was because Tristram kept telling me it was true.'

'He said that explicitly?'

'Pretty much. It was just a way of undermining me, chipping away at my self-confidence.'

'Why would he do that?'

'You'd have to ask him, except I doubt he could tell you. Lack of self-esteem? A fear that I might be the favoured one, after all? A desire for control? Straightforward spite? Probably a mix of some or all of those. For a long time, I was inclined to let it ride. He's my brother, after all, and you have to cut your family some slack, don't you? But gradually I realised he was a nasty piece of work who didn't give a flying one for anyone but himself.'

'What happened with him?'

'We both went off to boarding school. Our parents were just from a background where that was what you did. I don't think it would ever have occurred to them to send us to the local state school.' She laughed. 'I'm not even sure they could really afford boarding school. My dad was a solicitor like me. He earned a decent salary because he worked for some tax firm in the City, but it wasn't the megabucks you might earn today. They must have spent a fair part of their income on an experience which, in our different ways, Tristram and I both hated. My misery was just the usual thing – wishing I could be back at home, disliking all the petty rivalries, hating the formality of it all. But I was good academically so after a while I became more resigned to it. Tristram never really did. When I saw him during the school holidays, he seemed permanently angry. With the school, with our parents, with life, with everything. He wasn't as strong as I was academically – though he probably could have been if he'd put any effort into it – so he didn't have that to hide behind. His behaviour and disciplinary record got worse and worse. The school complained to my parents, and my dad tried to impose some standards on him. But that just made it worse.'

'This all sounds like typical teenage angst,' Ginny pointed out.

'That's all it was, really. But nobody knew how to handle it. My parents didn't have the skills or the emotional intelligence to get a grip on it. The school weren't really interested. Their solution for dealing with disruptive pupils was, in the end, just to expel them.'

'Is that what happened?'

'Eventually. Part of the trouble was that we weren't rich. I mean, we were comfortably off. But we didn't have money to splash around. There were kids at Tristram's school who were seriously wealthy, and he wanted to hang out with them. I'm not sure what those kids really thought of Tristram, but he was tolerated because he had a reputation as a rebel or what passes for a rebel in that environment. At some point – I'm not quite sure when or how – he'd started to get into drugs. Soft stuff, at first, but it became more serious. The dealers saw him as a conduit into a lucrative market, and of course Tristram fell for it. Started dealing to his so-called mates at school. That was perfect for him. Made him look cool and gave him a ready source of income. But he didn't get away with that for very long. There was some kind of incident. Nobody ever told me the details, but he was under the influence and he lost it, tried to assault a teacher. Expelled and sent home pretty much then and there.'

'Must have been a shock to your parents?'

'Oh, God, yes. Almost as much of a shock as me coming out.'

Ginny laughed. 'Insult to injury?'

'Something like that. But I'm not sure they ever came to terms with what had happened to Tristram. It was a practical problem as well as a personal blow. None of the other fee-paying schools wanted him after what had happened, so they had no choice but to send him to the local comp.'

'Horror of horrors,' Ginny said.

'Okay, state school girl, point taken. But he was an outsider. The kids at the new school just thought he was a posh boy. So he took the easiest route to ingratiate himself into their favour, which was to carry on with his dealing activities. It just went downhill from there. He had a few brushes with the police. Got away with it for a while, mainly because the police thought he was a nice middle-class boy who'd temporarily gone off the rails. But he was determined he wasn't going to stay on at school once he turned sixteen, and then it just got worse.'

She took a breath, as if conscious that now she'd started talking about this, she was going to find it difficult to stop. 'In some ways, I felt for him. He was being exploited. He'd got himself in with some deeply nasty people, who no doubt used every trick in the book to drag him further in. He wasn't a junkie himself – that was one thing he did manage to avoid, as far as I'm aware – but he was a user and he was getting deeper in debt. The people he owed weren't the types to send the bailiffs round, if you get my drift. He'd borrowed money from my mum and dad, but they were smart enough to realise it was just a bottomless pit. He tried to borrow money from me, but I didn't have any at that time. So he did whatever he could to scrape some money together – shoplifting, petty theft, fraud. It couldn't go on, and it didn't. He ended up inside.' She stopped, picked up her glass and finished her wine in one mouthful. 'That's more or less the story. He's been in and out since then. Never held down a job, as far as I'm aware. Just a vicious circle.'

'What about your parents?' Ginny asked. 'How did they take all this?' Isla's parents had died within a few months of one another a couple of years before, her father from a heart attack and her mother from an aggressive form of cancer. Ginny had only met them a few times. She'd managed to get along with them in a reasonably civilised manner, though she'd been left in no doubt they'd never bring themselves to approve of their daughter's relationship or, presumably, sexuality.

'As you'd expect. They spent a long time – far too long, in retrospect – trying to give Tristram the benefit of the doubt, hoping that eventually he'd find his way through and return to the middle-class fold. Eventually, even they realised it wasn't going to happen and they gave up on him. Or he gave up on them, when he found he couldn't extract money from them anymore. Do I sound bitter?'

'Sounds like you might have good reason to be.'

'I sometimes wonder if I've been too hard on him. But I don't think so. He's a parasite. He didn't even make the effort to come to Mum or Dad's funerals. I was relieved that he didn't, but if he'd come to Dad's it would have meant a lot to Mum. Mind you, if he had come back, he'd probably have ended up stealing Mum's jewellery.' She smiled. 'No, I am bitter. I won't make an effort to conceal it.'

'I hadn't realised it was quite that bad.'

'Maybe I'm exaggerating. That's what Tristram would tell you.' She took a sip of the wine, seeming more relaxed now she'd unloaded what Ginny suspected was years' worth of baggage. 'And that brings me back to the key question. What do I do about the letter?'

'As far as I can see, you've only got three real options.'

'Go on,' Isla said. 'Tell me how I reduce it down to three.'

'The first option is that you simply ignore the letter.'

Isla nodded. 'It's very tempting. But he can be remarkably tenacious when it suits him. If he does appear on our doorstep, I want to be in control. I don't want him just turning up out of the blue.'

'So your second option is to write back to him. Short and sweet. Keep it very plain and unequivocal and just make it clear you don't want to see him. Not now. Not ever.'

'And third option?'

Ginny took a sip of her wine. 'The third is to see him.'

CHAPTER EIGHT

S unday offered no day of rest.

Helena Grant was back in the office early, with the intention of making sure everything was in place prior to the arrival of Brian Nightingale the following morning. In fact, she'd already had an email from Nightingale confirming he'd be arriving in Inverness that evening and asking if she fancied joining him for dinner. In the light of the information that McKay had seen fit to share with her and Ginny, she'd pleaded a prior commitment.

She didn't know whether Nightingale would be happy about that, but she was determined he should have no other causes for complaint. In fact, she felt that, in the circumstances, they'd made pretty good progress. They'd interviewed all the other guests on the site by early afternoon on the Saturday, along with a handful of other potential witnesses – the cleaners and other staff employed on the site, some of the local restaurateurs and shop-owners who'd encountered the Dawsons during their stay.

They'd obtained and examined the CCTV footage from the handful of cameras on the site, and had identified images of a black or dark-grey BWM 5 series entering the site at around 4pm on the Friday and leaving at around 8.15pm. The registration didn't match any of the guests' cars, and was the most likely candidate for the car sighted outside the Dawsons' chalet. If so, then the car had not been present at the time the Fannings had heard the disturbance. Even so, whoever had been in the car was clearly a key witness to be tracked down.

The car itself proved to belong to a small independent car-hire company in Inverness. The car-hire office appeared to be closed on Saturday afternoon and Sunday. The two company directors, Craig and Andrea Gillan, had been identified through the Companies House website, with a registered address on the outskirts of the city. A visit from a local uniformed officer had found no one at home. In the end, Grant had decided to leave that one for Nightingale on Monday morning. It would give him something to do.

More poignantly, by Sunday afternoon they'd tracked down the next of kin for Paul and Maria Dawson. Maria Dawson's parents were both still living and now resided in Oxfordshire. Paul's parents were dead, but the police had eventually identified a brother living in West Sussex. Both had now been visited by officers from the relevant local force who had broken the news. At this stage, only limited information had been provided about the nature and cause of the deaths, but the relatives had been informed that the police were not currently seeking anyone else in respect of the deaths of the couple or their children. DNA samples had been taken to confirm the identities of the deceased, although Grant assumed this was nothing more than a formality.

This had all been reported back to Grant in the usual anodyne language, confirming that the appropriate actions had been taken. Reading between the bland lines, she couldn't help wondering what the real impact would be on those involved. What would it be like to discover your only child and your grandchild had been murdered by your son-in-law? What would it be like to discover that your brother had brutally killed his wife and children before taking his own life?

But from a professional point of view, it was another necessary part of the job completed. The inquiry team was now largely in place, with all the key roles assigned, ready for Nightingale to take over on Monday morning. He might even complain that she'd exceeded her brief by taking key decisions out of his hands, but she imagined that such a complaint would receive short shrift even from the likes of Michael Everly.

'I hope the bugger appreciates how much we've done for him,' McKay said, as they gathered for a final debrief on the Sunday afternoon. 'MIR all set up, team mostly in place, half the work done. He can just swan in and take the credit.'

'It'll reflect well on all of us,' Grant pointed out. 'Good professional job. Word gets around.'

'Aye, that's what worries me.' McKay was wandering restlessly round her office in his usual manner. 'They'll think we're a soft touch. Go and take over a case in the Highlands if you want a break. They'll do it all for you.'

'You are going to be co-operative, aren't you, Alec?'

'I'm going to be my usual helpful and supportive self.'

'That's what I was afraid of.' She watched as he peered inquisitively at her small bookcase, though as far as she could recall its contents had remained essentially the same since she'd been in this office. 'On your own head, then.'

'It usually is.' He straightened up and turned back to face Grant. 'You reckon we're going to get more of this, Hel?'

'More of what?'

'Pressure for cross-divisional working.'

'It's the way things are going, isn't it?' Ginny Horton said.

'Or the way the force is going. Break down the barriers, remove the silo thinking.'

'Aye, I believe they run training courses and everything.' McKay spoke in a tone of mild disgust. He finally sat down on the seat next to Horton. 'Sharing best practice. Building the knowledge base. That kind of bollocks.'

'Can't see anything wrong with that stuff myself,' Horton said, mildly. 'But I'm not as old as you, Alec.'

'Not many are, these days. Or that's the way it sometimes feels. Ach, I've nothing against that stuff in theory, but the buggers don't really mean it, do they? They don't want to hear about our good practice. They just want to impose the way they do it. They want to have everything under their control.'

Grant gave a mock yawn. 'They'll do what they want, regardless of what we say or do. I'll go along with it for the sake of a quiet life.'

'This one should be straightforward anyway, shouldn't it?' Horton said, in a tone that implied she'd prefer to move the conversation on.

'That'll be why they've cherry-picked it for Nightingale. All he's got to do is put together a neat file for evidence for the Fiscal. Hard to see how even he can screw it up. I just feel those poor kids deserve a little better.'

Grant sighed. 'This is the point, Alec, when I remind you you're talking about a higher-ranking officer.'

'Oh, aye, I'd forgotten. Hard to see how even a DCI can screw it up.'

'I can see you're not going to make it easy for yourself.'

'I don't believe in favouritism. I'm not going to make it easy for anyone else either.'

'What about this hire car?' Horton said. 'Where does that fit in?'

McKay nodded. 'Well done for dragging us kicking and

screaming back to the topic at hand, Gin. It's a good point. That's the very small pebble in the shoe for me. The one thing that doesn't quite fit. Who was this visitor? Family friend? Some business associate of Paul Dawson's? And did their visit in some way contribute to what happened later?'

'There's still a lot we don't know,' Grant agreed. 'We don't really know anything yet about Dawson's business activities. If he was in some sort of financial trouble, that might give us a motive. That's a key area for Nightingale to look at.'

'I'll see if it occurs to him,' McKay said.

'Presumably we didn't get any clues from the visits to the next of kin?' Horton asked.

'Not really. I guess Nightingale will want to talk to them again once the dust settles, but my impression from the notes is that neither the brother nor the parents-in-law knew much about Dawson's business. They both seemed to think he was doing well, but that was about it.'

'You never know what's going on below the surface, though.' McKay was thinking about his own brother-in-law, who had fooled everyone into believing he was thriving while the world was falling apart around him.

Grant was pulling together the papers on her desk. 'I'm glad to say that's all a problem for Brian Nightingale. I'm looking forward to focusing on the ten thousand other tasks I've got on my plate.'

'You okay about this, Hel?' McKay said. 'If it's any consolation, we'd all much rather be working with you.'

'Well, that's very sweet of you to say so, Alec. But if I'm completely honest, I'm rather looking forward to watching someone else having to deal with you for a change.'

'That's the spirit,' McKay said. 'Always look on the bright side. Brian Nightingale's gain is your loss.'

'Aye, Alec,' she said wearily. 'Something like that.'

CHAPTER NINE

Brian Nightingale stood at the entrance to the hotel restaurant waiting to be seated, just as the sign beside him had instructed. The restaurant supposedly opened at 5.30pm, but it was already gone 6pm, and there was no obvious sign of any waiting staff. For the moment, Nightingale also seemed to be the only prospective diner, but he supposed the place was always relatively quiet on a Sunday evening.

After a few moments, he walked cautiously into the restaurant, clutching the file of papers under his arm. There was some noise emanating from the kitchen, but he assumed it wouldn't be appropriate to start poking his nose in there. He cleared his throat loudly, in the hope of attracting some attention.

'Can I help you, sir?'

He turned to see a smartly suited waitress standing at the entrance to the restaurant. She looked pointedly down at the sign beside her.

'Are you open for dinner?'

'We open at 5.30, sir.'

'Ah, it's just that I couldn't see anyone around so I wondered–'

'Is it just for yourself, sir?'

He thought he could detect a note of judgement in her voice, though presumably the hotel was well accustomed to accommodating lone business travellers. 'Yes, just a table for one, please.'

'Of course.' She led him through the restaurant and showed him to a table in a gloomy corner at the far end. The waitress handed him the glossy menu. 'Can I get you a drink, sir?'

'Glass of red, please.' He was allowed one glass on expenses if away overnight. He'd made a point of purchasing a bottle from Marks & Spencer on his way from the station so he could treat himself to another glass or two later. Otherwise, it was going to be a very long evening.

While he waited for the drink, he perused the menu. It was irritatingly chatty and informal, with headings like 'Something to kick off!', 'Classic delights!' and 'A taste of the exotic!'. The exclamation marks alone were almost enough to kill his appetite. Everything was 'pan-fried', 'oven-roast' or 'char-grilled', and none of it looked particularly enticing. He eventually settled on garlic prawns and fillet steak with chips as the least risky options.

Once the waitress had taken his order and he'd had his first sip of the wine, he opened the file in front of him. If he had to dine alone, he might as well make good use of the time. He had a job to do.

The first job, which he hoped would be relatively straightforward, was to take over as SIO on this Dawson killing. His tactics there were straightforward. He'd focus simply on the facts and discourage any speculation. After all, they knew what had happened. There little serious doubt as to the perpetrator. His role was essentially to confirm that everything was as it seemed to be with enough evidence to satisfy the Fiscal.

He was less confident about the other part of the job.

When they'd first put the proposition to him, he'd been tempted to say no. It hadn't really been that he'd had any strong ethical objections. It was more that he felt this left him too exposed. 'So you want me to be – what? A kind of spy in the camp?'

The chief superintendent had closed his eyes briefly, as if Nightingale's words had been almost physically painful to him. 'I really wouldn't put it like that, Brian. We're really just looking for a few observations. A fresh pair of eyes, as it were.'

'To what end?' The question had sounded blunter than he'd intended.

'Just general intelligence, really, if I can put it like that. We need to have a better understanding of what's out there.' He'd had the air of a Roman emperor discussing the further-flung reaches of the empire. 'The extent to which their approach and values are aligned with ours.' He'd paused. 'I hope you've seen enough in your career to be confident of our good faith. When we believe in an officer's potential, we're only too happy to invest in appropriate levels of support.'

That had been a clear enough shot across the bows, Nightingale thought. He knew full well he'd been looked after a few times when his behaviour had arguably crossed a line. If they were looking for some payback on that, he wasn't in a position to argue.

He'd been given a list of the officers of interest, along with a summary of their careers and pertinent details from their personal files. He assumed the latter had been appropriately filleted and redacted, but there was still a sufficiency of interesting material in there.

While he waited for his starter, he flicked through the file.

The first name on the list was DCI Helena Grant herself. In Nightingale's memory, Helena Munro was a callow trainee in her early twenties, still struggling to cope with Jackie Galloway's in-your-face management style. Their respective time in Galloway's team had overlapped only by a few weeks prior to Nightingale's move south. It was clear that, one way or another, Grant's career had thrived since.

At some point in the intervening period, she had married Rory Grant, whom Nightingale had known a little during his time as a DS and DI in Strathclyde. Grant had decided to move to the Highlands to take up a DCI role and had presumably met and subsequently married Helena Munro shortly afterwards. Grant, then newly promoted to superintendent, had died unexpectedly a few years before, leaving Helena Grant as a childless widow.

Helena Grant was highly regarded by the senior team in Inverness and seen as a serious contender for further promotion, particularly if she was prepared to consider a move to the central belt. Grant herself had remained non-committal about that, claiming to be satisfied with her current role in major investigation. She'd certainly had a few notable successes in recent years, including some high-profile cases.

Nightingale waited while the waitress delivered his garlic prawns. The prawns were overcooked and chewy, but the garlic sauce was palatable enough mopped up with the complimentary slice of baguette. Nightingale picked up his now half-empty glass, and swallowed the remainder of the wine. He waved to the waitress, who was watching him from the far side of the still empty restaurant.

'Could I have another glass?' he said as she approached. 'Actually, I might as well get a bottle. I'll need to pay for it myself, if that's okay?'

'I'll bring the machine over. Just the house red?'

'Maybe the Shiraz.'

He continued working his way through the file. There were a couple of other DCIs and he skimmed quickly through their details without finding anything of particular interest.

The next name on the list was more intriguing. DI Alec McKay was a man whose reputation tended to precede him. Most of Nightingale's colleagues had an opinion about McKay and few of them were straightforwardly favourable. It was generally acknowledged that he was a good honest copper and an excellent detective. But that description was generally accompanied by words such as 'chippy', 'difficult', 'awkward' or, most commonly, 'smartarse'. Nightingale was slightly surprised to discover that these epithets were much less common among McKay's colleagues in Inverness, who generally seemed to express an unexpected warmth towards him. Nightingale's conclusion had been that McKay was difficult when it suited him. It would be interesting to see which McKay turned up for work over the coming days.

He refilled his glass and continued working through the file. There were a couple of DIs and DSs before he came to the next member of the major investigation team, DS Virginia Horton. In the photo in her personal file, she came across as attractive in a quintessentially English rose manner, with pale skin, wide eyes and dark bobbed hair. It was a look that had always appealed to Nightingale. She looked almost too young and innocent to be an effective copper, he thought, though that image was belied by her track record.

He'd been mildly disappointed to discover that, not only was Horton married but that her spouse was female. There'd been a time, not too many years before, when Nightingale would have been tempted to treat both those facts as a challenge. But he was realistic enough now to recognise that, aside from any other barriers, he was nearly old enough to be Horton's father.

The waitress arrived bearing his steak. Inevitably, it had been cooked more than the medium rare he'd requested, but it wasn't unpleasant. It was improved by the Shiraz which was a cut or two above the initial house red. There were times when Nightingale could derive pleasure from eating alone and tonight he was happy to settle into the moment, a brief opportunity to relax before the challenges of the next week or so.

After Horton, there were a handful of DCs he'd been asked to look at. Nightingale smiled at the amiable picture of DC Josh Carlisle that stared up from the file at him. Nightingale would have liked to say that Carlisle reminded him of himself at that age, but he didn't think he'd ever looked that innocent and guileless. Carlisle was a member of the major investigation team, Nightingale noticed, so might well be part of the inquiry team in the Dawson case. Perhaps he was someone Nightingale could work on. It might be useful to groom a loyal protégé up here.

Nightingale finished his steak, dipping his final chip in the meat juices. He held up the wine bottle. Nearly empty. It was fortunate he had another back in his room. And he could always grab a beer or two from the bar before he headed upstairs.

The waitress appeared and collected his plate. 'Everything okay?' she asked, in a tone that implied she wasn't likely to be interested in his response.

'Fine, thanks.'

'Anything else? Coffee or dessert?'

'No, thanks. I'll sign the bill on my way out.'

As he rose from the table, he looked around. Apart from his own presence, the restaurant was still empty. It was still not 7pm, and he guessed there was time for the place to fill up later. Even so, the place felt dead, as if he was stuck at the arse-end of the world. He wondered what it was like in the depths of winter.

He tried to smile at the waitress as she handed over the bill for his examination and signature, but her attention seemed to be elsewhere. He scrawled his name across the bottom of the sheet, and then handed it back to her. She took it with a sniff and entered it into the cash register. Finally, she deigned to offer him a smile, but only, he assumed, because her gaze immediately slid to the tip jar on the bar. He dug into his pocket and dropped in a couple of pound coins, smiling back. He wondered vaguely about asking what time she finished, but this one really was young enough to be his daughter. Maybe his granddaughter.

She nodded her thanks. 'Enjoy your evening.'

CHAPTER TEN

'You're in early.' McKay slumped down at his desk and turned on his computer. It generally took several minutes to boot up and connect to the network. These days, McKay knew how it felt.

'I might say the same about you.'

McKay glanced up at the clock on the wall at the far end of the office. Just after seven. He was usually in around this time, especially when they had a major investigation under way. But then so was Ginny Horton. 'Big day, isn't it? New teacher.'

'If you say so.'

'No giggling at the back, Horton.' McKay looked at his computer screen, which was showing no obvious signs of life. 'Coffee?'

'I'll come with you.' She followed him along the corridor into the kitchenette. McKay filled the kettle and set it to boil, while Horton dug out mugs from the cupboard. 'Good evening?'

McKay shrugged. 'Usual. Chrissie cooked an excellent roast. Yorkshire pudding and everything. Then I fell asleep in front of the TV. That was about it.' He wasn't about to tell her that his dreams both then and later in the night had been haunted by what he'd witnessed in the chalet. He could remember no details now, other than a single image of two eyes staring from a blood-drenched face, a face begging him to do something though he'd had no idea what. He'd woken earlier than usual, tossing and turning in the bed until he'd finally given up on the idea of sleep. 'You?'

'Not bad. Isla's having a few problems.'

'What sort of problems? If it's any of my business.'

'It's not a secret. She's been contacted by her brother.'

'I didn't even know she had a brother.'

'She doesn't talk about him much. Tristram.'

'I can see why she doesn't talk about him much.'

'He's the black sheep of the family. Been inside a few times. The issue is that he wants to come up to see Isla.'

'And she doesn't want to see him?'

'It's not that straightforward. But, as far as I can see, he's basically a manipulative bastard. He's screwed up his life, but he's got no one but himself to blame for that. I think she's better well away from him.'

'And how does she feel?'

'Pretty much the same, I think. But it's trickier to take a hard-nosed approach when it's your own brother. And she doesn't want him turning up unexpectedly. She spent most of yesterday fretting about what to do.'

McKay was pouring the boiling water into the mugs. 'And did she reach a decision?'

'Eventually. Sort of. She's clear she doesn't want to see him. She was in two minds as to whether just to ignore his letter or to tell him explicitly to get lost.'

'And?'

'In the end she wrote the letter. Well, we both did. Tried to keep it short, not very sweet, and as unambiguous as possible.'

McKay grunted as he pulled a carton of milk from the

fridge. He sniffed it before splashing some into the mugs. 'Sounds the best approach. Leave the bugger in no doubt he's not wanted. Otherwise, that type will always try to inveigle their way back into your life.' He handed her one of the mugs. 'Of course, he might still do that anyway. He doesn't sound like one to take "piss off" for an answer.'

'That's what worries me. She reckons he must have some ulterior motive for wanting to see her. Most likely, he wants money. In which case, he may not give up until he gets it.'

'But if he gets it, he'll be back for more. That's how it works.'

'I just need to make sure that Isla realises that. And that she actually posts the letter today.'

McKay opened the door of the kitchenette and peered down the corridor. 'Seems like the circus is coming to town. We'd better get back to the office and look busy.'

By the time they reached the open-plan office, Chief Superintendent Everly was already at the front of the room, chatting to Helena Grant and a man he vaguely recognised as Brian Nightingale. As they entered the room, Everly waved him over. 'Alec. Good morning. Come and join us.'

'Morning, Mike. Good to see you hobnobbing with the *hoi polloi*.'

'Just wanted to introduce Brian Nightingale here. You're aware that he's joining us temporarily to take over as SIO on the Dawson case?'

'Aye. Helena told us she was leaving us by mutual consent.' He could see Grant glaring at him from behind Everly. 'But, seriously, good to have you on board, Brian. Must be strange coming back to the old stamping ground.'

'I thought I was long forgotten up here.'

'Much missed, never forgotten. Look forward to working with you.'

'Likewise. I've heard a lot about you, Alec.'

'All lies. Well, mostly, I imagine.'

'I'm sorry this has been sprung on you, Alec. Must be a bit unexpected.'

'One DCI's pretty much like another. It's just a matter of getting you properly house-trained.' He smiled innocently at Helena Grant.

Nightingale gave an awkward laugh. 'I'm sure you're right, Alec. I thought we could hold a formal kick-off meeting later in the morning, but in the meantime it might be useful if you could talk me through the state of play so far. Helena's told me something about it, and I've had a brief skim through the file, but I was thinking you could talk me through the local colour.'

'The local colour,' McKay said slowly, 'is primarily a deep blood red.'

'Let's go and have a chat in one of the meeting rooms, where it's a bit quieter. Do you want to join us for this, Helena?'

Grant was still chatting to Michael Everly. 'I'm sure Alec can fill you in very comprehensively. It's probably best if I keep my nose out of it now you've taken over the case. Sends the right message.'

'Of course. Okay, Alec. We've booked meeting room two for the morning. I thought it might be useful to have a few one-to-one chats across the team while I'm getting my feet under the table.'

McKay led the way across the corridor to the meeting room. The room, primarily used for this kind of session, was scarcely large enough to hold more than the two of them. McKay made his way to the end of the room and sat down at the table.

Nightingale sat himself down and regarded McKay with suspicion. 'I thought it would be better if we were completely straight with each other from the off.'

'Always for the best, I find.'

'You come with something of a reputation.'

'Is that right?'

'"Chippy", "awkward" and "difficult" are some of the words I've heard about you.'

'I thought you meant something negative.'

'Another phrase I heard used of you was "A right fucking pain in the arse".'

'If you give me a minute, I can probably guess who said that. Or at least narrow it down to half a dozen.'

Nightingale shook his head. 'You think you're a real smartarse, don't you, Alec? Didn't anyone ever tell you no one likes a smartarse?'

'You're not the first. Sorry to disappoint you.'

'An answer to everything, haven't you?' Before McKay could prove his point, Nightingale leaned forward and jabbed his finger in McKay's direction. 'Just don't try it with me, son. I've eaten bastards like you for breakfast.'

'No wonder you look so dyspeptic,' McKay said.

'I expect you to play ball, McKay. That's all.'

'Look, Brian, we seem to have got off on the wrong foot. I'm not here to make your life difficult. I'm just here to do a job. And, though I say it myself, it's a job I'm actually not bad at, if I'm allowed to do it my way. And I know this place inside out. I know how to get things done here, and – though it may surprise you – I even know how to win friends and influence people, admittedly in my own special way. To put it another way, you'd much rather have me inside the tent pissing out.'

'I'm the boss here, McKay. I don't want you to forget that.'

'And I wouldn't want it any other way. Someone needs to carry the can.'

Nightingale opened his mouth then closed it. It appeared that, for the moment at least, he'd run out of words. 'Tell me about the Dawson case,' he said finally.

It took McKay only a few minutes to provide a succinct

summary of the investigation to date, including the interviews and other activities that had been carried out or were underway.

'You seem to have done a pretty thorough job so far,' Nightingale grudgingly conceded.

'I hope so. But that's Helena. Doesn't cut corners.'

'You don't think there's much doubt this Paul Dawson was the killer?'

'I wouldn't have said so. But it's an assumption for the moment. We haven't had any pathology results or the examiners' report. We've no explanation as to why he might have committed an act like that. There are a lot of questions.'

'And this visiting car. Where does that fit in?'

'That's the next on the list for me. We need to find out who the visitor or visitors were. At the very least, they should be able to give an insight into Paul Dawson's state of mind. Not to mention the rest of the family.'

'Assuming that the visitor or visitors didn't in some way contribute to that state of mind.'

'Exactly.'

'Okay, we'll treat that as the first priority.'

McKay took that as signalling the meeting was at an end. He pushed himself to his feet. 'If I know Ginny Horton, she'll already be well on with that. I'll go and find out.'

Nightingale had remained seated. He looked up at McKay. 'Remember what I said, Alec. No one likes a smartarse.'

'Aye, so people keep telling me.' McKay smiled. 'For some reason.'

CHAPTER ELEVEN

'This the place?' DC Josh Carlisle said. The satnav had brought them to the middle of the street, but was uninformative about the precise location of their destination.

'That's the trouble with places like this,' Ginny Horton said. 'Too posh to have their house names or numbers on the gates like normal people.'

They were parked in an upmarket residential area on the outskirts of Inverness. The houses were new builds, but in a different league from the off-the-shelf estates that increasingly dominated the edges of the city. These were all large houses, each individual; architect-designed for those who valued distinctiveness above practicality. They were positioned to ensure their large picture windows offered a striking view of the Moray Firth. The good weather was holding, the waters a sparkling azure under a clear sky.

'My guess is that one,' Carlisle said. He pointed to a sizeable bungalow just ahead of where they were sitting.

'Any reason for picking that one as opposed to any one of these others?'

'Not sure. It just looks the right sort of place.'

'Right sort of place for what? For a couple who own a car-hire company?'

'I suppose.'

Horton shook her head. 'Either you've got much more finely attuned social antennae than I've ever given you credit for, Josh. Or you're guessing.'

As it turned out, whatever gifts Carlisle might or might not have deployed, his assessment was correct. The house was indeed the home of Craig and Andrea Gillan, owners of the car-hire firm.

Horton had called the car-hire company as soon as the office opened at 8am that morning. This time, the phone had been answered by a pleasant-sounding receptionist with a sing-song voice. 'Gillan Cars,' she'd announced cheerfully. 'Morag speaking. How can I help you?'

'I'm hoping you can. This is DS Horton from Police Scotland major investigations. We're trying to trace someone who rented a dark 5-series BMW from you last week.' She read out the car registration. 'We don't know when the car was hired, but it was being used last Friday afternoon.'

The receptionist had initially argued that she couldn't provide that information over the phone, without verifying Horton's identity. Fair enough, Horton had thought. The woman was just doing her job. 'We're investigating a potentially serious crime, so time really is of the essence. I can send someone in to collect the information if necessary. Could you at least check you've got the details so we can make sure we don't have a wasted trip?'

'I suppose so.' There was the sound of fingers tapping on a keyboard as she presumably brought up the relevant records. 'Oh, that's odd.'

'What is?'

'That car wasn't shown as rented out last week. The last

client who rented it reported a technical problem, so it was being repaired at the start of the week.'

'And on Friday?'

'It was brought back to us on Wednesday so it should have been here on Friday. We've a booking for it later in the week.'

Horton was wondering about the possibility of fake plates, but it seemed an odd coincidence that the plates should relate to a similar model and make of car in a similar location. 'So the car's sitting outside your offices now?'

'It should be. Hang on—'

Morag put the call on hold while Horton waited, tapping her fingers on the desk. It was a few moments before the receptionist returned. 'It's not there.'

'Not there?'

'The car. The BMW. It isn't there.'

'You're sure?'

'I've checked the car park.'

'Are you saying it's been stolen?'

There was a pause, and the sound of a drawer being unlocked and slid open. 'No, I don't think so. We've very secure fences round the site, and there's no sign that the gates have been damaged. And the car keys are missing. They're normally held in a secure cabinet in the office, and that's not been damaged.'

'So what can have happened to the car?'

'There's one other possibility. Which is that Craig or Andrea borrowed it.'

'The owners?'

'Yes, they do borrow the cars occasionally. Usually if there's some problem with one of theirs. They're supposed to sign it out if they do...' Horton had heard more bumping at the end of the line, presumably as Morag checked another file. 'No, they haven't done that.' She sighed. 'It's always the way. If we forget to do something...'

'But you think they borrowed the car over the weekend?'

'I can't think what else might have happened to it. I definitely remember it being brought back on Wednesday, and I think it was here till Friday morning. I don't work Friday afternoons because I cover Saturday morning.'

'So who's there on Friday afternoon?'

'Craig or Andrea usually cover when I'm away. Andrea was here on Friday when I left, so I assume she covered the rest of the afternoon. That might be the explanation. Craig had dropped her off because he'd had to come into town and was planning to pick her up at the end of the afternoon. Maybe he couldn't make it for some reason so Andrea used the BMW to get home.'

'Was the car there on Saturday morning?'

There was silence for a moment. 'I'm not sure, to be honest. I didn't really notice. It's normally parked at the back of the office, and I didn't have any particular reason to go round there.'

'What about the Gillans? Have you heard anything from either of them since Friday?'

'No, but that's not unusual. They've got a range of business interests, so they only spend part of their time here. They usually leave me to run the place day-to-day.'

'Do you have a contact number for them?'

'I've got their mobiles in case there are any problems. But I don't know...'

'As I say, Morag, this is a major investigation. We do need to speak to them as a matter of urgency.'

'I just don't want to get into any trouble.'

'I'll make sure you don't, Morag. I just need the numbers.'

'Well, if you're sure.'

'I'm sure, Morag. And if we need anything else we'll come in to see you.'

After she'd finished the call, Horton had tried the two numbers, but both had simply rung out to voicemail. She'd left messages asking the couple to contact her urgently, but so far there'd been no response.

After a brief discussion with McKay and Nightingale, she and Carlisle had headed out here to try to track down the Gillans directly. Now, they stood at the gate of what Josh Carlisle had correctly identified as their residence. From here, they could finally see the house name on a sign beside the front door.

It was an impressive-looking house, set in a large well-maintained garden, angled to provide a view out over the Kessock Bridge and the Moray Firth, the dark bulk of the Black Isle facing them. 'Doesn't look as if they're short of a bob or two,' Carlisle commented.

'I'd say not. Wonder what their business interests are, other than the car-hire stuff.'

There was no response to the doorbell. Horton pressed it three times, holding it down for longer on the third occasion. She looked at Carlisle and shrugged. 'Looks like we've had a wasted journey. Don't know if it's worth checking round the back, just in case.'

'It's open,' Carlisle said.

'What is?'

'The door. It's not closed. Look.' He pushed the front door gently with his fingertips. It swung open. 'It hadn't caught on the latch.'

'Well spotted.' Horton took a step forward. 'Hello! Anyone home?'

There was silence from inside the house. Horton pushed

the door further open and stepped into the hallway. 'Mr Gillan? Mrs Gillan? It's the police.'

She looked back at Josh Carlisle, who was still hovering outside the door, looking uncomfortable about entering.

'They left the house unsecured,' she said. 'We're just checking that everything's okay in here before we secure it.' She paused. 'I learnt at the feet of the master, you realise, Josh.'

'I'm not sure I've quite got the master's ability to front it out,' Carlisle said.

'Who has? But I think we're okay giving the place a quick check over.' She moved through the hallway, still calling the Gillans' names, and peered into the living room. There was no sign of any disturbance or anything out of place, but it looked as if the house had been left relatively suddenly. There was a plate with the remnants of a sandwich on the low table in the middle of the room, with a half-drunk mug of cold coffee beside it. A paperback book was splayed face down on the sofa.

She continued through the hallway and looked into the kitchen. Again, there was nothing unexpected, though there was the same sense that the occupants had departed suddenly. A pile of unwashed crockery sat on top of the dishwasher, ready to be stacked. An opened bottle of milk sat on the table.

Horton returned to the hallway. Carlisle was still standing by the front door. 'Anything?'

'Not really. Except that it looks as if they might have left in something of a hurry. I'm going to take a look upstairs.'

Horton's sense of unease was growing. She told herself there was no sign of anything wrong. It wasn't as if her own house was left looking immaculate if she and Isla were running late in the morning.

She reached the upper landing. There were five doors – presumably four bedrooms and a bathroom. She pushed open the nearest door, realising she was holding her breath as she did so.

This was clearly the master bedroom, with a balcony giving views out over the firth. It was empty, the duvet on the double bed thrown back as if its occupants had only recently departed. There was a door leading to an en-suite bathroom. Horton stepped over and peered inside. Again, it was empty.

She returned to the landing and tried the next door. Another bedroom, apparently used only as a guest room. It was tidy and looked as if it hadn't been occupied for some time.

The third door was a bathroom. Again, its pristine condition suggested that it wasn't being used, presumably because the Gillans had their own en suite. Finally, she pushed open the last door. She'd expected this to be another bedroom, and she'd been partly right. This room also had a view out over the firth and in some ways it was a more impressive space than the master bedroom, with large windows and skylights that gave it an airy, spacious feel. The room was effectively divided into two spaces. The far end looked as if it was used as a guest bedroom if required, with a sofa that could be converted into a double bed, and a small shower room. The nearer end as set up as an office, with a desk set up to take advantage of the views. There were a couple of filing cabinets and a table holding a printer and a flatbed scanner. The desk itself was immaculately tidy. There was an Apple Mac desktop, a desk diary, and an array of pens held in a neat rack.

The area beside the desk was less tidy. It looked as if a stack of files had been pulled out of a cabinet and scattered across the floor. Some of the files lay open, as if someone had been searching through the contents. Others were tossed aside, as if rejected.

There was nothing necessarily suspicious about the mess, Horton thought. It was the state someone might leave their files if they'd been hurriedly searching for a particular document, rather than anything that might be left in the aftermath of a burglary. Again, it suggested that the Gillans might have departed the house in a hurry.

If Alec McKay had been here, he wouldn't have hesitated to start examining the files and would have concocted some spurious justification for doing so. Despite her confident words to Josh Carlisle, that wasn't really her style, and she was conscious she'd already been in the house for longer than she'd intended.

She made her way downstairs. Carlisle was still standing by the front door, casting anxious glances towards the street in the manner of someone keeping watch during a robbery. 'Don't worry, Josh. You don't look remotely suspicious. Nothing upstairs. Just all looks as if they might have left in a hurry for some reason.'

She followed him outside and then, after a moment's hesitation, closed the door firmly behind them. 'Let's have a quick look round outside, just in case.'

There was no sign of the BMW, but a Mercedes convertible was parked next to the house in front of a double garage. Horton peered into the interior but could see nothing of interest. She walked around to the side of the garage and pressed her face against its only window. As far as she could see, the garage was empty. She walked back to the front of the garage to rejoin Carlisle.

For a moment, she thought he'd disappeared. Then she heard a raised voice from out on the road and, a moment later, Carlisle's own, slightly plaintive tone. Horton sighed and hurried out to see what was happening.

An elderly woman with a precisely enunciated English accent was haranguing Carlisle at length and high volume. He was holding up his hands as if expecting her to strike him physically and was clearly struggling to interject a word into the exchange.

'But I saw you,' the woman was saying. 'Standing inside the doorway, keeping watch while your companion ransacked the place. If I hadn't appeared, I don't know what might have happened.'

Before the woman could speak again, Horton hurried over. 'Can I help you, madam?'

The woman stared at her. 'I very much doubt it. Unless you happen to be a police officer.'

'Funnily enough, that's exactly what I am.' Horton had already produced her warrant card. She held it in front of the woman's face. 'DS Horton.'

For the first time, the woman looked mildly confused. 'This man—'

'Is my colleague, DC Carlisle.'

'What?'

By now, Carlisle had produced his warrant card and was holding it out sheepishly for the woman.

'Why didn't he say so?'

'I did try—'

'And why was he breaking into the Gillans' house?'

'He wasn't. We were here to visit the Gillans and we realised the front door had been left unsecured. So we checked that all was well.'

'Why wouldn't it have been well?'

'Perhaps because someone might have broken into the house, as you were fearing.'

It took the woman a moment to absorb this. 'I see.'

'Do you know the Gillans, madam?'

'We're neighbours.' The woman gestured to a house across the road. 'I don't know them particularly well, but we keep an eye out for each other. You hear such awful stories about break-ins and burglaries. If you don't mind me saying so, we need more of you and your colleagues on the street.'

'I'll pass on your views, madam. Have you seen the Gillans this weekend?'

'This weekend?'

'Since Friday afternoon.'

The woman frowned. 'They've not been around all weekend. I thought I saw their car leave sometime on Friday afternoon. I noticed because it wasn't one of their own but one of the hire cars they use sometimes.'

The woman clearly had an eye for detail, Horton thought. 'What time would that have been? When they left, I mean.'

'I'm not sure. Mid-afternoon. Around three?'

'Did you notice what sort of a car it was?'

'It's a dark-grey BMW, but I couldn't tell you much more than that.'

'And you haven't seen them since then? Over the weekend, I mean.'

'No sign of them. There've been no lights in the house so they must be away, though that's quite unusual for them. They're rather the workaholic type.'

'You've not seen anyone else visit the house over the weekend?'

'Not until your car turned up today.'

'Well, thank you, that's very helpful. Mrs...?'

'Erskine. Fionnuala Erskine.'

'If you see the Gillans return, perhaps you could ask them to contact us. And if you see anyone else around their house, perhaps you could let us know?' She produced a business card and handed it over to Mrs Erskine, who regarded it with apparent suspicion.

'Are they in some sort of trouble?'

'We'd just like to talk to them as potential witnesses in an investigation. If you do see anything, please do let us know. I'd also suggest that, in your own interests, it's perhaps better if you don't accost any potential housebreakers. Some of them may be less easy-going than my colleague here.'

They left Mrs Erskine still standing by the Gillans' gate and climbed back into the car.

'Fionnuala Erskine?' Carlisle said.

'It's the class system,' Horton said. 'Useful witness, though.'

'You think so?'

'She's a curtain-twitcher. I bet nothing happens on this road without her knowing about it. So we can now be pretty certain a dark-grey BMW was here on Friday – which sounds like the car that was caught on the CCTV at the chalet site – and that they haven't been back since.'

'So does that get us very far?'

'Not really.' Horton thought for a moment. 'The real questions are why the BMW was at the chalet park in the first place. And where the hell the Gillans are now.' As she reached to start the car, her phone buzzed in her coat pocket.

'Alec?' She fell silent as she listened to what McKay had to tell her, then said, 'We'll get straight down there.'

She ended the call and turned back to Carlisle. 'Well,' she said, 'it sounds as if we might have the answer to at least one of those questions.'

CHAPTER TWELVE

'So what are we expecting to find down there?' Carlisle was staring out at the passing landscape as they headed down the A9 towards Aviemore.

Horton had her eyes fixed on the road. 'A burnt-out dark-grey BMW, apparently. According to Alec, it was reported by some tourists earlier this morning. Uniforms are already out there. They've found a burnt-out car in a patch of woodland just by the loch.'

'The one we're looking for?'

'Seems likely, doesn't it? They haven't yet reported the reg or any other details. Alec only had the barest details from the control room.'

They passed through Coylumbridge, the large hotel to their left, heading out towards the Cairngorms. In the past, this had been a busy ski resort but it had been badly affected by a combination of global warming and changing holiday priorities. There was new investment and hopes that the resort could be revived, but for the moment, with the main summer season just ended, the area was relatively quiet, and only a couple of cars passing them on the way to the loch.

They'd been told the car was off the road in woodland, just to the east of the main car park for the loch. It had been found earlier that morning by a couple wild camping in the woodland nearby. The local operational police hadn't initially treated the car as a priority, assuming it had been stolen and dumped by joyriders. Now, there was no mistaking the significance of the scene ahead of them, the trees pulsing with the reflected light from several marked cars, police tape stretched across the roadside. Horton flashed her ID through the window and was waved on into the woods.

It was still only late morning, the sun shining down through the dense forest of fir trees. The air was heavy with the scent of pine and through the trees Horton could see the light glittering on the surface of the loch. The examiners were already in place, and a tent was being erected over the car to protect any evidence, but she was able to see the registration. It was the vehicle they'd been looking for. As far as she could tell from the location, the car had left the road, descended a sharp incline and then struck a tree.

There was no sign of Jock Henderson today, but Pete Carrick was standing by the tent, suited up and ready. He turned as Horton approached.

'Morning, Pete. How's it going?'

'Not well. Considering what we've found.'

'I was told a burnt-out BMW.' She glanced over his shoulder to where the body of the car was gradually disappearing under the protective covering.

'A bit more than that, unfortunately. Two bodies. Driver and passenger.'

'Shit.'

'Quite. Not pleasant.'

'Seems likely it's the Gillans. The couple we're looking for.'

'We may have to wait on formal confirmation of that.'

'The bodies badly damaged then?'

Carrick was silent for a second. 'Very. I'm afraid. Not a lot left. It's an odd one. It doesn't make sense simply as an accident. I can't be sure till the collision people have looked at it, but I can't see how the car could have left the road unintentionally. You can see. It's a dry, pretty straight road. Even at high speed, you'd struggle to lose control, particularly in something like a Beemer.'

'People can lose control for all kinds of reasons, though. Illness, heart attack. Trying to avoid hitting a deer. We've seen them all.'

'Sure. And I'm not writing off any of those possibilities. But, for what it's worth, my impression is that that car was deliberately driven at the tree at high speed. It would need to be something like that to be consistent with the damage.'

'And that would be enough to cause the fire?'

'Your guess is as good as mine. They're pretty robust cars, designed to withstand a collision, but I guess there's a limit to that. Again, there's something about it that doesn't quite smell right to me. We'll have to see what the vehicle examiners have to say.'

Horton knew that Carrick wasn't prone to offer firm views outside his area of expertise, but he'd spent enough time working on RTC scenes to have a good idea what he was looking at. 'When do you think the collision happened?'

'Maybe a couple of days ago.'

'That would fit with the other timings we've got.'

'I'm glad one part of this is predictable, anyway.'

'I'm not even sure about that. The intriguing thing is that it looks as if there's a link between this and what happened on Saturday. This seems to have been the car that visited the Dawsons on Friday afternoon.'

Carrick raised an eyebrow. 'Really? That puts a rather different complexion on things, doesn't it?'

'Certainly doesn't simplify anything. What do you reckon you're likely to be able to get from this, once the various experts have crawled over it?'

'Who knows? Car and the bodies are pretty badly damaged, so don't know what's feasible. The good news is that the weather's been pretty kind over the last couple of nights, so with a bit of luck that'll have helped preserve anything worth having. We'll see what we can do.'

'I'm sure you'll do your usual brilliant job, Pete.'

'That's the difference between you and that boss of yours.'

'What is?'

'At least when Alec opens his mouth I can be sure he's taking the piss.'

'Never not sincere, me, Pete. And, to be honest, I never have much difficulty telling the difference between you and your boss.'

She went back to join Josh Carlisle who had been chatting to one of the uniforms. As she approached, Carlisle pointed towards the loch. 'The guy who found the car was asked to stay put. He's over near the car park. Shall we have a word?'

'Might as well. Don't know how much he's likely to be able to tell us, but you never know.'

They drove around to the car park. The area had been sealed off, and the car park itself was empty except for a van at the far end. Horton and Carlisle walked past it, into the woods away from the edge of the loch.

Ahead of them was a small tent and a man seated in a folding chair. He climbed to his feet as Horton and Carlisle approached and introduced himself.

'I hope we're not in any trouble. I've been wild camping

here with my girlfriend,' the man said. 'We understood it was legal up here, but some people don't seem to like us doing it.'

'Wild camping's legal in Scotland. All we're ever concerned about is that people behave responsibly, especially with regard to fires and cleaning up after themselves. As long as you do that, most people won't mind.'

'We're always scrupulous about that. Sorry, I'm Jake Albert.'

'Pleased to meet you, Mr Albert. Where's your girlfriend this morning?'

'I drove her up to Aviemore earlier. The plan was for her to do a bit of shopping for us while I went for a walk. I was due to pick her up, but I've just called her to say I might be a little late.'

'Thank you for waiting.'

'No problem. Chloe's no doubt getting her revenge by knocking back a full English in the café.'

'We just wanted to have a quick chat about your discovery this morning.'

'Sure. Don't know how much I can tell you, though.'

'How long have you been here? Just overnight?'

'We've been here a few nights, actually. We were planning to move on but it's such a lovely spot. We arrived on Friday.'

'So you were here on Friday evening?'

'We arrived here about five. We parked up in the car park by the loch and then came to find somewhere to set up the tent.' He gestured back through the woods in the direction of the car park. 'We've a van we use. Means we can doss down in the back of it if the weather should turn really bad, but we prefer to be out here. Anyway, we found this spot, which seemed ideal. There's even a stream running down through the woods over there. We got ourselves set up and prepared dinner.'

'Did you see or hear anything unusual on Friday evening?'

'That's what I've been thinking about. We did actually, though we didn't think anything of it at the time.'

'What time was this?'

'Maybe about nine. We'd actually just got into the tent. We tend to sleep with the daylight when we're camping. There's rather a lot of that up here in the summer, so we try to take advantage of the short period when it is dark. We'd eaten and had a couple of glasses of wine, and then we were ready for sleep.'

'And what happened?'

'We heard a car. It was so quiet that we could hear it coming from some distance. We expected it would just pass by. But then we heard a noise that puzzled us. I suppose, knowing what I know now, it must have been the noise of the collision, but it didn't really sound like that. Afterwards, there was just silence. We kept our heads down, to be honest. Probably a bit cowardly in retrospect, but you never know what might be going on in places like this.'

'And you didn't see or hear anything else? No sign of the fire, for example.'

'Sounds daft, doesn't it? But, no, we didn't. We were inside the tent and we slept pretty soundly till well after it was light. I imagine if we'd gone out in the darkness we'd probably have seen it through the trees, but we didn't. I remember commenting to Chloe the following morning that there was an odd burnt chemical smell in the air, but we didn't know what might be nearby and it soon dispersed.'

'You didn't discover the car till this morning?' There was a note of scepticism in Carlisle's voice.

'We just didn't happen to walk that way,' Albert said. 'There was no particular reason why we should. We've been for a number of long walks over the last couple of days – that's one of our reasons for being here – but we walked around the mountains or round the loch. It was only this morning, when I was on my own, that I decided to walk the opposite way, just to see if there was anything worth seeing.'

'Which turned out to be a crashed and burnt-out car,' Horton said.

'Exactly. So then I called the police. I didn't really go near it, and I assumed it was probably stolen. Expensive car. Someone will be missing that.'

'Have you seen anyone else in the woods since Friday?'

'A few people,' Albert said. 'Mainly just tourists going for a walk. Though most of those tend to stick by the loch. One or two more serious walkers. But nobody suspicious, if that's what you mean.'

'And you've not seen or heard anything else unusual since Friday?'

'Nothing at all. It's just deathly quiet here at night. No traffic, no houses nearby. Nothing. Apart from a few noisy owls and other creatures of the night. That's why we decided to stay longer.' He looked at his watch. 'Do you need anything else from me? I'd better go and get Chloe before long. We're planning to press on today. Head further north.'

'That's fine. I'd be grateful if you could leave us contact details, just in case any further questions arise once we've carried out a detailed examination of the car. Otherwise, thanks for your time and enjoy your holiday.'

She left Carlisle to take details from the young man and walked further into the woods, heading in the direction of the burnt-out car. She'd initially felt slightly sceptical that the couple had seen and heard so little of the events on the Friday evening, and she'd wondered if there was something they weren't saying. But if they'd wanted to avoid getting involved they could simply have left without reporting their find. And, given the density of the woodland and their distance from the car, it was probably unsurprising that they'd witnessed nothing of significance. It was fortunate that they'd seen or heard anything at all.

Horton's unease was less about Jake Albert's account than about the whole scenario. None of this seemed to make any sense. What would have brought the Gillans to this remote spot? What would have caused them to crash the car in that way?

Which brought Horton round to the really key question.

What the hell did this have to do with what had happened to the Dawsons?

CHAPTER THIRTEEN

For once, Helena Grant had closed her office door. It wasn't something she did often, preferring a literal open-door policy, even if that did mean Alec McKay came and poked his nose through it a little too frequently.

Grant would have preferred a desk in the open-plan office where most of the major investigation team were now located. She enjoyed the sense of teamwork, of collective energy, that the room engendered. When they were in the middle of a major inquiry, she spent more time down there than she did in here. But, just at the moment, she wasn't in the middle of a major inquiry. She'd been excluded from it and was sitting down here with mostly administration to contemplate.

Not that she didn't have more than enough to do. Her job was primarily a managerial one, and there was no shortage of work that needed completing relating to recent and ongoing investigations. She knew she ought to be grateful she'd been given the additional time and space to complete tasks that, in some cases, had been hanging over her for weeks.

In fact, what she was mainly feeling was frustrated. After the traumatic events at the start of the year, she'd thrown herself back into work as the most straightforward way of putting all that behind her. There were those, including Alec McKay, who'd questioned whether this was a wise strategy. It wasn't just that her life had been in serious danger. It was also that what had seemed increasingly like her future had been brutally snatched away from her. She was yet again back where she'd started, and this time she didn't even have any positive memories to console her.

She wasn't one for moping or for undue introspection, and she'd known that it wouldn't help if she took more time off work. So she'd done the opposite. She'd returned to the office as soon as the doctor was prepared to sign her off and taken on a higher workload than ever. So far it had worked, at least in the sense that she hadn't had the time to dwell either on what had happened or her own future.

In reality, the decision to appoint Brian Nightingale as SIO on the Dawson investigation hadn't changed much. After all, she'd already had a pretty full workload, and would have had to delegate or postpone other tasks to focus on the investigation. It was just that she knew that a live inquiry would have been a much more effective distraction from her own troubles than the stack of administration that now faced her.

Shutting her office door had felt almost like a symbolic act. She didn't want to find herself lurking on the edge of the investigation like an unwanted gatecrasher at a party. If Nightingale wanted her input or advice, she'd be happy to provide it, but she couldn't imagine he would be rushing to consult her. If he needed local knowledge, Alec or Ginny could respond to any queries.

She began working on one of the more routine tasks, on the basis that it was at least something she could motivate herself to do without having to concentrate too hard. The danger, she supposed, was that it might allow her space to think.

The knock on the door was so soft she thought at first she'd imagined it. A moment later, it was repeated, slightly louder.

'Yes?'

After a moment, Mike Everly's face appeared around the door. 'Not disturbing you, am I? I thought you might be in the middle of something.'

'Only admin. And that seems to be largely self-generating.'

'Tell me about it.' He'd entered the room now, carrying two takeaway cups of coffee. 'I just picked these up from the canteen. Thought you might be in need of one.'

'Now you come to mention it, caffeine would be very welcome.'

'Can you spare me a few minutes? Just wanted a chat about something.'

Here it comes, Grant thought. *No such thing as a free coffee.* 'Yes, of course. Any excuse not to get on with this stuff.'

He was a decent-looking man, Grant thought, if you liked that kind of thing. She knew from the whispers she'd heard around the office that quite a few of her female colleagues did. She'd heard a few comments about the fact that he was supposedly unattached, with a divorce somewhere in his past.

'What can I do for you?'

He looked mildly uncomfortable. 'Well, first of all, I just wanted to check how you felt about Brian Nightingale. I thought you might feel a bit resentful about his arrival.'

'Just means I can devote myself to my first love. Admin.'

He laughed. 'If you say so. Just wanted to assure you it was nothing personal. You're held in very high regard.'

'If you're not careful, I'll think you're protesting too much. You clearly want something.'

'It's funny you should say that...'

'I knew it.'

'Actually, I was just wondering what your ambitions were.'

'Ambitions?'

'Career-wise, I mean. Where you see yourself in five years. That sort of stuff.'

'It's not something I ever really think much about.' It was a sincere response. There had definitely been a time when she'd worried about that kind of thing, but she hadn't thought much about it for a good few years now. Not since Rory had died. What was that John Lennon line about life being what happens while you're busy making other plans? Or in Rory's case – and Lennon's too, she supposed – death was what happened.

'I suppose the question is,' Everly went on, 'whether you're happy as a DCI up here, or whether you see yourself progressing further.'

'Which would probably mean being prepared to move away from here,' Grant added. 'I really don't know. I'm happy doing what I'm doing. I've not lived up here all my life, but I'm a local girl and I don't have any great hankerings to move back to the big city.'

'I suppose you've got a good circle of friends and relations up here?'

She thought about that. She had some friends, certainly, and some good ones. But it was a small and select group. As for relatives, that was an even more exclusive group. Her parents were long gone. She had a brother down south she saw maybe once every five years. She had a few cousins and other relatives locally, but she hardly knew them. 'Fewer than you might think, to be honest. Look, Mike, what's this all about?'

'Nothing really. Not at this stage. It's just that, as I say, you're highly regarded. I've been giving some thought to career planning.'

'Career planning? That'll be a first.'

'It's not something the force has been good at. In the past it's generally been every man for himself–'

'With the emphasis on man,' Grant added.

'Probably. Anyway, all I'm doing is giving some thought to people who might have the potential to progress. And that includes you.'

'I'm not exactly a youngster.'

'You're not exactly old, either, if that's not too tactless a way of putting it. You're a good way off retirement. Plenty of time to progress if you want it.'

'You should be looking at people like Ginny Horton or Josh Carlisle. They're the real future.'

Everly nodded. 'I'm sure I will. But I just wanted to get a sense of how you felt about it.'

'To be honest, it's not something I've thought about for a good while.'

'I imagine Rory's death might have influenced your priorities. Again, apologies if that sounds insensitive.'

'No, you're right. It did affect my thinking. Rory was always very career-minded. Not in a ruthless or selfish way. Just trying to gain the experience and knowledge he needed to help him move up the ladder.'

'He'd have made a good chief officer.'

'We'll never know, will we?' Grant said. 'All the time and effort and concentration he devoted to developing his career, and then he was gone. I wondered whether he might have thought he'd wasted his life.'

'He was a bloody good copper.'

'I'm sure you're right. But it was hard for me to look at it objectively after his death.'

'So you put your own career ambitions on hold?'

'It just didn't seem important anymore. I just got on with the job.'

'And very well, by all accounts,' Everly said.

'I didn't really do it for anyone else's approval. I did it because it was the only thing I could do.'

'Maybe it's time to give it some more consideration, then.'

She picked up the coffee he'd brought her and took a large swallow of the now tepid liquid. 'Did you have something specific in mind?'

'How long have you been in major investigation?'

'More than ten years, scarily. But it's where most of the action is. I'm not sure I'd want to move anywhere else.'

'Fair enough. But I was wondering if you might be interested in some project work. I'm looking for contributors to a review exercise. Tulliallan have got a bunch of consultants in to look at how we do things. See how we can work more efficiently, make better use of technology. Deliver more for less.'

'Cutting jobs?'

'That's not the intention. But we have to squeeze maximum value from everything we do.'

This kind of initiative seemed to come round every few years. As far Grant could see, it generally just resulted in a period of disruption, after which everything settled back into more or less the same pattern, with a few new job titles or some changed terminology. 'If they've got expensive consultants working on this, I don't see what I could add. I've no experience of that sort of thing.'

'The consultants have their fancy techniques, but they don't really understand policing. We've got to ensure any proposed changes are realistic. We're looking for a small group of experienced officers and staff to review their recommendations. Identify what looks good and workable, and anything that looks problematic or less feasible.'

'If I were cynical,' Grant said, 'I might think this sounds like doing the consultants' work for them. What's that phrase about borrowing the client's watch to tell them the time?'

'It could be a good opportunity for you, Helena. It'll be high profile.'

'This wouldn't be full-time?'

'It would be a project alongside your core work. I've been asked to submit three names on behalf of the division, and I'd very much like yours to be one of them.'

'When do I need to make a decision?'

'If you were able to let me know in the next few days, that would be very helpful. I've a couple of other individuals in mind if you should say no, but you're very much top of my list.'

'Okay. I'll let you know. Sorry if I sound a bit uncertain – it's all a bit out of the blue – but I'm grateful for the offer.'

'I appreciate it's something different for you. But maybe it would do you good to step outside your comfort zone. There is one other thing. I don't know if it's a consideration, positive or negative.' He laughed awkwardly. 'I've been asked to chair the group. If you were part of the team, it would give me a chance to, well, see you in action, as it were.'

She laughed, trying hard to keep any note of awkwardness from her own voice. 'I'm not sure how to take that.'

'I just meant in terms of your working style...' Everly trailed off, clearly recognising he was in danger of digging himself even deeper. 'Anyway, I'll leave you to your admin. Give it some thought and let me know.'

Once he'd left the room, she rose and closed the door gently behind him. Even more than before, she felt as if she wanted to be by herself for a while. If only so she could think about what had just happened.

CHAPTER FOURTEEN

B rian Nightingale was looking worried.

That wasn't too surprising, McKay thought. He was feeling anxious himself, though he suspected the nature of his anxiety was rather different from Nightingale's.

'I don't like the way this is going.' Nightingale was pacing up and down at the front of the meeting room while they waited for the rest of the team to arrive. Nightingale had called the meeting at relatively short notice after Ginny Horton had reported back on what had been found at Loch Morlich. Possibly, McKay speculated, because Nightingale hadn't known what the hell else to do.

'The water certainly seems to be getting muddier.' For once, McKay was sitting calmly at the table if only because it wasn't feasible for two of them to wander restlessly around the room. 'Let's see what more Ginny has to tell us when she gets here.'

Nightingale finally lowered himself into a chair at the head of the table. 'It doesn't make sense. None of it makes sense.'

'It must make sense,' McKay pointed out. 'We just don't know what kind of sense yet.'

'Thanks for that, Alec. Takes us a long way forward.'

'Just trying to help.' McKay could see things were slipping away from Nightingale. He could almost bring himself to feel some sympathy. The inquiry had been complicated in ways that Nightingale had never envisaged. It was impossible for them to ignore the apparent connection between the Dawsons' fate and what had happened to the Gillans.

McKay was also troubled by this development. For his own part, he welcomed the prospect of something more challenging than a tragic but apparently straightforward murder-suicide. His own worry was that he might be stuck with Nightingale for even longer than he'd originally feared.

Once the rest of the core team had joined them, Nightingale called the meeting to order. 'Morning, people. Thanks for coming at short notice. I thought it might be worth us all getting together to review the next steps. What's the latest on the car, Ginny?'

'Not much new. I had a chat with Pete Carrick before we left. The examiners are still working on the car and the scene, but he gave me an update about what they've found so far. Which, to be honest, isn't much. The car's badly damaged, particularly the interior so that's destroyed much of the evidence in terms of fingerprints and DNA. It's possible forensics might give us more clues, but Pete didn't sound too optimistic.'

'And what about the cause of the collision?' Nightingale sounded impatient. 'Any more on that?'

'The collision and car teams are going to have a look at it, but the initial view is that it's unlikely to have been a straightforward accident. Straight dry road, no obvious reason for the car to have left the road at that point. And there would have been time and space to brake or turn before the car hit the tree.'

'Meaning what?'

'Meaning that, most likely, there had to be either some additional cause for the car leaving the road, which might be driver illness, a fault with the car, or–'

'Or the driver deliberately choosing to plough into the bloody tree,' McKay growled.

Horton nodded. 'Quite.'

Nightingale was leaning back in his chair, watching the rest of the team. 'We've got to be careful here. This is all just speculation. We don't know why the Gillans' car was at the Dawsons' on Friday afternoon, and if there's any kind of direct link between their deaths and the Dawson killings. There's a risk we're trying to construct some kind of grand conspiracy around what's still probably nothing more than two unconnected tragedies.'

Aye, you wish, pal, McKay thought to himself. 'Fair point, Brian. We're too smart for our own good up here.'

'Let's see what the various boffins come up with on the Gillans. We don't want to start jumping to any conclusions until we know what we're dealing with. In the meantime, I'd suggest we focus on finding out more about the Dawsons. Assuming that this is what it seems to be – and let's discount any more outlandish theories for the moment – something must have triggered Paul Dawson to do what he did.' He looked around at the team, as if about to impart some ineffable wisdom. 'According to the experts, there are generally only a limited number of motives for this kind of family annihilation.'

McKay suspected Nightingale had simply carried out an internet search on the term, just as the rest of them had. He was tempted to jump in and steal Nightingale's thunder but decided that, for once, silence might be the wiser option.

'The perpetrators are generally male, which would fit with Paul Dawson's role here. The main motives seem to be to punish the spouse for some perceived wrongdoing; to punish the family for some perceived failing; to eliminate the family because it's seen as an unwanted burden, typically because the killer's own financial status has collapsed; or sometimes as a means of saving the family from some imagined even greater threat.'

McKay decided he might as well humour Nightingale. 'So in principle any one of those could be pertinent here? Maybe Dawson thought his wife was having an affair or had failed him in some other way. Maybe Dawson felt the whole family had failed to live up to his exacting standards. Maybe his business had run into trouble. Or maybe the Gillans brought Dawson news of some potentially greater threat to his family's well-being.'

'Greater than being stabbed to death by their own husband and father?' Horton asked.

'Aye, well, it's all relative, isn't it? But you're right, Brian. The first step's to find out more about the Dawsons.'

'Thanks, Alec.' Nightingale was clearly unsure whether McKay was being ironic. 'We need to start with a more detailed conversation with the next of kin, assuming they're up to talking to us.' He glanced at the notes he'd clearly prepared before the meeting. 'I've been in touch with Hampshire and West Sussex police to see if they can assist us with that. I'm not sure it's a good use of our time to be traipsing all the way down there unless we're confident they've got something useful to tell us. I'll keep you all posted on that.'

'What about Paul Dawson's business?' Horton said. 'I did a quick search on the Companies House site over the weekend, but it didn't tell me much. Registered address was in Jedburgh, but it looked like it was probably his accountant's offices. Accounts are up to date, but that only means the latest set related to the year before last. Last year's not submitted yet. I'm no expert, but as far as I could judge the company looked very profitable at that stage. Things might have changed since, of course.'

Nightingale nodded approvingly. 'Do we know the nature of his business?'

'No clues in the Companies House stuff. I did a search online in case he had a website, but couldn't find anything informative. From the accounts, I'd guess he was some kind of one-man band. If so, the last accounts suggest he'd been making a tidy living from it.'

'But, as you say, that might have changed. The last year or two haven't been easy for a lot of people in business. And if he was the director of a limited company, he might not have been eligible for much in the way of government support. It's an avenue we need to explore. Maybe start with the accountants. Do you want to take that on, Ginny? May be worth taking a trip down there. I'll speak to our friends in the south, make sure we don't tread on anyone's toes.'

'Fine by me,' Horton said. 'We need to check out their home address too. There must be friends and neighbours who can tell us something.'

'I'll see if I can drum up some resource from Lothian and Borders to do some interviews down there. We also need to get access to their home and see if that provides us with any insights. If they can do some of the legwork locally for us, it'll allow us to focus on the areas where we can add most value.'

Nightingale was beginning to look back in his element, McKay thought. He'd clearly put all his earlier uncertainty behind him and was focusing on the process. McKay didn't have a problem with that. It was how most investigations were resolved.

'There is one other small question that's been nagging at me,' Ginny Horton said. 'The Dawsons had their children with them. If they lived in Scotland, shouldn't they have been back at school by now?'

Nightingale's expression suggested that the question, relatively trivial as it was, had momentarily knocked him off his smooth course. 'It's a good question. Maybe they'd taken time out of school, though they don't usually like you doing that just for a holiday these days.'

'More likely they weren't at state schools,' McKay said. 'If the Dawsons were as well off as the company accounts suggested, maybe they'd sent the kids off to private schools. From what I remember, even the Scottish ones tend to work more to the English term dates than the Scottish state ones.'

'Another thing to check out,' Nightingale said. 'If Dawson had fallen on relatively hard times, private school fees aren't cheap. Might have been another source of concern to him.' Nightingale looked around the team. 'Right, does that give us enough to go on for the moment? I'll get the various tasks allocated and make sure it's all on the system.'

McKay sat back and looked expectantly at Ginny Horton. Sure enough, he'd trained her well and she didn't let him down.

'I take your point about grand conspiracy theories, Brian,' she said. 'But I'm keen that we don't ignore the Gillans. There's clearly a link to the Dawson case so we still need to treat their deaths as a priority.'

'Yes, of course. Fair point.' Nightingale looked around the room, as if hoping someone might offer him a solution.

McKay leaned forward. 'Why don't I run with that one for the moment, Brian? I'm sure you're right that it may go nowhere, but Ginny makes a good point. We can just treat it as a separate strand of the investigation. It keeps the whole thing clear-cut.' *And your hands clean if the whole thing proves to be a massive waste of time,* McKay added to himself. He had a feeling that that aspect of his proposition might prove appealing to Nightingale.

'It's definitely a thought.' Nightingale tapped his fingers gently on the table, as if mentally weighing up the options. 'It might be the best use of your experience and expertise, Alec. I can see that.'

'As you say, Brian. It's important to focus on the areas where we can add most value.'

'Quite so. Okay, that's settled then. For the moment, Alec, you follow up on the Gillans. Keep me posted over the next day or so, and we can decide whether or not it's a wild goose chase.'

'Most likely.'

'Thanks, everyone. I'll set up a full briefing session for the whole team for the end of the afternoon, once we've got everything allocated. If you need anything in the meantime, just let me know.'

They rose from the table, Nightingale making a show of striding out of the room as if heading for another key meeting. McKay lingered for a moment in his seat, apparently checking emails on his phone. Ginny Horton leaned over and whispered gently in his ear. 'You cunning old bastard.'

'What?'

'You've taken on the element of this case that most interests you. And, for the moment, you're rid of Nightingale's interference.'

McKay shrugged. 'It does seem to have worked out that way. But it's win-win.'

'Is that right?'

'Aye. Nightingale's rid of my interference too.'

CHAPTER FIFTEEN

I sla could already feel the nights drawing in, even though it was still high summer, the wheat and barley unharvested in the surrounding fields, the evenings still pleasantly light.

But one of the first things that had struck her when she'd moved up here was how quickly the days shortened and lengthened after the solstices. It was now more than two months since midsummer. The days when the gloaming could stretch to midnight were long gone. As she arrived back at the house after another extended working day, the sun had already set over the Black Isle to the west and the reddened light threw long shadows over the garden, darkness thickening under the trees and bushes. It had been a fine day, but she could taste a chill in the air.

She wasn't surprised to see Ginny's car absent. She'd already texted Isla to say that she was likely to be another half hour or so. Isla locked her car and, pulling her house keys from her handbag, she approached the front door.

She'd realised – though only as she climbed out of the car – that she was feeling tense. It was the business with Tristram. She'd struggled earlier to screw up the courage to post her response to him. She'd actually walked past the postbox on the first occasion, unable to bring herself to pull the letter from her pocket. It was only as she was returning, clutching her sandwich and drink in a plastic bag, that she forced herself to take out the letter and – before she could stop herself – toss it into the box.

She'd expected to feel better once she'd done the deed, but she hadn't, not really. She still didn't know whether she'd made the right choice or whether the very act of making contact with him was opening some kind of Pandora's Box.

As she inserted the front door key into the lock, she glanced uneasily over her shoulder. She knew she was being foolish. He wouldn't receive the letter for another day or two. And if he was going to turn up here anyway, there wasn't much she could do about that.

She told herself she had no reason to fear him. Tristram had caused her all kinds of grief over the years, but he'd never been physically threatening to her. He was a relatively slight and seemingly gentle individual. That was one of the methods he used to inveigle his way into people's trust. He had an undeniable charm and he gave the impression he was safe to be around. It was only as you came to know him that you realised that, while he might present no physical danger, he was more than capable of damaging you in other ways.

She closed the front door firmly behind her, as if trying to shut out her own past. She made herself a coffee and carried it through to the living room, drawing the curtains across the large patio windows before turning on the TV. It was just past 8pm and she flicked aimlessly through the channels until she found one showing the news headlines. She'd heard from Ginny that, as the police had now released the names of the Dawson family, the investigation had made the national news. Sure enough, a couple of items down, the deaths were reported by an earnest correspondent outside the entrance to the chalet camp. There was little detail in the report, other than the fact that, at present, the police were not seeking anyone else in connection with the killings.

She sipped her coffee, only half-watching the screen. Then, unexpectedly, she glimpsed something that made her catch her breath. At the same moment, she heard a rattling at the front door and a key being turned in the lock. She started, spilling a splash of coffee on her shirt.

Isla was still dabbing at herself with a tissue when Ginny appeared at the living-room door. 'Not quite as late as I feared.' She peered at Isla. 'You okay?'

'I just spilled some coffee. It's nothing.'

'You clearly need a glass of wine instead.'

'If you insist. I'll go and get changed. Thought we could just pull something out of the freezer for supper.'

'Fine by me. I'll see what I can find.'

Five minutes later, Isla and Ginny were sitting back in the living room, each with a glass of wine, a batch-cooked chilli con carne defrosting in the microwave. 'You okay?' Ginny asked. 'You look a bit shaken.'

'I don't know. It's just–' She stopped. 'It sounds stupid.'

'Go on.'

Isla took a breath, already feeling foolish even for mentioning it. 'It was just – well, I was watching the TV news. There was a short report on the investigation you're involved in.'

'We were told there was likely to be. What about it?'

'They had a report from the site where it happened. Some reporter doing a piece to camera. It's just...'

'What?'

'There was a small crowd behind the reporter. Just a handful of people, presumably locals from the site or the village. You couldn't really see them clearly because the camera was mainly focused on the presenter, and most of them were some distance away. But, well, for a moment, I thought I saw Tristram there.'

'You can't have. It's just that he's on your mind at the moment. It will have just been somebody who looked vaguely like him.'

'I know. It was just a shock. At the time, I was absolutely certain it was him. Even though, when I think about it, it probably didn't really even resemble him that closely. It was just that there was something about him.'

'There's probably a psychological term for it,' Ginny said. 'When something or someone's on your mind, and you start imagining you're seeing them everywhere.'

Ginny returned to the kitchen and set the chilli on to heat while she put on some rice. She returned a few moments later with the bottle of wine to top up their glasses. 'I've got some slightly annoying news. On the work front. Looks like I'm going to have to be away for a couple of days.'

Isla felt an unexpected clutch of anxiety in her stomach. 'Why's that?'

'I've got to go down to the borders for a couple of days. We've arranged for the Dawsons' house to be given the once-over, so I'm going to be there for that. And I need to have a chat with Paul Dawson's accountant. We want to find out more about the state of his business.'

'Do you need to go down to do that? What are phones for?'

'That was my feeling. Doesn't seem like the best use of time. But it's this new guy, Brian Nightingale. He has his own ways of working, let's say.'

'So how long will you be away?'

'Just overnight tomorrow.'

Isla looked up. 'Tomorrow?'

'Sorry. I know it's short notice. I thought it was better to get it over with. If I drive down in the morning, we can do the house check in the afternoon. Then I can stay overnight and see the accountant the next day. Should mean I can get away fairly early and be back here at a sensible time.'

'Yes, that makes sense...' Isla trailed off.

'If you'd prefer me not to go, I'm sure I can organise it some other way.'

'No, don't be daft. How many nights have I spent away over the years? You hardly ever do. I'll be fine.'

'I hadn't realised how anxious you are about Tristram. I'll have a word with Brian first thing–'

'No.' Isla had spoken more sharply than she'd intended. 'I don't want you to do that. I've let this get to me more than I should.'

'But if you do want me to stay, that's really not a problem.'

'I know. But if you do I'll just feel guilty.' She smiled. 'And you don't want to make a bad impression on this Brian guy, do you?'

'I'm not sure what to make of him, to be honest. He'd obviously thought he'd come up for an easy time and he was shaken that the investigation's taken an unexpected turn. But he seems capable enough. And I've seen no signs of the sex-pest tendencies that Alec was warning us about.'

'But?'

'I don't know. I've a sense he has some agenda. That he's here to do something more than just get on with the job.'

'Presumably he's not going to be around for long?'

'I'm hoping not. It depends a bit on how the investigation goes. I imagine he'll be doing everything possible to get the case sorted.'

The beeping of the microwave signalled that the chilli was ready. Ginny started to rise, but Isla held up her hand. 'I'll get it. Sounds like you've a long day ahead of you tomorrow.'

'Well, I won't object to being waited on hand and foot.'

'No change there, then.' Isla grinned. 'I'll bring it through. We can have it in front of the TV for a change.'

While she waited for Isla to return, Ginny idly watched the TV. It was still on the news channel, and they were showing the headlines on the half hour, including a repeat of the report on the Dawson case Isla had seen earlier. Ginny watched with curiosity, wondering what it was that Isla had actually glimpsed behind the reporter.

As Isla had said, there was a small crowd clustered behind the presenter. They'd obviously been kept at some distance, and it really wasn't possible to make out individual features. There was only one moment, as the camera operator cut away from the reporter to show a wider shot of the site that the crowd momentarily became more visible. The camera swept across the small cluster of faces. Somewhere in the middle were the features that had presumably attracted Isla's attention.

This time, though, it was Ginny's turn to catch her breath. Like Isla, she had caught only a momentary glimpse of the face and there was no way she could be certain.

She had no way of knowing whether Tristram had really been in the crowd. But Ginny thought she had spotted someone else. Someone who seemed unexpectedly familiar.

CHAPTER SIXTEEN

'Do you always work this late?'

Helena Grant looked up in mild irritation. Something she'd learned in the course of the afternoon was that one of the benefits of an open-door policy was that, paradoxically, people rarely troubled you. As soon as you closed your door, every bugger in the building seemed to take it as carte blanche to come blundering in. 'It depends how busy I am.' The words sounded more pointed than she'd intended, but maybe that was for the best.

It was Brian Nightingale's face peering round the door, in the tentative manner of someone trying to pretend they haven't already disturbed you. 'Is it okay to come in?'

She repressed a sigh. 'Feel free. I'm just finishing up anyway. How's it going?' She'd already had a briefing from Alec McKay – another person who hadn't been deterred by a closed door, but she'd never seriously expected he would be – but she had no intention of telling Nightingale that.

'Not bad. A few developments we hadn't expected, but nothing we can't cope with.'

'That's good. If there's anything I can do to help, just ask.'

'You look busy enough anyway.'

'I'm not going to deny that. How's the team been? Alec not been too much of a nuisance?'

'I think Alec and I have the measure of each other.'

Grant doubted that very much, at least where Nightingale was concerned. In her experience it was easy to underestimate Alec, but rarely a wise thing to do. 'Good to hear.'

He'd entered the room fully now, and gestured towards the seat beside her desk. 'Do you mind...?'

'Go ahead. Something I can do for you, Brian?'

'Just wanted to say hello properly, really. Was conscious it was a bit rushed this morning.'

'Well, hello, then. Properly.' She smiled, unsure what else to say. 'It's good to have you working with us, Brian.'

'I really just wanted to have a bit of a chat with you about the team.'

'The team?'

'Just to get your views informally. I'm not expecting you to say anything out of turn, but it would just be useful to get a sense of their different personalities and what they can contribute. That sort of thing.'

'You've a lot of experience, Brian. I'm sure you can form your own impressions of them. I don't really know what I can add to that.'

'You've known them all a long time.'

'That's true. But maybe that just colours my judgement. Maybe I should ask you for your opinions once you've worked with them for a while.'

'I've started to get a sense of them. Just really wanted to check that I was pitching things right.' He seemed to hesitate. 'If you are finishing up here, last night's invitation still holds.'

'Invitation?'

'To join me for dinner. I'm stuck on my own in a budget hotel. I just thought that if you were at a loose end...'

'It's a nice thought, Brian, and I appreciate how tedious it is being stuck in a hotel. But I'm really too exhausted tonight to be good company. Some other time, maybe.'

He didn't look disappointed, she thought. It was more that he looked challenged, like a chess player who had received the response he expected to his opening moves and was now planning his subsequent tactics. 'Maybe later in the week.'

'You should ask Alec. He'd happily go for a beer with you. That way you'd get all the gossip.'

'I'm sure. What about Ginny Horton?' Is she one for socialising?'

'Ginny? Not particularly. I mean, she's sociable enough, but she's a bit of a home-bird.'

He nodded thoughtfully. 'Well, some other time then.'

She waited till he'd closed the door behind him before murmuring, 'How about never, Brian. Never's perfect for me.'

Almost immediately there was a further knock on the door, and Mike Everly peered into the room. 'Oh, you are there. Thought I must have missed you,' he said.

'You caught me just in time. I'd just reached my admin limit. Something I can do for you, Mike?'

'Nothing urgent.' He stopped. 'Well, actually, I was just wondering if you fancied going for a quick drink?'

Bloody typical, she thought. *Eight months without any kind of social life, then two invitations on the same evening.* 'A drink?'

'Well, I was really just wondering if it might be helpful to have a more informal chat about what we were discussing earlier.'

She looked pointedly at her watch. 'I very much appreciate the thought, Mike. But it's getting a bit late for me. Can we take a rain check for another time?'

'Yes, of course. I meant to pop over to ask you earlier, but got caught up in things. If you want to have more of a chat in the morning, let me know.' Unlike Nightingale, Everly did look genuinely disappointed at her response.

'I'll do that, Mike. Thanks for the offer, anyway.'

'I'll remember to ask earlier in the evening next time.' Everly smiled.

After he'd left she felt awkward and slightly guilty, as if she'd just committed some kind of social faux pas. There were times, she thought, when life seemed almost unbearably complicated. Times when she was relieved that all she had waiting for her at home was a glass of wine and that ready meal for one.

CHAPTER SEVENTEEN

'A re you sure?' McKay poured boiling water into the two mugs, gave them a quick stir and handed one to Ginny Horton. 'There you go. Don't say I never do anything for you.'

'Much appreciated,' Ginny Horton said. 'I take it I have to add my own milk?'

'What do you think I am? A waiter?'

She grinned and bent to retrieve a carton of milk from the fridge. 'No, I'm not remotely sure. He was only visible on the screen for a fraction of a second and not clearly even then. I replayed it a couple of times, and each time I grew less certain.'

'And Isla had already suggested she saw her brother?'

'That's my point. There's a danger you just see what you want to see. Isla's obsessing about Tristram at the moment. I'm up to my ears in this case, so I convince myself it's someone completely different.'

'It's possible the two of you are just losing your minds. I've seen it coming for a long time.'

'Bugger off, Alec. This is the last time I come to you with valuable intelligence.'

'Valuable intelligence, is it? That some guy you glimpsed for a nanosecond on the box bears a passing resemblance to a guy you interviewed at Loch Morlich?'

'That's pretty much it,' she acknowledged.

'Even if you were right, it doesn't prove anything. The couple told you they were leaving and intending to head north. Maybe they didn't make it any further than the Black Isle. If so, he might have been just another gawper hoping for his moment of fame in the background of a murder report.'

'It's a coincidence, though. Given the link between the two incidents.'

'A link he wouldn't have been aware of. I'm assuming you didn't mention it?'

'Of course not. I just talked to him about the car.'

'He's probably just curious because he's realised that the Highlands are an unexpected hotbed of crime.'

'I sometimes think you were the original smart alec.'

'No doubt named in my honour. Seriously, though, Gin, I will follow it up, just in case. Assuming he was there, that is.' He grinned. 'What time are you off?'

'Was planning to set off shortly. Brian said he wanted a word before I left but he was on the phone when I checked.'

'Give my regards to all those poor benighted souls toiling away in the far reaches of the borders.'

'I'm sure they'll return your good wishes, Alec.' She looked up to see Brian Nightingale peering through the door of the kitchenette. He tapped on the glass and beckoned.

'Looks like you've got the summons,' McKay said. 'Don't let me keep you.'

'Horton picked up her mug and stepped out into the corridor to join Nightingale. 'Morning, Brian. Just grabbing a quick coffee before I head south.'

'That's what I wanted to talk to you about.' Nightingale was already striding towards his office leaving Horton trailing in his wake. 'Slight change of plan.'

'Oh, yes?' She followed him into the office, registering the fact that there was an overnight bag sitting in the middle of Nightingale's desk.

'I assume you won't have a problem if I travel down with you?'

'Of course not. But why...?'

'Couple of reasons. I was thinking about it overnight. Strikes me that Paul Dawson's at the heart of this, so we need to know as much as possible about his background and circumstances. I'd like to be there when they look around the house. I also thought it might be useful for me to introduce you to the folk in Lothian and Borders myself. I know some of them pretty well, so we might get more out of it if I'm there.'

None of this rang particularly true to Horton. Her view was that the SIO's role ought to be primarily managerial, and she couldn't see that Nightingale's presence was likely to add much to her work over the next couple of days. He'd surely have been more usefully employed co-ordinating activities up here. 'Whatever you think. I've booked a pool car to drive down in. Happy to drive unless you'd prefer to.'

'I'm more than happy to be a passenger.' Nightingale glanced up at the clock. 'I guess we'd better be off soon.'

'I'll grab my stuff and meet you downstairs.'

'Fine. See you shortly.'

Still feeling slightly bemused, Horton returned to the office to fetch her bag and laptop. McKay raised an eyebrow as she entered. 'What was all that about?'

'He's coming with me.'

The eyebrow was elevated a notch higher. 'Has anyone told him he's the SIO on a major inquiry?'

'He thought he could add some value.'

'In fairness, his absence will probably improve things for the rest of us. It's you I'm more concerned about. I assume you've got no choice in this?'

'What am I supposed to say? "No, Brian, I really don't want you to come with me"?'

'I'd be tempted.'

'Your future's largely behind you. I still have to be careful.'

'Not too careful, though. Make sure you take care of yourself.'

'I'll do that, all right. See you in a couple of days. I'll keep you posted if we find anything useful down there.'

'We don't know if there is anything useful down there.' McKay was still watching her, but his expression had changed. The usual levity was gone. 'Like I say, Gin. Take care.'

CHAPTER EIGHTEEN

McKay found the Gillans' house easily enough and parked outside the gateway. The Mercedes convertible Ginny had mentioned was still parked outside, and there was no sign that anything else had changed since her visit. McKay walked slowly down the drive and approached the front door.

Behind him, a voice called, 'I say! Can I help you?' It was a sharply enunciated, unmistakably English accent. Presumably the woman that Ginny had encountered previously. McKay had to give the woman her due. She took her neighbourhood watch responsibilities very seriously and seemed capable of moving at the speed of light, given how quickly she'd arrived from whatever vantage point she had been occupying.

He turned. 'I really don't know. What did you have in mind?'

'This is private property, you know.'

'Aye, but the Land Reform Act gives me the statutory right to roam. So I'm roaming.'

Her expression was one of disgust, although it was unclear to McKay whether her disgust was aimed at him or the legislation. 'I won't hesitate to call the police.'

'I can save you the time. I am the police. DI McKay.' He walked back up towards the gate, now brandishing his warrant card. 'Mrs Erskine, I presume.' He'd managed to dredge up the name from the notes Ginny had supplied.

She seemed both impressed and slightly disconcerted that McKay knew her name. She leaned forward to peer suspiciously at his documentation. 'You're really a police officer?'

'I know it's difficult to believe. My senior officers often have a similar problem. But I'm afraid it's true.'

She was gazing past him at the Gillans' house. 'Are they in some sort of trouble? We seem to be seeing an awful lot of police officers. Plain clothes ones, at that, and now a detective inspector. I'm assuming you're not here about a speeding offence?'

'A little more serious than that.' McKay smiled. 'Although I should stress that we want to talk them only as possible witnesses.'

'That's what your colleague said.' There was a sceptical note in her voice.

'Your neighbours seem rather elusive. I take it you've seen nothing more of them since my colleague spoke to you?'

'I haven't seen them since Friday. I've kept an eye out just in case.'

'How well do you know them?'

'Well, they're neighbours. That's about it, really. I wouldn't describe us as friends.' She sounded as if the very idea was distasteful.

'So you wouldn't have any idea where they might have gone?'

'I'm afraid not. I couldn't tell you anything about their private lives.'

'And there've been no other visitors since they left?'

'Other than your colleagues and now yourself, no.' She paused. 'Actually, no, that's not quite true. There was a vehicle here late yesterday afternoon. I nearly came out to talk to them, but then I realised it was a delivery of some kind.'

'A delivery?'

'Yes. Not the mail, but some private company. It was just a plain grey van. A small van. Not one of those transit types.'

'I don't suppose you noticed the registration?' McKay might not have bothered asking this of any other observer, but his hunch proved correct.

'I did, actually,' she said proudly. 'I made a note on my phone. Just in case.' She pulled an aged Nokia from the pocket of her cardigan and, after a moment thumbing through the screens, she read out the number for McKay to jot down. She looked up at him. 'Do you think the van's significant?'

'I don't imagine so,' McKay said. 'Did you see if the driver actually made a delivery?'

'He had a cardboard box. About so big, I suppose.' She held her hands a foot or so apart. 'Square. He took it to the front door and rang the bell, but obviously there was no response. Eventually, he left the package tucked just inside the porch out of sight of the street.'

'How well did you see the driver?'

'Not very well, to be honest. He was wearing a peaked cap and dark glasses.' She smiled as if seeking McKay's approval for her observational skills.

'That's very helpful. It's useful to know what's going on.'

'I make a point of knowing that. You can't be too careful.'

'Anyway, thank you, Mrs Erskine. I won't delay you. I'm sure you've plenty to be getting on with.'

She looked mildly disappointed, as if she'd been hoping he might ask her to join him in the investigation. 'Yes, of course. I'll get in touch if I should see any sign of the Gillans.'

'Please do. That would be very helpful.' McKay smiled and stood waiting pointedly until she finally took the hint and turned to cross the street to her own house. He waited a few moments longer then made his way back down the Gillans' drive. No doubt Fionnuala Erskine would be watching his every move.

He walked towards the front door and peered inside the narrow porch. He saw the package immediately. It had been placed just inside the outer door, sheltered from the weather and hidden from any passing eyes.

McKay paused and frowned.

The package had been damaged. There was tearing along the top and sides of the cardboard, as if someone or something had tried to gain access to its contents.

There was something about the sight that McKay found disturbing, though he didn't immediately know why. As he drew closer, he saw, initially to his relief, that the rips looked to be nothing more than the work of some animal. A moment later, it occurred to him to wonder what the box might contain that would be of interest to a wild creature.

McKay reached into his pocket and took out a pair of disposable plastic gloves, which he carefully pulled over his hands. His unease was growing. The animal – perhaps more than one animal – had clearly made a determined effort to gain entry to the box, but had been defeated by the robust packaging. McKay dug again into his pocket and found the Swiss Army knife his sister-in-law had bought him the previous Christmas. He drew the blade down the hefty tape sealing the package, then using the blade he carefully lifted the flaps of the box.

With no idea what to expect, he pushed back the two flaps and peered inside.

Whatever he might have been expecting, the reality was more baffling than anything he might have imagined. Inside the box was a small metal cage, the type used by children to accommodate small pets. At first, McKay thought the cage was empty, but as he tipped the box slightly the sawdust in the base shifted. Lying at one end was the inert body of a hamster.

CHAPTER NINETEEN

'Decent place.' Brian Nightingale stared up at the ivy-covered stone facade of the large villa in front of them.

'It's that all right.' Ginny Horton wasn't sure of the age of the house. She guessed late Edwardian. It didn't quite have the grandeur of a Victorian house of this type. She was no expert, but she associated this kind of solid, bourgeois dwelling with the later period. In any case, Nightingale was undoubtedly correct. It was an imposing place, set in a sizeable and well-maintained mature garden, although the proximity of the neighbouring houses suggested that parts of the villa's original land had been sold off over the decades. In a village on the edge of one of the neat market towns that dotted the borders, it would be worth a bob or two. She wondered what would happen to it following the death of the Dawsons.

The local man, a DI Graeme Dangerfield, was standing in the porch waiting for them, a set of keys in his hand. 'Supplied by Maria Dawson's parents,' he explained. 'They were keen to do what they could to help.'

'I imagine they, more than anyone, are looking for an

ALEX WALTERS

explanation,' Horton said. 'I don't know how you come to terms with something like this.'

Dangerfield shook his head. 'I don't think you can. Those poor kiddies. So what's the plan here?'

'I thought first just have a look round,' Nightingale said. 'Get a sense of the place and what it tells us, if anything.'

'I take it we've no reason to treat it as a crime scene?'

'Not unless we find something that tells us otherwise. This is more about getting a sense of the family. We're in the process of getting access to their bank accounts and suchlike, and we're going to speak to Paul Dawson's accountant tomorrow. So that should tell us if this was in some way related to his business interests. We're keen to find anything that might give us an insight.'

Horton had understood that Nightingale was acquainted with Dangerfield, but she had a sense now of a wariness between the two men, as if each were sizing up the other.

'Shall we take a look?' She had already pulled on a pair of disposable protective gloves, but she noticed that neither of the two men had bothered to do the same.

Dangerfield turned to unlock the door. He cautiously pushed it open and stepped forward into the hallway. There was a caution to his movements, as if he expected his entry might in some way be challenged.

The interior of the house was as impressive as its exterior. The hallway floor had been stripped back to its original glazed tiles, draped now with expensive rugs. The doors and fittings were heavy oak. Overall, the Dawsons had retained the original feel of the house while giving it some appropriate modern touches.

'Doesn't look like the house of someone whose business is struggling,' Nightingale said. 'But I guess you can never tell.'

124

'Place might be mortgaged up to the eyeballs.' Dangerfield peered into the living room. 'Where do you want to start?'

'Is there an office?' Nightingale said. 'From the Companies House details, we're assuming he ran his business from home. Some sort of consultancy, according to the accountant, though he didn't know too much about the detail of what Dawson did.'

'Let's see what we can find.' Nightingale pushed open the doors of all the ground-floor rooms. These all seemed to be used for domestic purposes – the kitchen, two apparent living rooms, a separate dining room and a downstairs lavatory and shower room.

'We can come back to these,' Nightingale said. 'Let's check upstairs.'

He led the way up the wide staircase with its ornately carved bannisters. A second, narrower staircase led from the landing to a third floor and what had presumably once been servants' rooms.

The second-floor rooms comprised a set of five bedrooms – a master bedroom with an en-suite bathroom, three bedrooms which had clearly been used by the three children, and a fifth bedroom used as a guest room. The only other room on this level was a large bathroom, dominated by an imposing roll-topped bath.

Horton stood for a moment in the doorway of one of the young girls' rooms, with its garishly pink bed linen and glittery piles of dolls. It was a poignant sight now, but the children had clearly not lacked for material possessions at least. Each of the rooms had an expensive games console, and there were numerous toys scattered around.

Nightingale was already on his way to the third floor, Dangerfield trudging close behind him. From upstairs, Horton heard his voice. 'Right. Here's what we're looking for.'

She dragged herself reluctantly away from the children's rooms and followed the two men upstairs. The third floor comprised two large rooms built into the eaves. Both of these had been converted into office space, with desks, padded office chairs, filing cabinets and the other familiar furniture of a modern workspace. The rooms had windows with views over the village and the surrounding countryside, and skylights that gave the rooms a light, airy feel. A pleasant place to work, Horton thought.

There were two desks, and she guessed that the largest would have been used by Paul Dawson. The accountant hadn't mentioned any employees in the business, so it seemed likely that the second desk was used by Maria Dawson in some capacity. Something for them to check out the next day.

The desk was clear of any papers or documents. Nightingale turned on the PC but was greeted only with a request for an access password.

'We can get our IT people to check out the computers,' Dangerfield said. 'Unless you prefer to do it at your end?'

'Might as well do it here if that's possible. Once they've got into them, we can see if it's worth taking a closer look.' Nightingale was sounding slightly dispirited, as if he'd begun to realise the futility of their task here. He pulled open one of the filing cabinets and lifted out a couple of fat files. The first contained a set of glossy brochures. 'Dawson Associates,' he read from the cover. 'Driving wellness in the workplace.'

'How do you drive wellness?' Dangerfield asked.

'What even is wellness?' Nightingale said. 'The opposite of illness, I suppose.' He held up a stack of brightly coloured leaflets. 'Not just wellness: leadership; coaching; mental health in the workplace. No wonder he went off his head.' Nightingale glanced at Horton. 'Am I being politically incorrect?'

'You know exactly what you're being.' Horton had already decided that she wasn't going to tolerate any nonsense from

Nightingale, however much it might be wrapped up as banter. She'd been exploring the desk and, in one of the drawers, had found several boxes of business cards. 'Paul A Dawson, CPsychol, MCIPD. Consultant and Coach.' She handed one to Nightingale. 'Chartered psychologist. Chartered Member of the Institute of Personnel and Development.'

'If you say so. It's all psychobabble to me.' Nightingale was still delving into the drawers of the filing cabinet. 'These mostly look like client files. Test papers.' He passed one of the files to Horton. 'For assessing how bonkers you are, presumably.'

'Psychometric questionnaires. Tools for exploring your personality. I don't imagine you've ever done one of those, Brian.' She gave him her sweetest smile.

'They got me to do one on some training course a couple of years back. Utter nonsense.'

'Didn't like what you found, eh, Brian?' Dangerfield winked at Horton.

'At least we have an idea of what he did now. And the client files suggest he had plenty of business. A few big-name companies, too.'

'No doubt charging them squillions for the privilege.' Nightingale closed the filing cabinet and walked over to a low bookcase set against one of the walls. It was packed with what appeared to be psychological textbooks as well as a mix of academic and popular management books. Nightingale pulled a book at random from the shelves and flicked aimlessly through it. 'People make a living doing this kind of stuff?'

'A pretty decent one if this place is anything to go by.' Dangerfield walked over to the window and peered out at the view. 'Is this telling us anything?'

Nightingale was still looking around him. 'We'll need to get someone to go over these files. Just in case there's anything significant in them. My guess is probably not, but maybe we can make a final decision once we've spoken to the accountant. Shall we check downstairs?'

They made their way downstairs and checked out the bedrooms. These were, if anything, even less informative than the office. There was nothing that seemed out of place in a typical family house. The rooms had been left tidy, with again nothing to suggest that the Dawsons hadn't expected to return as scheduled from their holiday. Nightingale carried out a quick check of the drawers in the dressing table in the master bedroom, but again found nothing unexpected. 'I'm getting the feeling we're wasting our time here now. Let's check downstairs.'

They started with the kitchen. Again, there was nothing unexpected. The fridge was empty, except for a handful of longer-life items. The freezer, on the other hand, was relatively well stocked. Nothing to indicate that the family hadn't embarked on their holiday with every expectation of returning as normal. But that revealed nothing. Even if there had been serious issues on Paul Dawson's mind, he wouldn't necessarily have shared anything with his wife.

The living room was no more revealing. Apart from some shelves holding a handful of paperbacks – mostly recent bestsellers, as far as Horton could judge – there was little personal in the room. Again, it had the air of a room that had been tidied in advance of a family holiday, with any personal detritus cleared away.

By now, Horton was convinced they were wasting their time. They had gained nothing so far from the visit other than confirming Paul Dawson's profession. This was one of the many tasks that were necessary in this kind of enquiry but which, in the majority of instances, yielded nothing of value. The real question was why she, let alone Nightingale, was wasting their time travelling down here to carry it out.

Leaving the two men to finish checking out the living room, Horton wandered out into the hall. There was even less of interest out here as far as she could see. There was a small table with a single drawer, which proved to be empty, and a built-in cupboard containing a selection of outdoor coats and a single pair of adult-sized wellington boots. The only other item of possible interest was an untidy heap of unopened mail behind the front door, presumably items delivered since the Dawsons had departed on their holiday.

She flicked idly through it. The vast majority comprised nothing more than advertising leaflets from local businesses, interspersed with the occasional targeted marketing letter. Near the bottom of the pile she came across one envelope which looked slightly different from the rest. The address was printed but using an old-fashioned label, and the letter had a stamp rather than a printed frank. It looked more personal than the rest of the mail. She held up the envelope to examine it more carefully.

'What's that?' She looked up to see Nightingale reaching out to take the envelope from her.

She moved it out of his grasp. 'Probably nothing. But maybe you should wear some gloves, just in case?'

He stared at her for a moment then nodded. 'Okay.' He paused. 'I don't suppose you have a spare pair?'

'Here you go.'

He avoided her eye as he pulled on the gloves, then took the envelope from her. He peered at the front of the envelope. 'Addressed to Paul Dawson. Addressee only.'

'One of the things that caught my eye.'

Nightingale turned over the envelope. It was self-sealing and seemed to be already coming open. He hesitated for a moment, then slid his finger gently under the flap. He reached inside and drew out the contents. A single sheet of paper, folded like a letter. Nightingale carefully unfolded it and held it up for Horton to see.

It was a printout of a photograph. A young woman, probably in her mid-twenties, sitting at a table gazing up at the camera. There was nothing remarkable about her. She had short-cropped dark hair and was wearing a pair of glasses that looked slightly too small for her face. Horton's impression was of someone who preferred not to be the centre of attention, but who'd been caught inadvertently by the camera lens. She had an opened file in front of her, but the setting looked more like a professional workshop than a college. The paper carried no other information. Nightingale's expression was quizzical. 'Interesting.'

'Very. Why would anyone send that to Dawson?'

'Maybe some former client?'

'Seems a bit odd to send it with no note or explanation, though.'

'Maybe it was a follow-up to something they'd discussed. But, yes, it's odd.' He looked up at her. 'I don't suppose you've an evidence bag as well?'

CHAPTER TWENTY

McKay stood at the top edge of the lawn, staring down at the view in the late-afternoon sunshine. The Moray Firth was a pale blue under the summer sky, partly shadowed now by the bulk of the Black Isle to the north. From here, he could see the elegant curves of the Kessock suspension bridge, the roads busy with the approach of rush hour.

He heard a shuffle of feet on the path behind him.

'You'd be no good at playing Grandmother's Footsteps, Josh.'

'Guv?'

McKay turned. Josh Carlisle was looking mildly bemused as he frequently tended to when speaking to McKay.

'How's it going?'

'They've got the site sealed off.'

'What about the package?'

'Been shipped off to forensics.'

McKay looked back at the house. He felt unaccountably relieved at the removal of the object in question, as if its bizarre presence had been casting some sort of ill-omened spell over the residence. 'Are the examiners inside yet?'

'We're just opening up the house.'

McKay had made the executive decision to open up the Gillans' house. They still had no definitive evidence that the Gillans' deaths were anything other than a tragic accident. But the delivery of the strange package had further complicated the picture. There had been no marking on the package – no address or information about the sender or the delivery – and no explanation of its contents.

Why would anyone go to the trouble of sending the Gillans a dead animal? A dead hamster, for Christ's sake? Presumably, it was intended either as some message or warning to the Gillans sent by someone unaware of their deaths, or it was intended as a message to whoever might visit the house following the discovery of the Gillans' bodies.

Either way, he felt it was a sufficiently bizarre development to justify treating the whole house as a crime scene. Carlisle had already confessed to him that Ginny Horton had given the interior an unofficial once-over during their earlier visit, but had found little other than some evidence that the Gillans seemed to have departed in a hurry.

At that point, though, they'd had no strong reason to think that any harm might have come to the Gillans. Horton had been looking for nothing more than some possible clues to their whereabouts. Now the context was rather different.

Even so, McKay was irritated at being forced to make these decisions in isolation. He didn't trust Brian Nightingale's motives or good intentions, and he knew any operational decision was potentially vulnerable to retrospective criticism. Normally, that wouldn't have troubled McKay too much – he was generally inclined to seek neither permission nor forgiveness for his actions. But at the moment he preferred to keep his backside well covered.

'Any word back from Brian yet?' he asked Carlisle.

McKay had tried to call Nightingale earlier but the call had simply cut to voicemail. After trying a couple of times, McKay had given up in disgust, delegating the task to Carlisle. McKay didn't fully trust himself not to express his opinions too bluntly when Nightingale finally deigned to take the call.

'Nothing. Maybe there's some problem with the phone.'

'That'll be it.' McKay's next move would be to try Ginny, but he knew Nightingale would find further cause to complain if he hadn't been told about this directly. Whichever way McKay played this, he was probably on a hiding to nothing.

He made his way round to the front of the house. Jock Henderson, fully suited except for his helmet, was standing in the middle of the front lawn, apparently smoking a leisurely cigarette. 'Afternoon, Jock. You drawn the short straw again then?'

Henderson dropped his cigarette butt on to the grass and very deliberately screwed it into the lawn with his heel. McKay could almost hear a collective tut of disapproval from the surrounding neighbours. 'You know how we always make that joke about how we should stop meeting like this?'

'You always make that joke, Jock. I make good ones.'

'Aye, well. We *really* should stop meeting like this. Can't you find me a nice straightforward crime? I mean, a bloody hamster, for Christ's sake.'

'I'll bear that in mind, Jock. At the moment, it's all I have to offer. That and two dead people in a burned-out BMW, and a family knifed to death in their cosy holiday chalet. And the thought that they're potentially all linked. I'm only sorry I won't actually be able to see Brian Nightingale's face when he finds out about the hamster.'

'Nightingale. I saw that old bugger was back,' Henderson commented. 'I hope he's changed his ways.'

'I don't know what you're talking about, Jock. I never listen to office tittle-tattle.'

'You don't need to. You generate half of it. Mostly the scurrilous half.'

'I have to do something to stave off the boredom. As for Nightingale, we'll see. He knows there are still a few of us around who have an idea why he left here in the first place. It was a long time ago. He may be a changed man by now.'

'Aye,' Henderson said. 'And you might stop taking the piss, but I'm not going to put any money on it.' He extinguished his cigarette under his heel as before. 'I'd better get back in the house. If I leave it all to the youngsters, they're bound to screw it up.'

'And that's your job. Anything else I should know before I go? Did you get anything from the box?'

'Forensics will take a detailed look at it, but it was just a plain cardboard box. Not new. No identifiable markings as far as we could see. What about the delivery van?'

'We're getting it checked out. One of the neighbours got the registration.'

Henderson looked around them. 'Aye, it seems like that kind of area.'

'Never knock a good witness, Jock. My guess is that it'll either turn out to be some local courier who took a delivery in good faith and knows nothing, or – more likely – the plates were faked. But you never know. We've had stupider villains.'

'Whoever's behind this doesn't strike me as stupid. They're leaving us floundering so far.'

McKay left Henderson to continue his work, and walked over to Josh Carlisle who was chatting to one of the uniforms. 'Any word from our dear leader?'

'I've tried a couple more times. Asked him to call back urgently, but no response yet.'

McKay sighed and took out his own phone. He'd been intending to break the news about the dead hamster when he spoke to Nightingale direct, if only so he could enjoy hearing Nightingale's response. But if Nightingale was not picking up voicemails, he had no choice. He thumbed the number in his address book, and the call was answered almost immediately. 'Alec?'

'Hi, Ginny. I don't suppose that boss of ours is anywhere around, is he? He seems to have been oddly elusive this afternoon, and I've a bit of strange news he needs to hear.'

CHAPTER TWENTY-ONE

'What can I get you?'

Helena Grant still wasn't at all sure that this was a good idea. Equally, she wasn't sure she'd actually had much of a choice. All she could do was make the best of it, which would involve staying sober and not saying anything stupid. 'I'm driving so I'd better stick to something soft. Lime and soda, maybe?'

'One of the benefits of living within walking distance of the city,' Mike Everly said, 'is that I can treat myself to a pint or two when I'm not on the duty rota.'

He'd turned up in her office towards the end of the afternoon and said, apparently jokingly, 'Right, last chance. I'm at a loose end this evening so that offer of a drink still stands, if I've not left it too late.'

She hadn't felt she'd had an option but to accept. She'd also been giving more thought to whether she should take part in the consultancy review and this had seemed like a good opportunity to chat informally about it. It was only when they'd reached the pub that she began to have second thoughts. She'd driven them both into town and found a parking space in one of the backstreets behind the riverside bar. Now, sitting here, looking out at the sunlit waters, she felt uncomfortably as if she was on a date.

She wasn't one to say 'never again', but for the moment she had no desire for any kind of romantic relationship. She was more than happy to spend time with Mike Everly as a colleague or even a friend, but she was wary of any possibility that it might evolve into something more serious.

'You're looking thoughtful.' Everly slid her drink across the table to her.

'Just staring into space. It's felt like a long day.'

'Still working on the admin?'

'It's amazing how it builds up. You finish one piece and almost immediately get more filling your inbox.'

'Tell me about it.' Everly took a swallow of his beer. 'I do occasionally wonder if there are more useful things we could be doing. Stuff like policing.'

'Aren't we supposed to fit that into our spare time?'

'Something like that. Speaking of which, I understand the Dawson case is becoming more convoluted than we'd envisaged?'

'So I've heard. You probably know more than I do. What's Brian's view?'

There was a moment's silence, and she had the sense that Everly was weighing his words carefully. 'I haven't had a chance to talk to him yet. He's down in the borders today.'

Grant couldn't read Everly's tone and it wasn't her place to offer an opinion on Brian Nightingale and his behaviour. 'Probably not what he was expecting, I'm guessing.'

'Probably not. But that's the nature of the job, isn't it?' Everly sounded as if he wanted to change the subject. 'You'd know more than most. I was looking at some of our recent cases. One or two surprises in there.'

'If you mean I'm a magnet for trouble, you're probably not far wrong.'

Everly laughed. 'I wasn't going to put it like that, but you seem to have had more than your share. I was intrigued by this Ruby Jewell character.'

He'd obviously been taking a pretty thorough look through the files. 'She's still out there. One of our failures.'

'She certainly seems very elusive. I take it that's not her real name.'

'It's what she was calling herself when we first came across her. We think she's most likely Maggie Donaldson, daughter of a local businessman, Archie Donaldson, currently a reluctant guest of Glenochil Prison. But we don't know that for certain.'

'And she's wanted in connection with several murders. Not to mention...'

'My own attempted murder. That's the one.' She took a deep swallow of her drink, recalling the moment, only months before, when she'd been minutes away from death.

'Sorry. I didn't mean to bring it up like that. Mr Tactful, that's me.'

'I'm over it now. Or at least I mostly am. But if you're asking me how the hell she's still out there, the answer is I don't know. I was convinced – on both occasions when she came into our sights – that we'd catch up with her sooner rather than later. The last time we had the surrounding area pretty much shut down but somehow she still got through. She's got a weird gift for – I don't know, really – for invisibility or anonymity. You see the image she wants to project, but you never really see *her*. Does that make any kind of sense?'

'I think so.' Grant couldn't tell if there was a note of condescension in Everly's voice.

'She changes her image, and it's as if she's a different person. And on top of that, she's very smart. She ran rings around her father and I'm afraid she's done the same to us. To be honest, she could be anywhere by now.' Grant looked around, somehow feeling uneasy. 'Or she could be that young woman working behind the bar.'

'You're joking.'

'I'm joking about the woman behind the bar. Or at least I think I am. But I'm not joking about what Jewell's capable of. She scares the hell out of me. I'd like nothing more than to see her safely behind bars.' She realised Everly was looking at her with interest, and she knew she'd said too much. 'Well, you did ask.'

'I did. But maybe we should change the subject. Have you given any more thought to this consultancy project?'

The truth was that, despite herself, she'd thought of little else since Everly had first mentioned the idea. She still hadn't reached any kind of decision. Part of her brain was telling her it really wasn't for her. It wasn't what she did. She was a detective, first and foremost. That was the work that dragged her out of bed every morning. Much of it was mundane, some more dramatic, but she'd never found it boring. She loved even the most tiresome, painstaking parts of it, the endless routines needed to give you the one breakthrough that mattered. The sense that, in the end, you were doing something worthwhile, something that made a small difference.

She had a good arrangement here. A team she mostly liked and enjoyed working with. A decent lifestyle. An opportunity to live in a strikingly beautiful part of the world. When she allowed herself to stop and think about it, she realised that she was, by and large, pretty content. How many people could say that?

But another part of her brain was telling her this was precisely the trouble. She was still young enough to have a future in front of her. She wasn't a middle-aged cop eking out the last few years till retirement. She wasn't even someone like Alec McKay who'd found his only vocation and had no ambition to do anything more or different. Alec was only a year or two older than she was, but she knew he was now here for life – or at least until someone, most likely Chrissie, dragged him unwillingly into retirement.

Grant was more than happy here, but she still had hankerings for something more. The current set-up wouldn't last forever. McKay might well be part of the furniture, but people like Ginny Horton and Josh Carlisle would move on. Perhaps it was time for her to seek a new challenge, and the project sounded like a low-risk opportunity to stick her toe in the new waters.

'I've been thinking about it,' she said to Everly. 'It's an attractive idea and I think I'm definitely ready for a new challenge.'

'Do I sense a "but" coming?'

'Only that I like my current job. I wouldn't want to feel too divorced from – well, real police work. I spend too much time pen-pushing as it is.'

'Like it or not, the higher you climb up the ladder, the more pen-pushing you have to do. But the project role would give you the chance to get a feel for some of that, as well as potentially opening some doors for you. If you decide they're not for you, then you've not lost anything. But I think you might be surprised. You're a very capable officer, Helena, and with the right sponsorship you could go a long way.'

'You make me sound like a charity walk. Sponsorship?'

'Maybe that's not the right word. Support. Guidance. Someone pushing your case.'

'Someone like you?'

He took another mouthful of beer, perhaps so she couldn't easily read his expression. 'I wasn't really thinking of me though

I'm happy to do whatever I can to support you. But through the project you'll meet a number of senior, influential people. If you impress them, you'll establish some important allies.'

'And if I don't?'

'That's a hypothetical we don't need to worry about. As I say, you're a very capable officer.'

She wished she shared his apparent confidence. That was the other part of her concern, she supposed. The prospect of taking on the project work felt intimidating. It was work she'd never done before, in the company of people she'd never previously had to deal with. She didn't know what to expect or whether she'd be up to it.

Which, she told herself, was exactly why she needed to do it. She'd been stuck in a rut for too long, nervous of stepping outside what she knew. She needed to take a few risks. 'Okay, then, you've talked me into it. I'll do it.'

Everly's smile broadened. 'That's great, Helena. You won't regret it. This really could be the stepping stone to big things for you. I'm sure you'll enjoy it. I'll sort out the formalities in the morning, but it'll be good to have you on board.' He looked over his shoulder towards the bar. 'Look, the food's pretty decent here. If you've nothing pressing, how do you feel about grabbing a bite to eat?'

She hesitated, conscious that this risked turning into precisely the kind of evening she'd intended to avoid. On the other hand, Everly had been nothing but entirely professional, and she'd just committed herself to working relatively closely with him for some months to come. 'Why not? It's that or something microwaved at home.'

'I'll get us a menu. And, well, here's to the project. And to us.' He held up his nearly empty glass in a mock toast.

'To the project,' she echoed cautiously.

CHAPTER TWENTY-TWO

'You're kidding.'

'Aye, it's that old one about the dead hamster in the cardboard box,' McKay said from the other end of the line. 'Always has them rolling in the aisles.'

'But why?'

'For once your guess is as good as mine. When are you planning to head back up?'

Horton had handed him her phone when McKay had called and was standing listening. McKay, probably not accidentally, was speaking loudly enough for her to hear his responses.

'Is there anything I can usefully do this evening?' Nightingale asked.

Horton guessed McKay would be biting back the reply he wanted to give to that question. She heard him say, 'Probably not. The examiners are going over the house at the moment.'

'Not much point in me rushing back tonight, then. I imagine you've got it all under control?'

'Aye, all going swimmingly up here. We're still looking into how and when the Gillans' BMW arrived at Loch Morlich. We're getting all the CCTV in the area checked out in the hope of spotting something, but it's a long shot. The more interesting news is that the plates on the van that delivered the box to the Gillans' house turned out to be fake–'

'So the box was actually delivered by the killers?'

'Looks like it. Or someone working with them. We've a witness who saw the driver, though only from a distance. Again, we're checking out the local CCTV and road cameras. It's the sort of neighbourhood that has no shortage of security. So plenty going on.' McKay paused. 'How are you getting on down there?'

'Not so bad. We've been over the Dawson house.'

'Anything useful?' Horton knew McKay well enough to detect the scepticism in his tone.

'Some useful background stuff on Dawson's work. Some type of occupational psychologist.'

'That right?' This time the scepticism was more evident, though possibly aimed at Dawson's work rather than Nightingale's achievements.

'Ironically dealing with stuff like wellness and mental health at work. Physician heal thyself, and all that.'

'Who'd have guessed that kind of stuff might turn out to be a waste of time?' McKay said.

'We also found something interesting in the post there. Envelope addressed to Paul Dawson. Inside, just a printout picture of a young woman. No note or explanation.'

'Presumably someone of significance to Dawson?'

'We'll get copies of the photograph circulated,' Nightingale said. 'And do an image search on the internet. It shouldn't be difficult to identify her. Some of Dawson's friends or associates must know who she is. It may turn out to be nothing, but it's worth checking out.'

'We need anything we can get,' McKay said.

'I get the picture, Alec. I'm here at the end of the phone if you need anything.'

'That's reassuring to know. Signal improved, has it?'

'Sorry?'

'I was trying to get hold of you earlier, but there was no answer. Assumed there must have been no signal. I was lucky to get hold of Ginny.'

'It's not a great signal here, no. Must have been while we were in the back of the house.'

'You need to get back here to civilisation.'

'I'll bear that advice in mind, Alec. Have a good afternoon.' Nightingale ended the call and handed the phone back to Horton. 'I assume he's been told he's a chippy little bugger?'

'Many times,' Horton said. 'It's almost as if he doesn't care.'

'One day he might be forced to care.'

It wasn't clear to Horton if this was a prediction or a threat. Nightingale looked around them. They were still in the hallway of the Dawsons' house, Dangerfield waiting outside. 'We need to have this place looked over properly. We can't take anything for granted. None of this seems to make any sense. We'll need to work closely with the team down here on this, so we might as well go back in with Graeme now. We can see what resources we can draw on. They'll be as up to their ears as everyone else, so it might help if we can oil the wheels informally.'

'Whatever you think best.'

Horton paused to take a final look around the Dawsons' hallway, thinking now about that final time when the family had left the house to embark on the Highland holiday. She wondered what their state of mind had been, whether at that point Paul Dawson had already known what the future held.

She stood there for a moment longer and then, carefully closing the front door behind her, went to join her two colleagues.

CHAPTER TWENTY-THREE

McKay spent the rest of the afternoon co-ordinating door-to-door interviews with the Gillans' various neighbours. The numerous marked and unmarked vehicles in the vicinity of the house, along with the uniformed officers sealing off the site, had inevitably drawn a small crowd of onlookers, including Fionnuala Erskine who had been smugly sharing her limited knowledge with anyone prepared to listen. The small crowd had eventually been persuaded to disperse and McKay had arranged for a team of uniformed officers to cover the houses in the immediate vicinity. He himself, with a slightly sinking heart, had accompanied Fionnuala Erskine back to her house in the hope of extracting a more detailed description of the delivery driver.

In the course of the short walk to her front door, she informed McKay that she was a widow, that her husband had died suddenly of a heart attack a couple of years before, and that she largely devoted herself now to what she unironically referred to as 'good works'.

Though her house was less imposing than the Gillans', it was still a sizeable residence for a woman living by herself.

'Nice place,' McKay commented as they entered the hallway, 'but don't you find you rattle round in it a bit?'

She nodded. 'I did at first, but I'm used to it now. I didn't want to move after Angus passed on. Too many memories.'

McKay grunted an acknowledgement, barely taking in what she was saying. He followed her through into the living room, accepting her offer to seat himself on the sofa but declining a cup of tea. The room was tidy almost to the point of obsession. She took a seat in the armchair opposite him. 'So I was right then?'

'Right?'

'About something having happened to the Gillans.'

'I'm not at liberty to say anything more at this stage, I'm afraid. Can I ask you again about the van you saw?'

'Have you been able to track it down? Presumably you can do that with the registration?'

'We're just in the process of doing that.' McKay had no intention of revealing to Erskine that the van had had fake number plates. 'In the meantime, I wondered if you could remember anything more about the driver.'

She was clearly eager to help, which in McKay's experience, was not necessarily a desirable quality in a potential witness. 'I'm trying to visualise him, but I was some distance away. My impression was that he was youngish–'

'And definitely male?' It was better to assume nothing.

'I'd have said so.'

'Anything else? Height?'

'Average height, I'd have said.' This was what witnesses tended to say unless the individual in question was unusually tall or short. 'For a man, I mean. Above average for a woman.'

'That's very helpful. And how were they dressed?'

'As I say, some sort of overall. A dark colour. Black or dark blue. No coat or jacket. The shoes were a light colour. Probably trainers or something like that.'

'And you saw the driver's face?'

'Only a glimpse really. Just as he came back from the front door. As I said earlier, he was wearing a face-mask and a peaked cap – I think that was black or dark blue too, but to be honest I couldn't swear to it – so I couldn't see much of the face. He was white, but I'm not sure I could tell you much more than that.'

'You're doing very well. Anything else? Anything unusual in the way he walked or moved?'

'Not that I noticed. I just had the impression of someone who was relatively young and fit.'

McKay finished jotting down the description in his notebook. 'You make a good witness, Mrs Erskine. Not many people have your powers of observation.' *Or nosiness,* he added silently to himself. He wasn't sure how useful this was likely to be, but at least they had something. 'What time was this delivery yesterday? Can you remember?'

'Actually I can. I noticed the time because I was listening to the radio and the news had just been on. It was about five. I got up to make myself a cup of tea, and that was when I noticed the van.'

That would be useful in helping them to check the CCTV and traffic cameras in the surrounding area. "Is there anything else you can tell me about the Gillans? Anything unusual in their habit or behaviours? Any recurrent visitors recently?' It was a necessarily vague question but Erskine struck him as the kind of woman who would notice anything worth noticing.

'To be honest, I hardly know them. There's a fairly close-knit community in the neighbourhood, but they've never really been part of it.'

'How long have they lived here?'

'Just a couple of years. I made a point of going to say hello when they first moved in. They were pleasant enough, but that was about all. I've not really had much contact with them, other than the occasional brief chat if we happened to run into each other in the street. Even then, they weren't ones to stop and talk. Always gave you the impression they were in a hurry, had something better to do. You know the type.'

McKay could imagine that Mrs Erskine might have a similar effect on a number of her neighbours, but said nothing. 'What about visitors? Did they seem to have many?'

'Not that I noticed. There was the occasional unfamiliar car parked outside, but I never knew whether it was just one of their hire cars. Beyond that, I'm afraid I don't really know.' She sounded disappointed, as if she'd failed in her duty to McKay.

McKay pushed himself to his feet. 'That's been most useful, Mrs Erskine. I won't take any more of your time now, but if anything else occurs to you that you think might be relevant, please do give us a call.' He imagined she would need little prompting.

'Of course.' She jumped up to show him back to the front door. 'I'll be keeping an eye out for you.'

McKay had little doubt she would. He said his goodbyes and stepped back out into the afternoon sunlight. The shadows were lengthening now, the evening approaching. Across the street, a couple of uniformed officers were still guarding the scene, the police tape and remaining marked cars incongruous in the otherwise anonymous suburban setting. In the house, Jock and his team would no doubt be painstakingly carrying out their work.

The investigation was progressing in the only way it could, but all McKay could see or feel, at least for the moment, was a dense cloud of unknowing. His mind kept drifting back to what he'd witnessed in that chalet. To the blood-covered bodies. To those three dead children.

It wasn't just that they lacked answers. They didn't even know what the right questions might be. There were too many missing pieces, and the story just made no sense.

Just in that instant, he could almost bring himself to feel some sympathy for Brian Nightingale.

CHAPTER TWENTY-FOUR

The sun was setting behind the squat bulk of the Black Isle, the front garden already deep in shadow. Isla glanced around her as she made her way to the front door. She fumbled in her bag for the keys, glancing over her shoulder. She'd had a sudden sense she was being observed, but there was no one visible in the garden or the road beyond. The shadows had thickened still further, though it was light enough to see all but the most shaded corners. It was a calm evening, only a gentle breeze stirring the leaves.

Isla stepped inside and closed the door firmly behind her. After a moment's hesitation, she relocked the door with the deadlock and closed both sets of bolts. They generally double-locked the front door only before retiring to bed. Tonight, she needed the additional reassurance.

She walked through the house, turning on the lights and closing the blinds and curtains. For some reason, her nervousness had increased since she'd entered the house. She didn't know what was wrong with her. She felt dread, almost a sick feeling in her stomach, as if she knew something bad was about to happen.

The house was oppressively silent. Taking a breath to calm herself, she turned on the television, mainly just to hear people talking. Then she returned to the kitchen and turned on the oven. She rummaged through the freezer and found a portion of lasagne they'd cooked a few weeks earlier. She transferred it to an ovenproof dish and placed it in the oven to cook through. Then she pulled a bottle of red wine from the rack, opened it, and poured herself a generous glass.

She returned to the living room and sat down in front of the television. An amiable TV chef was touring some supposedly obscure part of Asia. Exactly the kind of undemanding comfort-watching she needed.

As she settled back, glass clutched in her hand, the front doorbell rang.

She started, almost dropping the wine. It was obvious she was at home, so she could hardly hide behind the sofa and pretend to be elsewhere. Reluctantly, she made her way through to the hallway. As she did so, the bell rang again, more insistent this time. She straightened and, making sure the hefty chain was in place, she unlocked the door.

'Evening, sis. Long time, no see. Bad penny and all that.'

Oddly, as soon as she saw his face, her earlier anxiety vanished. It was just Tristram. Just her brother. Just the kid she'd grown up with. A kid who was, and presumably remained, a pain in the backside, a poisonous influence, and generally a bad lot. But in the end just her brother.

He was well, she thought. He was dressed in jeans, a black T-shirt, and an expensive-looking jacket. There was a trace of grey in his hair, but he still looked younger than his years.

'Tristram.'

'At least you recognised me. Can I come in? It's turning nippy out here. Why'd you want to come and live in the far north anyway?'

She hesitated. Even though her nervousness had gone, she knew the smartest move would just be to tell him to bugger off. To go away and never disturb her life again. That would be the clever thing to do. That was what Ginny would advise.

'Hang on.' She half-closed the door, unfastened the chain, then stood back to allow him into the house. 'Living room's through there.'

'This is good of you, sis.'

'I haven't done anything, except not throw you out.'

'It's a start.' He stopped and made a pantomime gesture of sniffing the air. 'Something smells good.'

'It's a lasagne portion for one.'

'Oh, that's a pity. I haven't eaten since this morning.'

This was how it was going to go, she thought. It would be one story after story, each designed to inveigle his way back into her life. She knew the tricks, she could see the sleight of hand, but she'd almost certainly end up falling for it. 'I'll see what I can find. Go in there.' She gestured to the living-room door, and turned into the kitchen.

He ignored her instruction, as she'd known he would, and followed her, standing in the kitchen doorway as she dug into the freezer. She found another lasagne portion and stuck it in the oven beside her own. Hers had barely begun to cook, so they'd be ready at the same time. She'd give him some food, tell him what she really thought, then get rid of him.

He'd wandered silently into the kitchen, picking up the opened bottle of wine. 'Decent stuff. You're obviously doing well for yourself.'

'It's £5.99 from Tesco. If you're after money, you've come to the wrong place.'

'Perish the thought, sis. I'm just here to say hello, mend a few fences. You got my letter?'

'I got your letter, and I wrote back.'

'Well, that's nice.'

'Not really. I told you I never wanted to see you again.'

'Ah. Lucky I haven't got it yet, then, I guess.'

'Not for me. Look, what is it you want, Tristram?'

'Maybe a glass of that plonk.'

'Help yourself.' She gestured to the cupboard beside him. 'Glasses in there.' Then she added, as a thought struck her, 'How did you get here?'

'How did any of us get here?' He was delving in the cupboard for a glass. He found something suitable and poured himself a large measure of the wine.

'Don't try to be smart. It's not one of your strengths.'

'You're probably right about that. You mean how did I get here tonight?' He took a sip from the glass. 'A mate dropped me off, actually.'

'And how are you proposing to leave?'

'That's not very hospitable, sis. I've only just got here.'

'And I don't want you to be in my house any longer than you need to be.' She knew she was already losing the battle with him. She'd done what she always did. She'd offered small concessions – the food, the wine, not telling him to piss off as soon as she opened the door – in the hope he'd accept them and expect nothing more. But that wasn't how he thought or worked. He just banked whatever you gave him and moved on to the next thing. She shouldn't even try to engage with him.

'Can we try this again?' he asked. 'We don't seem to have made a good start.'

Exasperated, she turned and left the kitchen. If she was going to have to do this, she at least needed a fortifying glass of wine in her hand. She returned to the living room, threw herself on to the sofa and took a mouthful of her drink. The television was still playing silently.

As she'd expected, he'd followed her and was standing in

the doorway, carrying not only his own glass but also the wine bottle. She'd forgotten how quickly and easily he made himself at home, regardless of what kind of welcome he'd received.

He sat down at the other end of the sofa, placing the bottle on the table between them. 'To answer your question, I can phone my mate to pick me up. Assuming you don't want me to stay.'

'For the avoidance of doubt, Tristram, and just in case I haven't made myself crystal clear already, I don't want you in this house for any longer than absolutely necessary.'

'Sisterly love, eh? Speaking of which, how's your other half?'

'All the better for not meeting you.'

'Pity she's not here, though. I'd like to meet her.'

'I've told her all about you, so the feeling's unlikely to be mutual.'

He smiled, as if he'd won some kind of victory. 'Glad to hear you still talk about me, anyway.'

'What is it you want, Tristram? What's this all about? Are you in some sort of trouble again?'

'Straight as an arrow, these days. I've learnt my lesson.'

'That'll be the day. So why are you here?'

'Just like I say. I want to mend fences, build bridges, whatever the phrase is. There's only the two of us now, sis. It just seems stupid we should be at loggerheads.'

'There's only the two of us because you destroyed Mum and Dad.' It was harsh and not entirely fair, but she knew how much pain Tristram had caused their parents. 'You didn't even turn up for their funerals.'

'I didn't think I'd have been welcome. They'd made it clear they'd finished with me, just as you have.'

'Don't play the victim. You've no one to blame for what happened except yourself.'

'I'm sure you're right about that, though these things are never straightforward, are they?'

She gave no response to that, other than to pick up the bottle to refill her glass, making a point of not offering it to him. His smile had broadened, the look of a chess player who'd manoeuvred his opponent into a tricky position.

'So this is it, is it?' he said. 'I come here to offer you an olive branch, and all you want to do is throw me out.'

'My only mistake was letting you through the door in the first place. I don't trust you, Tristram. It's as simple as that. You've only ever contacted me when you've wanted something.'

'So I've learnt my lesson. There's nothing I want from you, sis. If you want to know, I'm doing okay for myself.'

'Is that right?' She had no interest in his life. Every new fact she learned about him had the effect of drawing her further into his influence. 'I don't care, Tristram. I don't care what you're doing or where you're living or who your friends are or anything else about you. I just want never to see you again.' She pushed herself to her feet. 'You can have the food. You can even have another glass of wine if you like. Then I want you to go. And not come back.'

At first glance, his expression resembled that of a friendly dog being banished from the house. But behind the pathetic facade, there was still a glint of mischief in his eyes. This was nothing but a game to him, just as it always had been. A way of testing how far he could play with her emotions.

She marched into the kitchen and took the portions of lasagne from the oven. She transferred them to plates, grabbed knives and forks from the drawer, and took the food back through to the living room.

Tristram was on his feet, standing by the far wall, peering at some framed photographs of Isla and Ginny. It was a sequence of photographs that essentially told the story of their relationship. Their first proper date, the day they'd moved into this house, the low-key celebrations of their civil partnership and then of their marriage. He turned back to Isla. 'This her? She's quite a looker.'

She ignored him, holding out one of the plates. 'Here's the food. Eat and go.'

'It's your warmth and hospitality I miss more than anything, sis.' He took the plate and sat back down on the sofa to eat. She noticed he'd already poured himself a second glass of wine.

She sat in one of the armchairs, as far away from him as possible, to eat her own lasagne. She just wanted to get this over with, although she could tell that Tristram was making no effort to hurry.

'Good stuff.' He gestured to the plate with his fork. 'You do the cooking or is it your friend?'

She offered no response, continuing to fork the food into her mouth. Finally, her plate still unfinished, she slid it on to the table between them. 'I want you to go now, Tristram. Call your lift. You'll have finished eating by the time they get here.'

He looked down at his plate, and then leaned forward to place it on the table beside hers. 'Don't worry, sis. I've got the message. The lasagne's great, but I'll leave it there. I'll go and wait for my mate outside.' He climbed to his feet with apparent weariness, and stood for a moment zipping up his jacket. 'I'm sorry you've responded like this. I really did come with the best of intentions. There's nothing I want or need from you, but I'd like to rebuild our friendship.' As he made his way to the front door, he turned back to her. 'That's all, sis. Give it some thought.'

She didn't follow him to the front door, but stood motionless, listening, until she heard it close behind him. As it did so, the emotion suddenly hit her. She dropped back into the armchair and a moment later, realised she was crying.

CHAPTER TWENTY-FIVE

Graeme Dangerfield looked at his watch. 'I'd love to, Brian. But I'm driving. In any case, the other half will kill me if I'm late for supper because I've been in the pub.' He rose from the table. 'I hope this afternoon was useful. We'll do what we can on the resource front, though we've the same pressures you have. But we'll definitely get the examiners into the Dawson house first thing.'

Brian Nightingale was staring into his empty glass, as if wondering where the beer had gone. 'You're really going to leave me to drink alone?'

Dangerfield glanced at Ginny Horton, who was sitting at the table beside Nightingale, and raised his eyebrows. 'I'm sure Ginny will keep you company, Brian.'

'No disrespect to Ginny, but I'm not sure she's as up for a session as you are, Graeme.'

'Those days are long gone, even for me. Glass of wine at home's more my scene these days. This is the first time I've been in a pub for months.'

'You ought to be making the most of it, then.' Nightingale had suggested repairing to the pub at the end of their meeting with the local team, but his offer had been taken up only by Dangerfield. She suspected Dangerfield himself had joined them only out of politeness. She noticed that he'd paced his drinking very carefully and she reckoned he'd downed no more than a pint in total compared to Nightingale's three. So far, Ginny had dutifully stuck to lime and sodas.

'I'll leave you to it, folks. If you need anything tomorrow, Ginny, just give me a call.'

'Thanks, Graeme. Will do.'

Nightingale was still peering into his empty glass. 'Cheers, Graeme. I'll be in touch.' He was silent for another moment, watching Dangerfield until he was out of earshot. 'Miserable git.'

'I thought he was a friend?'

'He was, once. I did him a few favours as well, back in the dim and distant, but it doesn't seem to cut much ice. He wouldn't give me the steam off his urine.'

'He seemed to be offering us what support he could.'

'You reckon that'll come to anything? He'll give us the examiners' time because he's got no choice. In any case, that won't come out of his team's budget. But there'll be bugger all else.' He picked up his glass again. 'The tight bastard wouldn't even stump up for another pint.'

Nightingale wasn't exactly drunk, she thought. He was the kind of character who could probably hold his drink, though perhaps not as well as he imagined. But she could tell his tongue had been loosened, and she was already having an uneasy feeling that she might not appreciate everything he had to say.

'We going to have another one here?' he said.

'Why don't we head in to dinner?' She looked around at the bar they were sitting in, with its surfeit of brass ornaments and hunting scenes. 'The food looks decent, and I could probably face something stronger than lime and sofa if I've a few solid calories inside me.'

He looked down at her glass. 'That's a fair point, I suppose.'

'Glass of wine would go down very nicely with a decent supper.'

They'd been booked into a small high-street hotel in one of the towns close to the police offices. It seemed a decent unpretentious place, and she was looking forward to sampling the food. She swallowed the last of her drink, and followed Nightingale through the reception and into the restaurant at the rear of the building. They were greeted by an effusive head waiter who deftly steered them to a table by the window. It was still light outside and they were looking out over an area of greenery, with a small river visible at the far side of the grassland. Nightingale paused while the waiter brought the menus, then turned immediately to the wine list. 'Do you fancy some wine? We could justify a bottle between the two of us.'

'I don't know–'

'If there's a problem with the expenses policy, I'll cover it. I don't like having to stint when I'm on the road.'

'I'll leave it up to you.' She'd already decided that if Nightingale wanted something he was likely just to take it. There was little point in arguing.

'Very wise. Red okay?'

'Whatever you think. I probably prefer red generally.'

'A woman of good taste, I can see.'

He ordered a bottle of what she'd noted was a relatively pricy Barolo, and they both made their choices from the menu. She had the sense that everything Nightingale did was intended to impress, though she was unsure why he'd think she'd care that he'd ordered the most expensive items on the menu. The only aspect that mildly interested her was how Nightingale would justify this on his expense claim, but she guessed he was accustomed to getting his own way there as well.

The waiter brought the wine and Nightingale made a point of going through the whole laborious tasting routine, nodding approvingly as the label was shown to him, swirling and sniffing the sample in the bottom of his glass, before taking an appreciative sip. 'Excellent,' he proclaimed, in the manner of a Roman emperor declaring his judgement on a gladiatorial combat.

'Well,' Nightingale said, 'this is nice. We can finally get to know each other properly.'

'I suppose so.'

'You seem quite a tight little team up there.' His tone suggested that this wasn't necessarily a desirable characteristic.

'We've been through quite a lot together in the last few years. I guess that helps bring you together. I hope we've not made you feel unwelcome.'

'On the contrary. Though Alec seems a bit of a character.'

'Alec's just Alec. You get used to him. And his bark's a lot worse than his bite.'

'He's given me a few nips so far, but nothing to worry me.' He paused and swirled the wine gently in his glass. 'I must say, he does have a bit of a reputation around the force. He's put a few people's backs up over the years. In one or two cases, quite influential people.'

'Again, that's Alec. He's not interested in any kind of career advancement or office politicking. He tends to say what he thinks, and he's not always a great respecter of authority or rank.'

'The sort who doesn't suffer fools gladly? Problem is, it doesn't always pay to take senior officers for fools.'

'I'm not aware he's ever done that. Anyway, he's one of the best at what he does.'

'He's certainly had a few notable successes in recent years. You all have. These things get noticed. I just wonder how much credit McKay can take for some of that. I can't help noticing he's surrounded by some very capable women.'

Here it comes, Horton thought. *Divide and conquer.* 'Who do you have in mind?'

He swallowed the remainder of his glass of wine, then picked up the bottle to refill it. He waved the bottle vaguely in her direction, but she had barely touched her own drink. 'Well, present company, obviously. You've a good reputation, Ginny. People see you as a very safe pair of hands.'

'What people exactly?'

He took another mouthful of wine. 'Oh, you know, word gets around. But people in the right places, if you get my drift.'

She decided it wasn't worth pursuing that one. 'You said women. Plural.'

'I understand that Helena Grant's very well regarded, too. Again, she's seen as very competent, very solid.'

'She's more than that, in my view.' Horton waited while the waiter served their starters. She noticed Nightingale had already emptied his glass. 'Apart from anything else, I've found both her and Alec to be superb mentors. I've learnt a lot from them, and I imagine people like Josh Carlisle would say that same.'

Nightingale had ordered langoustines, which he was painstakingly dissecting with his knife and fork. 'She seems to be a very formidable woman.' As he was speaking, he briefly placed his fork back on the plate and almost absent-mindedly refilled his glass. This time, he didn't even bother to offer the wine to her.

'Why are you telling me this, Brian?'

There was silence for a few moments as he worked at the

langoustines. 'I just think it's fair that you should be aware that everything's being looked at. Everything and everyone.'

'In what way?'

'The whole force is under pressure, Ginny. So they're looking at how they can squeeze their assets and resources even more. More synergy, more economies of scale. Better use of IT systems to underpin it all. Changing working practices. Sweeping out some of the dead wood.'

'So what does that mean?'

'I'm not sure I'm supposed to say too much. I suspect we all need to be prepared for big changes. And not everyone will come out the other side.' He started working on another langoustine. After a few moments, he abandoned his attempts at precision and began to pull apart the langoustines with his fingers. He glanced up at her apologetically. 'I'm not sure there's any other way to do it.'

Horton wasn't sure if he was referring to the seafood or the reorganisation of the police force. 'I still don't understand why you're telling me all this.'

He finished with the langoustines, wiping his hands briskly on the napkin. 'I want you to know who your friends are, Ginny.'

'And who are my friends?' She was aware that a frostiness had crept into her voice. 'You?'

He picked up the bottle to top up his glass. 'This is nearly done. Should we order another?'

Horton looked at her own glass. She'd drunk barely a quarter of it. 'I'm fine.'

'Can't be too careful, though. I don't want to leave you bereft of alcohol.'

'That's not–' she began, but he was already waving to the waiter.

She waited till the waiter had removed their plates and

taken the order for more wine before she continued. 'I don't like this talk about "friends", Brian. It makes me uncomfortable. I just come into work to do a decent job and work co-operatively with my colleagues. I don't want to have to contend with so-called friends and enemies on the job.'

He shrugged. 'Change is going to happen whatever you or I might think of it. I just want to make sure I'm standing on the right side when it does.'

'With all due respect, Brian, how do you claim to know all this? You're a DCI and I'm only a lowly DS, but you're not sufficiently highly ranked that the powers-that-be would share their confidential and sensitive plans with you.'

The waiter had filled up Nightingale's glass and topped up the missing few centimetres of Horton's. Nightingale took another copious mouthful of wine before continuing. 'I keep my ear close to the ground. You may be too young to have realised it yet, but it's just the way policing works. You do people favours. You help them out when you're in a position to. And then, when you need to, you call the favours in. It's just how it goes. And I've been on both sides of it. It's not done me any harm. In fact, it's saved my career once or twice.'

She could easily believe that. 'I still don't really understand. What kind of favours?'

He leaned over the table, spilling a splash of wine from his glass on to the white tablecloth. Before she could draw back, he'd reached out and taken her hand. 'Well, Ginny,' he said, 'that's really up to you.'

CHAPTER TWENTY-SIX

C hrissie McKay had taken her mug of tea out on to the decking at the back of the house to enjoy the late-afternoon sunshine.

They'd been living over here for more than a year, and she was increasingly sure they'd made the right decision. It had been her idea initially, so she'd never felt able even to consider the possibility they might have made a mistake. But the first few months were tougher than she'd expected, and certainly tougher than she could ever have acknowledged to Alec.

She'd persuaded Alec that, after everything they'd been through, they needed to make a new start. Nothing dramatic – they were both a bit too old for that – but something that would drag them out of their rut and give them a chance to put the past behind them. The idea was that they'd sell their house in Inverness and move out to this bungalow on the Black Isle. It was hardly a major move – just a dozen miles or so, and they had friends out here. Alec could commute back into Inverness, and she'd try to find herself a little job somewhere on the isle or over in Dingwall. She hadn't worked since Lizzie had died, and had gradually found herself transformed almost into an old-fashioned housewife, something neither she nor Alec had really wanted. She wasn't bothered about what she did. Just something that would keep her occupied, give her some sense of achievement, and enable her to spend time with others. The last point was important, given the times when Alec's job became all-consuming. Times like now.

In the event, the Covid pandemic had put paid, at least in the immediate term, to her plans of finding a job. Those early months in the lockdown had been difficult. Although he spent more time working from home, Alec was still going into the office regularly because police work didn't stop. Chrissie had been trapped in the house, unable to make meaningful contact even with their friends in the neighbourhood.

But things had gradually improved. The restrictions had slowly been loosened, and she'd begun to involve herself in the local community and volunteer groups. Although she hadn't yet found herself the paid job she'd hoped for, she found plenty of activity to occupy her time.

Today, she'd had a free hour or so after completing some administration for the community group she was involved in. Alec was deeply involved in yet another major investigation, and she wasn't expecting him back for a while yet. It had been a relatively warm day and she decided to drink her tea outside, enjoying the tranquillity and the views.

It was the silence here that always surprised her. She just wasn't accustomed to it, after years of living in the city. Inverness was hardly a bustling metropolis but there was always traffic on the main roads, the distant sounds of voices, dogs barking. Here, particularly at night, the silence could seem absolute and almost eerie.

She could see the stream of cars crossing the Cromarty Bridge, but could hear nothing of them. Except for the occasional car on the adjacent roads, the only man-made sound she normally heard up here was the low hoot of a train passing on the far side of the firth. Now, on a windless afternoon, she could hear nothing but a faint burble of birdsong from the thick hedges that lined their rear lawn.

There were only a few streaks of white cloud in the sky, and the low sun over Ben Wyvis was throwing long shadows from the trees and houses on both sides of the firth. The tide was in and the waters were still, mirroring the surrounding landscape.

She had no doubt now that they'd made the right decision. Their marriage felt stronger than ever, and she was confident that they were finally putting their past behind them. It wasn't that they were forgetting Lizzie or what she'd meant to them, but they were gaining some perspective on what had happened. They were creating new memories for the two of them, rather than obsessing about what lay in the past. They were finally looking forward rather than back.

She could see that in Alec's behaviour. He was always more than capable of making himself a royal pain in the backside. But he seemed more relaxed, calmer, more in control of his own emotions. He was no less focused on the job but he'd achieved a better balance between that and the rest of his life.

Unexpectedly, she heard a vehicle on the rough track alongside the house. She looked at her watch. It was too early to be Alec, and she didn't normally get many other visitors at this time of the day. She swallowed the last of her tea, then made her way back into the house.

She'd expected to hear the front doorbell, but there was no sign of anyone through the frosted door panels. She could still hear the vehicle outside, but it sounded as if it was now heading back down the track. Probably someone who'd driven up here by mistake, looking for one of the neighbouring houses.

She opened the door in time to see the rear of a grey van disappearing round the bend halfway down the track. At first, she thought that her assumption had been correct. It wasn't surprising. The backroads in the area could be confusing.

Then, as she turned to re-enter the house, she noticed a package had been left just beside the front door. She stopped and peered at it. From where she stood, she could see no sign of any address or other labelling. It was a plain, unmarked cardboard box, sealed with a thick band of parcel tape. Her first thought was to take it into the house and check what was inside. If it had been delivered here in error, there would presumably be some kind of documentation to identify the intended recipient.

But some instinct made her hesitate. Still staring at the package, she made her way back into the house to get her phone. She didn't generally phone Alec at work, except in emergencies, but he answered almost straightaway. 'Chrissie?'

'There's nothing wrong. I just wondered if you had a minute to talk?'

'I'm just finishing up here. Waiting for a last word with Jock and his merry men. What is it?'

'Have you ordered anything?'

'Ordered? How do you mean?'

'Some kind of package.'

There was an unexpected silence at the other end of the line. 'What kind of package?'

'Something's just been delivered. I'm assuming it's been dropped here by mistake but I can't see any name or address on it. Or any kind of marking, for that matter.'

'What's it like? Can you describe it to me?'

She was surprised by how seriously Alec seemed to be taking the situation. 'It doesn't really matter. I shouldn't have bothered you. It can wait till you get back.'

'That's okay. But just tell me what it looks like. How big is it?'

'Hang on.' She walked back through the hall and peered out of the front door. 'It's more or less square. Well, cubic, I suppose. About a foot or so tall and wide, maybe a bit more. Just a plain cardboard box, sealed with parcel tape. Do you want me to have a look inside?'

'No.' Alec's sharp response took her by surprise. 'No, don't do that.'

'What is it, Alec? Do you think...?'

'It's almost certainly nothing. Like you say, just something delivered in error. But don't touch it. Just go back inside and keep yourself locked in. I'm coming straight over.'

'Alec, you don't–'

But he'd already ended the call. She tried to call him back, but the call just rang out, either because Alec had stuffed the phone back in his pocket as he headed for his car, or because he knew that if he answered she'd keep trying to persuade him he didn't have to leave work for this.

She stared at the package for a moment longer then decided she had no option but to follow Alec's advice. She returned to the house, locked the front door behind her, and sat down to wait for his return.

CHAPTER TWENTY-SEVEN

Ginny Horton woke at first light with an awful sense of dread. It was the kind of dread you associate with the morning after the night before, she thought. When you know you've done something awful but your brain hasn't yet managed to drag together sufficient memory to tell you what it is.

Still not yet fully awake, she rolled over in the bed, disconcerted to find that she was lying here alone, the other half of the bed cold to her touch.

It took her a few more seconds to make sense of where she was. And a few more seconds to recall what had happened, what had prompted that waking sense of dread.

She wasn't at home. She wasn't waking, as she generally did, with Isla sleeping peacefully beside her. She was in a hotel in some small town in the Borders, and she was alone. That, in turn, prompted the memories of the previous night to flood back into her brain.

She lay for a few more moments trying to sort her recollections into some coherent order. She'd done nothing wrong. It was important she kept reminding herself of that. She'd done nothing wrong. In fact, she'd done exactly the right things. It was just that Brian Nightingale might not share her view.

It had started with that moment at the dinner table when he'd reached for her hand. She'd been startled by the suddenness of his movements and had pulled her own hand away more sharply than she'd intended. Nightingale had reached further to try to prevent her and had knocked over her largely untouched glass of wine, spilling a red pool over the white tablecloth.

The waiter had been oversolicitous, fussing about the table, mopping up the wine and replacing the cloth as if the fault had been his. Despite her objections, he'd insisted on presenting them with a complimentary bottle of wine. The last thing she'd wanted was another bottle of wine at the table, given that Nightingale had largely polished off the contents of the first two by himself.

Eventually, everything was sorted. Nightingale had apologised for his clumsiness, although not, she noticed, for trying to grab her hand in the first place. As she'd expected, he made a show of filling her glass and then promptly refilled his own. By now, the effects of the alcohol were beginning to show in him. A casual observer might have thought he was sober enough, but she could see his movements were becoming less well co-ordinated, his speech less coherent. Her guess was that he was a habitual drinker, skilled at concealing its effects. Even so, several pints and two bottles of wine in, it was beginning to show.

She turned down his suggestion of desserts or coffee, but eventually agreed to join him in the adjacent lounge while they finished off the complimentary wine. She reasoned this was unlikely to take long, given that Nightingale had already polished off half the bottle.

She followed him out into the lounge, wondering if he could

be trusted with both the bottle and his own glass. For the moment at least, he looked steady enough on his feet and, as if making a point, he took them to the furthest corner of the lounge. He placed the bottle and glass on the low table, then sat himself down on a sofa, gesturing for her to join him.

'You were asking about favours,' he said. 'That's just the way it works in the force. You scratch my back, and all that. But there are plenty of people out there more than capable of bearing a grudge. If you don't give them what they want, they'll get their own back at some point. Again, that's just the way it works. That's what you need to understand, Ginny.'

'I'm sure you're right, Brian. To be honest, I'm not really interested in all that office politics stuff.'

He waved his wine glass in her direction, narrowly avoiding spilling the contents. 'It's not just office politics, Ginny. It's about relationships, about the way we interact with each other.' As he'd been talking, she noticed he'd been gradually moving along the sofa in her direction. 'How do you interact with your fellow officers, Ginny?'

'I don't know what you mean.' She looked over her shoulder, thinking that it really was time she made her excuses and left. There were still a few people in the restaurant, but before too long she and Nightingale might be the only people in here.

'It's a simple enough question. I mean, you're a woman in what's still a mainly male environment. That might make some women feel uncomfortable. But then I suppose you're not the same as some women–'

She had no idea where this might be going, and no desire to find out. She was on the point of saying goodnight as politely as she could manage when she realised her mobile was buzzing in her bag. Ignoring Nightingale, she reached down and turned it to read the screen. Alec. Not exactly the proverbial knight on the white horse, but right now more than sufficient.

She accepted the call and made a point of saying his name. 'Hi, Alec.'

'I don't suppose that boss of ours is around? It looks as if he's having more signal problems. He should change his network.' This was all spoken in a voice loud enough to be heard by Nightingale at the other end of the sofa.

'Yes, he's just here. Is something wrong?' In her relief at receiving the call, it had only just occurred to her that it was unusual for McKay to disturb her outside working hours. He normally did it only when something major had arisen.

'Depends on your point of view, I suppose. Another development, anyway. Another package.'

She could see that Nightingale had overheard the news. 'Containing?'

'A child's toy. One of those pink glittery plastic pony things.'

'What?'

'Quite. And that's not the end of it. There's also a personal downside.'

She'd already detected something odd in McKay's tone, but she hadn't been able to work out what it was. 'In what way?'

'The box in question was delivered to my house. The initial recipient was Chrissie.' He paused and she could tell there was something else he wanted to say. 'It wouldn't have mattered. Except the toy was similar to one Lizzie had as a child.'

'Oh, Alec.'

'It could have been worse. Luckily, some instinct stopped Chrissie opening it and she called me. As soon as she described the box, I raced back home and, taking appropriate care, I opened it myself.' He stopped. 'She saw it, though.'

'Do you think it was sent deliberately?'

'I don't see how anyone could have known what toys Lizzie had as a child. I think it was probably just a lucky guess. Lots of young girls had those toys. Either way, it feels like someone wanting to send me some kind of message.'

'How is Chrissie?'

'She's the resilient sort. But it's left us both a bit shaken.'

'I'm not surprised. Is there anything I can do?'

'You could pass me over to DCI Nightingale. I assume he's heard everything I've just said.'

She looked over at Nightingale who nodded. His expression suggested that the last thing he wanted to do was talk to McKay. Not least, she suspected, because Nightingale knew he was going to struggle to talk coherently. In other circumstances, she might have been tempted to protect him. As it was, she handed over the phone.

'Brian.' McKay was speaking in a voice loud enough for almost the whole restaurant to hear. 'You heard all that?'

She could see Nightingale was struggling to focus. It looked as if the effects of the evening's alcohol had hit him quite suddenly, perhaps because he'd unexpectedly had to shift back into work mode. 'Yes. Yes. That's – well, it's awful, Alec.'

'As long as you don't tell me you're my best mate and that you love me.' McKay had clearly registered Nightingale's condition. 'I take it you've had a more enjoyable evening than I have.'

'Just, you know, oiling the wheels...'

'Is that right? I hope you've not been leading young Ginny astray.'

'I've been giving her the benefit of my wisdom...'

'And what did you do for the rest of the evening?' She could hear the irritation in McKay's tone. Given what he'd faced today, she could hardly blame him.

'Aye, very funny, Alec.' Nightingale picked up his glass and downed the rest of his wine. 'So what's it you actually want?'

The sibilants clashed into one another, rendering the question almost incomprehensible.

'What I want, Brian, is some sort of idea what time you're likely to get back here tomorrow. We've a lot to go through.' He paused. 'On the other hand, it might not be a good idea for you to be hitting the road too early in the morning.'

'I'll get there when I get there, Alec.' Nightingale was trying to sound authoritative, Horton assumed, but he sounded only peevish.

'Aye, that's helpful. But don't rush. I'm sure we can manage without you.' McKay sounded as if he'd had more than enough of talking to Nightingale. 'You can hand me back to Ginny now if you like.'

Nightingale stared at the phone for a moment, as if unsure how he was supposed to perform this manoeuvre. Finally, he held out the phone for Horton to take.

This time McKay spoke more quietly. 'Is our friend as pissed as he sounds?'

'Pretty much so.'

'I take it you're not?'

'Not remotely.'

'If it was anyone else, I'd ask you to take care of him. He sounds like he might need it. But, given his past reputation, I'd suggest you take care of yourself.'

'I can do that.' She was trying hard to keep her responses neutral, hoping that Nightingale was hearing nothing of what McKay was saying. 'You're sure you're okay, Alec. Must have been a shock for you both.'

'I just tried to treat it like another job. Got the evidence sent off for forensics to work whatever magic they can. It kept me busy for a while. Harder for Chrissie.'

He said his farewells and ended the call. She was about to tell Nightingale that she wanted to call it a night when her phone sounded again. Isla, this time. Horton mouthed the name to Nightingale to excuse herself, and took the phone out to the hotel reception. The last thing she wanted was to chat to Isla with Nightingale listening in.

As it turned out, the conversation was more fraught than she'd expected. Isla had called to break the news about her brother's unexpected visit. She sounded not exactly shaken, but troubled by what had happened. 'I don't know if I handled it the right way,' she kept repeating. 'I just cut him dead. I felt like such a bitch once he'd gone.'

'From everything you've told me, you did exactly the right thing,' Horton said. 'You've told me what a manipulative bastard he is. This is exactly how he wants you to feel. If you're feeling guilty, then there's more chance you'll change your mind and do what he wants.'

'But what if he's sincere this time? What if this time he really does just want to rebuild bridges?'

'You've known him all your life. How likely do you think that really is?'

'I know. It's just...'

They'd gone round that conversational loop several times, Ginny trying to offer Isla the reassurance she needed, Isla almost but not quite convinced. It had been clear to both of them that they weren't getting anywhere useful, but neither of them could quite bring themselves to end the call.

Somewhere in the middle of all that, she'd been conscious of a disturbance behind her in the restaurant. After a few minutes, she became aware that one of the waiters was standing at the rear of the reception. He'd moved into her line of sight with the aim of attracting her attention. 'I'm really sorry, Isla. I'm going to have to go. There seems to be some kind of problem here. Look, let's talk about this properly once I'm back. I'm sure you've done the right thing.'

She turned back to see the waiter hurrying towards her. 'I'm really sorry to have interrupted. It's just that we've a wee problem on our hands. Your friend–'

'Colleague,' she found herself saying, as if it mattered. 'He's just a colleague.'

'He's being a bit difficult. I wondered if you could...'

She nodded, already conscious of the sinking feeling in her stomach, and followed the waiter back into the lounge where she'd been sitting with Nightingale.

Nightingale was standing unsteadily at the entrance to the restaurant, the now empty wine bottle clutched in his hand as if he'd been about to wield it as a weapon. Another of the waiters was trying to placate him, receiving a stream of invective for his trouble. As Horton entered the room, Nightingale turned to her, staggering slightly as he did so. 'Ginny. Thank Christ. Can you reason with these bastards? All I want to do is buy another bottle of wine. I can't get the fuckers to take my money.'

'I imagine they think you've already had enough, Brian. And so do I. Why don't you just call it a night?'

'Oh, Christ, you too. Little miss goody fucking two shoes. It's not even fucking nine o'clock. I'm not stopping drinking yet.'

'I'm afraid you're going to have to, sir,' the waiter said. 'If you continue to cause a disturbance, I'm going to have to call the police.'

'Oh, that's fucking rich. Listen, sonny, I am the fucking police.' He stumbled again, this time as he tried to reach into his pocket, presumably for his warrant card.

'Brian.' She'd spoken sharply enough to catch his befuddled attention. 'Let me get you upstairs before you get yourself into real trouble.'

Nightingale turned towards her, his mind now seemingly distracted. 'Hear that, lads. She wants to get me upstairs. You might have thought she was just an uppity dyke, but she can't resist my fucking charms...'

'Do you want me to call the police?' the waiter had asked her. 'This isn't acceptable.'

She sighed. 'Not yet. Give me a chance to try to deal with him. Brian, this is your last chance. I'm going to take you up to your room and you can sleep this off. It's either that, or I ask these gentlemen to call the police. And if I do that, your career will be well and truly screwed. And don't think that your so-called "friends" will cover up for you, because I'll be the one pursuing the complaint.'

He stared at her, his expression suggesting she'd broken some sacred bond between them. The arseholes' code of old-style policing, maybe. 'Last chance, Brian,' she repeated.

He finally seemed to get the message. 'You bastards. You fucking bloody bastards. All I want's one more drink. Is that too much to ask?' But his tone had changed. No longer belligerent, but pleading and pathetic.

With the help of the waiters, she'd finally got him upstairs – the hotel had, inevitably, been too small to have a lift – and into his room. He'd stopped arguing, but he'd continued to make inappropriate comments about her sexuality. At one point, when they were halfway up the stairs, she thought he'd tried to use their enforced proximity to grope her. She'd been tempted to break his fingers, but instead she'd pushed his hand away and tried to maintain what distance she could from him.

This had all been just a few hours before. Now she was lying in the half-light, trying to think through the implications. She knew full well she'd done nothing wrong. She'd handled the situation about as well as possible in the circumstances. She'd almost certainly been right to protect Nightingale and to prevent him entirely screwing his career.

But there were other considerations. Ironically, she'd

performed for Nightingale exactly the kind of favour he'd been talking about, although she suspected he'd had something rather different in mind. But she wasn't sure Nightingale would necessarily see it that way. He wouldn't see her as having dug him out of the mire. He'd see her as having something over him, and that would worry him.

That thought led on to another. She'd protected Nightingale last night, and that had probably been the right thing to do at the time. She hadn't wanted to leave him to the mercy of the local uniforms. But that didn't mean she should continue to protect him. His behaviour had been utterly unacceptable – the drinking, the aggression, the inappropriate comments about her, the attempted groping on the stairs. It had been unacceptable in itself and might well be symptomatic of deeper issues. She should report it through the relevant channels. It was a duty she owed to her colleagues, to the force, maybe even to the public.

Which was fine in theory. The reality was that, however justified the cause might be, whistle-blowers were never popular. It wasn't just that Nightingale would think she'd betrayed him. It was also that many of her colleagues would think the same, whatever they might personally think of Nightingale. It was the police officers' form of *omertà*. However badly someone might behave, it was better for the problem to be swept under the carpet. If she reported Nightingale, she'd be taking a large and potentially risky step into the unknown.

That dilemma was what had wakened her so early in the morning, along with her continuing anxieties about Isla and her brother. She looked at her phone. Nearly 6.30am. She knew she was unlikely to sleep again. She might as well get up, get showered and dressed, and prepare herself for the day ahead.

She was due to see Paul Dawson's accountant at ten. The original plan had been that she'd drop Nightingale off at the divisional HQ so he could co-ordinate with the team down here. In the event, they'd done most of the necessary glad-handing the previous afternoon, and she suspected that Nightingale wouldn't be in either the condition or the state of mind to do any more this morning. Unless he surfaced before she left, her inclination was to leave him to sleep and then pick him up on her return. She could leave a note at reception, and if he preferred he could always get a cab into the police HQ.

It didn't seem an unreasonable plan, but she was conscious Nightingale might well complain that she'd broken their agreement and left him abandoned at the hotel. It was exactly the kind of trivial complaint he'd come up with if he thought his own reputation was under threat.

Well, bugger him, she thought. It wasn't her job to act as his nursemaid. If he couldn't get himself up in time, he deserved to be left behind. Whatever she did, the car journey back was likely to be uncomfortable for both of them.

She thought back to the previous evening, when the two waiters had finally succeeded in getting Nightingale back into his room. He'd fallen fully clothed on to the bed, and had almost immediately fallen into a noisy restless sleep. They'd decided there was no real option but to loosen his clothing and then to leave him where he lay.

After they'd left the room and as Horton was closing the door behind them, one of the waiters had turned to her. 'Maybe not my place to say it, but that guy's got a real problem.'

She'd nodded. 'I know. And believe me, he's not the only one.'

CHAPTER TWENTY-EIGHT

'Please do come in. I'm afraid it's a little cluttered.'

That was something of an understatement, Ginny Horton thought. The accountancy practice of Norrington and Grieves occupied a couple of offices above a row of shops in Jedburgh. There was a reception and administrative office, currently occupied by a middle-aged woman who sat systematically tapping data into a computer. Behind that was a slightly larger office notionally occupied by Roger Grieves, although the majority of the available space seemed to be taken up by piles of paperwork and stacked files. If Norrington existed, he didn't seem to be in this building.

'Sorry it's a bit chaotic. We're in the middle of negotiating for some more storage space.' He leaned over to move a heap of papers from a chair to the floor. 'Please do take a seat. Can I get you a coffee?'

'No, that's fine. I won't keep you any longer than I need to.'

Grieves took a seat behind a desk as cluttered as the rest of the office. He was a short rotund man, with a shiny bald head and a substantial greying beard. He looked as if joviality was his

A PARTING GIFT

natural mode and he was making an effort to look sombre. 'Take as long as you need. I want to do everything I can to help. It's an awful business. I still can't quite believe it.'

'That's really why I'm here, Mr Grieves. We're trying to understand the circumstances; what might have led Paul Dawson to commit this kind of act.'

'There's no question that he did it, then? I was hoping...' He left the sentence hanging.

'All the evidence indicates that, I'm afraid. Can I ask for your views of Paul Dawson? What sort of man was he?'

'I'm not sure what to say really. I only really knew him as a client, although I'd known him for a long time. More than ten years. We started working for him when he first set up his business.'

'His business is some kind of consultancy, I understand?'

'I'm not sure I entirely understood it myself. Paul was an occupational psychologist. His background was in human resources. Training and development, that kind of stuff. All a bit of a mystery to me. I know his background was in retail, training sales teams. He'd worked for various big companies and then for one of the large consultancies. He was offered some kind of redundancy package, and took the opportunity to go solo and set up his own consultancy practice.'

'Successfully?'

'Pretty much so, I think. He was basically a sole trader with a few associates helping him out as he needed them. He'd initially had ambitions to grow the business more, but in the end he'd accepted it was better kept small. He was making a decent living for himself without all the stress of trying to run a larger business.'

'And he was happy with that? He didn't see that as a failure?'

'That's what he told me. That it had been a conscious decision on his part. He'd seen people he knew trying to build consultancy businesses, the pressures of trying to sustain a sufficient flow of business, and he just thought it was too much stress. I honestly don't know if he had any regrets.' He shrugged. 'He was making a more than decent living, though.'

'He wasn't having any financial difficulties?'

'Not at all. The pandemic lockdown had been a bit of a challenge for him at first, as it was to a lot of people. But he'd found ways through that. He was running his workshops online, and he'd found effective ways of working remotely. If anything, he reckoned that made the work more profitable because he was still charging the same but not incurring the costs for travel and venues. Obviously, I don't really know what his future order book looked like, but I did his quarterly VAT so saw his figures pretty regularly. The last year was probably the strongest he'd had.'

'When did you last see him?'

'I'm trying to think. The last time I saw him face to face was probably a couple of months back. He'd called in to drop off some documents. We took the opportunity to have a chat. Nothing particularly profound. Just talking about family and holidays, and all that.'

'What did he say about his family?'

'The usual stuff. How the kids were doing at school. His wife, Maria, was thinking about going back to work.'

'How did he seem about that? Her going back to work, I mean.'

'Fine, as far as I could tell. He'd been encouraging her to do it for a while. If anything, I think he'd felt bad about the fact that she'd stopped working in the first place, but given how much he was working away at the time, I'm not sure they had much choice.'

'How did he seem generally?'

'No different from usual. But, as I say, this was two months ago, so I couldn't say if he'd been the same more recently. I've spoken to him on the phone a few times, and he seemed fine. All this just came completely out of the blue as far as I was concerned.'

'Did he talk about his holiday plans at all?'

'He did, actually. They've generally been abroad in previous years. Places suited to the kids. They'd been delaying booking this year, hoping the pandemic situation might become clearer. In the end they decided to stay in the UK, but he'd left it late to book so they had to take what they could get.'

'Did he say why they'd chosen the Highlands?'

'Just somewhere to get away, I think. Somewhere remote. He'd spent time up there a few years back.'

'I don't suppose the names Craig or Andrea Gillan mean anything to you?'

'I don't think so. Should they?'

'Possible friends of Paul Dawson?'

'Doesn't ring any bells, I'm afraid.'

'Anything else you can tell me that you think might be relevant?'

'I can't think of anything. It's been a huge shock. I can't say I knew the family well, but from everything Paul said you'd have thought everything was pretty idyllic for them. I can't begin to imagine what might have triggered something like this.'

'We may never know for certain. We're just trying to understand as much about the circumstances as possible.'

'I don't envy your job. It can't be pleasant, delving into something like this.'

She offered no response to his observation. 'Many thanks for your assistance, Mr Grieves. We're likely to need to look more closely into Paul Dawson's business and finances so we'll be in touch with you about that. If anything else occurs to you in the meantime, please give me a call. I'll leave you a card with my details.'

Back outside, she was left only with a sense of frustration. As with the previous day's visit to the Dawsons' house, she felt as if she'd largely been wasting her time. That was part of any investigation, of course. You couldn't tell what might or might not be useful till you'd done it. But she was far from sure this trip south had really been justified.

That thought took her back to Brian Nightingale. If her trip had been a waste of time, his seemed doubly so. Sure, he'd shaken a few hands with the local team the previous afternoon, but he could probably have done the necessary liaison over the phone. He might have had some agenda to justify his travelling down here, but whatever it was had been lost in last night's drunken chaos.

She paused and looked around her for a moment before heading back to her car. Jedburgh looked like so many of the Border towns, a place seemingly preserved from an older, more serene age. The buildings were picturesque and well-maintained. There were quaint little independent shops and cafés, and little sign of the boarded-up shopfronts and ubiquitous charity shops that dominated so many high streets. It was a prosperous area, and she could imagine the Dawsons would have fitted in well here.

So what was it that had led Paul Dawson from here to that dreadful massacre in the Highlands? What had been going on in his head to make him do that? How did that link to what had happened to the Gillans?

She still had no answers that made any kind of sense. Grieves had perhaps given her one or two clues that could be followed up as they began to talk to the Dawsons' neighbours and tried to identify some of their friends. But it still felt as if they were a long way from any breakthrough.

And in the meantime all she had to look forward to was the prospect of a long drive back with a very hungover Brian Nightingale.

CHAPTER TWENTY-NINE

McKay spent the rest of the morning working through the material they'd gathered so far. It was still painfully thin. The interviews with the other chalet guests had yielded little of value. Most had barely noticed the Dawsons, except as yet another family staying on the site. One or two had exchanged greetings or had a brief conversation with Paul or Marie Dawson, but could add nothing to what was already known.

The visit to the Dawsons' house had yielded little beyond some insights into Paul Dawson's occupation and the mysterious image received in the post. Ginny's interview with the accountant might reveal more, but McKay wasn't getting his hopes up. After that, they'd be more dependent on the local team interviewing the Dawsons' neighbours or anything they could glean from the family's phones or computers. That work was all underway, but McKay's frustration was growing.

They'd gathered little from the CCTV or traffic cameras. They had one sighting of the BMW heading south on to the Kessock Bridge which confirmed the approximate timings they'd gleaned from the Fannings and the CCTV on the holiday site, but so far found no further sightings to confirm its subsequent direction. Similarly, they had a sighting of the van leaving the Gillans' neighbourhood which confirmed the timing provided by Fionnuala Erskine, but no further sightings in Inverness or beyond. They were still gathering and analysing further footage, so some breakthrough might emerge, but McKay wasn't feeling unduly optimistic.

He knew his mood was coloured by Brian Nightingale's behaviour. He'd tried to contact Nightingale several times that morning but succeeded only in reaching his voicemail. McKay had left a message on the first occasion, but hadn't subsequently bothered. There was no response from Ginny Horton's number either, so he assumed she'd already begun her interview with Dawson's accountant.

The priority was to find out what had happened to the Gillans since Fionnuala Erskine had seen the BMW leaving their home on the Friday. Their working assumption had been that Andrea Gillan had borrowed the BMW to drive home and then the car had been driven up the A9 to the chalet site and the Dawsons. After that, the vehicle had travelled south down to Loch Morlich, presumably still driven by one or other of the Gillans.

They had only limited information about what had happened at the loch – nothing more than the testimony of a couple some distance from what had happened who had not witnessed the crash and had supposedly failed to see or hear any signs of the car being torched. According to Ginny's interview notes, the latter claim wasn't entirely implausible – and the couple might have simply wanted to minimise their role as potential witnesses rather than risk further disrupting their holiday – but it did limit the value of their evidence.

The thought of the young couple – Jake Albert and Chloe Frost, according to Ginny's notes – reminded McKay he'd done nothing with what Ginny had told him the previous day. She'd thought she'd spotted Albert in the background during the news report from the chalet site. In a moment of uncharacteristic generosity McKay had said he'd check it out. It was only now, when actually faced with the task, that it occurred to McKay to wonder how exactly he was supposed to do that.

Ginny had at least told him the channel she'd been watching. Sighing, he looked up the relevant number and, after being transferred several times, eventually found himself talking to a reporter called Iain Pershore based at a news desk in Inverness. 'Aye, I know the story, of course,' Pershore said. 'It was Cassie who did that report. Cassie Sinclair. She's out on a job at the moment, but I can get her to call you when she gets back. What is it you want to know?'

McKay knew he had to choose his words carefully. Any hint of a story, particularly one involving their own reporter, and he'd never get these people off his back. 'It's probably something and nothing. When these kinds of reports are shown on TV they always generate calls from the public.'

'Tell me about it. We get them too. We pass on anything that's potentially useful but most of them are time-wasters.'

McKay was cursing himself for not thinking through his story before calling. Now, he had no option but to wing it. 'This one's unusual. One of the criminal justice social workers locally, reckons that in the background to the report she spotted one of her clients – a guy who's out on licence. One of the conditions of his licence is that he's excluded from the Black Isle area. If he was there rubber-necking he'd have been in breach.'

The story sounded barely half-baked to McKay, but Pershore seemed to buy it. 'I can pass it on to Cassie, but I don't know how much she'll be able to help you. We try not to take much notice of anyone standing in the background, unless they started causing trouble. She probably won't even remember.'

'I assumed so. I was just wondering if there was a way for me to view the report itself.'

'If that's all you need, I'm pretty sure that report's still up on our news app. If you go into the local section, you'll find recent reports. This is a pretty big story so it should still be there. If you just want to check out whether it's your guy in the background, that'll be the quickest way to do it.'

'Easier than I expected then. Thanks.'

'No worries. I'll pass it on to Cassie as well, just in case.'

Feeling mildly guilty, McKay ended the call and turned back to his computer to track down the news app. As he did so, a voice from behind him said, 'Not like you to be spending time in the office during a major inquiry. Has Brian Nightingale chained you down?'

He didn't turn, not least because he didn't want her to know how pleased he was to hear her voice. 'In a manner of speaking. He basically seems to have left me to run the show.'

'It's called delegation.' Helena Grant threw herself down on to the chair by McKay's desk. 'I should try it.'

'It's called going bloody AWOL.' He finally looked up from his screen. 'Good of you to make a brief return to the *hoi polloi*.'

'I didn't want to tread on Brian's toes, so I thought I'd better keep my distance for a day or two. I only came in just now because he didn't seem to be around. Where is he, anyway?'

'Your guess is probably as good as mine. Although, for what it's worth, my bet is that he's still in bed somewhere in the Borders recovering from the mother of all hangovers.'

She gazed at him for a moment. 'You might have to rewind that. In bed? In the Borders? With a hangover? In the middle of a major investigation?'

'Like I say, just a guess. But an educated one.' He recounted to her the events of the previous day, ending with his phone conversation with Nightingale.

'He was drunk?'

'Well and truly stoshied, I'd have said. He was doing his best to conceal it. You know, talking in that overprecise way drunks do, which just makes them sound even more drunk.'

'I take it Ginny wasn't in the same state.'

'More pissed off than pissed, I think.'

'What are they doing down in the Borders anyway?'

'Christ knows. Brian has his own sense of priorities. Just like his phone has its own distinctive form of signal problems. No response for most of yesterday afternoon till I managed to contact him via Ginny. No response again this morning.'

'Not ideal.'

'You always were the mistress of the understatement, Hel. Thing is, I've made a few discreet calls this morning. It looks as if Nightingale comes with a bit more of a reputation than we'd realised.'

'In what way?'

'A couple of things about our pal Brian. First, he has a reputation as a serious drinker. I don't know if he'd count as a full-blown alcoholic. If he is, he's clearly a relatively functioning one. Seems to hold his job down satisfactorily most of the time. But there've been a few incidents when he's been out of control. Just started drinking and not stopped until he was more or less comatose. Once or twice when he's caused severe embarrassment by doing it in highly inappropriate circumstances.'

'He's got away with this?'

'That's the second thing. He's seen down south as something of a teacher's pet. Very close to some of the senior team.'

'Why would they get close to someone who's a potential embarrassment?'

'To go back to the school analogy, it's because he's a snitch. He's useful to them.'

'In what way?'

'I don't know. I just know he's not to be trusted, and that if he's been sent up here, even on a temporary basis, that's not likely to be good news.'

'He's not exactly burnishing his reputation at the moment.'

'As long as Ginny doesn't somehow end up carrying the can for it.'

'Ginny's too smart for that.'

'Let's hope so.'

'On the subject of hobnobbing with the top brass, I've got a bit of news too.' Grant told him about Mike Everly's offer and her decision to accept it.

'Congratulations. Sounds like you've a real chance to impress.'

'Or a real chance to make a complete arse of myself. It all feels like very new territory for me.'

'You'll be fine on that front. Whether you'll be able to bite your tongue sufficiently is another question.'

'I'm more capable of doing that than you are.'

'Aye, but you don't want to be setting the bar that low. Seriously, it sounds like a really good opportunity. Apart from anything else, you'll be in a position to prevent these consultants from doing anything really stupid.'

'That was one of the things that persuaded me, to be honest. I've seen too many of these projects go belly-up because no one bothers to ask the people who actually have to do the job. We all whinge about that, so it would seem a bit feeble not to take up the opportunity when it's offered.'

'Fair point. And what do you reckon to Mr Michael Everly?'

'To be honest, I like him more than I expected to. He gets a bit caught up in the management jargon at times, but I think his heart's broadly in the right place. He seems more supportive than some senior ranks we've had up here.'

'When does all this start?'

'Kick-off meeting in the next week or two. Then we'll see. Mike reckons I should be able to do it alongside my day job.'

'The question is whether you can also do it alongside Brian Nightingale's day job. If he doesn't surface soon, you may need to.'

'Let's hope he gets his act together. Sounds like you've a lot on your plate.'

'More than enough.'

'In which case, I'd better leave you to it.'

He nodded. 'Don't be a stranger, though. I know what it's like when people start mixing with the rich and famous.'

'Piss off, Alec. You don't get rid of me that easily.'

He watched her flounce jokily off across the office and turned his attention back to the computer. It took him only a couple of minutes to track down the news app, and then a few moments longer to find the report he was looking for.

He clicked play and found himself watching a female reporter he vaguely recognised – presumably Cassie Sinclair – speaking in front of the familiar backdrop of the chalet site. The report itself was relatively anodyne, little more than a rephrasing of the police's media statement backed up by some predictable accounts of the shock of the other guests and staff. She gestured to the location around her to give an impression of the setting in which the tragedy had occurred.

A few people were milling around in the background. McKay guessed the majority of those watching were either other guests or staff. The site was comparatively remote and he couldn't imagine even the most curious of the local residents making the trip up there just to witness a TV news reporter.

It was only in the last few seconds, as the cameraman

panned around the site, that McKay spotted the couple Ginny had been referring to. He rewound slightly to get the best possible view.

The image wasn't particularly clear. He had the impression the couple had positioned themselves to avoid being caught on camera and had been taken by surprise. They were trying to skip back out of sight, and the woman turned her head away.

But just for a brief moment they were caught facing the camera. The bearded man was unfamiliar to McKay, so he couldn't immediately confirm or deny Ginny's hunch. She'd have to look at that on her return.

But the woman seemed much more familiar, even though it took him a few seconds to place her. But even as he identified her, he was struck by another idea, even more unexpected. He told himself it couldn't be true, that a low-resolution image on a computer screen could expose more than real life. But somehow, the more he looked, the more convinced he became.

'Shit,' he said.

CHAPTER THIRTY

The journey back was awkward, but less grisly than Ginny Horton had expected. Brian Nightingale had been waiting for her in the hotel lounge. He looked sallow and unwell, and he'd glowered at her as she'd entered, but said nothing either about what had happened the night before or her decision to leave him sleeping that morning.

He offered little beyond grunts of acknowledgement until they were in the car heading north. He'd clearly been happy for her to drive, which at least freed her from the dilemma of deciding whether he was in a fit state to take the wheel. He barely looked in a fit state to be a passenger.

It was only when they were well on the way that he finally spoke a coherent sentence. 'How was the accountant? Anything useful?'

'Not particularly,' she said. 'He confirmed that Dawson's business was doing okay, so it doesn't look as if he had money worries. The only negative was whether he might have failed to grow the business the way he'd originally hoped.'

'That hardly sounds like a motive for doing what he did,' Nightingale grunted. He fell silent and, after a few more minutes, dropped back into a doze. His lolling head wasn't the most prepossessing sight, but at least Horton was relieved of the need to make further conversation. He remained asleep for most of the rest of the journey, stirring only when she stopped briefly for fuel just outside Perth.

'Do you want a sandwich or anything?' she'd asked. She assumed he'd risen too late to get breakfast at the hotel.

'Oh God, no. Maybe just a bottle of water?'

It was a fine day for the last stretch of the drive up through the Cairngorms, the autumn sky an unblemished blue, the sun still high. The road was relatively quiet in the middle of the day, and she was able to keep up a good speed even on the stretches of single carriageway.

As she drove, she mulled over the dilemma that had disturbed her sleep earlier that morning. Nightingale's relative quiet and his failure to mention the events of the night before had, if anything, increased her uncertainty. Maybe his behaviour the previous evening had been nothing more than an aberration, the unfortunate outcome of meeting up with some old acquaintances. Though that didn't lessen the inappropriateness of his words and behaviour.

She arrived back at divisional HQ slightly behind schedule, having navigated a lengthy tailback on the A9 caused by a broken-down vehicle by the Inshes junction. Nightingale stirred as she pulled into the car park. He took a large swig from the bottle of water, his condition seemingly improved by several hours' sleep. 'Have I slept all the way? I can't believe it.'

'Pretty much,' she said. 'At least you didn't snore.'

'Sorry about that. I was going to offer to take over part of the way.'

'No worries. I like driving. It's like my running. Gives me time to think.'

'I'd heard you go running. I was told you take it pretty seriously.'

'I try to. The job gets in the way sometimes. It's easy at this time of the year. Harder when winter comes.'

'I can imagine.' He was silent as she manoeuvred the car into a narrow space. As she turned off the engine he said, 'Look, Ginny, about last night...'

She almost laughed at the cliché. 'I'm not going to spare your feelings, Brian. It wasn't good.'

'No. I don't know how it happened.'

'You drank too much, that's how it happened. It's not complicated.'

'Anyway, I know I owe you an apology.'

'Me and those two waiters.' She was tempted just to smooth the waters, to say 'yes, apology accepted' and move on. If nothing else, she was finding the conversation almost as awkward as he must be. But a few words of muttered apology, even if sincerely intended – and she wasn't entirely convinced about that – weren't really enough. 'Look, Brian. I don't want to make a meal of this, but in my view what happened last night wasn't acceptable. We were down there on force business, and at the very least what you did had the potential to bring the force into disrepute. On top of that, you did and said some things I felt were inappropriate.'

She wasn't sure what response she'd expected. She'd spoken before she'd allowed herself time to think or hesitate. If she didn't say something immediately, it would be increasingly difficult for her to express her views later. She didn't expect him to be comfortable with her response, but she'd hoped he might at least accept it and that it would prompt him to think about his actions.

It had been a vain hope, she realised almost immediately. Nightingale just shook his head, his expression suggesting that all his worst expectations had been fulfilled. 'And that's it, is it? I try to apologise. I admit I've behaved badly. I try to make amends as best I can. And you just throw it back in my face. I know what it is. None of you bastards up here want me around. You've been gunning for me since I arrived.'

'Brian–'

'Don't pretend. At least Alec fucking McKay's honest about what he thinks of me. You just behave like Little Miss Perfect till you've got the chance to get one over on me. And now you'll do your best to screw me over. You really are a cold-hearted bitch, aren't you?'

'For Christ's sake, stop playing the victim. Anything that happened last night was your fault. You can't just expect me to sweep it under the carpet because you give me a half-hearted apology.'

He jabbed a finger in her direction. 'Do your worst. Make a formal complaint, if you like. If you try to bring me down, I've plenty of favours I can call in. Plenty of people who'll happily destroy your reputation to protect me. Who the fuck will support you? Helena Grant as part of the bitch mafia? Alec fucking McKay who's got about as much credibility down south as Father fucking Christmas? Just think about that before you start making threats. Think about your own future.'

The explosion of fury seemed almost to have come from nowhere. She'd issued no threats, and had done nothing but state her views as calmly and dispassionately as she'd been able. Before she could say anything more, Nightingale had climbed out of the car, slamming the door loudly behind him.

She watched him stride off towards the building entrance, wondering if it had already occurred to him that he'd left his overnight bag in the car boot. In other circumstances, she'd have retrieved his luggage with her own and taken it in for him. As it was, she'd just drop the keys of the pool car back into reception and let him come and find it when he was ready. That would probably add to his anger towards her, but she suspected there was already little she could do about that.

The real question now was whether she had the courage to do what she was increasingly sure was right.

CHAPTER THIRTY-ONE

Helena Grant sat curled up on her sofa, working her way steadily through the files that Mike Everly had sent over. She was feeling mildly guilty, as she still tended to when she worked from home. It had become more commonplace during the pandemic, of course. Although the nature of policing meant that most activities had to be carried out in the office, they had been encouraged to work from home whenever possible.

Grant had never felt entirely comfortable with the idea, though she knew this was mainly because she'd become too set in her ways. Even Alec McKay had been persuaded it wasn't necessary for him always to be in the office from the crack of dawn to the end of the evening, though that might have had more to do with the rekindling of his relationship with Chrissie.

In her own case, the dynamic was the opposite. Following the dramatic ending of her previous relationship, she'd seen the office as a refuge. It was somewhere she could go and forget about her personal life, could throw herself into her work and depend on the support of people who, with a few exceptions, were primarily colleagues rather than friends. Home held few attractions for her.

It was the project that had brought her back home this afternoon. Earlier that morning, in preparation for the forthcoming kick-off meeting, Everly had emailed over to her a stack of detailed material relating to the consultancy work so far. She'd realised from a first glance that she'd struggle to make sense of it if she tried to read it on screen, so she'd printed the key documents off and then, on a whim, brought them back home to read. She told herself it was a sensible decision. If she'd stayed in the office, she'd have struggled to concentrate, distracted by the noise, the interruptions, the countless other claims on her attention. But she still had a sense that she was bunking off school.

On the other hand, the documents needed her full attention. There was a mass of material – reports, discussion papers, research analysis – much of it phrased in ways that felt almost like a foreign language. Even the most mundane words – agile, champion, road map – seemed to have different meanings. Her first thought, as she skimmed through the text and charts, was that she was well outside her comfort zone. Her second thought was that she was perhaps too far outside, and that she should bail out of this before she made even more of a fool of herself.

It took her a few more minutes, fortified by a strong coffee, before she persuaded herself that she was up to the job she'd taken on. She was an intelligent woman, accustomed to working with data and evidence. She had well-developed analytical skills. But she was trying to make sense of a document that, in part, was written in an unfamiliar language. As she worked her way through the material, she began to develop a suspicion that there was less to it than met the eye. She found herself increasingly highlighting passages, scribbling question marks and comments in the margins.

The overall thrust of the reports was sound enough, she

thought, but some of the conclusions and recommendations were based on very shaky evidence. She was imagining how this material would be received if she were presenting it in court or to the Fiscal.

She knew she had to be careful not to dismiss the consultants' conclusions too casually. There was a tendency among working police officers to mock anything that smacked of 'management-speak', as if the force had no scope to improve its effectiveness or organisation. Sifting through the jargon and obfuscation, there was considerable good sense in the recommendations, which she could envisage improving their work. It was just a question of distilling those gems from the mass of verbiage surrounding them.

Feeling in need of refreshment, she put the papers aside and went into the kitchen to make herself another coffee. Returning to the living room with the refilled mug in her hand, she walked over to the window and gazed out at the view.

This was why she'd chosen to live here, what had sold the house to her on first sight. From this slight elevation, she could look out across the Beauly Firth to the far shore, the dark mass of Inverness visible to the left, the sweep of the landscape opening up to the right. On a fine day like today, the waters were a pale blue, sparkling in the afternoon sunlight.

She was turning to resume her work when she noticed the grey van parked at the rear of her own car, immediately in front of the house. She was sure it hadn't been there a few moments earlier when she'd risen to go to the kitchen and she wondered vaguely who it might be. They didn't get many vehicles down here. Occasionally, delivery drivers would park here to kill time between gaps in their schedule. But usually they parked further along the road where there was a better view of the firth.

As she watched, she saw a man jog hurriedly down the path back to the van. He had his back to her, a baseball cap pulled low across his face. He jumped back into the van, did a U-turn and pulled off down the street. She watched the vehicle disappear, noting its registration through force of habit.

She hadn't heard the doorbell, but maybe he'd just left something. She walked back into the hallway and opened the front door. There was a neatly wrapped cardboard box sitting to the left of the door.

She'd heard, just before leaving the office that afternoon, about McKay's strange delivery. She stepped out on to the path and walked round the package. There was no obvious address label or other marking. After a moment, she fetched her phone and took photographs of the box from various angles. She texted the images to McKay and then dialled his number. He answered almost immediately. 'Hel?'

'Are you free for a few moments?'

'I've just been summoned by Brian Nightingale who wants to see me immediately. So, sure, take as long as you like. I see you've just sent me a text as well, so I'm clearly popular.'

'I just wanted to get your view on something. Have a look at the picture in the text. Does that look familiar to you?'

There was silence for a moment as he looked at the photographs. 'That's at your house?'

'Left just now. Grey van.' She recited the registration number. 'I only saw the guy from the back. White, average height. Wearing a black jacket, jeans and a baseball cap. Think he was wearing a face-mask, though I only saw that for a second.'

'That's a different reg from the one we were given for the delivery at the Gillans' house. We need to get the package removed and checked out.'

'I'm inclined to look at it first. I don't want to end up making a fool of myself.'

'You won't do that. But your choice.'

Without saying any more to McKay, she went back inside the house. She found some disposable gloves and a sharp kitchen knife, then returned to the package. Leaning over, she slit down the parcel tape across the top of the box. Once she'd cut through all the tape, she folded back the twin flaps and peered cautiously inside.

Her first reaction was to laugh. The box contained what looked like some form of rag doll, a toy she might once have had as a young child.

'What is it?' she heard from the phone.

She raised the phone back to her ear. 'I'm not sure, exactly.' She had crouched down by the box and pulled it towards her to peer inside. 'Some sort of doll.'

'Doll?'

'Like a cloth doll or a rag doll.' She reached into the box and, taking care to minimise her contact, she tried to lift up the doll to get a better look. As she did so, any thought of laughter disappeared. 'Christ.'

'What is it?'

'I was right. It is a rag doll. Quite an old, slightly threadbare one. Like a toy some child no longer wants...'

'That's very poetic, Hel, but–'

'But it has a severed head. It's an old, slightly threadbare rag doll. With a severed head.'

CHAPTER THIRTY-TWO

'I said immediately, Alec. Not in fifteen minutes.'

'Aye, so I was told. I came as soon as I could.'

'I'm not accustomed to people disobeying my instructions.'

'I'm not accustomed to being treated like someone's personal lackey.'

McKay was in Nightingale's office. Nightingale had told him to take a seat, but McKay, characteristically, had ignored him and was prowling round the room, as if seeking some point of vulnerability. He knew the constant movement was irritating Nightingale, which seemed a sufficient motive in itself.

'You're not beyond being disciplined, Alec.'

'And what are you going to discipline me for? Taking an urgent operational call so that I was briefly delayed in attending a routine meeting with you?'

'I was thinking more of insubordination.'

'We're not in the army. I'm just telling you what happened.'

'What was this call anyway?'

'From Helena. She's working at home and she's just taken a delivery.'

'A delivery? You don't mean—'

'A doll.'

'A doll? Had she ordered a doll?'

McKay stopped prowling and dropped himself into the chair opposite Nightingale's desk. 'Oddly enough, no. But that wasn't the only interesting thing about this doll.'

'Go on.'

'Its head had been severed.'

Nightingale blinked. 'What?'

'Someone had cut off its head. And slashed open its body.'

'But why would anyone send something like that?'

'That's the question, isn't it? We have to assume it's some kind of signal or message, like my delivery yesterday, but it's hard to see quite what it's intended to communicate.'

'Other than "we know where you live"?'

'That's the bit that Helena's most likely to take to heart, but it must be something more than that. The doll itself looks old and well-used. I've had it sent to forensics.'

'And no other clues or indications in the box?'

'Like the others. No labels or information. Just a plain cardboard box. Delivered by a guy in a grey van. I'm getting the plates checked out.'

Nightingale unexpectedly slammed his fist on the desktop, with the air of a student teacher trying to regain control of his class. 'Christ, this is a fucking mess. We seem to be getting nowhere. Why the hell was this doll sent to Helena Grant?'

'That's what intrigues me,' McKay said. 'Deliveries to me and to Helena. Suggests there's something personal about this. Though I've no idea how that would link to the Gillans or the Dawsons.' McKay rose and resumed his roaming around the office. 'We've got people looking at the Gillans' business interests but we've not so far uncovered anything suspicious. The car-hire business seems to have been Andrea Gillan's personal baby. She built it up as an offshoot of her husband's commercial hire business, and it produced a decent profit. The commercial business is a bigger and more complicated set-up, with various agricultural subsidiaries. It's a bit of a tangled web of companies, and it's possible there's something dodgy concealed in there. But the number-crunchers reckon it might just be set up to deal tax-efficiently with the seasonality of the various operations.' He shrugged. 'I don't pretend to understand the detail. But we're only at the start of pulling that apart so it's possible we might find something more interesting in there.'

McKay had mainly been detailing all this because he wanted to remind Nightingale that the team had been beavering away over the past couple of days. He was growing tired of humouring a man who couldn't be bothered even to be present at the investigation he was supposedly leading.

McKay's own priority was to get back to Ginny, to test out the wild hunch he'd had when viewing the TV news report. The more he'd thought about it, the less convinced he'd felt. He recalled a training course, a few years before, in which the trainer, some kind of forensic psychologist, had talked about the phenomenon of motivated perception – the tendency to see what we want to see. McKay couldn't recall much of the detail but he remembered some of the experiments the trainer had described. The core message had been that human perception was notoriously unreliable, particularly when faced with an ambiguous image or incident.

That was no doubt the case here. Isla had thought she'd spotted her brother. Ginny had believed she'd seen the witness from Loch Morlich. McKay had thought he'd seen – well, something else again. Something which, the more he considered it, barely made any sense. They were each of them imposing their own preferred order on something that, in reality, was little more than a blurred set of pixels.

'We need to find something soon,' Nightingale was saying.

'I'm hoping this might have some significance.' He slid a sheet of paper across the desk towards McKay, who leaned forward to examine it.

'This the image you found in Dawson's mail?'

'Copy of it. We've got the original bagged up.'

McKay gazed at the image for a moment. Then he picked it up, held it out in front of him and squinted at it.

'I wasn't asking to you admire it,' Nightingale said.

McKay was still staring at the picture, his head tilted slightly to one side. 'Can I borrow this?'

'Take it. It's just a print-off. I'm getting the tech people to see if we can do a reverse image search on the internet to identify her. If that fails we can try it on the Dawsons' relatives and any friends or associates we identify and include it in a media appeal.' Nightingale was watching McKay's face. 'Mean something to you?'

'I don't know. Maybe nothing. Probably just motivated perception.'

'Probably just what?'

'Seeing what you want to see.' McKay's eyes remained fixed on the image. 'Or, in this case, perhaps seeing something you should have seen long before now.'

CHAPTER THIRTY-THREE

Later in the afternoon, Isla forced herself to leave the house and take the short walk down to the shoreline. She felt she didn't make enough of where they lived. It was a glorious place, particularly on a fine early autumn afternoon like this. She stood at the edge of the narrow beach and gazed out across the waters of the Moray Firth towards the Black Isle. Immediately ahead of her was the jutting promontory of Chanonry Point, the favoured site for dolphin-spotting in the area. To her right, curving out as if to meet Chanonry Point, was Fort George, an imposing army base built after Culloden and still, for the moment, used as a working garrison. There were no signs of dolphins today, just the dancing whitecaps raised by the mild breeze.

She told herself she just wanted an opportunity to take some air and clear her head. Ginny would no doubt have achieved the same effect by taking herself off for a run along the coast, probably covering more ground in her first five minutes than Isla had managed in the last twenty. That was fine. Isla was no runner, and preferred a gentle amble along the waterline, the clear sea lapping against the stones just a metre away from her feet.

Today, she'd stopped at one of the benches to enjoy the view, allowing herself a few moments just to think again about the events of the previous evening. She still didn't know what to make of Tristram's behaviour, and continued to feel bad about driving him away so abruptly.

She'd spent the morning in the office but then, with a stack of formal documents to read through in preparation for a meeting the following day, she'd decided it would be more productive to spend the afternoon working from home. As soon as she'd entered the house, she'd regretted her decision, wishing she'd stayed out until Ginny returned that evening.

But she knew she couldn't just put her life on hold. She couldn't lock herself in the office on the possibility that Tristram might turn up again. Equally, she couldn't cower inside, afraid to open the door until the moment Ginny returned home.

She looked at her watch. She still had plenty of reading to get through and she didn't want to be working late into the evening. Reluctantly, she turned from the shore and began to make her way back to the house, gulls cawing noisily behind her.

She turned into the driveway and stopped. A package had been left beside the front door. A square, seemingly unmarked cardboard box.

That's odd, she thought. She wasn't aware they'd ordered anything, and there was no reason anyone should have bought them a present at this time of year. She walked forward and peered at the box. As she'd thought, there was no obvious address or other label.

She unlocked the front door then picked up the box and carried it through to the kitchen. It felt slightly heavier than she'd expected, and she could feel something loose bouncing inside as she moved, as if the contents had not been tightly packaged. She placed it carefully on the kitchen table, turning it round to see if she'd missed some indication of its provenance. There was nothing. That in itself seemed odd. If it had been delivered by some courier company, there would surely be at least some kind of address label.

She hesitated. Being the partner of a police officer tended to engender suspicion, particularly as Ginny had had a previous experience of being targeted at this address. Isla knew she was just feeling jittery at the moment. Ginny's absence, combined with her brother's visit the previous evening had left her more than usually prone to anxiety.

She shook her head, angry at her own foolishness. Then she walked across to the drawer where they kept the kitchen knives, digging around until she found one suitable for cutting through the parcel tape.

CHAPTER THIRTY-FOUR

'What do you think?'

Horton rewound the relevant few seconds for a third time. 'I mainly think it's a really lousy image and I haven't a clue. The more I watch it, the less certain I become.'

McKay nodded. 'Aye, that's pretty much what I felt. There was a moment when I felt absolutely convinced. Then I watched it again and hadn't a clue why I'd felt so sure.'

Horton ran through it a fourth time, pausing the recording at the moment when the man turned towards the camera. 'I mean, it easily could be him. The build's about right. The hair's similar. But it's all so small and blurred. I imagine there are countless people who look like that.'

'That's how I feel about the woman,' McKay said. 'I mean, it easily could be her, but there's nothing particularly distinctive about the way she looked.'

'So why did you think it was her?'

'She's part of the case. She was just on my mind.'

'I mean, you're right. There's a possible resemblance. But I'm not sure I'd have thought of her if you hadn't said it.'

'There you are then. You've had plenty of other stuff going

on since you spoke to her, so she wasn't at the forefront of your mind. Whereas I've been thinking of nothing but the Gillans for the last forty-eight hours and she's been part of that.'

'In a small way, I suppose.' Horton sounded doubtful. 'She didn't make much of an impression on me. She was just a pleasant young woman trying to be helpful.'

McKay was thinking back to his own impressions of Morag in the hire-car office. He'd be struggling to add much to Ginny's summary. Why he'd thought of her when he'd seen the face on the news report, he had no idea. Except that there was one other thought he hadn't yet shared with Ginny.

'There's something else. This isn't going to make any sense to you, because it doesn't make much sense to me. But when I glimpsed that face in the report, two names jumped into my head. The first was Morag. The second was Ruby Jewell.'

'Ruby Jewell? You're kidding.'

'Given her track record, she's not someone I'm inclined to joke about. I know it's a stupid idea. I'm just telling you what jumped, unprompted, into my head.'

Horton played the brief clip again. 'I mean, it's possible. But anything's possible with that resolution. So what is it you're saying? That this could be Morag or it could be Ruby Jewell?'

'Or that Morag could be Ruby Jewell.'

'But that's ridiculous. You've met Ruby Jewell. You've spoken to her. You couldn't spend time with Morag and not know if it's the same person.'

'You'd think so, wouldn't you? Except I met and spoke to her as a potential witness in a murder enquiry last Christmas and I didn't make the connection at all.'

'But that was different. You were outside in the dark, first thing in the morning, and she was wrapped in a scarf and hat. And you encountered her in a context where you had no reason to expect to.'

'It still baffles me I didn't make the connection. And we expected we'd have no trouble catching up with her after her encounter with Helena, but she's evaded us at every turn. I'm not the superstitious type, but there's something almost inhuman about her ability to shapeshift.'

'Okay, but how is it possible you didn't see the resemblance in person, but you spotted it when you looked at this low-resolution blob.'

'I'm just telling you the thought that popped into my head when I looked at the report. I'm not suggesting it makes any sense.' He paused. 'I tried to phone Morag just in case her voice gave me any clue, but there was no response on the phone. Just went to voicemail.'

'You do know this sounds slightly insane, Alec?'

'I don't deny she's under my skin a bit. She's always seemed one step ahead of us, and she's always given the impression she's playing with us. The character I met as Ruby Jewell was a larger-than-life figure, all bright over-the-top clothes and dyed hair. I saw the image she was projecting, not the person behind that image. It might have been the same with Morag. She was the opposite – just an unassuming local Scottish lass. The sort of person you hardly notice if they're serving you from behind a counter. It's almost as if, in that case, you're seeing the lack of image rather than the person behind it. I'm not making much sense, am I?'

'Not really. I know what you mean about her, but she doesn't have magical powers.'

McKay was silent for a moment. 'There's one other thing.'

'Go on.'

They were sitting side by side at McKay's desk, and had been watching the news report on McKay's PC. 'That picture you found in Dawson's mall. It didn't ring any bells?'

'Oh, for goodness' sake, Alec, you're not suggesting...'

He'd had the picture face down on the desk and now turned it over. 'Take another look.'

'You're getting obsessive, Alec. I looked carefully at the picture when we first opened it, and it meant nothing to me.' She picked up the image and gazed at it again. 'I've not seen Ruby Jewell the way you have, so I can't make that comparison. I'm just trying to see how she might look like Morag.' She held the image further away and squinted at it. 'I suppose I can sort of see it. Facially, at least. But that would probably be true of thousands of people. The hair's completely different. This woman's wearing glasses. She looks older than Morag.'

'But a lot of that is just superficial. It's not difficult to change your appearance in that kind of way.'

'I still can't really see it, Alec. I'm not saying you're wrong, but it's much more likely you've just got this lodged in your head. I can't say I blame you. She's a dangerous woman and she scares the hell out of me. But we can't go chasing ghosts.'

'She's out there somewhere, though, Gin.' McKay had picked up the picture again and was gazing thoughtfully at it. 'We need that facial recognition technology, or one of those super-recognisers.'

'We've got access to that expertise in the force. But I don't fancy your chances in persuading Brian to invest his budget in it unless you've something more substantive to give him.'

'It would be typical of her, though, wouldn't it? Hiding right under our noses.'

'She's a smart woman. But she's only human.'

'She's a psychopath. I don't even know what drives her.'

'I think she just wants to hurt people. To kill people. It's as simple as that. She latches on to people and their causes, but that's nothing more than a way of justifying her bloodlust. That's my view. But we'll catch up with her eventually–' She stopped at the sound of her phone buzzing. 'Sorry, bear with me. It's Isla. She's been having a few issues of her own at the moment.'

'No worries. We can chat when you're finished.'

He'd expected Ginny to leave the office to talk to Isla if they had something personal to discuss. But the call didn't last long enough for that.

'Oh, Christ. Really?' Horton was silent for a moment, then said, 'Don't touch anything. I'll get right back. Twenty minutes.'

She ended the call and turned back to McKay. 'We've got another one.'

'Another one?'

'Another one of our boxes. Isla opened it without realising.'

'And?'

'Looks like we've something else to add to our collection.'

CHAPTER THIRTY-FIVE

Helena was startled by the ringing of the front doorbell. It wasn't long since the examiners had left, having completed their work and taken the box itself back for forensics to work their magic. McKay had arranged for a couple of uniforms to check around the immediate area on the off-chance the van driver might have chosen to linger somewhere. He'd offered to come out himself, but she'd told him he shouldn't waste the time.

It had taken a couple of hours out of her afternoon, and it was only now that she'd settled back down to the project work. She was feeling mildly hassled rather than fearful.

Then the doorbell had rung. The sound was rare enough in the house and in the circumstances it was sufficient to set her heart racing. She walked over to the window. There was an unfamiliar car parked in the road outside. At least it wasn't a grey van, though that brought only limited reassurance.

She made her way back to the front door. After she'd had some issues on a previous case, she'd had a spyhole fitted and, before opening, she peered through to see her visitor.

Mike Everly.

The sight of him was unexpected but not unwelcome. She'd been feeling more tense than she'd realised and she welcomed the opportunity for some reassuring company. She opened the door to greet him. 'Mike?'

He was looking uncharacteristically awkward. 'I just thought I'd better check you were okay. I just heard about the package.'

'I'm fine. Just slightly uneasy that someone has my address. It's good of you to come out. But you really didn't need to.'

'Staff welfare's very important. And you're a key member of the project team now.'

'Are you sure you weren't just checking I wasn't swinging the lead?'

'Definitely not. I'm happy to trust people to work as they think best.'

She left him in the living room while she went to make coffees for them both. When she returned he was standing at the window, gazing out at the waters of the firth below. 'Beautiful view.'

'I was lucky to find this place. Rory and I had a place in Inverness. Even when he was alive it was bigger than we needed. Afterwards, I needed a new start. This was just the kind of place I was looking for.'

She decided she was talking too much, and she sat down with her coffee. After a moment, Everly left the window and sat down at the far end of the sofa, a discreet gap between them. 'I envy you the view. I'm just renting a place at the moment. It's fine but it doesn't have much to recommend it.' He gestured to the project files she'd left on the coffee table in front of them. 'What do you make of it all?'

She'd envisaged having more time to get her thoughts in order before having this conversation. She was intending to pull together her notes, write up a short summary and some

217

conclusions, and then prepare a coherent and considered response for Everly. As it was, she hadn't even finished reading through the material. She knew Everly was only making conversation and wouldn't expect anything beyond off-the-cuff thoughts. Even so, she didn't want to make a fool of herself.

She forced herself to pause and think before continuing, deciding she might as well be honest. 'I was afraid it was all going to be beyond me at first. The language is a bit...'

'Impenetrable? Tell me about it. I'm prone to management-speak but this lot... Some of them are even worse face to face. I should have warned you about that. The first time I read their stuff, I was tempted to ask for a translation.'

'I'm glad it's not just me, then.'

'I don't want to be too cynical. A lot of the tools and techniques they use are very good, but they do sometimes try to blind us with pseudoscience.'

'There was a lot I thought they'd got spot on. And they highlighted some issues I don't think we've even really thought about. There's a lot of good stuff in there.' She paused. 'There's also stuff I don't think would work in a million years. It's not that it's necessarily wrong. It's just that they're trying to import ideas that wouldn't work in our culture.'

'Maybe it's our culture that's wrong?' Everly suggested.

'There's plenty that could be improved about our culture. But it's evolved that way for a reason. It supports our priorities and the nature of our work.' Feeling more confident and enthused now, she talked him quickly through a couple of examples she'd noted down as she'd been reading.

Everly was looking pleased. 'This is exactly what I wanted from you, Helena. You're open to ideas, but you're also steeped in practical experience. Actually, I'm not sure this smart-suited bunch will know what's hit them when they meet you.'

'I didn't mean–'

'No, seriously, Helena. You're more than a match for them. They're a smart bunch with their MBAs and PhDs, and it's right that we take on board what they have to say. But we've got to be prepared to challenge and question their ideas.' He smiled. 'I think you'll be a real asset to the project.'

She wasn't sure how seriously to take Everly's flattery, but there was nothing in his tone to suggest it wasn't sincere. 'That's reassuring. It wasn't quite how I was feeling when I first sat down with all this earlier.'

Everly looked at his watch. 'Look, feel free to say no if you've other plans, but I wondered if you fancied getting a bite to eat? It would be useful to talk a bit more about your impressions of the consultancy work, if nothing else. I could drive us somewhere and then drop you off back here afterwards.'

She hesitated. She thought about telling him that she still had plenty of reading to be getting on with, or even pretending that she had something else scheduled for that evening. But she knew she was being cowardly, afraid of embarking on even the most unromantic of relationships after all the pain she'd experienced. Nothing Everly had said suggested he had anything in mind other than a relaxed but professional discussion.

Alongside that, there was another part of her head telling her that, after her experience that afternoon, she didn't want to spend the whole evening in the house by herself. The prospect of some human company was definitely more attractive.

She smiled at Everly. 'That sounds like an excellent idea.'

CHAPTER THIRTY-SIX

Isla was gazing thoughtfully at the picture Ginny had taken. 'Yes, I think so. I mean, I can't be sure it's the same one, but it looks very similar and about the right age and condition.'

'You don't think it could just be coincidence?'

'Well, obviously it could be. But it seems unlikely, doesn't it?'

Ginny exchanged a glance with McKay who was sitting at the far end of the kitchen table. They'd both travelled over here in response to Isla's call, using separate cars so McKay could head either home or back to the office afterwards. Ginny had no intention of leaving Isla alone again that evening. 'It's an unusual colour.'

'I used to call him – it – Honey because of the pale-yellow fur. I don't think I ever saw another one in quite that colour. I don't even know where it came from originally. I have a feeling I might have inherited it from my mum.'

'So, unless we've got a very odd coincidence, this is either the same one or someone's gone to some trouble to procure a duplicate.'

McKay leaned forward. 'And there's only one person, other than yourself, who could have known about Honey?'

'I think so. My parents are no longer with us. There might have been friends at the time who saw him, but it wouldn't be anyone I've seen in years.'

McKay picked up Ginny's phone and gazed at the image as if expecting it to reveal something more to him. But it was just a teddy bear. A little larger than average, and, as Isla had said, an unusual light shade of yellow-brown. Nothing else distinctive. Except that, like the rag doll sent to Helena Grant, its head had been nearly severed from its body.

McKay couldn't recall what cuddly toys he'd had as a child. His main childhood memories were of crashing die-cast toy cars together. But if he'd been presented with a beloved childhood toy mutilated in this manner, he'd have found it deeply disturbing. He looked up at Isla, but her face remained blank and unrevealing.

'Why would he do this?' Isla said. 'I mean, is this intended as some sort of retribution for the way I treated him last night?'

Ginny looked over at McKay, who said, 'That's one question. But I'm afraid it's not the biggest one.'

'I don't understand.'

It was Ginny who responded. 'This isn't the first of these packages. There've been a series of similar deliveries over the last twenty-four hours or so. Including deliveries to Alec and to Helena and one which implies a link to the Gillan deaths. The same size and shape of box. The same lack of any kind of labelling or marking. All apparently delivered by the same grey van, albeit with different fake plates. One of them containing a soft toy with a severed head similar to this one. The others containing equally strange items.'

'So if we assume your brother is in some way connected

with this,' McKay said, 'that suggests he was also involved with the sending of the other packages.'

'You think Tristram...?'

'I'm not jumping to any conclusions,' McKay said. 'Do you have contact details for your brother?'

'I've only an address. In London. He wrote to me a few days ago, but he didn't give a phone number or any other means of contacting him.'

'We'll need to get the letter checked out,' McKay said. 'Just in case. And we'll contact the Met about getting someone to visit his place. You think he's likely to be still up here?'

'I've no idea. He was here last night. That's all I know. I didn't give him any reason to hang around. But Tristram can be persistent when he wants to be. I thought that was what this was all about at first. Just a way of putting more pressure on me.'

'I appreciate this must be difficult for you, but, given the possible link with the Gillans' deaths, at the moment your brother's the one concrete lead we have. We do need to track him down. Do you have anything else that might help us? Other friends or contacts who could help us trace him?'

'I'm afraid any friend of Tristram's has been no friend of mine for a long time. I really have no idea what sort of life he's leading now or who he's mixing with.'

'You say he has a police record?'

'He's been inside a couple of times to my knowledge. And fines and a suspended sentence before that. Drugs-related mainly.'

'We'll see what we've got on file. That should give us a relatively recent likeness and maybe other contact details.' He offered a smile. 'We're very grateful for this, Isla. Thank you.'

She looked up at him, and for the first time that afternoon he saw the spark of some kind of passion in her eyes. An unexpectedly cold passion. 'I just want you to get hold of the bastard. Find out what he's up to.'

Ginny reached out and placed a hand on Isla's arm. 'Don't...'

'That was why I threw him out last night. I could feel it starting again. I could feel myself being sucked in. He gave me a load of crap about wanting to rebuild our relationship. There were moments when I was almost fooled by it.' She gestured to the picture of the teddy bear. 'But if you want to build bridges you don't do something like that. You don't decapitate your sister's favourite childhood toy and stick it in the post to her.'

McKay gazed back at her, his face impassive. 'We'll find him, Isla. We'll find out what he's up to. I've asked enough questions for tonight.' He nodded his farewells to Isla and followed Ginny out into the hallway. He waited while she slid the letter from Tristram into an evidence bag and handed it to him.

McKay glanced towards the half-open kitchen door and said quietly, 'This is getting to her, isn't it?'

Ginny opened the front door and stepped outside with him before responding. 'I think that's what Tristram wants. I don't know him. I've never even met him. But my sense is that he's playing with her. He wants to damage her. Not physically, but psychologically. Emotionally. She wasn't going to say it to you, but she's told me before how much that bear meant to her as a child. It was the one toy she clung to when she was very small. And one day it went missing. She blamed Tristram because hiding her toys was the kind of thing he did. He vehemently denied it, and in the end everyone assumed she'd just dropped it somewhere. She's told me the story just as one of those childhood anecdotes when she's been trying to explain what Tristram was like, but I could always tell it meant a lot to her.'

'So you think Tristram kept it all this time just to play a stroke like this?'

'I think it's possible.'

McKay was silent for a moment. 'You'll be all right, the two of you?'

She smiled. 'You mean tonight or generally?'

'I meant tonight. But both, I suppose.'

'We'll be fine. I'll make sure of that. Whatever that bastard might try to do.'

CHAPTER THIRTY-SEVEN

She hesitated as she reached out to open the car door. 'I don't want this to come across the wrong way. But would you like to come in for coffee?'

Everly laughed. 'I'll take the offer only at face value. But, yes, I'd love to.'

Helena Grant had decided it was still early enough in the evening for her question not to be misinterpreted. They'd had a pleasant early supper at a pub a few miles away, but it was still only around eight thirty. The sun had set, but the sky was clear and the evening had the translucent quality unique to the Highlands. She'd enjoyed the conversation with Everly, which had ranged from discussing the project to chatting about their respective careers. She was more than happy to continue the conversation a while longer.

She led him into the house. 'Make yourself comfortable. I'll go and make the coffee. Decaf or the real thing?'

'Whichever you're having. I still sleep soundly enough to overcome the caffeine, but I'm happy with the decaf.'

'These days, if I drink the real stuff at this time of night I can guarantee I won't sleep. You really must have a clear conscience.'

'That must be it. Decaf's fine. Just black for me. No sugar.'

She returned a few minutes later with the coffees. He was standing by the window, gazing out across the firth towards the lights of Inverness. 'It's an impressive view even at this time in the evening.'

'It's one of my favourite times of day here, to be honest. Especially earlier in the summer when it stays light almost till midnight.'

He returned to join her on the sofa. 'I love the long days. I'm not sure I'll ever quite get used to the midwinter, though. You hardly seem to see the sun.'

'You get used to it. I like it. As long as I can shut out the world.'

'Not always easy in our line of work. Sometimes the world intrudes when you don't want it to–' He stopped. 'I'm sorry. I'd forgotten what you went through last winter. Not something to make light of.'

'It's all history now. It's not something I like to think about, but it doesn't keep me awake at night.' She lifted up her coffee mug. 'No more than caffeine.' She smiled. 'How are you finding it up here, anyway?'

'Everyone was welcoming when I first arrived. But people are always a bit wary of a new broom, aren't they? I hope everyone's accepted I'm here to protect the interests of the division. Unless you've heard differently, of course?'

She wasn't sure she could answer his question with any confidence. He was generally seen as personable, easy to talk to, fair and considerate in handling staff issues, and probably an improvement on some of his predecessors. But she wasn't sure that the officers and staff actively trusted him. 'No,' she said, 'I've heard nothing to contradict that. Though I'm not sure I envy you. Whatever you do, some people will complain about it.'

'If people have genuine causes for concern, it's important to listen to them. That's one reason for wanting to involve people like you in the work, Helena. So we can pick up and respond to concerns before it's too late.'

'Well, we'll see how it works out.'

He took a sip of his coffee. 'On a related topic – that is, people dealing with something new – how do you think Brian Nightingale's going down?'

The question took her by surprise. 'I don't know really. I've not had many dealings with him myself. It's not always easy to settle into a new patch.'

'The only reason I ask – and I don't want you to tell tales out of school – is that he had a bit of a chat with me this afternoon.'

'About what?'

'About the team. He feels he's not always getting the support he needs; that one or two people are not being fully co-operative; that they're a little too prone to doing their own thing.'

'Did he mention any names?'

'You can probably guess one of the names he mentioned.'

'Alec, obviously.'

'Obviously. The other one surprised me, to be honest. That's why I wanted to get your view.'

'Go on.'

'Ginny Horton. From what I've seen, she always strikes me as a pretty straightforward sort of individual.'

Grant wasn't sure that was quite how she'd describe Ginny – she'd discovered over the years that Ginny had some surprising hidden depths – but she'd never been difficult to work with. 'Definitely. Ginny's hard working, diligent. Sure, she's bright and she's more than capable of coming up with insights or avenues for investigation that the rest of us have missed. But she's a stickler for the rules. I don't see her going off on a frolic of her own.'

Everly nodded thoughtfully. 'That was my impression. Maybe she's just got on the wrong side of Brian somehow.'

'Did he say what she'd done?'

'A lot of it was trivial stuff. He acknowledged that. But he reckoned it was a cumulation of minor things. He'd decided to join her on this visit to the Borders because he thought it would be useful to take advantage of his personal contacts down there. She was obviously unhappy with him joining her and made it clear she didn't want him. Then she was unco-operative when they were checking out the Dawsons' house. Kept making jokes at Brian's expense.'

'None of this sounds like Ginny.'

'It's just what Brian told me. There was some sort of argument between them over dinner last night. Brian reckoned it was just a bit of a spat, but then she went off to see Dawson's accountant without waiting to give Brian a lift into the office as they'd arranged. Brian said he had to cancel his planned meetings with the local team and ended up kicking his heels into the hotel till she got back.'

'I've never found Ginny remotely difficult to work with. Maybe it's just a personality clash?'

'That's what I said to Brian. If he's got concerns, he should have it out with her. They're probably rubbing each other up the wrong way without even realising it.' He paused. 'Alec might be a different matter, though.'

'In what way?'

'Come on, Helena. You know as well as I do that he's not the easiest of individuals to deal with.'

She couldn't in all honesty deny what Everly was saying. She'd developed a strong working relationship with McKay over the years, and she'd come to respect and even like him. Even so, there were times when he could be utterly infuriating. Even if he was much less of a maverick than he liked you to think, he was more than capable of following his own tangent if he thought it necessary. The fact that he was generally proved right didn't necessarily increase his popularity.

'When push comes to shove, there's no better or more loyal team player than Alec. Trust me on that. I owe my life to him. Literally.'

'That's why I wanted your views. Brian reckons that one reason he wanted to take the trip down to the Borders was to test Alec out.'

'Test him out?'

'See how he'd perform left to his own devices. Clearly, he's done that effectively when he's been working with you, but he knows you and how you want things done. Brian wanted to see how Alec would fare working for an unfamiliar SIO.'

'And?'

'Brian reckons he got on with the job well enough.'

'But?'

'But, basically, Alec just took off on his own. He made all the decisions – designating the crime scenes, involving the examiners, submitting material to forensics – without making any real attempt to consult with Brian.'

'Alec's an experienced detective. He probably assumed he could handle that stuff without disturbing Brian. Was there anything Brian would have wanted done differently?'

'He says there are a few areas where he'd have handled it differently, but he doesn't see that as the main issue. It's more that, in the middle of an inquiry of this magnitude, Alec didn't bother to discuss his intentions or actions with the SIO.'

'And the SIO was readily available?'

'On the phone, yes. Brian said he had a few signal problems

yesterday afternoon, but that Alec made no attempt to contact him today until he got back to the office this afternoon.'

To Grant's ears, all of this sounded more than plausible. She didn't have much doubt about Alec's attitude towards Nightingale, and she could easily imagine Alec wouldn't have been too concerned about seeking Nightingale's input. But then most of what he'd done over the last couple of days had presumably been pretty straightforward. It sounded as if Nightingale was making a fuss about not very much at all.

'That's not really the problem, though,' Everly went on. 'Or at least Brian thinks that's just a symptom of the problem.'

Grant took a sip of her rapidly cooling coffee. 'Which is what?'

'McKay's attitude. Insubordination is the word that Brian uses.'

'That's a bit strong. Slightly chippy might be closer.'

Everly smiled. 'Look, I know you feel obliged to defend Alec, Helena. In your position, I'd be exactly the same. But he really doesn't have the best of reputations. He's known for being difficult.'

'That doesn't make him bad at his job.'

'No one's suggesting he's bad at his job. His track record speaks for itself. It's more a question of whether he can work with Brian.'

'Perhaps that's Brian's problem.' The words sounded blunter than she'd intended, but they reflected her mood.

'Maybe. But he's the SIO. He has to run the investigation as he thinks best. I've no reason to think he's not running it well.'

'So what does he want? With regard to Alec, I mean.'

'Nothing serious. He fully accepts it may just be a personality issue. But he's considering taking him off the case. Not my problem really, of course. Brian needs to take it up through the major investigation hierarchy. He was just seeking my views because we're old friends.'

Grant looked up. 'I didn't realise that. That you were old friends.'

Everly took a mouthful of coffee before responding. 'Well, *friends* is probably overstating it. But we go back a fair way.'

'So what did you advise him?'

'I didn't really, to be honest. It's got to be his decision. But I told him not to be rash. I know Alec's a good copper, and the best ones aren't always the easiest to handle. It might not reflect well on Brian if the powers that be think he can't handle someone who's a bit challenging. On the other hand, if he thinks Alec's impeding the investigation, he's got to do what he thinks is necessary.'

'It's not my place to advise him either,' Grant said. 'But, for what it's worth, I think he'd be crazy to stick Alec on the bench. For all his faults, Alec gets results. And, for the avoidance of doubt, he gets them the right way.'

'Well, it's Brian's decision,' Everly said. He looked at his watch. 'I'd better be getting going or you'll begin to suspect I'm after more than a cup of coffee.'

Grant wasn't sure how she was supposed to respond to that. In other circumstances, she might have felt herself tempted by the prospect of taking things further with Mike Everly. But the preceding conversation had left her uneasy, and she just wanted to be alone. She gestured towards the table. 'I've still got a lot of reading to do.'

'I'd better leave you to it then.' He smiled. 'But I'd like to do this again sometime, if you're up for it. Dinner, I mean.'

'Yes, that would be great.' She was aware she sounded less enthusiastic than she might have earlier in the evening.

'Are you feeling okay?'

'Fine, just a bit tired, that's all. I'm obviously not used to reading lengthy consultancy reports.'

'No, well, which of us is?' He laughed and pushed himself to his feet. 'Right, I'll let you get some rest. I've already taken up too much of your evening.'

'Not at all. It's been great.' She stood up and followed him to the front door. 'Sorry if I'm being a bit of a party pooper at the end.'

Outside, it was still a fine evening, but she could see clouds gathering above the firth to the east, dark against the still pale sky. The forecast had predicted rain before morning. She was wearing a relatively thin silk shirt, and as she watched Everly walk back down the path to his car, she found herself involuntarily shivering. This was it, she thought. The real end of the summer.

CHAPTER THIRTY-EIGHT

It was barely seven, but the traffic was slow on the Kessock Bridge and there was already a tailback from the Longman traffic lights. It was the rain, McKay supposed. More people chose to drive and they set out earlier to avoid the traffic. Which, of course, just meant that the traffic built up earlier.

McKay invariably worked long hours during large-scale investigations, and it wasn't unusual for his days to start earlier than this. He was always like this in the middle of a major investigation. The adrenaline started pumping, and he just wanted to keep going, keep plugging away until they got their breakthrough. It was when he felt most real.

The force of the rain was unexpected. He'd seen from the previous evening's weather forecast that the warm spell was expected to break today. That was hardly a surprise. In McKay's experience good weather didn't last long in these parts. The summer had been as mixed as usual, an early spell of warm weather succeeded by a mix of showers and cooler sunshine.

But now the summer felt well and truly gone. The sun wasn't yet up and it still felt like midnight. A dense persistent rain had been falling for most of the night and was showing no sign of slackening. The lights of Inverness were smeared into swirls of orange and white by the sweep of the wipers across the windscreen, a chain of crimson brake lights ahead.

It was another twenty minutes before McKay finally pulled into the police car park. He pushed open the door and peered out into the gloom. 'Bugger.'

The smart thing to do would be to dig out his umbrella from the boot, he thought. Instead, he jumped out into the wet morning and raced across to the entrance, his head down against the teeming rain. As he reached the doors, he realised someone else had had a similar idea and was pounding in from his left. McKay reached the door first and, feeling almost impossibly virtuous, held open the door for his fellow runner.

It was only when he stood back that he realised that the individual in question was Brian Nightingale. 'Morning, Brian. Practising the drowned-rat look for the ladies?'

Nightingale stopped and glared at McKay. He was looking even more sallow and unwell than usual, McKay thought.

'That mouth of yours is going to get you into trouble one day.'

'You wouldn't believe how many times it has already, Brian.'

'I'd believe it only too well. Can we have a word?'

'Now? It's just that I've a few things I need to–'

'Later then. Ten, my office.'

McKay opened his mouth to respond but Nightingale had already vanished, pressing his ID card to the barrier and rushing for the lift that had just arrived. McKay was happy to let him go. The last thing he wanted was to share a lift, even for a few minutes, with Brian Nightingale. He turned to use the stairs and saw Helena Grant enter through the main doors. Clearly more sensible than either he or Nightingale, she was in the process of folding her soaked umbrella.

'The gang's all here,' McKay said. 'You've just missed Brian.'

'How was he?'

'His usual charming self. Wants a word with me later, apparently.'

'I'm not sure if I should tell you this, Alec, but a little bird tells me that he's gunning for you.'

McKay took a few steps back to ensure they couldn't be overheard. 'In what way?'

'He thinks you're trouble. Insubordinate.'

'Only in my usual mischievous way.'

'I'm sure. But he wants to take you off the investigation.'

'On what grounds? I'm the one who's kept the bloody thing running while he was swanning off to the Borders.'

'I'm just telling you what I've heard. My guess is that if he does something, he'll arrange it on some bland bureaucratic basis. Find some other task for you to do or some way of sidelining you. He's not going to want a fight.'

'Too bloody right he doesn't. Not with me.'

'No one with any sense would pick a fight with you.'

'That doesn't rule out Brian Nightingale unfortunately. But why would he want to do this? He must know he's not capable of handling this one on his own.'

'Would he know that though? People like Brian tend to have an inflated sense of their own abilities.'

'I saw the look in his eyes when he started to realise that this wasn't going to be the piece of cake he was expecting. He looked scared shitless.'

'Maybe that's the point. Maybe he thinks you'll show him up.'

'That's not how I work, Hel. You know that. I'm a team player.'

'Aye, I know that. But you've an odd way of showing it sometimes. Brian's not as familiar with your funny little ways as I am. Maybe you should cut him a little slack. Rein in your usual tendencies. Let him think he's boss. I've never really been under that illusion, but he might fall for it.'

'The man's a liability, Hel.'

'In that case, he needs your support, doesn't he? There's one other thing.'

'Go on.'

'I hear he's gunning for Ginny, too.'

'Ginny? What's she supposed to have done? I can see why I might not be flavour of the month, but even he can't have a problem with Ginny–' He stopped suddenly. 'Jesus. The bastard.'

'What?'

'You know I told you Ginny said she had a few problems with Nightingale while they were down on their jaunt? He knocked back too much of the vino over dinner and ended up making a nuisance of himself.'

'And you discovered he had a bit of a track record in that direction.'

'Exactly. So he knows Ginny's got something on him. That'll be why he's gunning for her. Get his retaliation in first.'

'Is she intending to lodge a formal complaint?' Grant asked.

'That's her decision. She was mulling it over. It's not an easy decision. You can bet Nightingale's got the old pals' network sewn up.'

'Especially if he's undermined her credibility in advance.'

'You want me to say something to her?'

'I shouldn't really have even spoken to you about it. It's something I was told in confidence.'

'Our friend Michael Everly, then.' McKay grinned.

'I'm saying nothing. But I thought you ought to know. You're more than capable of looking after yourself, but Ginny's maybe not quite as streetwise. She may need some protection.'

'I wouldn't underestimate her. But I take your point. I can't keep an eye on her if Nightingale's slung me off the case.'

'Just bear that in mind, Alec.'

'I will. How's the project work going anyway?'

'Only just getting into it. More interesting than I'd expected. I'm beginning to think there's probably something useful I can bring to the party.'

'Not a poisoned chalice, then?'

'That's the worry. I'll see how it goes.' She seemed about to say something more, but her gaze flicked past him out towards the car park. 'Speaking of which, Mike Everly's heading this way. Maybe best if we're not seen chatting this morning.'

'Aye, he might jump to the right conclusion.' Taking his cue, McKay moved towards the stairs, leaving Grant to take the lift. A few steps up he turned back. 'Thanks for the heads-up, Hel. Appreciated.'

CHAPTER THIRTY-NINE

McKay booted up his computer then went to make himself a coffee while the machine went through its usual endless routine. He was the first into the open office that morning. Through the glass partition he could see Nightingale at his desk, painstakingly tapping at his keyboard with two fingers. *Spreading some kind of poison,* McKay thought.

At the top of his inbox there was a short email from Wally Kincraig, sent only a few minutes before. It said only: 'Alec. Let me know when you get in. Something interesting.' McKay read through the message a couple of times, as if expecting it to divulge greater meaning. Then, picking up his untouched coffee mug, he rose and made his way down the corridor to Kincraig's office.

Kincraig was one of the forensic accountants who'd been attached to the team, charged with the task of working through the Gillans' business and personal finances in the hope of finding something that might provide a clue to their killings. Kincraig had retired from the force a few years earlier and was now living down in Fife, but still carried out occasional consultancy work for the force. He was currently sharing an office with a couple of other supposed financial wizards, but McKay could see through the glass that the other desks were currently unoccupied. He tapped on the door and entered. 'Morning, Wally. You always in this early?'

'I'm staying with my younger sister and family while I'm up here. Trust me, I like to be out of the house before the meltdown when she's trying to get the kids off to school. Anyway, there's plenty on at the moment.'

'Tell me about it. How are you getting on?'

'Pretty well with the Gillans. Craig and Andrea Gillan seem to have done their own bookkeeping, with an accountant preparing the annual accounts. The books are all in a decent shape – on the surface at least – so it's not been difficult to make sense of them. We've had good access to everything we need.'

'And?'

'It's mostly straightforward. Makes a pleasant change, actually. We're usually dealing with the types who go out of their way to make their business dealings as impenetrable as possible. Nest of companies within company, usually ending up registered in some offshore tax haven. Nice to be faced with a set of relatively straightforward company accounts.'

'But you've found something interesting?'

'Looks like it. On the face of it, everything ties up nicely. Orders, money in, money out, all neatly recorded and consistent.'

'But?'

'What intrigued me was the sheer volume of orders they took. There are two or three strands to their agricultural business. The agricultural supplies stuff looks largely above board, as far as I can tell. They bought in bulk products, took a turn on them, and sold them on to local farmers. But the biggest part of their business was equipment hire. Everything from small stuff to combine harvesters and the like. Farmers hire what they need across the various seasons, so there's careful planning and juggling of resources at the busy times. Ultimately, the size of the business is limited by supply and demand. Demand because obviously there's a limited, if relatively large pool of customers in their catchment area, who tend to want the same equipment at more or less the same time. Supply because there are limits on how much equipment it's feasible to own. At the top end, we're talking big expensive machines. That's a costly investment if the equipment's not used to capacity. One of the challenges for the Gillans would have been to ensure they had enough equipment to meet demand, but not so much it was standing idle more than they could afford.'

McKay had been engaged in his familiar prowl around the office, carrying his coffee mug with him, but now sat himself down opposite Kincraig. 'This is all fascinating stuff, Wally. I don't know if you've ever considered writing a column in the *Farmers' Weekly*. I'm just not clear how it links to the Gillans' deaths.'

Kincraig grinned. 'Keep listening then. Like I say, it was the volume of orders that caught my eye. Orders for vehicle hire. I couldn't square it with the inventory of equipment that the Gillans owned. They couldn't have fulfilled the order book.'

'Could they have sub-hired equipment from someone else?'

'That was something I considered. But there's no record of it. And obviously that would have involved a significant outflow of cash.'

'So how did they work this magic?'

'The simple answer is that they didn't. There's no way they could have. Everything looks fine on paper. There are orders, invoices, payments received, all the right paperwork. It's just that there's nothing of substance behind it.'

'You're sure about this?'

'Pretty sure. It's still early days and it's not easy to make everything tie up, so we'll need to pin down the detail. But I'm confident the broad picture's correct. My guess is that it's inflated the company's turnover by at least 100 per cent. In other words, their business on paper is twice as large as it is in reality.'

McKay was uncharacteristically motionless for a moment, trying to make sense of what Kincraig had just told him. 'So what about the orders? Where do they come from?'

'I've done some checks. As far as I've discovered so far, they're all genuine companies in the sense that they're all registered with Companies House, but most of them have nothing to do with the agricultural business or farming.'

'So the orders...?'

'Are fakes. Not even particularly convincing fakes if you look at them carefully. But until now no one's had any reason to do so.'

'Not even their accountant?'

'Not really. He's an accountant, not a farmer. They presented him with a stack of documents, and he just took them at face value. It obviously never occurred to him to make the calculation that I did, even though it was staring him in the face if he'd known anything about the nitty-gritty of the business. If I'm honest, it only occurred to me because my dad was a farmer and I remember all the fuss there used to be about getting hold of equipment at the peak times.'

'So let me get this straight. The Gillans were creating fake orders. For work that never happened. And they then issued an invoice. That was paid.'

'That's about the long and short of it, yes.'

'So who did they issue the invoice to? Sorry if I'm being dense.'

'The invoices weren't issued. Not really. They were

prepared and recorded in the system. But not sent to anyone. Not in the form they appear in the books anyway.'

'So who paid them?'

'That's the question, isn't it? The Gillans obviously took a lot out of the business financially. Not so much that it would have been suspicious if the turnover figures had been legit to start with. But more than seems consistent with their lifestyle. I've not had a chance to work through the bank details yet, but my guess is that when I do the picture will quickly get muddier than any of their tractors. It's clear they moved substantial sums out of their own domestic accounts, but we don't yet know where that money ended up.'

'So what are we talking? Money laundering?'

'I'd guess so. All smartly done. On a relatively large scale, but not so much that it would attract the attention of anyone who didn't understand the nature of the business. As far as I've been able to tell so far, they paid the tax that was due at each stage, including corporation tax, VAT, PAYE and NIC. They didn't use anything beyond the usual accountant's tricks to avoid tax, so there was no reason for the Revenue to notice anything. Pretty much a model business, except that half of it was fake.'

'What about the car-hire business?'

'I've only scraped the surface of that so far. But it looks like it might be a similar picture. Smaller scale, but possibly even more of it faked. It's easier with private hire because most of the bookings are domestic customers. The orders are mostly made informally, the payments by card or bank transfer. Invoices are issued to individuals so there's no company detail. But again, just from a superficial look, the volume of orders doesn't square with their available cars. It's also a pretty seasonal business up here. The volumes are normally highest in the summer months, but they somehow managed to keep their vehicle utilisation up even during the off-peak months.'

'So who's behind this?'

'Give me a break, Alec. We've managed to come up with this in a few days. Don't expect miracles.'

'Aye, they take a little longer. I know. But there can't be too many contenders up in this neck of the woods.'

'You'd think not. Though maybe it doesn't have its origins up here.'

'What about Paul Dawson? You had a chance to look at his accounts yet?'

'Not yet. Ginny's put us in contact with his accountant, who's agreed to let us have what he's got and we're getting anything relevant sent up from his house. We're still waiting on authorisation to access his bank accounts. I've had a look at the published accounts. He was obviously doing well for himself. Maybe a bit too well compared to his lifestyle.'

'So it could be a similar picture?'

'Could be. Consultancies potentially give you a lot of scope. Theoretically, like the hire stuff, they're limited by volume. A consultant can only work so many hours in the day, so you're limited by how many consultants you've got available. And, just like tractors, you can't afford to have them sitting around not working for too much of the time.'

'I'm sure those smart-suited buggers they've got sniffing round the force would love to hear you compare them to farm machinery.'

'At least you know what farm machinery's there for. But it's the same principle. You can get round it by sub-contracting, which is why so many business consultancies operate on an associate or body-shopping model. You have a core team to do the bulk of the work, but bring in freelance resource as you need it.'

'You're a mine of information, Wally. Some of it's even mildly interesting. And you think this might all be true of Dawson?'

'I think it's quite possible. He was doing bloody well for a one-man band, which makes me think there must be a number of associates working with him. Or, if the picture's the same as the Gillans, supposed associates. The other issue is fee-rates which can be – well, let's say highly flexible in that world. The top consultants can be charging a hell of a lot. If you were channelling money through the business, for whatever reason, you could conceal some of it just by using a premium fee-rate for some of that work.'

'But a figure like Dawson's going to be relatively small fry, presumably. We're not talking millions.'

'No, but we're not talking peanuts, either. If you had a few people like Dawson working for you, you could feed a lot through it unnoticed. Probably better than souvenir tat shops on Oxford Street or whatever.'

'We need to know the picture with regard to Dawson asap. If you're right, it would give us a connection between him and the Gillans, and this gives us a potential motive for the killings.'

'It doesn't tell us who's behind them, though.'

McKay picked up his now empty coffee mug and peered into its interior, as if hoping that it might magically refill. 'It doesn't, but it gets us closer.' He paused, thinking. 'You come across any references to an Archie Donaldson in the Gillan material? Business associate, something like that?'

'Not so far.' Kincraig frowned. 'Isn't that bastard inside?'

'Well and truly. Glenochil, last I heard.'

'Thought we'd broken up his businesses, good and proper.'

'We did largely. Or so we thought. The NCA were crawling all over it. They even succeeded in confiscating some of his assets under the Proceeds of Crime Act.'

'So why'd you mention him?'

'Because he was always a slippery bastard. And money laundering was one of his things. Not his only thing. He dealt in pretty much anything he could make some money from, whether it was drugs or human beings.'

'Sounds a lovely guy.'

'A real charmer. And skilled at keeping himself at arm's length from the worst of it, at least until the end. Then he met his match, but that's another story.'

'His daughter, wasn't it? The one we've never caught up with.'

'Aye, thanks for reminding me. We never confirmed whether she really was his daughter, but that's the assumption.'

'You think Donaldson might still be in business? From behind bars?'

'It's not unheard of, is it? I think we closed down most of his operations, and I suspect his daughter might have creamed off a few choice pieces for herself. At the time, I thought that was her primary motive, that she was trying to muscle in on his business. But we had another run-in with her a few months back, and I'm not sure that's really what drives her. The money's a means to an end. She's a sadistic bugger, and she's on some kind of bizarre, perverse moral crusade.'

'Crusade?'

'Against her dad and his associates. Against what they stood for. I could even sympathise with her if she didn't use such extreme techniques to make her point.'

Kincraig looked baffled now. 'I'm not sure I really follow.'

'That'll teach you to blind me with your accounting science. You ought to know by now that I can talk fluent shite better than anyone. Ignore me. I'm just blethering bollocks to myself.'

'No change there then.'

'Aye, so they tell me. But, seriously, thanks for all that, Wally. It takes us a big step forward.'

'I'll write up what we've got so far. We need to plug on with trying to track all the bank accounts linked to the Gillan business. Then I need to get on to Dawson. If you can persuade Brian Nightingale to push more resource in our direction, I don't reckon anyone here will object.'

'I'll see what I can do, though I suspect my influence in that direction is severely limited. I'm not sure I'm flavour of the month with DCI Nightingale.'

'I'm not sure who is,' Kincraig said. 'As far as I can see, he's mainly concerned with looking after himself.'

'Hush your mouth, Wally. I couldn't possibly comment. Right, I'd better leave you to it before one of us says something we might live to regret.' He paused at the door to the office and turned back. 'And if you do come across any reference to Archie Donaldson in connection with the Gillans or with Paul Dawson, let me know, eh?'

CHAPTER FORTY

McKay glanced at his watch as he left Kincraig's office. Still only 8.30. He was tempted to go along to Nightingale's office to pass on the information he'd just been given. Apart from anything else, he knew how much it would infuriate Nightingale if the intended purpose of the meeting – presumably to give McKay some sort of bollocking – became deflected by positive progress in the investigation.

As it turned out, Nightingale already had a visitor. Ginny Horton, presumably getting her own form of bollocking. He wondered about barging in anyway but decided that was unlikely to go down well with either party. He couldn't see Ginny's face but there was a redness to her neck which suggested some kind of emotion. From her stance, he suspected it was anger rather than anything more passive.

In a fair fight, Ginny was more than capable of looking after herself. The question was whether she could hold her own against someone as slippery as Brian Nightingale. Helena was right, he thought. It would pay McKay to bite his tongue if that meant he could stay around to keep an eye on Ginny.

When she emerged from Nightingale's office a few minutes

later, McKay kept his head down, tapping away on his computer as if he was doing something useful. From the corner of his eye, he watched as she threw herself down on to her seat and began banging away at her own computer. Her face was concealed behind the monitor, but he didn't have much doubt about her mood.

If she'd wanted to talk to him, she could have stopped by his desk as she'd returned to the office. On the other hand, he knew that Ginny wasn't one to seek sympathy if she thought she could cope on her own. She probably wanted a few minutes to recover her composure. Instead of approaching her desk directly, he left the office, headed for the kitchenette along the corridor, and made two coffees.

When he returned a few minutes later, she was still working away at her computer, tapping much more gently now. He slid one of the mugs of coffee towards her. 'Okay?'

She looked up. 'Been better, I guess.'

He pulled up a chair and sat down beside her desk. 'Feel free to tell me to bugger off,' he said cheerfully. 'People generally do.'

'No, I'm happy to talk. I've nothing to hide.'

'I saw you were in with Nightingale.'

'He called me in there. Gave me a real dressing-down.'

'For what?'

'Mainly for – in his words – abandoning him at the hotel. Failing to take him into the local office as we'd agreed. Reckoned that had embarrassed him with his contacts down there because he couldn't make the meetings he'd set up with them. Said it had impeded the investigation because it prevented him from setting up the liaison arrangements he'd intended. Oh, and he claimed I behaved unprofessionally when we visited Dawson's house the previous day. I supposedly made some sarcastic remarks and behaved in a way that made him look foolish in front of a colleague from another division.'

'I don't suppose he expressed any views about his own behaviour in the evening?'

'Funnily enough, he skated over all that. I wasn't sure it would be wise for me to raise it.'

'Maybe not. This is all bollocks, Gin.'

'Well, of course it is. That's not the point. A lot of it is my word against his – I bet his mates down south will have his back if it comes to it.'

'It's not your job to make sure he drags himself out of bed in the morning.'

'He'll just claim he wasn't late and that I didn't wait for him. If I complain about his behaviour in the restaurant, he'll claim I'm exaggerating.'

'There were witnesses.'

'I can't imagine the hotel would want to get involved in any complaint.'

'So what did Nightingale say exactly?'

'It was all "more in sorrow than anger" stuff, really. How he knows I'm a good conscientious officer but I've maybe picked up a few bad habits from those I've been working with...'

'Well, there's no denying that. I can only apologise, Gin.'

She finally gave him a smile. 'I was sorely tempted to punch him in the face.'

'I don't think that would have helped your cause.'

'I'd have felt better.'

'We'd all have felt better, but not a price worth paying. So how did he leave it?'

'That he's not going to take any formal action this time. He just wanted to give me an informal shot across the bows...'

'...Discourage you from making a complaint about him?'

'Obviously he didn't say that.'

McKay shrugged. 'Just don't take it to heart. Everyone knows he's an arse.'

'It's just infuriating that he'll probably not get called out on his bad behaviour. There are too many men like him in the force. Men who do whatever they like and bully their way through.'

'You're not wrong. Look, Gin, if Nightingale tries to pull any more of his strokes, let me know.'

'That's very sweet of you, Alec. But I don't need you or anyone else to protect me.'

'Perish the thought. You've always scared the hell out of me. That's not the point. You're young. You've a career to think about. A reputation to build. I'm just an old fart. Okay, not quite ready for the knacker's yard but I'm not going anywhere career-wise. If anyone needs to go down in a blaze of ignominy to bring Nightingale to his knees, I'd much rather it was me than you.'

'I'd rather it was neither of us. It's not needed, Alec. I can take care of Nightingale.'

'I'm sure you can. But if you need it, the offer's there.'

'Thanks, Alec. I won't need it, but the offer's appreciated.'

'Speaking of Nightingale, I need to see him myself.'

'You getting a bollocking too?'

'Aye, but we've scheduled that for later. I've got a bit of news for him. We may have our first breakthrough on this one.'

'Are you going to share with me?'

'Later. I'll share with Nightingale first. Don't want him to think I've not followed the protocols.'

'Heaven forbid.'

'No point in giving him any more ammunition than I can help. I'll leave you to it, Gin. But stay strong.'

CHAPTER FORTY-ONE

Nightingale was on the phone, so McKay tapped gently on the glass to announce his presence. Nightingale gestured furiously towards the phone as if McKay might not have previously noticed it.

He continued to smile and raised his hand to his mouth to mime asking Nightingale if he'd like a coffee. Nightingale ignored him, but McKay made his way along to the kitchenette. It was clearly going to be one of those days when he found himself repeatedly preparing coffee to help lubricate the wheels of his conversations.

He made two more coffees, deciding that Nightingale was probably the type who took both milk and sugar, and carried them back to Nightingale's office. Nightingale had finished his call, though his expression suggested he was no keener to see McKay. McKay raised the two mugs so Nightingale could see what he'd brought, and then, without waiting for Nightingale to respond, pushed open the door of the office.

'I told you to come at ten,' Nightingale said bluntly.

'So you did. And it's firmly in the diary. I thought you might

ALEX WALTERS

like a coffee.' McKay placed the mug gently on Nightingale's desk.

'What do you want?'

'I don't want anything. On the contrary, I come bearing good news.'

'Is that so? What sort of good news?'

'Our first break on the Gillan case.'

Nightingale looked more surprised by the news than McKay had expected. 'What sort of break?'

McKay outlined, as simply and clearly as he could, the gist of what Wally Kincraig had told him. 'So it looks as if the Gillans were involved in something shady.'

'Kincraig is sure about this, is he?'

'Seemed pretty sure. Obviously, it's early days and he hasn't started delving into the detail of the various accounts yet.'

'I don't want to go jumping the gun on this. Not until we're sure of our ground. The Gillans were solid middle-class types. We need to be confident we're right before we start accusing them of wrongdoing.'

'Kincraig seemed confident of the wrongdoing. In the scale and nature of it he's still following up. The same with Paul Dawson.'

'From what you've said, we've even less to go on in Dawson's case. We don't even have the detail of the accounts yet. Admittedly, there's not likely to be much public sympathy in his case, but even so...'

'I'm not suggesting we present any of this publicly yet, but it gives us a line to work on. Kincraig says they really need more resources over there so they can get things moving faster.'

'I bet he does. I was already wondering whether we really needed their support on this. The likes of Wally Kincraig don't come cheap.'

McKay took a breath. 'The point is that we have good

252

evidence the Gillans were engaged in dubious practices. It looks as if Dawson might have been involved in something similar. If nothing else, that gives us the possibility of a link between them. It also provides a potential motive for murder.'

'It doesn't explain why Dawson decided to kill the rest of his family, though.'

McKay hadn't expected Nightingale to be effusive about the news, but he had at least expected the development to be received with a degree of warmth. 'No, it doesn't explain that. But it casts a different light on the case. Maybe we're looking at something closer to organised crime than we'd assumed.'

'I hope not. As soon as they start hearing phrases like "money laundering" and "organised crime" we'll have the National Crime Agency on our backs. There'll be the whole of Gartcosh up here grabbing the glory before we can turn round.'

Nightingale did have a point there, McKay supposed. He wasn't personally too troubled about the NCA grabbing the glory, but he'd never found them the easiest to work with. They'd been involved in the Archie Donaldson case, and while they hadn't been an active hindrance McKay had never been entirely sure what value they'd added. 'Fair point. So for the moment we don't make a big stooshie about it. But it's an avenue I'd like to pursue. That's why I've come to talk to you about it.'

Nightingale took a mouthful of the coffee McKay had brought and grimaced. 'There's sugar in this.'

'I thought you took sugar.'

'Look, McKay, I might as well be blunt with you. I'm not sure I want you pursuing any avenues on this case. I'm not sure I want you on this case at all.'

McKay donned the blankest of his expressions. 'And I'm not sure I understand.'

'There's nothing to understand. I'm considering moving you off the investigation.'

'On to what?'

'It's a question of making the best use of all our available resources. I was thinking of having a word with Charlie Farrow, see what he's got on at the moment. He might need extra support.'

This largely confirmed that, for the moment at least, Nightingale was bluffing. McKay had transferred into Farrow's team on a previous occasion and it hadn't gone well. Farrow was now well and truly winding down to retirement and all he wanted was a quiet life. The last thing he'd be looking for was an opportunity to manage Alec McKay. 'I'm still not clear why you'd want to do this, Brian.'

'Because, Alec, you're a fucking pain in the fucking arse. I hope that's clear enough for you.'

'It's clear enough. But it's not really grounds for taking me off the inquiry. I've done a decent job.' McKay smiled genially. 'For example, covering your fucking arse when you decided to go AWOL to get pissed and try to grope Ginny.'

Nightingale blinked. 'What did you say?'

'Didn't I make myself clear enough to you? I thought I was speaking your language.'

'Is this intended as some kind of threat, McKay?'

'Threat? Heaven forbid. I don't make threats; promises, sometimes. But never threats.'

'If you want to get into some sort of fight with me, McKay, my promise is you'll lose. And lose badly.'

'I don't know what you mean. I was simply justifying why I should stay on the case. You'd already have been screwed without me. We both know that.' McKay's smile was unwavering. 'By the way, how's the phone signal today?'

Nightingale's mouth moved but no words emerged. Finally, he said, 'You've gone too far, McKay. As far as I'm concerned, you're history.'

'What's that thing they say? About history being written by the victors? But then there don't need to be any winners or losers, as long as we can just all get along. Isn't that right?'

'I can have you disciplined. You know that, don't you?'

'I imagine you can.' McKay leaned forward and the smile disappeared. 'I don't generally play dirty, Brian. Not if I can avoid it. It makes me feel... sullied. But when I do play dirty, I'm good at it. I've been having a few chats with mutual acquaintances down south. It sounds to me like you've got a problem. Maybe not a serious problem, just yet. But heading that way. Your behaviour with Ginny the other night was symptomatic of that.'

'You don't–'

'Oh I do. When I was trying to track you down the following morning, I ended up making a call to the hotel. I ended up talking to the manager who confirmed to me that a couple of the waiters had reported trouble with an inebriated guest the previous evening. He'd been surprised because the guest's booking had been made in the name of Police Scotland. I apologised on behalf of the force and said we'd look into it.'

'That's bollocks.'

McKay raised an eyebrow. 'Is it? I'm afraid I inadvertently recorded the call.'

'You're bluffing.'

'I'm not here to judge you, Brian. I reckon you've a problem and you need to get some help with it. It's not my place to compel you to do that. I know you've already caused some embarrassment back on your own patch, and it looks like you've been protected so far. I'm not sure why, though I have my suspicions. But I wouldn't be surprised if that's why you've been shipped up here. Get you out of their hair before you cause them further problems.'

'You don't know anything.'

'I don't know everything. Not yet. But I know enough.'

'What is it you want?'

'Me? I don't want anything. I just want to be allowed to get on with my job. Properly and unhindered. And I want Ginny to be allowed to do the same. I'm not interested in your squabbles, Brian. I'm not interested in you screwing over others to cover your own arse. I'm not even interested in helping you to deal with whatever demons you seem to be fighting. That's your business. I just want to do my job. Is that clear?'

'You'll come to regret this, McKay.'

'Maybe. But then I can just add it to the pile of other regrets I've accumulated in my life. In the meantime, just let me get on.'

'And what does that mean?'

'It means I stay on the investigation.' McKay paused, watching Nightingale's eyes. 'And it means I want to talk to Archie Donaldson.'

CHAPTER FORTY-TWO

B rian Nightingale hesitated for a moment at the entrance to the hotel restaurant then turned left into the bar. If he had to be stuck in this godforsaken place, he might as well enjoy himself. He wasn't in the best of moods. He'd been dwelling for most of the afternoon on his conversation with Alec McKay. McKay no doubt thought he had Nightingale over a barrel, but that just showed how little McKay really knew.

There was some truth in what McKay had said. Nightingale had allowed his own standards to slip a little too often in recent months. It wasn't that he had any kind of problem – he couldn't believe McKay had even had the nerve to suggest that – but he'd allowed his focus to drift. He'd been too casual in his approach.

But he was on safe ground. There were people watching his back. As long as he continued to be useful to them, they'd carry on doing so. That was why Nightingale was here in the first place. McKay might be a smartarse, but he had no idea what he was up against. Nightingale was quite happy to bide his time for the moment, give McKay enough rope.

The barman looked at him quizzically. 'Evening, sir. How are you doing tonight?'

Nightingale looked at him as if suspecting some unspoken agenda behind the question. 'I'm fine, thanks.' He gestured towards the one draught ale available. 'I'll have a pint of that, please. And I might treat myself to a single malt chaser.' He pointed to one of the Speyside whiskies lined up at the rear of the bar.

'Very good, sir.' The barman busied himself pulling the pint. 'Something to celebrate?'

'Just survival. Made it through another day.'

The barman slid the beer across the bar towards Nightingale, then drew a measure of whisky. 'Water, sir?'

'Just a couple of ice cubes.' Nightingale took a swallow of the beer. He paid with his personal credit card, then picked up the drinks and carried them to a table in the corner.

He ought to have been a bit smarter after he'd arrived up here. He should have realised what a hostile environment he was stepping into. Sure, he'd known he'd be looked after if it came to it. But he should have watched his own back more carefully. Now, he was having to play catch-up, giving McKay more leeway then he'd ideally like. But in the end that would be for the best. It would just give McKay the opportunity to make even more enemies.

The first warming sip of the whisky made Nightingale feel better, more in control. This was what he'd been needing all day. It took him only a few more minutes to finish both the rest of the whisky and the beer. He contemplated going straight into the restaurant but then, after a moment's hesitation, returned to the bar.

'Same again?'

As Nightingale nodded, he thought for a moment that the barman had raised a disapproving eyebrow and wondered about remonstrating with him. But the barman had already turned away to pour the whisky and Nightingale realised he was in danger of making a fool of himself. 'Thanks.'

'Are you dining with us tonight, sir?' the barman asked as he pulled the beer.

Nightingale nodded. Apart from his one night in the Borders, he'd eaten in the restaurant every evening since he'd arrived up here. That was probably another mistake. Yet another mediocre steak in a plastic room served by a surly waiter. After tonight, he'd make more of an effort, have a stroll into town to see what culinary delights it might offer. He didn't have high expectations, and he had no great desire to eat alone in a restaurant filled with happy families and couples, but it would offer a change from this mausoleum.

'Would you like me to reserve you a table, sir?'

Nightingale looked over at the restaurant. As far as he could see, there were no more than three people in the restaurant. All men, all eating alone. It didn't look as if they'd have too much difficulty squeezing him in without a booking. He took the barman's words as a not-too-subtle nudge that Nightingale perhaps shouldn't drink too much more without having something to eat. That, of course, was none of the barman's fucking business. On the other hand, Nightingale was forced to recognise there was some wisdom in this view. 'Yes, why not?'

'I'll book you in, sir. Half an hour or so?'

'Fine.'

It took him less than that to knock back the second round of beer and whisky. Maybe it wasn't wise to drink too much, but it was definitely making him feel better. The anger and frustration he'd been feeling immediately after his meeting with McKay had largely melted away. Even the bravado he'd felt when he'd first entered the bar was gradually being replaced by a firmer confidence in his own abilities. It wasn't the drink talking. The drink just allowed him to see himself more clearly, more objectively. He had a tendency to underestimate himself and his own abilities, hiding behind the support and protection he received from others. But they gave him that support and protection for a reason: because they appreciated his value to them.

In the restaurant, he ordered himself his usual garlic prawns and fillet steak. He knew neither would be anything more than mediocre. As on previous evenings, he ordered himself a bottle of red. The waitress nodded, though as with the barman he thought he detected some disapproval in her expression.

The food was largely as he'd expected, although the steak was perhaps a little more skilfully cooked than on previous evenings. Given his challenging day, he decided to treat himself to the restaurant's 'platter of local cheeses', giving him the opportunity to order another large glass of red wine.

The cheese was fine, if over-chilled, and did actually seem to comprise a selection of locally produced products rather than the plastic supermarket cheese he'd been half-expecting. The wine went down equally well and rather more quickly. He contemplated ordering another glass, but decided he'd rather return back to the bar. He rose to his feet, conscious he felt slightly less steady than he'd expected.

'Are you okay, sir?' The waitress paused from collecting the plate and looked up at him.

'I'm fine. Just felt slightly dizzy when I got up.'

Her expression was sceptical, but she offered no response. Nightingale made to move towards the entrance, stumbling slightly against her. 'Ach, sorry. Seem a bit clumsy tonight.'

'Perhaps you'd better sit down,' she said. He noticed there was no 'sir' this time. He made his way towards the restaurant entrance. He felt steadier now. He could tell that the waitress had thought he was slightly drunk, but he knew he was just tired after a long day.

The bar was empty, except for a couple of middle-aged men talking earnestly in one corner. A large television screen was silently showing a football match, although no one other than the barman was watching.

Nightingale lowered himself on to a stool at the bar and ordered a large Scotch, this time choosing a different malt from the one he'd drunk earlier. The barman seemed to hesitate slightly, but then turned and poured the drink. He added a few cubes of ice before placing the glass in front of Nightingale.

Nightingale stared at it for a second. 'Did I say I wanted ice?'

'No, sir, but I thought–'

'So why did you give me ice?'

'It was just that earlier–'

'But this isn't the same whisky, is it?'

'Well, no, but–'

'So why did you assume I wanted ice?' Nightingale wasn't even sure why he was making an issue of this. If the barman had asked him whether he wanted ice, he'd probably have said yes. It was just that he'd had enough of people thinking they could make a fool of him. Bloody Alec McKay playing the tough guy and trying to threaten him. All the bloody youngsters in this place smirking at him behind his back, as if he was some old lush who couldn't hold his drink.

'I'm sorry, sir. I can pour you another.'

'Don't bother. I'll manage with this.' He realised, as he sat sipping the whisky, that the exchange had achieved nothing except to make him feel mildly foolish. He finished the drink too quickly, then turned back to the barman, whose eyes were fixed on the television screen. 'Right, now you can pour me one without ice. If you can manage to tear yourself away from the TV.'

The barman looked at him and the disapproval was now

unconcealed. 'Are you sure, sir? It's just that you seem to have had rather a lot to drink already.'

Nightingale glared at him, his fury mounting. 'Are you saying you're not prepared to serve me?'

The barman hesitated, but clearly wasn't in the mood for a battle. 'Of course not, sir. I was just wondering–'

'It's not your job to bloody wonder, is it? Just like it's not your job to spend the evening watching bloody football. It's your job to serve me a drink when I bloody ask for one.'

'Sir–'

'Don't "sir" me. Just get me a bloody drink.'

'Of course. Would you like the same again?'

'Same again. No ice.'

The barman placed the drink in front of him. Nightingale said, 'This one should be on the house.'

'I'm afraid I can't do that, sir.'

'Who says you can't do that?'

'The rules say so, I'm afraid. I'm just not allowed to. I offered to replace your previous drink.'

'So what's the bloody difference? You'd presumably just have thrown it away. Or drunk it yourself. You can put this on the fucking house.'

'That's not the point, sir. I don't have the authority...'

'Don't tell me. It's more than your job's worth.' Nightingale was already telling himself not to push this any further. He could sense the barman was growing increasingly irritated, and that this was unlikely to end well.

'If you're dissatisfied, sir, perhaps the best thing is if I call the manager for you.'

Before Nightingale could object, the barman had walked to the far end of the bar to pick up a telephone. He spoke a few words too quietly for Nightingale to overhear, then walked back. 'He's just on his way, sir. I'm sure he'll be able to take care of you.'

The manager arrived a few moments later. He was scarcely older than the barman, but he looked unfazed by Nightingale's aggressive glare. 'Does there seem to be a problem, sir?'

Faced with the direct question, Nightingale struggled to find a response. His initial complaint about the ice seemed almost embarrassingly trivial. 'No, it's nothing. Just a misunderstanding about the drink I ordered.'

'I'm sorry to hear that, sir. It's just that we don't tolerate aggressive behaviour towards our staff.'

'Aggressive behaviour?'

'Daniel here tells me that you were being aggressive. That you swore at him.'

'It was just a misunderstanding, that's all. I was perhaps a little – forceful.' Nightingale found he was struggling to articulate the last word.

'If you don't mind me saying so, sir,' the manager said, 'I wonder if you've perhaps had a little too much to drink this evening.'

Nightingale stared at him. 'What?'

'We've all done it, sir. But it might be better if you were perhaps to call it a night now.'

Nightingale was aware that, remaining on the stool, he was allowing the manager literally to look down on him. He tried to push himself to his feet, but experienced the same dizziness he'd felt leaving the restaurant earlier. He steadied himself against the bar. 'I'm perfectly sober.'

'I'm afraid you don't seem so, sir. Perhaps I could get someone to assist you to your room?'

'I'm buggered if I'm going to let you put me to bed like some naughty schoolboy.' The sentence hadn't quite emerged as clearly as he'd intended, but he assumed the meaning was clear.

'In that case, sir, I'd suggest you make your own way to bed. I don't want to be forced to take any more formal action.'

'What the hell do you mean? Just you fucking well try it.' Nightingale jabbed his fingers towards the manager's chest. 'You just try it and you'll fucking well regret it.'

'Sir—'

Nightingale already knew he was making a big mistake. He was losing control of the situation and could see no easy way to drag himself back. His brain felt clouded, and he was struggling even to articulate the words he wanted to say. His body no longer felt quite under his control. He realised now, too late, that the effects of the two large whiskies, combined with the other drinks he'd consumed earlier, had crept up on him more quickly than he'd expected. It wasn't that he was drunk, he told himself, but he'd drunk a little too much to argue his position in the way he wanted. Even so, he couldn't see a dignified way to extricate himself. 'I'm telling you. Just don't fucking try it.'

He didn't know where things might have gone next if the couple hadn't appeared. He wasn't even sure where they'd come from. They hadn't been in the bar and he couldn't recall seeing them in the restaurant. Now they were standing just behind the manager.

They were probably in their late twenties or early thirties, dressed in the smart-casual gear he associated with plain-clothes cops. He wondered if they were people he'd met at the divisional HQ. Neither of their faces struck him as immediately familiar, but that might have just been his slightly woozy state. Certainly, they seemed to recognise him.

'Brian,' the woman said. 'Here you are. Sorry we're a bit late.'

The man grinned at the manager. 'Hope he's not been causing trouble. He likes to wind people up.'

The manager blinked. 'Well...'

'He doesn't mean a word of it. Are you ready to go, Brian? We're running a bit late.'

'Go?'

'Christ's sake, Brian. Don't say you've forgotten. It's a good job we came to find you rather than leaving you to your own devices. You'd still be sitting in the bar while we were all out painting the town red.'

Nightingale had no idea what was going on. Was this some sort of joke being played by his new colleagues? Or had there been some sort of invitation he'd missed? He supposed it didn't really matter. It gave him an opportunity to extricate himself from the mess he'd got himself into here. It might even give him the chance to have a few more drinks, possibly at someone else's expense. 'Where are we going?'

'Just into the city centre. Couple of places we know. You can stay as long as you want to, and bail out if you think you've had enough.'

That settled it for him. However this might have happened, it gave him the exit route he needed, and he wasn't committing himself to anything except possibly more drinks. 'Sounds perfect,' he said. 'Lead on.'

CHAPTER FORTY-THREE

McKay had found himself a small meeting room well away from the major investigation offices and, more to the point, well away from anywhere Brian Nightingale was likely to be. He was pushing things to the limit and taking a risk by doing so, but he'd reached the point where he didn't much care.

When Nightingale had, with obvious reluctance, agreed that McKay could make contact with Archie Donaldson, he'd done so on the basis that McKay kept him fully informed. 'As far as I'm concerned, Alec, this is a wild fucking goose chase. Even if you're right about the Gillans and Paul Dawson being involved in something dodgy, we've no evidence that Donaldson's involved.'

'Copper's gut, that's all. And Donaldson's the sort who'd have his ear to the ground.'

'To be honest, Alec, I don't much care what you do. But I want you to keep me up to speed. No fucking surprises.' He'd paused. 'And you don't fool me, McKay. This is more about Donaldson's daughter than Donaldson, isn't it?'

McKay had done his wide-eyed innocent act, knowing he

was fooling no one. Nightingale clearly wasn't quite as dim as he might appear. 'Daughter? How'd you mean?'

'One of your few recent failures, Alec. Involved in multiple murders, and yet she skipped out of your hands with no trouble at all. Some people might even find that a touch suspicious.'

'Aye. And some people don't have two brain cells to rub together.'

McKay had wanted more than a telephone conversation with Donaldson, not least because he wanted to see for himself how Donaldson might react to McKay's questions. He'd assumed he might have to trek all the way down to the prison, but the pandemic lockdown had clearly motivated the Scottish Prison Service to embrace the benefits of technology. After a brief conversation with the governor, McKay had agreed that the easiest and most efficient approach would be to conduct the interview online. McKay had booked the session for 10am.

He supposed he ought to be keeping Nightingale informed about this arrangement, but some instinct told him that it would be better to go ahead with the meeting first. As it turned out, when he'd made a half-hearted attempt to track down Nightingale earlier, there'd been no sign of him. Maybe another heavy night. It gave McKay the excuse he needed, anyway. And it was obviously just coincidence that he was conducting the session in a meeting room that Nightingale was unlikely to be aware of.

He sat himself down in the small room and booted up the laptop, wondering how he ought to play this. The last time he'd seen Archie Donaldson, other than in court, had been on that bleak morning in the dump of a hotel Donaldson had owned. Donaldson had always tried to keep at arm's length from the more sordid elements of the businesses he owned, but it had all caught up with him. And it was his daughter, the woman who had been styling herself Ruby Jewell, who had ultimately brought him down.

The truth was that McKay didn't really know why he wanted this meeting with Donaldson. Money laundering had been a big part of Donaldson's activities, but the man had been inside for more than a year and they had no evidence that any parts of his business were still operational. McKay had no reason at all to connect him with the Gillan or Dawson killings, other than perhaps his own, not entirely rational obsession with Jewell and her current whereabouts. Nightingale had been right about one thing. Jewell had given them all the slip, and McKay didn't like that.

On the dot of ten, McKay dialled in as he'd been instructed to be greeted by the amiable face of Chief Officer Malcolm Benedict, a bald-headed barrel of a man who wished him a cheerful good morning. 'Technology all seems to be up and running. If you have any problems, we've got our tech guy on standby, but we're all getting used to working like this now. Usually goes smoothly.'

'Thanks, Malcolm. And thanks to you and your colleagues for organising this. Much appreciated. I've just got a few questions I'd like to ask Mr Donaldson in connection with a current investigation. Hope it won't take too long.'

Benedict nodded. 'No worries.' He turned, leaned forward and moved the laptop so Donaldson's face became visible. 'All yours.'

Donaldson's appearance shocked McKay. When McKay had last seen him standing in the courtroom, he'd appeared a solid, robust figure. Worn down by everything that had happened to him, no doubt, with new worry-lines etched into his face. But he'd had the air of a man intending to bounce back. At the time, McKay had had little doubt that Donaldson would do so. That type generally did. He was given a lengthy sentence, commensurate with the scale of his crimes, but he'd be out eventually. McKay suspected that, despite the best efforts of the NCA and the Revenue, some aspects of Donaldson's business empire would continue to tick away somewhere. Eventually, he'd be back, still mysteriously self-sufficient, and it would all start again. With men like Donaldson, that was just how the game worked.

But perhaps not in this case. The man on the screen in front of McKay looked like the shadow of the person he'd previously been. He'd lost considerable weight, but the result was to leave him looking gaunt, pale and unhealthy. His hair was lank and thinning, and his eyes lacked the energy and spark that had once characterised his manner.

'Good morning, Archie. You don't mind if I call you Archie?'

Donaldson grunted. 'Long as I get to call you Alec.'

'Knock yourself out. How are you this morning?'

'Shite. And don't bother telling me I look well, because then I'll know you're talking bollocks.'

'I wasn't going to,' McKay said. 'You look like you feel. Shite.'

'Aye, well, that's maybe not so surprising.'

'That right?'

'You'd look and feel like shite if they'd given you six months to live.'

This was news to McKay. No one had thought to mention the fact to him when he'd called to set up the meeting the previous day. 'Sorry to hear that, Archie.'

'Not as sorry as I was, I'm guessing.'

'Probably not. What's the cause?'

'The big C. All the smoking years catching up with me. The docs are still debating whether there's more they can do, so the prognosis isn't certain yet. But I'm assuming the worst.'

'Aye, well, fingers crossed then, Archie.'

'I know I'll be in your prayers, Alec.'

'Always, Archie. Always.'

'So how can I help you today, Alec? I'm assuming you've not set all this up just to enquire about my health.'

'Sadly, no. I've got a few things I'd like to discuss with you, Archie. I want to test you out on a few names.'

'Fire away.'

'Do the names Craig and Andrea Gillan mean anything to you?'

Even before Donaldson spoke, his eyes had answered McKay's question. There was something about the way they'd blinked and narrowed that told McKay both that his question had taken Donaldson by surprise, and that the names did indeed have some significance. 'Should they?'

'That's the question. They're business people like yourself. Or they were.'

Yet again, McKay spotted another half-concealed tell in Donaldson's expression. McKay would have been hard-pressed to explain what he'd seen, but he had little doubt that, for a second time, Donaldson had been surprised.

'Were?'

'Were. It hasn't reached the news yet, even if you get to hear it in there. But they're both dead.'

This time, Donaldson's expression gave nothing away. He'd perhaps realised that, one way or another, he'd already revealed too much. 'I'm sorry to hear that. Or I might be if I had a fucking clue who they were.'

McKay heard Benedict say something, presumably admonishing Donaldson for the bad language. 'You're sure you've had no dealings with them, Archie?' McKay had brought with him a small pile of printouts. They were nothing more than pages he'd printed randomly from the files of an unconnected recent case. He picked them up and riffled through them, as if searching for a particular reference. Then he stopped, ran his finger along a couple of arbitrary lines, and looked up at Donaldson. Donaldson had no idea what documents McKay might be consulting. 'No business dealings?'

'Not that I can recall. But I've had dealings with a lot of people over the years. I couldn't swear to it.'

'No, I can see that.' McKay picked up the papers again as if to check the reference. 'Must be difficult to remember everything. Perhaps even quite major things. Especially when you've other problems to be worrying about. Let's put that aside for a second, then. What about the name Paul Dawson? Does that mean anything to you?'

This time Donaldson seemed less surprised. 'Aye. Because we do in fact get to hear the news in here.'

'Always good to be well informed.'

'Dawson's that bastard who killed his wife and kiddies, isn't he?'

McKay was always struck by the hierarchy criminals constructed to justify their own crimes. Donaldson had been involved in people trafficking and human slavery, but, in his head, that was presumably a lesser crime than killing your wife and family. It wasn't a point McKay felt inclined to debate in either direction. 'That's the one. You've seen his picture on the news, then?'

'I guess so.'

'But you didn't know him?'

'How would I have known him?'

'He was in business, just as you were.'

'You might be surprised to learn that I'm not acquainted with everyone in business, Alec.'

McKay had picked up the papers again and was toying idly with them. Donaldson had hardly looked a picture of joy at the start of the interview, but he was now increasingly anxious. 'No, well. And I'm guessing the old memory's not what it was. You've a lot on your mind at the moment. I feel almost guilty for having to bring this up.'

'I don't know what game you're playing, Alec. But those names mean nothing to me.'

'If you say so, Archie. By the way, how's that daughter of yours doing?'

'Daughter?'

'What was it she was calling herself? Ruby Jewell? Quite a name. But then quite a character.'

'As far as I'm concerned she's not my daughter. And how the hell would I know how she's doing? She's the last person I want to see, and I'm guessing the feeling would be mutual.'

McKay decided it was time to try his hand and push Donaldson harder. 'We've reason to think that Jewell, or whatever she's now calling herself, may be linked to the deaths of Craig and Andrea Gillan, and possibly to the deaths of the Dawsons. Would that surprise you?'

This time McKay was left in no doubt that his words had struck home. Donaldson offered no immediate response, but his face had told McKay all he needed to know. Before Donaldson could speak, McKay continued, 'Look, Archie. You've told me you're not a well man. Six months to live, maybe a little more, maybe a little less. Six months that you'll spend in the delightful confines of Glenochil Prison. And in the meantime Jewell, your own daughter, is out there laughing at you. She's killed three people who were still contributing to your business. Money being siphoned in your direction by people who'd remained undetected by the National Crime Agency or HMRC. Presumably your intended pension pot.'

'I've no idea what you're talking about,' Donaldson said, but any remaining spark had gone from his voice.

'I wouldn't be surprised if you've lost a few more from your clandestine network over the last year or so, Archie. A few other unexplained deaths that have gradually squeezed the cash flow out there. Am I wrong?'

'I don't know what you're talking about.'

'Aye, just keep up that line, Archie. It's very convincing. The question is are you happy to let Jewell just keep laughing while she destroys what's left of your life?'

Donaldson leaned forward. 'There's nothing left of my life. That's the point. There's nothing left to destroy. I'm dying.'

'Not quite yet. And there's the possibility of release on compassionate grounds. I imagine the authorities would look more favourably on that if you'd been co-operative on other matters. You might even get out before Jewell destroys what little's left of your old empire. Have a few bob left to end your life in comfort.'

'What is it you want from me, McKay?'

'What I want, Archie, is for you to do something you've probably never done before.' McKay smiled. 'I want you to tell me the truth. The truth. The whole truth. And nothing but the truth. To coin a phrase.'

CHAPTER FORTY-FOUR

I sla stopped in the doorway and peered out into the gloom, swearing gently under her breath.

It had been bound to happen, but she wished it hadn't happened so dramatically. Sunny weather never lasted for long up here. A day or two of sunshine would seduce you into thinking the forecast was set fair for the foreseeable future, and then the next day would turn out like this. Leaden skies, endlessly pouring rain, a chill eastern wind. It felt as if the summer had finally ended and a dour autumn had arrived.

Not that Isla normally cared too much. She and Ginny hadn't moved here for the climate, and she was generally content whatever the external environment might be throwing at her. Just at the moment, though, she felt as if what she wanted more than anything was just to get out of the office.

She'd wondered, that morning, whether it might be better to force herself to work from home. It wouldn't have been ideal – she had meetings today which couldn't easily be postponed – but she was conscious that, after the experiences with her brother and then with the parcel, she was looking for an excuse not to be alone in the house. She didn't like that feeling. She wanted the house to be a refuge for her and Ginny, not somewhere she felt fearful to spend her time. She'd have preferred to overcome her anxiety, force herself through it. Convince herself she was safe.

It was Ginny who'd persuaded her otherwise. She reminded Isla that the teddy bear in the parcel suggested that there must be some link between Tristram and the deaths of the Gillans. The link might be perfectly innocent, but until they knew for sure they shouldn't take any unnecessary risks. For the moment, it was better Isla didn't spend time alone in the house if she could help it. She added that they were starting to make progress in the investigation, so she was hopeful they'd have some answers before long.

Isla hadn't been convinced by the last point, but she'd accepted the sense in what Ginny was saying. She'd come to the office as usual, forcing herself to focus on the detail of her work, trying to ignore the distractions otherwise filling her brain. It had more or less worked. The anxieties had faded and she'd found herself settling back into the familiar work routine. The meetings so far had been tiresome and protracted, but had produced the required outcomes.

By lunchtime, though, she was troubled by a minor but nagging headache, a thickness behind her eyes. It was partly that she hadn't slept well the previous night, but it was also the result of forcing her brain to disregard the emotions troubling her. All that, combined with the over-bright lighting in the office and the relentless drumming of the rain on the skylights above the meeting room had left her feeling desperate for air.

But the sight of the pounding rain on the road outside had caused her to hesitate. Even the short trek to the retail park opposite would leave her soaked. She paused for a moment, then, holding her umbrella close over her head, decided to make a run for it.

Her judgement had been correct. By the time she'd crossed the main road and jogged across the car park, the rain had soaked even into her heavy waterproof jacket. It had insinuated itself inside her clothing, dripping uncomfortably down her neck and back. Even so, she felt invigorated by her run through the rain, as if she'd thrown herself physically back into the real world.

She bought herself a sandwich and a drink and headed back out to the car park. The rain showed no sign of lessening, and she had no option but to repeat her first rain-soaked run. She raised her umbrella and was about to step out when the car pulled up opposite the supermarket entrance. The front passenger window was lowered and, from inside, a voice called, 'Hey, sis. Do you need a lift?'

Bloody Tristram. He has an instinct for this, she thought. Almost as if he could home in on the moment when she was at a disadvantage and actually needed some help. The moment when she was least likely to turn him away. Her instincts were telling her just to ignore him, to turn and walk back into the supermarket. But that would seem churlish and ungrateful, or at least would be portrayed by Tristram as such.

She lowered the umbrella and walked over to where the car was waiting. She leaned and spoke into the car window. 'Don't worry. I'm only going over the road.'

She stepped back as the door was pushed open. 'That's fine.' This time it was a woman speaking. 'We can drop you round. It's no trouble. Save you getting any wetter. Hop in.'

Isla knew she'd already gone too far in engaging with these people. Now, without seeming rude, she couldn't see any easy way to extricate herself. 'Well, if you're sure...' She climbed into the rear seat of the car and looked around her. The driver was a woman she didn't recognise. Tristram was in the front seat, grinning widely.

Isle was already sensing something wrong, but the car was pulling away from the kerb. The driver turned into the car park, completed a circuit around the first line of parked cars, and then turned back out on to the main road. Tristram looked over his shoulder. 'If I were you, sis,' he said, 'I'd put on my seat belt. We've a little way to go.'

CHAPTER FORTY-FIVE

Chrissie McKay stared out at the landscape. The view was the main reason they'd bought this place. In other respects, it had been pretty much what they'd wanted – the right sort of size, a relatively new build and low maintenance, remote enough to be peaceful but not so much they were cut off from the world and Chrissie's friends. They'd seen a few places that more or less fitted that bill, but this place had all that, and a spectacular view out over Cromarty Firth.

Not today, though. Today, the rain had come in and the view was reduced to nothing but a grey haze. The normally imposing bulk of Ben Wyvis was invisible in the clouds, and the expanse of the firth was concealed beneath a blanket of mist. She could barely see beyond the end of the garden.

Chrissie didn't mind too much. It was one of the pleasures of living here. The view on a clear day could be breathtaking, but she'd also developed a delight in the way the weather and the climate could change. When they'd first moved here, she would simply sit at the window and watch the panorama change its character, sometimes even in the space of an hour. You could see the rain sweep in along the length of the firth, the mist encroaching across the waters. You could watch the tide creep out, leaving the face of the firth as still as a pond, reflecting the landscape around it.

As the seasons changed, she could sit in this spot and watch as the barley in the field below their garden was planted, sprouted, grew gradually to maturity, and was harvested, until the cycle started again. She could watch the leaves grow and thicken on the trees, turn in the autumn and fall as winter approached. She could watch the snows come and go on the mountains, feel the pounding of the wind and the rattling of the rain against their windows.

It had felt, in recent days, as if someone was intent on destroying hers and Alec's new-found happiness. Someone seemed intent on intruding into their idyll, raking up the unhappiness that had beset them in recent years. That thought had worried her. She knew she and Alec were making positive steps forward, but she also feared their current contentment might be fragile. She hadn't entirely come to grips with her own negative feelings, and she suspected that the same was true of Alec. That was the point, really. That was why they'd moved here. They needed to support each other in putting the past behind them and reaching out to the future. They could do it, but it wouldn't be easy.

The last thing they needed was some bastard deliberately trying to undermine what they were doing. Alec was probably right that it was just some low-life toerag who could be safely ignored, but in practice it wasn't that easy simply to move on.

She'd spent the afternoon working on a funding bid for one of the local community groups she'd become involved with. At this stage, it was, or should have been, a relatively straightforward task, collating data from various sources into one document. She'd been making good progress with it but this afternoon she'd been unable to concentrate. The words and numbers blurred in front of her as her mind flitted from one anxious topic to another. After a fruitless hour or so, she'd pushed the papers aside and headed into the kitchen to make a coffee. Since then, she'd been sitting staring out of the window, semi-hypnotised by the falling rain.

She was hoping that Alec wouldn't be too late home. He'd seemed in an odd mood that morning, both tense and excited. They were beginning to make progress, he'd told her, though as always he shared nothing of the detail. She knew that was how it ought to be but she sometimes wondered if it was good for him to have to keep his feelings to himself. She'd tried to call him earlier in the afternoon, mainly just to hear the sound of his voice, but his phone had cut to voicemail and she'd assumed he'd been tied up in meetings.

She was in this extended reverie when she was disturbed by the ringing of the front doorbell. She immediately tensed. Alec had told her to be careful in answering the door, advising her to check it was someone she knew before answering. It hadn't been advice she'd really needed, and they had very few visitors here. The postman was a familiar figure, and most of her friends wouldn't call without phoning first.

The doorbell rang a second time. She rose and made her way down to the hall. If she was careful, it was possible for her to gain a view of anyone at the front door from the kitchen window without being seen. She entered the kitchen and peered out. A young woman was standing by the front door, rain dripping from her hair. She looked soaked to the skin and deeply miserable, and no kind of threat. There was a car parked on the driveway behind her.

Chrissie returned to the hall and opened the front door, making sure she kept the chain in place. 'Yes?'

The young woman gazed at her anxiously. 'I'm really sorry

to disturb you. It's just that I've got a bit lost. I was just wondering if you could give me some help.'

'Where is it you're looking for?'

The woman gave her the name of a house. It was a name Chrissie vaguely recognised, though she couldn't immediately place it in the local vicinity. She'd spotted the name on a house somewhere in the surrounding backroads, but she couldn't immediately recall where. 'I'm sorry. It does ring a bell, but I can't remember where it is.'

'It must be somewhere nearby,' the woman said. 'We put the postcode into our satnav and it brought us to the bottom of your track.'

'I'm afraid the postcode covers half the village and a lot of the outlying houses,' Chrissie said. 'Satnav's not a lot of use once you get here. Do you have a contact number you could phone?'

'It was stupid of us, but I didn't think to ask for one. We're supposed to be collecting some items I bought from them online. We're already half an hour late, and they said they had to go out later.'

'I'm not really sure I can help you, I'm afraid. All I can suggest is you try some of the other neighbours. They might have a better idea than I do. We've not been living here all that long.'

'No one seems to be in. I imagine they're all at work.'

Chrissie was beginning to tire of the conversation. The woman seemed to be willing her to come up with some magical solution to her problem, but Chrissie didn't see how she could help. 'I'm not sure what else you can do, to be honest. Have you tried looking online? You might find the name on one of the mapping apps.'

'Perhaps you could have a word with Phil?' The woman gestured towards the car. 'I'm not very good at that sort of thing.'

Chrissie wasn't entirely sure what sort of thing the woman

had in mind. 'I'm not exactly a computer whizz myself. I just meant that if you have a phone–'

'It might be better to speak to Phil,' the woman said. 'I don't understand this sort of stuff. Bit of an airhead where technology's concerned.'

Chrissie looked at the woman in exasperation. She'd come across people like this before, hiding behind their own supposed ineptitude to avoid taking responsibility for anything. She also noted that Phil clearly had more sense than to expose himself to the pouring rain.

Even so, the last thing she wanted was to prolong this conversation. If it helped to move them along, perhaps it would be easiest for her to talk to Phil. She picked up the golfing-style umbrella they kept by the front door, and walked out to the car.

She was on the passenger side of the car and as she approached, the driver – presumably the mysterious Phil – pushed open the passenger door and leaned over to speak to her. 'Can you help us?'

She ducked her head into the interior of the car. 'I'm not sure I can. The house name does ring a vague bell, but I'm afraid I can't recall where I've seen it.'

'The satnav said it should be around here,' Phil said plaintively.

'I've just been explaining,' Chrissie said. 'Satnav's not much use out here. Have you tried looking at an online map? You might find the name on there.'

The man picked up a phone which had been sitting on top of the dashboard. 'That's a thought.' He pressed the screen, clearly going through the routine to open up an appropriate application.

Chrissie could feel the cold rain on her back, and she was growing stiff from bending awkwardly to peer into the car. 'Look, I'd probably better leave you to it. I need to be–'

Phil held the phone out towards her. 'Is that where we are?'

She peered at the screen, barely managing to suppress her frustration. 'No, that's the other end of the village. Hang on.' Sick of leaning into the car, she climbed in and sat in the passenger seat beside him, intending to show him the correct position on the map.

Almost immediately, she realised her mistake. As soon as she was sitting, the umbrella was snatched from her hand and the car door slammed behind her. She reached for the handle, but the door wouldn't open.

The rear door of the car opened and the woman climbed into the car behind her. The man had started the engine and, as soon as the rear door closed, he hit the accelerator and turned the car sharply round in the narrow driveway. A moment later, they were heading down the rough track at speed.

Chrissie opened her mouth to protest, but the man shot her a look that left her silenced. Behind her, the woman leaned forward over Chrissie's shoulder. 'If I were you,' she said, 'I'd put on my seat belt. We've a little way to go.'

CHAPTER FORTY-SIX

Helena Grant looked up at the tap on the door, half-expecting it to be Alec McKay. She hadn't seen him since their brief encounter the previous morning, and she'd expected he might want to share his subsequent experience of dealing with Brian Nightingale.

It was Mike Everly who poked his head around the already open door. 'Helena?'

'Come in.' She saw he was carrying the set of typed notes she'd dropped off with his secretary earlier. 'You can't have read those already.'

'I have actually.' He lowered himself on to the seat facing her desk. 'I wasn't really expecting this, to be honest.'

This, she presumed, was his cue for throwing her off the project. Despite his previous kind words, the notes would have exposed how shallow and ill-informed her views were.

'I just thought you'd read through the papers in advance of the meeting. You didn't have to produce this level of detail.'

'I'm sorry. I just started writing them to help get my own thoughts in order, and then I decided I might as well share them with you to check whether I've been thinking along the right lines. I'm sorry if...'

'No, don't be sorry. I just meant I didn't expect you to go to so much trouble. These are really excellent.'

'Really?'

'Absolutely. You've captured all the issues, and you've highlighted a number of points I hadn't spotted myself. It's very clear and concise, which is more than I can say for most of the material the consultants produce. In fact, I'm beginning to think that when we come to communicating the project outputs to staff we'd be better off issuing something like this rather than the kind of report they churn out.'

'It's all rather rough and ready.'

'It's all there, though. This is exactly what I hoped you'd bring to the group, Helena.'

'I'm just glad I'm on the right lines. This is all very new to me.'

'On the basis of this, I'd say you were a natural.' He paused. 'Look, Helena–'

She never found out what he'd been about to say next, because there was another tap on the door. This time, it really was McKay.

Everly looked slightly awkward, as if he'd been caught out in some misdemeanour. 'I'll leave you two to it. Thanks again for the notes, Helena.'

McKay gestured for Everly to stay seated. 'Actually, Mike, it was you I was looking for. I was wondering if you could spare me a few minutes.'

'Yes, of course. Do you want to go to my office?'

'It might be useful for Helena to hear what I've got to say. It certainly affects her.' McKay picked up a chair from the corner of the office and placed it beside Grant's desk, sitting himself next to Everly. 'I've just been talking to Archie Donaldson.'

Everly frowned. 'Isn't he inside? Helena and I were talking about the case the other day.'

'Well and truly inside. I was talking to him remotely.'

'I hope this isn't another instance of you going freelance, Alec. Brian's already expressed concerns about that.'

'Me? Not at all. I was speaking to Donaldson with Brian's full and express permission.' He paused. 'Although he might not have expected Donaldson to be quite as forthcoming as he turned out to be.'

'I'm not sure I understand.' Everly looked at Grant as if she might translate McKay's words into something more comprehensible.

'Donaldson's not a well man,' McKay said. 'In fact, he's a very unwell man. Cancer. They've given him six months.'

'I don't like to think of anyone suffering that,' Grant said. 'But I'd struggle to have too much sympathy for Donaldson.'

'In fairness, I don't think he's asking for it. But it is encouraging him to be more co-operative.'

'Hoping for compassionate release?' Everly said.

'No doubt. But there's another factor.'

'Go on.'

'It seems that, despite the best efforts of our friends in the NCA, Donaldson isn't quite as impoverished as we might have expected. Some aspects of his business have continued despite his incarceration. Notably, money laundering.'

'I think I'm seeing where this is going,' Grant said.

'Various people were on Donaldson's payroll,' McKay said. 'Very much at arm's length, you understand. Donaldson was always a master at keeping himself as far away as possible from the dirty work he was involved in. But, yes, among the people on Donaldson's payroll were Craig and Andrea Gillan and Paul Dawson. He'd bailed both their businesses out in the past and they owed him, but they were also raking in a nice bonus on top of their legit operations.'

'So how does that provide a motive for their deaths?' Everly asked. 'There's presumably no benefit to Donaldson in having them killed.'

'Not Donaldson, no. On the contrary. But someone who wanted to destroy Donaldson's business interests.'

'Someone like Ruby Jewell, for example?' Grant said.

'Quite. When we first discovered what Jewell had been doing to her father's business, back before he went inside, I thought her motives were more business than personal. That she was looking to muscle in on his territory. There was some of that, but it's personal as well. She just wants to destroy him and anything he's associated with.'

'It sounds like she may not need to,' Grant said. 'Given what you've said about his health.'

'I said that to Donaldson. He laughed. As far as she's concerned, that'll just be the icing on the cake. She's destroyed him financially. The Fates will do the rest.'

Everly was looking increasingly uncomfortable. 'I'm not sure I understand, though. I thought Paul Dawson killed himself after killing the rest of his family. Where does Jewell fit into that? And how did she kill the Gillans? They were driving the car.'

'I asked Donaldson that. He didn't really have a clear answer. But he had no doubt that Jewell had been behind the deaths. Either she somehow forced them into those acts or she was somehow responsible for what seemed self-inflicted.'

'But we've no evidence for any of this?' Everly said. 'I mean, this could just be some yarn that Donaldson's spinning to show he's being co-operative.'

'It could be,' McKay conceded. 'And that's exactly the kind

of thing that Archie Donaldson might do. But there was one other titbit he fed me. Which is really why I wanted to talk to you, Mike.'

'What's that?'

'It's about Brian Nightingale,' McKay went on. 'Donaldson reckoned he had Nightingale on his payroll.'

'Brian? That's ridiculous. I've known him for years. He's got his faults, but he's not bent. That just proves that Donaldson's churning out a load of bollocks.'

'I'm just relaying what Donaldson told me. And he told me he'd be able to provide evidence.'

'He's just bullshitting.' Everly turned to McKay. 'Unless this is you trying to stir up trouble?'

'Why would I do that?' McKay's face was, as so often, a picture of innocence.

'It's obvious there's no love lost between you and Brian. He's already raised complaints with me about you. There's every reason for you to try to bad-mouth him back.'

'Except it wasn't me bad-mouthing him. It was Archie Donaldson. The interview was recorded and there were witnesses present.'

'None of that would be admissible in court, Alec. It wasn't a formal interview.'

'I wasn't thinking about court. I was thinking about my own reputation. Some people seem inclined to question it.'

'Okay, then, suppose we go with this for the moment. What was it that Donaldson told you?'

'He told me Nightingale had been on his payroll for a long time, along with various other cops both up here and elsewhere in the force. We're not talking big money here, as far as I could tell, but occasional backhanders for information received, blind eyes turned, favours rendered. That kind of thing. Donaldson reckoned he had quite a coterie of officers in his heyday. Of course, a lot melted away when Donaldson was sent down and there was only a tiny hardcore left. Nightingale went back a long way and stayed loyal, not least because Donaldson had a lot of dirt on him.'

Everly gave a snort of disgust. 'This all sounds like utter bullshit, Alec. I can't believe you fell for it.'

'I haven't said I did. I'm just the messenger. But I think it's a message we need to listen to. A major villain is claiming that one of our officers is corrupt, and tells us he can provide evidence. I think we have a duty to investigate, don't you? I think professional standards need to be informed as a starting point.'

As she watched McKay, Helena Grant realised why he'd wanted to have this conversation with Everly in her presence. He'd been concerned Everly would want to brush it under the carpet. She could tell from Everly's expression that he didn't want the hassle; he didn't want to face the reputational can of worms this kind of investigation would open up. 'I think Alec's right. We can't just ignore it. We have to put it on a formal footing.'

Everly stared at her for a moment, his expression suggesting that he was more disappointed by her response than by McKay's opinions. *Maybe it turns out I'm not senior management material after all,* she thought. *Perhaps I lack the requisite discretion gene.*

'It's not as simple as that,' Everly said, as if to confirm her thoughts. 'This kind of thing can just blow up in your face. It can expose all kinds of issues. I'm not disagreeing that we need to take action. But we need to handle it sensitively.'

McKay's expression had turned to one of mild disgust. 'And how do you propose we do that?'

'Well, perhaps we should see what Brian has to say?'

McKay exchanged a glance with Grant. 'You're suggesting we speak to Nightingale before we make this formal? Tip him off, as it were.'

Everly glared at McKay. 'I don't like that kind of language. It's prejudging Brian's guilt. We're not "tipping him off". We're just giving him the chance to hear the accusations that have been made.'

'With respect, Mike,' Grant said quietly, 'I don't think that's how standards would see it. If there are accusations of criminality or misconduct being directed at Brian, they'd want him suspended immediately so that an independent inquiry could be carried out.'

Everly's anger hadn't reduced, but it was clear he was struggling to muster an argument. 'Okay. But we know how these things go once standards get involved. Even if Brian is ultimately cleared, the stigma stays with him. No smoke without fire. I don't want to destroy a man's career on the word of someone like Donaldson.'

'We all understand that,' Grant said. 'But I don't think there's an alternative.'

'As far as I'm concerned there isn't,' McKay said. 'I don't want you to take this the wrong way, Mike, but I actually don't much care what you think. I've no desire to screw over my own career to protect the likes of Brian Nightingale. Whatever you might want to do, I'm going to raise this formally with standards.'

'You might not want to screw over your own career, Alec, but I reckon you're going the right way to making it happen. If you go around making enemies, sooner or later someone's going to want to bring you down.'

'I don't know what you mean, Mike. Everybody loves me. It's my sunny disposition and winning charm.'

Everly had risen to his feet and was towering over McKay. 'You're a fucking smartarse, McKay. That's all. One day you'll pay for it.' He turned back to Grant. 'I'm sorry for the language, Helena. But you're maybe better off not associating too much with this guy. You've still got a future ahead of you. Or at least you have if you make the right decisions.'

CHAPTER FORTY-SEVEN

After Everly had left, McKay rose and closed the door gently behind him. 'Sorry if I've ruined your prospects, Hel.'

She laughed. 'If my prospects really do depend on not doing the right thing, I'd rather not have any. Mike'll calm down. He must know you're right. Although next time maybe try to be a bit less provocative in the way you point it out? Just a little management tip for the future.'

'Aye, I'll bear it in mind.'

'You really think Nightingale's bent?'

'Well, it wouldn't be too surprising, would it? We already know he's got a few skeletons in his closet. He's something of a piss artist. It's exactly the kind of background which means you get compromised. And he always seems to have a few quid to splash around. Ginny reckoned when they were staying down in the Borders, he was sticking the booze on his personal account because he knew he wouldn't be able to swing it through expenses.'

'That doesn't prove much. Our only witness is that paragon

of honesty and good faith, Archie Donaldson, a convicted human trafficker, drug dealer and all-round villain.'

'I reckon Donaldson's spilling whatever he can now. He puts on the usual big brave face, but he's scared shitless. Donaldson's always seen himself as invulnerable. He was the big man, keeping himself distanced from the shite that made him rich. Even when that all came tumbling down and he ended up inside, I don't think he believed it. I visited him during his early days inside. He seemed as arrogant and bumptious as ever. He knew the NCA and the Revenue would extract whatever they could, but he thought he was smarter. I suspect he was right. In other circumstances, he'd have been more than capable of bouncing back. But now that's not going to happen.'

'Cancer can be beaten.'

'Of course. And he trotted out some stuff about there still being options the doctors can try. But that just sounded like bravado. I could see in his eyes he felt defeated. He doesn't believe he's going to survive. He just wants to make the best of the time he's got left.'

'And that involves spilling the beans to us?'

'He's got two motives. Partly, it's just about coming clean, wanting to get stuff off his chest. I'm prepared to believe he's genuine about that. But Everly's right. It's also that he wants to get compassionate leave. He's been a model prisoner and now he's bending over backwards to assist us. It'll no doubt all count in his favour when he comes to make his request.'

'Which doesn't necessarily mean he's not spinning us a load of nonsense.' She frowned. 'Why bring up Nightingale with you anyway? Why did he think you'd be interested in some Glasgow-based DCI?'

'Because he knows Nightingale's been working up here. I wasn't going to say it to Everly, but that was one of the details that made me think Donaldson was telling the truth. How would he have known that if he wasn't privy to what Nightingale was doing. But there's more to it than that. He reckoned Nightingale was brought up here specifically because the Gillans and Dawson were connected to Donaldson. In other words, someone didn't want us to start looking into this without being suitably supervised. Nightingale's role was clearly to stop us digging too deeply, or maybe to deflect us if we started digging in the wrong places. By which I mean the right places.'

'So do we think Donaldson was directly behind that?'

'My guess is not. I think it's more likely someone who didn't want us to start looking at Donaldson's business in case we uncovered dirt closer to home. If Donaldson's had Nightingale in his pocket, he's probably not the only one down south. They could have a lot to hide.'

'I'm beginning to understand why Mike was reluctant to open this particular can of worms. You don't know who might be involved.'

'If I was watching from the outside, I'd be ordering in the popcorn,' McKay agreed. 'As it is, I just want to make sure I'm not the one being consumed.'

McKay had stayed remarkably still while they'd been talking, as if his usual restlessness had somehow been sublimated into what he was saying. Now, finally, he resumed his roaming. 'There were a few other things Donaldson told me.'

'What sort of things?'

'Mainly about our friend, Ruby Jewell. He really believes she's the devil incarnate.'

'He's not far wrong.'

'I'm not going to disagree. Especially after what they tried to do to you. She's a very special kind of psychopath, even if she generally does get someone else to do her dirty work for her. She's a chip off the old block in that sense too.'

'So what did he tell you?'

'That she's still around. Still up here. She never left.'

'If it was anyone else, I wouldn't believe it. We had a full-scale search going on for her for months. Her picture's been all over the media. She and that associate of hers have been on the force's most wanted list all that time. I don't see how they've evaded us. Except we know that's what she does. But how does Donaldson know that?'

'Because she's been taunting some of the people who are still part of Donaldson's network. Periodic letters, phone calls, texts. Letting them know she's there, and that she's coming for them.'

'And I don't suppose any of them chose to report this to us?'

'What do you think? Jewell might scare the hell out of them, but anyone who's an associate of Donaldson isn't going to seek our help. But it sounds like she's being playing with them for months. Ginny found a picture in Dawson's mail. I had to look at it over and over again, but I'm pretty sure it was Jewell. That was sent just a few days before Dawson killed his family and himself.'

'So what's this all about? Just crushing her father?'

'That's a big part of it. But it feels like there's something more now. Why's she stayed up here?'

'Because she likes screwing around with us?'

'That's another part of it, certainly. She's run rings round us from the start. We've managed to stall her at one or two points, but she's always been at least a step ahead of us. The whole thing's a game to her, and it's a game she's bloody good at playing. But now it feels like something more. It feels as if she's building up to something.'

'Does she know Donaldson's dying?'

'The obvious answer is that she can't possibly know. Donaldson told me he's tried to keep the news under wraps. In his words, as soon as you're seen as dispensable, you become dispensable. When you lose authority, it's gone for good.'

'Quite the philosopher, isn't he?'

'He's right, though. His condition's not widely known in the prison, so it's hard to see how it could be known outside. Except...'

'Except we're talking about Ruby Jewell.'

'Quite. So that might be a factor. Or it might be something else. If she is behind what's been happening, it seems very personal. The packages sent to our houses – mine, yours, Ginny's.' He paused. 'That's another thing I discovered this morning. Spoke to forensics to see if they had anything more on the items in the packages.'

'And?'

'They've found DNA on all of them. DNA that matches the Dawson children.'

'Shit.'

'Not only that. They've also found minute traces of blood. A fine spattering. A pattern that would be consistent with the items being present when the Dawsons were killed. Even that poor bloody hamster.'

'But how could they have been removed...?'

'Unless someone had been back in there after the killings? They couldn't.'

'You're suggesting Jewell or someone returned there before the bodies were discovered?'

'We can't be sure. There could be other explanations for the presence of the blood. Forensics can't yet give a precise view on how old it is and there could be other explanations for the patterning. But it seems likely. And there's something else. The teddy bear that was sent to Ginny and Isla. That's the same. The DNA and the blood patterning. So it looks as if that could have been in the room too. That's even more intriguing. The bear looked very much like one Isla had as a child – if not the toy itself, then a copy of it. She thought her brother was behind it.'

'Her brother? Where does he fit into this?'

'It's a long story. Her brother's the black sheep of the family and Isla had cut him out of her life, but he's recently turned up again.'

'So what does that mean? That he's part of Jewell's coterie.'

'Your guess is as good as mine. Jewell does seem to have a knack for getting people to do her bidding. Maybe the teddy bear was just a coincidence, but it doesn't seem likely. But if not, and if the bear was in that room with the Dawsons, it raises a hell of a lot of questions.'

'And we don't have any forensic evidence that places Jewell in that room?'

'Who knows? We've never had the opportunity to take a DNA sample from Jewell. We've never even had her fingerprints. We tried to find prints when she went missing that first time, but she'd made sure she left nothing behind. Again, she's always been a step ahead. There are plenty of DNA traces in that room, some of which belongs to third parties, but nothing we've been able to tie to any nominal.' McKay had wandered over to the window and was watching with apparent fascination the rain battering the glass. 'Any progress we've made has been because she's wanted us to.' He turned. 'Speaking of which, I've made one other discovery this morning.'

'You've been busy.'

'Mostly on the back of my discussion with Donaldson. But this was something else. I wanted to follow up with the young woman I'd spoken to at the Gillans' car-hire place. I'd tried to phone the place but there'd been no answer, so I asked Josh Carlisle to pop out there to check what was going on. The place was closed and locked up, and it seemed as if it had been for a day or two. There was a pile of mail inside the door.'

'Not surprising, surely. I imagine your young woman had decided that with the Gillans gone there wasn't likely to be a job for her. She's probably just done a bunk.'

'That was what I thought, though I know the people in the commercial hire place are keeping it ticking over till the future of the business becomes clearer. But the young woman, Morag, had also given us a home address and mobile. I'd already tried her mobile which just went to voicemail, so Josh went to check out the address. Turns out it's a fake. Or, rather, a real address but not one where our Morag has ever lived.'

'So Morag wasn't Morag?'

'Apparently not.' McKay had returned from the window and once again sat down opposite Grant. 'And, embarrassing as it is to admit it, I think we can guess exactly who she was.'

CHAPTER FORTY-EIGHT

O n his way back from Helena Grant's office, McKay made a detour into the professional standards unit, hoping to have an informal chat with the DCI in charge of the local office. Despite his words to Everly, McKay felt uncomfortable about registering formal concerns about Nightingale. It wasn't that he had any time for Nightingale himself. It was just that exposing any fellow officer to the rigours of standards felt almost like a professional betrayal. Whatever the outcome, it would be an unpleasant and intrusive process that would potentially leave more officers than just Nightingale tainted.

But even putting aside his own feelings about Nightingale, McKay couldn't see he had much choice. Donaldson had made accusations about Nightingale, and McKay would be remiss if he failed to act on those accusations. He couldn't brush them under the carpet even if he'd wanted to, especially as he'd now discussed them with both Everly and Grant. He didn't have an excuse to delay taking action. But he did want to ensure he did everything by the book. The sensitivities he could leave to the experts.

As it turned out, the DCI in standards was tied up in a

lengthy meeting, and the rest of the team were similarly unavailable. McKay told the receptionist he needed to talk to someone as a matter of urgency, and she booked him in for the first available slot later that afternoon.

McKay had wondered whether Everly might take the opportunity to warn Nightingale what was coming, although he guessed Everly would have more sense. Whatever other qualities he might or might not possess, Everly was likely to be skilled at protecting his own backside. After the conversation with McKay and Grant, he wasn't likely to do anything that might compromise his own position. In any case, there seemed to be no sign of Nightingale. His office was empty, and it looked as if he hadn't yet turned up that morning. Maybe the heavy nights had finally caught up with him.

Ginny Horton was talking earnestly on the phone, but otherwise the main office was almost empty, with most of the team out and about dealing with whatever activities had been allocated to them. For the moment, the investigation was continuing along the same track, an established routine of interviews, data gathering and analysis. McKay hadn't yet thrown his own recent discoveries into the mix, and he was contemplating how best to do that. He had no issues with sharing the hard data – the news about the Gillans' finances, about the forensic analysis of the items in the packages, or about the disappearance of the mysterious Morag. All of those were straightforward factual developments which needed to be incorporated into their approach. He was less clear about how to present his discussion with Archie Donaldson – even putting aside the accusations about Brian Nightingale. Much of that still felt speculative and anecdotal, and McKay was aware that his own growing obsession with Ruby Jewell risked clouding his own judgement. These were decisions he needed to make before that afternoon's briefing meeting.

He was already feeling profoundly wrong-footed. Was it really possible he'd sat and talked to Ruby Jewell in the car-hire office with no inkling it was her? When he'd raised the possibility with Helena Grant, she'd dismissed it as absurd. 'Look, Alec, I share your views about her. She's a very dangerous woman. But she's not superhuman. It's just not possible you wouldn't have recognised her.'

McKay remained unsure. There had been no reason for him to expect to see Jewell there, and no reason for him to question that Morag was who she claimed to be. The woman who called herself Morag looked nothing like the woman he'd originally met in Donaldson's offices a couple of years before. But he recognised that the differences could be little more than superficial – a dramatic change in hairstyle, in clothing, in make-up. It probably wouldn't take a great deal.

If it had been Jewell in there, what was she up to? Had she been working there legitimately for some time, presumably under a false name, to gain the Gillans' trust or to gather information about their lives and routines? Or had she only placed herself in there after the Gillans' deaths to confuse the police about how and when the deaths had occurred. Their only real information about the Gillans' final movements had come from a single source – the mysterious Morag who had claimed that Andrea Gillan had been in the office on the Friday morning. The Gillans' neighbour had seen the BMW in the Gillans' drive and had seen it depart, but had not seen who was inside the car.

Their information about the ultimate fate of the BMW had come from the evidence of the equally mysterious young man Ginny Horton had interviewed by Loch Morlich. The man who might or might not have been spotted in the company of a young woman in the background of the news report from the site of the Dawsons' death.

McKay wasn't even sure whether any of this really mattered. It didn't materially change the fact or even the nature of the Dawsons' or Gillans' deaths. It just confused the timescales. But it felt as if a narrative had been deliberately constructed to create a false impression. They had assumed that one or both of the Gillans had visited the Dawsons on that fateful Friday afternoon, but they had no real evidence for that. Perhaps someone had wanted to ensure the police made the connection between the two sets of deaths.

Or, more likely, McKay thought, perhaps someone has simply been playing with them, sending them in ever more confusing directions, generating more and more confusion as they worked towards some unknown endgame. And, as he'd said to Helena, it was feeling increasingly personal, as if they were all being drawn inexorably into some spider's web.

McKay was conscious he was in danger of losing all perspective. This wasn't the way he worked. He'd never been one for puzzles or game-playing. He was bright enough, but his intelligence had always been of the straightforward kind. His skill was generally in stripping away the bullshit, getting to the nitty-gritty of whatever he was dealing with. Tearing apart the lies and obfuscation that surrounded most crimes. But this – and it had been true of all his dealings with Ruby Jewell – was something different. It was as if her primary motivation was simply to manipulate, to create doubt, to ensure others were dancing to her evermore confusing music. Any other agenda – revenge, money – seemed almost secondary to that.

He sat down at his desk, rubbing his temples, trying to clear the fog surrounding his brain. He was relieved to see Ginny Horton had finished her call and was walking across the office towards him. More than anything, he needed to talk all this through with someone like her. Someone sharp and clear-headed, someone prepared to tell him he was just talking bollocks.

But as she approached he saw the expression on her face and the words he'd been intending to say dried in his throat. 'What is it, Gin?'

'I need to pop out for a short time. Just home and back.'

'Problem?'

'I don't know. It's weird. I've just had a call from Isla's office. I can't understand it. They're saying she went out for a sandwich at about twelve but she hasn't come back. I've been trying her mobile but no response.'

McKay glanced up at the clock on the office wall. Nearly three. 'Maybe she met up with someone and went for lunch?'

'You've met Isla, Alec. Does she strike you as someone who'd just pop out of work for a three-hour casual lunch without bothering to let anyone know? Especially when she had back-to-back client meetings scheduled for the afternoon.'

'But you think she might have gone home for some reason?'

'I can't come up with anywhere else. I've just tried the Raigmore in case she had an accident, but they've no record so far of anyone who fits the bill.'

'There'll be some straightforward explanation, Gin–' He stopped as Horton's phone buzzed in her hand and her expression shifted from anxiety to relief.

'It's a text from her. Looks like you're right as always...' She trailed off and her expression changed again, this time to puzzlement. 'Alec, I think you'd better have a look at this.'

McKay took the phone from her. The text was a series of images. The first was a wide shot of a badly lit room containing a row of beds. The beds were nothing more than cheap wooden frames, each holding a thin bare mattress. There were bodies lying on a number of the mattresses, but in the first shot they were unrecognisable. The second image was a close-up of one of the beds. The figure lying on the bed, staring up at the camera and clearly terrified, was Isla. McKay flicked to the next image and stopped, his breath caught in his throat.

It was a similar shot; a similar frightened figure, eyes fixed on the camera.

Chrissie.

McKay looked up at Horton. 'What the hell is this?'

'It's been sent from Isla's number. Do you think they're real?'

McKay skimmed through the remaining images. There were only two more, both again showing individuals lying on the beds. The first, curled up awkwardly as if trying to evade an impending blow, was Brian Nightingale. The final figure, a man who looked to be in his early thirties, was unknown to McKay. He realised now that all four individuals had been secured to the bed frames with plastic ties. He flicked back again the image of Chrissie, hoping against hope that it had somehow been mocked up. To McKay's eyes it looked real enough, but he was no expert.

He pulled out his own phone and, thumbing through the list of recent callers, he dialled Chrissie's number. It rang for a few seconds and for a moment he thought it was going to cut to voicemail. But then suddenly a voice said, 'DI McKay. You were quicker than I expected. I assume you've seen our photographs by now.'

McKay forced himself to keep his voice calm, biting back the words he wanted to scream down the phone. 'What is this?'

'We thought you might like some photographs. As a souvenir, perhaps.'

It was a woman's voice, but beyond that he had no idea of the speaker's identity. It could be Ruby Jewell in one of the identities he'd encountered her. But then, he thought, it could be almost anyone. There was a strange anonymity to the tone. If he were asked to describe it subsequently he'd be unable to identify it as anything distinctive. 'A souvenir of what?'

'Of the occasion. Something to remember it by.' He had the sense that the speaker was silently laughing at him. 'You could also perhaps treat it as an invitation.'

'An invitation? To what?'

'A farewell party. But a warning. When you do come, I'd prefer you to come by yourselves. Just you, DS Horton and perhaps DCI Grant as well, if she'd like to attend. I know what a happy little family you all are. One other thing. You might want to consult with Chief Superintendent Everly, and let him know that DCI Nightingale is already here. He'd be most welcome to join us.'

'I don't–'

But the call had already been ended. He redialled the number but received an 'unobtainable' message. He looked up at Horton. 'You heard that?'

She nodded, her face ashen. 'Nice to issue us with an invitation. But how do we know where the hell they are? I mean, we can try to trace the phones but that takes time, even if the other phones are still operational.'

'We can set that in motion as a backup. But I don't think we need to. Those images aren't clear, but they show enough. She knew I'd recognise the place.'

'What do you think she's got planned?'

'Christ knows. But nothing good.' He took a breath, still forcing himself to remain calm. 'Right. Let's go and talk to Helena and Everly.'

CHAPTER FORTY-NINE

I n the end, they just took one car, the highest performance
  model available in the pool. McKay was driving. Helena
Grant sat beside him, Ginny Horton and Mike Everly in the
rear.

As McKay had expected, Everly had been the most difficult.
'I can't authorise an operation like this. Not without a proper
risk assessment and appropriate backup. It's more than my job's
worth.'

'I'm not asking you to authorise it,' McKay had explained
patiently. 'I'm asking you to come with us. You can claim we
kidnapped you if you like. I don't much care. And stickler as I
am for the rules, we don't have time for any risk assessment
bollocks. As for your job, Mike, with all due respect to you and
due deference to your exalted rank, I don't give a flying fuck
about it. I only care about my wife and Ginny's partner.'

Everly's mouth had opened, but he'd clearly struggled to
find anything appropriate to say. Finally, he offered, 'What
about backup?'

'You might have a point there. We can't turn up there mob-
handed. We don't know what she's got planned, and we don't

want to provoke her unnecessarily till we've got a clearer idea. But it would be wise to have some resources available nearby if we need them. She's not stupid. She'll realise we're not going into something like this empty-handed.'

McKay had half-expected Everly would still refuse to participate in the expedition. That prospect didn't much trouble him. In practice Everly was likely to be more of a liability than an asset. On the other hand, he'd clearly been included for a reason, and McKay was intrigued to know what that reason might be. In the end, Everly had said only, 'Okay. I'll organise that. I'll see you downstairs.' He paused. 'You really think this is Ruby Jewell?'

'I can't imagine anyone else pulling a stunt like this. She's clearly been building up to something. This feels like some kind of endgame.'

Everly had been silent for a moment. 'You were right about her, weren't you?'

'Was I?'

'Whoever she is, whatever she is, she's scary as hell.'

'Oh, yes. That. Aye, I was right.'

Five minutes later, they were in the car heading north on the A9. McKay had the blue lights and sirens going and floored the accelerator as they pulled away from the Longman roundabout across the Kessock Bridge. The rain was still hammering down, and he was conscious the roads might be treacherous, perhaps even flooded in places, particularly once they left the A9. He wanted to get there quickly, but he wanted to get there.

'You sure we're going to the right place?' Everly said from the back seat.

McKay didn't want to think about the question, but Everly was only articulating the anxiety in the back of his own mind. He was as sure as he could be that he was making the right judgement, but he couldn't be certain. 'We don't have any other options. We've got people trying to track the phones but no success so far. She assumed I'd know where to go, and I can't come up with any other likely options.'

He remembered the previous occasion when he'd made this journey. He'd been chasing Archie Donaldson, led on a pursuit that he later realised had been orchestrated by the woman he'd known as Ruby Jewell. At the time, it had felt like a conclusion, the resolution they'd been hoping for, spoiled only by Jewell's own elusiveness. She'd proved equally evasive in their last climactic encounter, when McKay had narrowly saved Helena Grant's life.

He realised now that those previous moments, dramatic as they had been, were nothing more than the endings of intermediate acts, steps Jewell had taken to bring them to what felt like a dénouement. He had no idea what was in her mind or how much she had really planned, but he had a sense that a destiny was being worked out tonight.

He reached the Tore roundabout and turned off towards Dingwall, just as he had on that previous occasion. He'd set the satnav before they'd set off but realised now he didn't need it. The route was imprinted on his brain, as if he'd made that journey only a few days before. He didn't even have to think about the point where he turned off the main road, or how to navigate the winding B-road that would ultimately lead to their destination.

He realised also that he'd ceased to worry that he'd made the right call in coming here. He had an increasing certainty that he was right. It felt almost as if he was being called, drawn here by some instinct outside his own control.

Even so, as he approached their destination his confidence faltered. The dark bulk of the building looked just as it had done the last time he'd been here, although the place appeared even more neglected and dilapidated than it had then. Despite the thickening gloom of the rain-soaked evening, the place was in darkness and there was no sign of human life.

McKay supposed that the absence of light was unsurprising. He'd asked Donaldson what had happened to the place after his arrest and conviction. It had been confiscated along with large parts of Donaldson's other property and assets, and attempts made to sell it, so far without success. McKay could understand that. A collapsing former hotel with a bad reputation wasn't likely to be much of a money-spinner.

But that presumably meant that the power and other utilities would have been disconnected. The place would be little more than an empty shell, with nothing but those rows of cheap beds to indicate its former role in Donaldson's sordid empire.

McKay drew the car to a halt into the area that had once been the hotel car park. 'This is the place.'

'Are you sure about this?' Everly said. 'It looks deserted.'

McKay twisted in his seat and glared at Everly. 'No, Mike, I'm not fucking sure. I'm working on nothing more than instinct, just like we all are. I'm praying I'm right. Do you have any better suggestions?'

'Come on,' Grant said. 'Let's go and take a look.'

As he opened the car door, McKay was buffeted by the rain, the wind roaring through the trees around them. He ducked his head, peering into the gloom.

It was only then that he knew he'd been right. He hadn't spotted her at first, standing in the shadow of the former hotel entrance. Even once he'd seen her, he couldn't say he recognised her. She was just a woman, probably in her mid-twenties. She bore no obvious resemblance to the Ruby Jewell he'd first met in Donaldson's office, or to the Morag he'd talked to in the car-hire showroom. She just seemed anonymous, a blank human canvas waiting for a personality to be projected on to it.

But he had no doubt it was her.

'Evening, Ruby,' he called to her against the pounding wind. 'Thank you for the invitation.'

CHAPTER FIFTY

McKay had intended to say more, but the young woman was no longer there. He took another step forward, his head still bowed against the teeming rain. In the shadow of the overhanging porch, the front doors of the building were standing open.

He glanced over his shoulder to see his colleagues gathering behind him. 'You think it's her?' Everly said.

'It must be.' McKay stepped into the porch. Beyond the doorway, the entrance lobby was lost in shadow, barely penetrated by the last of the daylight. McKay could hear only the rattle of the rain on the porch roof, the roar of the wind in the surrounding trees. 'Ruby?'

He felt mildly absurd calling her that. It wasn't her real name. It probably wasn't the name she was using now. It was just an identity she'd adopted briefly, slipping it around herself the way another person might pull on a jacket or coat. But it was how he thought of her, a means of pinning down the elusive personality that had so frequently slipped through his fingers over the past two years.

Holding his breath, as if entering a toxic environment,

McKay walked into the building. The last time he'd been here it had been thronged with people – uniforms and members of his own team, immigration officers, examiners, all dealing with the implications of what they had found here. The place looked as if it hadn't been touched since that day more than two years before. The room was unlit and thick with shadows.

McKay took another step forward, looking round for Ruby Jewell. The entrance hall was deserted, but his eyes followed the curve of the stairs to the upper floors. This would once have been an imposing place. A country house built for a self-made Edwardian businessman. Now it was nothing but a slowly collapsing shell.

Jewell was at the top of the stairs, at the edge of the first-floor landing. She said nothing, but turned and disappeared. She was leading the way, McKay thought, and as always there was nothing he could do but follow. He turned to the others. 'We don't know what we might be facing up there. Jewell has at least one accomplice and they're both potentially dangerous. We could be walking into some kind of trap. If we are, at least one of us should stay down here so we don't all get caught.'

'If Isla's up there, I want to come with you,' Horton said.

McKay nodded. 'Mike? Helena?'

'As the senior officer present, I ought to lead this. Helena should stay down here.'

Grant shook her head. 'Very gallant, Mike. But as the senior officer present, you should stay down here. If things go pear-shaped, we need someone to call in and co-ordinate the backup. Gold command and all that.'

McKay could see Everly was about to argue, but they didn't have time for that. And there was something else. Whatever they might encounter, McKay wanted to face it in the company of people he trusted. Everly might be a decent copper – McKay hadn't seen enough to judge – but McKay had been through experiences with Helena Grant and Ginny Horton that had created an inviolable level of trust between them. 'That seems sound to me. Mike, we're counting on you. If you see or hear anything that gives you cause for concern, bring in the backup straightaway. Otherwise, give us fifteen minutes. If nothing's happened by then, call them in anyway.'

Before Everly could argue, McKay began climbing the stairs, his eyes fixed on the point above him where he'd last sighted Ruby Jewell. There were three storeys to the building and the dormitory-style bedrooms which had once accommodated the victims of Donaldson's human-trafficking activities were on the top floor. As far as McKay could recall, the final stretch of stairs was steeper and narrower.

He looked back. Horton and Grant were just behind him. Everly was dutifully standing in the hallway below, gazing up anxiously. McKay climbed a few more steps, until his head was level with the first-floor landing, then paused, listening. He could still hear only the clattering of the rain against the windows and the periodic booming of the wind against the walls.

He reached the landing and looked around. The rooms on this floor had been guest rooms in the days when the building had been used as a hotel, and a corridor vanished into darkness ahead of him. He gazed up the next flight of stairs. He had to assume Jewell had continued up there, but he could see and hear nothing that betrayed her or anyone else's presence.

McKay waited until Grant and Horton had caught up with him, then signalled his intention to continue up to the third floor. At the foot of the stairs, he paused again, still listening intently. This time, he thought he heard something: the faintest of sounds from the floor above. Nothing more than the scuff of a foot along the floorboards.

It was barely light enough to see, even though McKay's

vision had adjusted to the gloom as he'd ascended the first flight of stairs. He could just about make out the dark bulk of an old cabinet on the landing above him, the paler rectangle of the doorway leading on to the upper floor.

He climbed slowly, trying to make no noise that would reveal his approach, until finally he could see through the doorway. The gloom up here was even more intense than the shadows on the lower floors, but he could see the two rows of beds stretching away from the doorway. At the end, waiting for him, was the young woman he thought of as Ruby Jewell.

He reached the top of the stairs. He could see now that the beds closest to Jewell were occupied by the figures he had last seen in the texted photographs – his own Chrissie, Isla Bennett, Brian Nightingale and the unknown young man. There was no sign, as far as McKay could see from the doorway, of the man who had been Jewell's accomplice. McKay stepped forward, alert for any possibility of an ambush.

Nothing happened. Jewell was watching him with a faint smile on her face. The individuals on the bed appeared conscious and unharmed, although all were now gagged. Chrissie was looking at him with an expression of relief that he hoped he'd be able to justify. Isla was looking past him at Ginny Horton with a similar expression. The faces of Nightingale and the young man were harder to interpret.

'What do I call you?' McKay asked. 'Ruby?'

'Why not? One of my livelier incarnations.'

'You're good at this, Ruby. You should have thought of a career on the stage.'

'This is much more fun. I have police officers at my beck and call.'

'Not my idea of fun, but each to his own. What's this all about, Ruby?'

She ignored his question. 'I could have gone on and on, you

know? Playing with you. Toying with you. Dismantling my father's business and financial interests. Helping others who had their own reasons for hating him. Taking my revenge.'

'That's what it was all about was it? Revenge on Archie Donaldson?'

'Mostly. That and the sheer joy of it. The pleasure of running rings round you and your colleagues.'

'We'd have caught up with you eventually.'

'You think so? Even though you sat and talked to me in the car-hire office without having an inkling who I was? And you were definitely one of the brighter ones. You came closer than most, and you stymied my plans on a couple of occasions. But don't fool yourself that I wasn't always a step ahead.'

'But you're here now.'

'Because I've chosen to be.'

'So why have you?'

The smile widened. 'It was when I heard about Donaldson's illness. I assume you know he's dying?'

'I'm wondering how you know.'

'I make it my business to know about him. But when I heard that, all the fun disappeared. The Fates have done my job for me. All his wealth, all his business interests – the little he still has left – are worthless to him. He's stuck in prison and he's dying. The best he can hope for is that he's allowed out at the end to suffer his last few painful days in freedom.'

'I can see you feel a lot of affection for him.'

'All I feel is slightly cheated. That I won't be able to play out all my games right to the end. There's plenty I could still do – plenty of his old associates I could continue to torment – but there's no point anymore. So I thought I should bring things to a close.'

McKay wanted to keep her talking. Mostly, this was because he wanted to buy himself time, have a chance to work out how to deal with this, how to extricate Chrissie, Isla and the others without risking any harm to them. But part of him simply wanted to understand Jewell, to comprehend what she had done and why she'd done it. 'And where do the Dawsons and the Gillans fit into this?'

He could see the grim amusement in her eyes. 'Small fry, really. I've been mopping up the dregs of Donaldson's former empire. Some of it your colleagues dealt with – it was entertaining to watch them confiscate his assets – but there was a lot they'd missed or just didn't bother with. It was a fraction of what he'd once had, but there was a sizeable amount still trickling through. Some of his former clients were content to continue to filter their money through his associates. He'd always been smart about that. He had a large network with apparently disconnected individuals dealing with relatively small amounts each. Small enough that they generally didn't come on to the radar of the Revenue or your colleagues, but the totality added up. Donaldson creamed off his share, and the remainder made its way home in cleaned up form. He'd intended it to be his pension once he finally emerged from prison, but I'd been working my way through the network, gradually finding ways of closing it down.'

'Were there other victims?'

'That's for you to find out. This was a national network. I used various methods to achieve my goals.'

'So why Dawson and the Gillans?'

'When I heard about Donaldson's condition, I thought it would be a nice touch to bring it back home. To his own territory. The Gillans had been close associates of his at one stage. Craig Gillan had been a farmer, and he'd made good use of the enforced labour Donaldson was able to provide. They'd sold up the farm some years back and moved into the hire stuff for an easier life, but they kept up the contacts with Donaldson and became part of the network.'

'And Dawson?'

'He was nothing, really. He'd worked for Donaldson years ago. He was notionally an HR manager in one of Donaldson's businesses but he developed a specific expertise in immigration issues. Which, given the nature of Donaldson's businesses, meant an expertise in where to procure fake documentation, work permits, that sort of stuff. That was the real service he provided, but it was all off the books, cash in hand. Donaldson had seen him as a potential protégé, someone he might have brought into a more senior role in the business. That was all kiboshed when Donaldson went down, but I thought it would be amusing to make him one of my final victims.'

'Are you saying you killed him and the Gillans?'

'In a manner of speaking. But you didn't miss anything. They killed themselves.'

'I'm not sure I understand.'

'No, you wouldn't. But it's one of my gifts, if you can call it that. I know how to destroy lives. I'd been working on Andrea Gillan for a while. I managed to get myself a summer job there – well, you met Morag, didn't you? Then I gradually worked on her. Drip by drip. Some of it straightforwardly psychological. Undermining her confidence and her self-esteem. She wouldn't even have realised I was doing it. But then she began to get anonymous communications that indicated that their criminal activities were being exposed and would soon be revealed to the authorities. Poor Andrea couldn't even confide in her husband because he was betraying her himself. She discovered he was having an affair and was preparing to set her, Andrea, as the scapegoat for their various dodgy dealings.' She laughed. 'She might have felt differently if she'd ever discovered who he was having the affair with.'

'You're saying you drove her to kill both of them? You couldn't have relied on that working.' It was a statement not a question, but McKay realised he wasn't sure he believed it.

'Probably not. It was just the most entertaining way of doing it. If it hadn't worked, I'd have found another way to deal with them.'

McKay found himself chilled by her dispassionate tone. 'What about Paul Dawson? You're not saying...'

'Oh, yes. That was an even longer game. I'd booked myself on to one of his residential programmes months before. Again, I lured him into having – well, first a one-night stand, then an affair. I worked on him gradually. He tried to end it, and I became an unstable, neurotic bunny boiler, threatening to break up his marriage and quite possibly harm his wife and children. I sent him pictures of us in the post – sometimes the two of us in compromising positions, sometimes with threatening messages, sometimes just pictures. He threatened to go to the police, but I let him know I'd learnt about his business dealings and said I'd expose him. I tightened and tightened the screw. Amusingly, he came up here on holiday partly to get away from me, buy himself some time. He didn't know I'd also started working on Andrea Gillan. The precise timing was accidental, but it worked out perfectly to muddy the waters. Dear old Andrea had actually sent me a suicide note explaining what she was about to do and where and when she was intending to do it. She saw me as a confidante, even though – or maybe because – I was the one who'd given her the means to do it.'

'I'm not sure I understand,' McKay said.

'I don't know what your smart pathologists will be able to do with their burnt-out bodies, but I'm sure they'll eventually find the traces of diamorphine. That was how Andrea killed Craig and herself. They were dead more than twenty-four hours before the car crash. We set up the crash with the two of them strapped up in the front, and then torched the car. I don't doubt your experts will be able to confirm that in due course, but I'd hoped that the fire damage would be enough at least to confuse the issue.' She seemed almost gleeful as she recounted the story. 'Andrea had wanted me to be the one to find the bodies, so she'd given me a set of house keys. We'd driven over there in the small hours of the Thursday night and moved the bodies into the boot of the BMW. Then I drove it to the Gillans' house on the Friday afternoon because Andrea had once told me she had a nosy neighbour who watched their every move. It just confused the timing on the Gillans' death.

'Finally, I drove up to see the Dawsons, turning up on their doorstep as the visitor from hell. Paul tried to pass me off as a business contact but it was obvious his wife wasn't fooled, and I said enough to both of them – about me, about Paul, about their marriage, about Paul's business dealings – to provoke the mother of all arguments after I'd left. I knew Paul was on the edge, but, to be honest, I hadn't expected it to work as well as it did.'

McKay felt a chill finger down his spine. 'As well as it did?'

'Pity about the wife and kids. But, you know, collateral damage.'

'Collateral damage?'

'It happens. It happened to the woman I thought of as my partner.' Jewell's partner in crime – and perhaps in other ways – had been killed in the grounds of this building while trying to attack Archie Donaldson two years before. It struck McKay that, for the first time since he'd met her, he could see genuine emotion in Jewell's expression. 'She died, and none of you bastards were able to prevent it. It probably never even occurred to you that I really cared about her. But I did. I've missed her every day since.'

There was nothing McKay could say. As far as he was concerned, the woman had simply been a psychopath who'd carried out Jewell's dirty work. He hadn't mourned her death at the time, and he'd find it hard to dredge up any sense of loss now. But he supposed that, for Jewell, that wasn't how it worked.

'That's why I organised this today,' Jewell went on. 'In part, I'm just tidying up the loose ends alongside my own farewell. But I also wanted you all to suffer. To suffer physically, but also to suffer emotionally. To see your own loved ones in danger and put you in a position where you have to choose. Your own life or those of the ones you love. With the risk that it might be both. I think it's a suitable punishment.'

'I don't understand. Punishment for what?'

'None of us is innocent. You know that. You and your wife here, for example, you killed your daughter.'

McKay forced himself not to react, not to allow Jewell the satisfaction of knowing how much she was twisting the knife. He glanced at Chrissie, but it was impossible to read her expression in the gloom. 'You've no idea what you're talking about.'

'Then DS Horton behind you. Allowing her stepfather to die without trying to rebuild a relationship with him.'

This is nonsense, McKay thought. A deliberate rewriting of the past to fit some deluded notion of morality that existed only in Jewell's head.

'And her partner, Isla Bennett here, rejecting her own brother, poisoning their parents against him, systematically denying him the inheritance that was rightfully his.'

McKay had expected some reaction from Isla to these words. But in fact it was the young man on the bed who jerked angrily at his binding, grunting muffled abuse at Jewell. It suddenly occurred to McKay that the young man must be Isla's brother. 'So why is he here too?'

'I can tell you that,' Helena Grant said from behind him. 'If that's Isla's brother, he was the man working with Jewell last year. He's the man I met as Bill Emsworth's supposed son. The one who left me to die with Emsworth.'

Jewell was smiling. 'He's just another loose end to be tidied up. Tristram had his own parental axes to grind and we've worked well together. He was another one who'd been well and truly screwed over by my father. I came across references to him when I was working in the office there. There was a lot of bad blood and it wasn't difficult to persuade him to help me.'

'Doing your dirty work, the same way your previous partner did?'

'Trist never really had the stomach for it, but broadly yes.'

'So why aren't the two of you skipping off into the sunset?'

'Like I say, just tidying up loose ends.'

McKay was still trying to work out where this was leading. If he kept Jewell talking, it wouldn't be long till Everly called in the backup. As it was, there were three of them blocking Jewell's escape. There was nowhere she could go. When the moment came, they'd simply arrest her.

Except that Jewell wasn't a fool and would be well aware of all that.

'And what about Brian Nightingale? Why's he here?'

'Every pack needs a joker,' she said. 'Brian was another one on my father's payroll. Still is, as far as I'm aware, which just proves Brian's happy to work for peanuts. The thing is, when Archie heard about the Gillans' and Dawsons' deaths, he twigged this was directed at him. He's already lost so much he didn't want to risk losing any more, and the last thing he wanted was for the authorities to start digging around in his affairs again. He made a few phone calls and arranged for Brian to take over the investigation. Apparently, Brian's seen as a valuable resource by some in the police   a man guaranteed to screw up any inquiry through his unique blend of ineptitude, laziness and drunkenness. He was brought up here to do precisely that.'

'But he didn't just turn up,' Helena Grant said. 'It must have all gone through official channels.'

Jewell nodded. 'Ah, yes. You're beginning to see now. And that would be official channels controlled by...?'

McKay turned momentarily and caught Grant's eye. She'd obviously realised at the same moment he had. 'Mike Everly,' he said.

That's right. The same Mike Everly you've left downstairs to call the cavalry on your behalf. I wasn't quite sure how that was going to play out, but I knew you wouldn't want to risk storming in here in numbers. And how long did you give him? Fifteen minutes? I'd say that's just about up.'

As she spoke, there was a deafening roar from the stairwell behind them, followed by a blast of hot air that buffeted them from behind.

'Perfect,' Ruby Jewell said. 'I'd say you have, at any optimistic scenario, perhaps three or four minutes before the stairs become utterly impassable. You need to make some decisions.'

CHAPTER FIFTY-ONE

McKay knew that, despite Ruby Jewell's tauntings, there was no time to make any kind of rational decision. He could already taste the acrid smoke in the air. There was no time for thought, only action.

He didn't even pause to tell Grant or Horton to save themselves. Whatever he said would make no difference to what they chose to do, and neither would rush to save themselves at the expense of others.

McKay fumbled in his pocket and found the Swiss Army knife he now always carried with him. He opened the knife blade as he ran across to Chrissie's bed and sliced through her ties. She stumbled awkwardly to her feet and McKay shouted, 'Just run. Head for the stairs. It's the only chance you've got.'

To his left, Jewell applauded mockingly, a game-show host congratulating a successful contestant. Ignoring her, he turned to Isla's bed and cut through her ties. Ginny Horton was on the far side of the bed, and she helped Isla to her feet. 'Go. Both of you. Now!'

He could see Ginny hesitate, but it was clear she understood the significance of McKay's words, and she turned and pulled Isla with her. McKay moved further along the room and cut the ties holding Tristram. Tristram jumped to his feet, and without hesitation made for the stairs. McKay could see a haze of smoke rising from the stairwell.

Finally, McKay turned to Nightingale and again cut the ties holding him to the bed. Nightingale looked scarcely capable of standing up. McKay took him by the arm and, half dragging and half supporting the other man, led him to the stairs. The air below was thick with smoke. At the head of the stairs, McKay turned back to Jewell, who had remained unmoving at the far end of the room. 'Come on. There's still a chance.'

'I don't want a chance. Not anymore. I'm done.'

McKay knew he had no choice. If he tried to take Jewell against her will, he'd risk losing the few precious seconds he had. As Jewell had said, he'd already made his decision. Or she'd made it for him.

He followed Nightingale down the stairs. The smoke was thickening. McKay pulled off his coat and held it over his nose and mouth. There'd been no time to remove the gags from those who'd been held prisoner, and McKay had no idea whether that would be a help or a hindrance in the circumstances. He reached the foot of the upper flight of stairs without incident, Nightingale just ahead of him.

The lower flight of stairs down to the ground floor turned at the middle landing, and McKay couldn't see what was happening on the ground floor. But a flickering orange light suggested fire was taking hold down there. There were five silhouetted figures on the stairs below – Chrissie, Ginny, Isla, Helena and Tristram, all making good progress. Nightingale still looked unsteady on his feet, and McKay wrapped his arm around him, trying to provide support as he dragged him further down the stairs.

As he turned the corner on the middle landing, McKay saw

that the fire was already raging at the rear of the entrance lobby, behind the reception desk. Even so, there seemed to be a clear run to the doors, still standing open to the rainy night. Below him, McKay saw first Chrissie then the others stumble across the room to the doors and out into the darkness.

Despite the relief sweeping through him, McKay forced himself to concentrate. Still supporting Nightingale, he made his way, more slowly and laboriously than he would have liked, across the room to the open doors. Behind him, the old reception desk exploded into flames, a line of fire running rapidly across the floor. There had been something in there, he thought, some accelerant.

It didn't matter. They'd all made it outside. Everyone, apart from Jewell herself, had escaped. The pouring rain and chill winds had never felt so welcome. McKay dragged Nightingale across to join Chrissie and the others standing at a safe distance from the burning hotel.

'Brian, pal,' McKay murmured as he finally released Nightingale to slump groggily against the car, 'when you're going through disciplinary hell in the coming months, I hope you'll spare a thought for the old bastard who made it possible for you to be there.'

CHAPTER FIFTY-TWO

Helena Grant stood a little way from the others, watching the scene impassively. Chrissie had thrown herself into McKay's arms as soon as he'd let go of Nightingale. Grant had expected all of them to show some visible signs of emotion, whether laughter or tears, but Chrissie had simply buried her head against her husband's shoulder and was holding him in silence. Isla and Ginny were clutching each other in a similar manner, as if seeking each other's reassurance that they'd made it out alive.

They were all in shock, Grant thought, none of them able to grasp what had just happened. Isla's brother was sitting on the grass, oblivious to the sodden ground, his eyes fixed on the flickering orange visible through the windows of the building. Nightingale was still slumped against the car, breathing heavily.

As she looked around, it occurred to her that Mike Everly was missing. She'd wondered, when Jewell had revealed Everly's role in protecting Donaldson, whether Everly might have been tempted to leave them to their fate, but he'd clearly called for backup as they'd agreed. The night was filling with sirens, pulsing with approaching blue lights. The first marked cars were drawing up on the roadside, and in the distance she could hear a fire engine.

She finally spotted Everly standing much closer to the now burning building than seemed sensible. He'd been out in the rain for much of the time they'd been inside, and he looked wet and cold.

'Mike,' she called. 'Come away from the building. It can't be safe there.'

He turned to her. 'She didn't come out. You left her in there. Young Maggie.'

'Maggie? You mean Ruby Jewell?'

'She was Maggie really. Maggie Donaldson. Though not even that, really. Why did you leave her?' His voice sounded odd, passion and emotion had been drained from it.

'We didn't want to. She had her chance, Mike. Just like the rest of us. She chose not to come. It was her decision.'

'But it can't just end like this. Not after all these years. Not after everything I've done. All the risks I've taken.'

'I don't understand, Mike.'

He looked back at the building. 'I've got to try to get her. I've got to have a go.'

'You can't, Mike. It's madness.' She gestured towards the glow from the window. 'Look at it in there.'

'I can't just leave her. Look, I'm soaking wet. If I can get through the smoke, I might have a chance.'

'It's insane, Mike. We don't even know how safe the building is now.'

He was already walking away from her, heading towards the front doors. 'I can't just leave her.'

'Mike–'

She had started to move after him, but he had already entered the building. She followed him towards the front doors. The flames had spread across the whole of the entrance hall and there was a line of fire blocking the stairway. She had thought, once he had seen the state of the fire, Everly might realise he was facing an impossible task and turn back. Instead, she saw him run through the wall of flames and then, apparently unharmed, scramble up the stairs.

There was nothing more she could do. Even from here, she could feel the heat of the fire and see it spreading slowly up the stairwell. She hurried back over to McKay. 'It's Mike. He's gone back inside.'

McKay stared at her over Chrissie's shoulder. 'He's done what?'

'Gone back inside. To try to rescue Ruby Jewell.'

'He'll never manage it. We gave her the opportunity to come with us, and she made her decision.'

'I told him all that. He was talking about Jewell as if he knew her, as if he'd protected her in the past.'

'But I thought–'

'That Everly was on Donaldson's payroll? That's what Jewell said. But she was never the most reliable of witnesses.' McKay looked over at the building. Flames were visible in all the ground-floor windows now. 'He's really gone back in there?'

'He managed to get through the entrance hall. The last I saw he was heading up the stairs.'

'Does he even know where to find her?' McKay shook his head. 'If I thought he had even a small chance of succeeding, I'd try to help him. But he hasn't got a prayer. It's just a suicide mission...' He paused. 'Maybe that's it. He can't believe he's likely to save her. Perhaps he knows he's just going to his death. Whatever his involvement with Donaldson and Jewell, he must know it's all going to come out now.'

He was interrupted by the noise of the fire engine entering the small car park. He and Grant stood back as the engine drew up in front of the building. As the fire officers bundled out of the vehicle, McKay stepped forward. 'There are two people still inside. One of our officers and a young woman. The woman had refused to leave. The officer went in to try to rescue her.'

'We'll do what we can. But I don't think there'll be much we can do until we've got the fire down here under control. Do you know how safe the building's likely to be?'

'No idea. It's been standing empty for a couple of years, and my guess is it was neglected for a long time before that. That's all I can tell you.'

'I'd suggest you stand well back now. We'll do what we can.'

McKay took the hint, and he led Chrissie back towards the edge of the car park, with the others following. 'That poor man,' Chrissie said. 'What made him go back inside?'

'I don't know,' McKay said. He exchanged a glance with Helena Grant. 'It seems it was something else we didn't know about Ruby Jewell or Maggie Donaldson or whoever she was.'

'Maybe they'll both make it out and be able to tell us.'

'Maybe,' McKay said. 'But somehow I've a feeling that, by the end, that wasn't what either of them wanted.'

CHAPTER FIFTY-THREE

'Should have had a cremation,' McKay whispered. 'Half the work's already been done.'

'Alec!' Helena Grant said. 'You can't say things like that. Disrespecting the dead.'

McKay looked round the church. 'Seems to me he's already being accorded more respect than he deserves. No one's had a bad word to say about the bugger so far.'

'What do you expect? *De mortuis nihil nisi bonum*, and all that.'

'I generally prefer *Illegitimi non carborundum*. Stands me in better stead at work.'

'It's a funeral, Alec. People don't generally use them as an opportunity to air their grievances.'

'It's not just that, though, is it? Seven people were killed. The Gillans and the Dawsons. Those three innocent kiddies. Now it's all going to get brushed under the carpet. Nightingale will get quietly pensioned off on medical grounds. Everly's conveniently dead. No one's going to start digging too deeply into what he might have been up to earlier in his career. Those two can't be the only ones. There must have been plenty of other bastards in on the deal. Yet it looks like the only person who'll face justice is Isla's brother, as an accomplice in the murders last year.'

'I'm not looking forward to being called as a witness in that. Poor Isla. And poor Ginny.'

'I'd say poor Tristram too. I reckon Jewell had a gift for getting people to do what she wanted. He was probably as much a victim as anyone. I don't think it was an accident that she picked someone close to Ginny. That's just the kind of game-playing Jewell would have loved.'

'Maybe Archie Donaldson will spill the beans in his final days. That would leave a few other people exposed.'

'I doubt it. I think some deal's being cooked up to allow him compassionate relief in return for keeping his mouth shut.'

McKay fell silent as the service finally started. He had no interest in following the service itself – McKay had never been one for the comforts of religion – but he took the opportunity to look around the church. The building was, as he'd expected, packed with mourners. Some of the great and the good were here, too. The chief constable, of course, and a senior representative of the Scottish Government, along with other dignitaries whom McKay half-recognised.

None of that was surprising. Everly had been a senior officer killed in the line of duty, while apparently performing a heroic act. The death of an officer on duty was, thankfully, a rare enough event in itself, and Everly's relative seniority was likely to attract even greater interest. In those circumstances, as Helena Grant had implied, no one was likely to be asking too many questions.

There would, inevitably, be an inquiry into the background to Everly's death. McKay had cynically commented that the investigation would no doubt focus on why Everly had been allowed to re-enter the building rather than one of his more junior colleagues offering themselves up for pointless sacrifice. But that was a problem for another day.

It had proved impossible to recover the bodies of Everly and Ruby Jewell until the fire crew had eventually succeeded in bringing the blaze under control. By that stage, the fire had already spread to the first floor, consuming most of the landing. There had followed a further delay while the structural safety of the building had been confirmed. Everly's body had been found on the first-floor landing, badly damaged by the flames. The assumption was that he had collapsed from smoke inhalation before even reaching the second floor. Ruby Jewell's body had been found, more or less where McKay and the others had last seen her, on the upper floor. She had also died of smoke asphyxiation, although her body had been untouched by the fire.

The post-mortems on the two bodies had revealed one further intriguing fact. Everly and Jewell had shared DNA. Everly, not Archie Donaldson, had been Ruby Jewell's father. That titbit of information had been passed on to them by Jacqui Green before – supposedly in the light of Everly's senior rank – the remainder of the investigation had been taken over by a team based out of Tulliallan.

'So what do we make of that?' Grant had asked.

'Explains a few things, maybe,' McKay had said. 'My guess is that, if we were in a position to delve a little deeper, we might find that Everly had been on Donaldson's payroll for a long time. Maybe got a little closer to Donaldson's wife than Donaldson realised.' He had paused. 'Or maybe Donaldson did realise. We know that Donaldson's wife died young and unexpectedly, but we've never had reason to check out the circumstances. And perhaps that was why Donaldson was so happy to offload his daughter at the earliest opportunity.'

'And what? Everly took care of her after that?'

'Maybe. Or maybe only when she reappeared at the time we arrested Donaldson. At that stage, Everly would have learned we were trying to track down Donaldson's daughter and perhaps put two and two together. That might be one reason we've had such difficulty finding her. Part of that was down to her own innate ability to reinvent herself, but I also wonder whether she was assisted by a few judicious interventions by Everly when he was down south.'

'You think that's possible?'

'I don't know. He talked to you about taking risks. I wouldn't be surprised if he engineered his move here after she reappeared last Christmas.' McKay had smiled. 'The funny thing is, I suspect she never even knew.'

'That Everly was her father or that he was trying to protect her?'

'Both. She gave us the impression Everly was working for Donaldson – which maybe he still was. I don't think she realised he was also working on her behalf.'

'This is all guesswork, Alec.'

He'd shrugged. 'That's all it's likely to remain. I don't think we'll be allowed anywhere near the case after this. Shame, because there are things I'd like to know.'

'Like what?'

'Like whether Jewell was really capable of talking people into killing themselves.'

'Why would she make it up?'

'Because she liked creating her own myth. That was why she set all this up. Putting on one last show to taunt her pursuers. Demonstrate she could do exactly what she liked. But the truth is she could have simply poisoned the Gillans. She could have knifed Paul Dawson and then proceeded to kill his wife and those poor kids in cold blood. We know from the objects in the packages that she was in the chalet after the murders had been committed. It looks as if she planted Isla's old teddy bear there to pick up the traces of blood and DNA. My guess is that she parked the car somewhere down in the village then walked back up. The question is, did she return just to pick up some souvenirs to send us or was that when she killed the Dawsons?'

'It's a horrible thought, either way.'

'It is. I've been thinking about Kevin, my brother-in-law. You remember he fell from the ramparts at Fort George. We thought he'd either taken his own life or been pushed. But maybe it was Jewell who talked him into jumping. She really was capable of anything.' He shrugged. 'Still, I don't suppose the likes of us will ever be allowed to know. All we can do is keep buggering on. Pity about your project work, though.'

'Maybe it'll be restarted after the dust has settled. I'm not sorry. It was interesting stuff, but I'd already begun to suspect I was being set up. I reckon they wanted to involve a few supposedly down-to-earth cops to help sell some of the less palatable outcomes.'

'I'll have you fully trained in the principles of high-level cynicism before you know it.' McKay had found himself hesitating. 'I did wonder if you were getting close to Everly. If so, I'm sorry. You've suffered enough on that front.'

'He was a charmer,' she had said. 'No question about that. And I admit I enjoyed his company. But, no, I'm not going down that route again for a good while.'

McKay had been replaying all this in his head as the service came to an end. He realised that he'd failed to listen to any of the eulogy delivered by the chief constable. 'All very moving,' he said to Grant.

'You thought so?'

'Aye. So let's move. There's only so much church I can take.'

Outside, it was a fine autumn day, the leaves just beginning to turn on the trees around the churchyard. The sky was clear of cloud, the sun sufficient to bring some warmth to the day even this late in the year. McKay and Grant stood back to watch the rest of the congregation pour out of the church.

'What about Ruby Jewell or Maggie Donaldson or whoever she was,' McKay said. 'Do you know if there are plans for a funeral?'

'I don't know how it works,' Grant said. 'I'm not aware she had any next of kin, but there must be some kind of process. You weren't thinking of going, were you?'

He smiled grimly. 'I might be tempted.'

'To pay your respects?'

'No. If I went, it'll be for just one reason.'

'Go on.'

'Because this time I want to make bloody sure she really is dead.'

THE END

ACKNOWLEDGEMENTS

My first thanks should go to Craig Gillan, who was generous enough to offer a winning bid in a Bloodhound Books auction in aid of Ukraine. Part of his prize involved having characters named after himself and his wife, Andrea. I can only apologise to them both for the fate that meets the fictional Gillans, although I should stress that I did inform Craig of this prior to using their names...

Otherwise, thanks go to all the usual suspects. To Helen, as ever, for her unstinting support, advice and editorial input. And to everyone at Bloodhound Books – to Betsy and Fred for their support for the series, to Tara Lyons for keeping everything together, and to Clare Law for her unfailing editorial wisdom. And to all the good people of the Black Isle and the surrounding areas, with apologies as ever for littering the glorious countryside with an inordinate number of corpses.

A NOTE FROM THE PUBLISHER

Thank you for reading this book. If you enjoyed it please do consider leaving a review on Amazon to help others find it too.

We hate typos. All of our books have been rigorously edited and proofread, but sometimes mistakes do slip through. If you have spotted a typo, please do let us know and we can get it amended within hours.

info@bloodhoundbooks.com

Printed in Great Britain
by Amazon